Sailor Girl

SAILOR GIRL

SHEREE-LEE OLSON

The Porcupine's Quill

Library and Archives Canada Cataloguing in Publication

Olson, Sheree-Lee
  Sailor girl / Sheree-Lee Olson.

ISBN 978-0-88984-301-1 (pbk.)

  I. Title.

PS8629.L85S34 2008   C813'.6   C2008-900342-X

1 2 3 4 · 10 09 08

Published by the Porcupine's Quill, 68 Main St, Erin, ON N0B 1T0.
http://www.sentex.net/~pql

Readied for the Press by Doris Cowan.

Represented in Canada by the Literary Press Group.
Trade orders are available from University of Toronto Press.

We acknowledge the support of the Ontario Arts Council and the Canada Council for the Arts for our publishing program. The financial support of the Government of Canada through the Book Publishing Industry Development Program is also gratefully acknowledged. Thanks, also, to the Government of Ontario through the Ontario Media Development Corporation's OMDC Book Fund.

ONTARIO ARTS COUNCIL
CONSEIL DES ARTS DE L'ONTARIO

Canada Council
for the Arts

Conseil des Arts
du Canada

for my parents

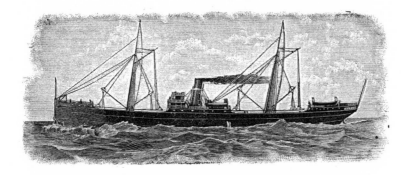

'You think, 'cause you been to college, you know better than anybody. You know better than them as 'as seen it with their own eyes. You wait till you've been to sea as long as I have, and you'll know.'

Two Years before the Mast, Richard Henry Dana, 1840

July, 1981: Greyhound

She was thirty per cent water.

Kate laughed to herself, thinking of Rebecca's line, code for when they had partied too intensely the night before. Parched. Dehydrated. Scalp too tight. They would wash down aspirins with ginger ale in the college smoking lounge, belching like schoolboys till the screws loosened, till they were back up to sixty per cent.

She braced her Docs against the seat in front of her and stretched her whole body till her arms trembled, snickering again at the image of Becks, bent double, helpless with laughter, ginger ale squirting from her nose. They had laughed that time till Rebecca started crying. Then they went down the street to the Beverley Tavern – two in the afternoon, just the wizened regulars communing with their brews – and smoked cigarette after cigarette, feeling wicked and mature.

That's what she needed now, a beer and a smoke. Possibly she was still drunk. Rebecca said a wine hangover was the worst. You wake up desiccated; just add water and you're drunk all over again. What's wrong with that? Kate said.

Across the aisle of the bus a blond woman was giving her the Look. Kate knew what she saw: she saw a delinquent. Aviator shades, slash of plum lipstick, cloud of rust-coloured hair escaping her braids. The woman's eyes flicked to her Docs. People were supposed to notice Doc Martens, it was why she had bought them, specifically why she had bought them in purple, when she absolutely couldn't afford them. They were boots for standing your ground. For kicking. For running if you had to.

The woman had a big Farrah Fawcett hairdo that was way too sensual for her crabbed face. It was good hair, though. Kate could not fathom the hair thing. Not only how ordinary women could achieve such extraordinary results, but also that they would go to such lengths to attract while repelling. She knew what Becks would say: Becks would say Farrah needed a good screw, that would put a smile on her face.

Kate smirked and levered her seat back with a thump, tipping the emerald bottle of Canada Dry against her lips. Eyes closed, licking at the last sweet bubbles that popped and fizzed against her tongue, wanting more, wanting water.

God, she could drink Canada dry.

Where she was going there was nothing but water, water and sky. A pilgrimage of water: the Great Lakes like giant footprints climbing to the centre of the continent. Ontario, Erie, Huron, Michigan. And then Superior.

The water was already here, filling the big tinted windows of the Greyhound, muscular waves furrowing the gunmetal skin of Lake Ontario, which stretched west and south and east to a smudged horizon. She didn't understand why no one talked about the lake in the city. It was as if there was a communal shame for the state of it, barricaded behind six lanes of expressway, trashblown and fouled. There was a beach somewhere near her apartment, but nobody she knew ever went there.

Oh, but now, riding the bus west toward the Welland Canal, the lake came roaring back, the wildness of it, the huge beauty. This was the thing she couldn't explain, the pull of the water, as if it were calling her blood. Becks said she was out of her mind to go back, it could happen again, but here she was. Going back.

They were pulling into Hamilton now. There was a rest stop of twenty minutes and Kate made her way to the washroom and waited till the room cleared. She stood in front of the mirror and pushed her sunglasses up. Her left eye still resembled a squashed grape, though the lividity had faded in the twelve hours since she took the call from the union man. Bill Stone.

The SS *Huron Queen* would be different, Bill Stone said. A different kind of boat than the *Black River*, a homesteader boat. Two lady cooks who needed a good worker. Decent crew, nothing like those malcontents and scumbuckets on the *Black River*.

Kate took out her makeup bag and brushed green onto her right eyelid, mimicking the damage on her left, then powdered her face all over, taking special care with the raised red line between her brows. Yanking down the collar of her turtleneck, she inspected her throat. After a week she was no longer shocked by what she saw: a circle of fingerprints, now fading; a bruise choker.

Outside on the platform her skin prickled in the heat, heat that had thickened in the hour since they pulled out of the Toronto terminal. She paced by the magazine kiosk, smoking a cigarette. Lady Diana's face was on every cover: the new patron saint of virgin brides.

The counter woman was poring over the *National Enquirer*. She raised her face and gave Kate an avid look. 'You see what they're saying about the dress? A hundred and fifty thousand pounds. What's that, three hundred grand?'

Kate stared blankly.

'Diana's wedding dress. A hundred and fifty thousand pounds!'

'That would be more like half a million dollars.'

'Half a million for a dress!'

Kate shook her head. 'No way. I think they make that stuff up. Have you got aspirin? And a bottle of ginger ale?'

'It's going to rain,' the woman said, taking Kate's last five-dollar bill. 'This humidity's gotta break soon.'

The sky had grown black when Kate found her seat again on the bus, squeezing past the new passengers, shoppers heading home to the smaller towns along the lake. Farrah's seat was empty now. The shoppers clucked as they settled, flicked on reading lights, buttoned their cardigans against the air-conditioned chill.

Kate took a long swallow of ginger ale and burrowed under her jean jacket, listening to the rain pelt the bus as it coughed and groaned through its gears. Past the steel plant, its slag mountains steaming in the sudden cold. Back to the highway, where she could see above the lake's chop a fleet of cumulus clouds, their hulls dark with weather.

She pulled the Minolta from her shoulder bag, feeling the bus sway in the wind, the excitement pour through her. She wedged an elbow against the armrest and raised the camera to her right eye, tracking the inky clouds through the lens, past fat raindrops exploding against the glass, past streaming ribbons of traffic, past the lacy scrim of trees.

Storm ships.

They made her glad she was going back.

PART ONE

❡ 1. The MV *Black River* in no way resembled Kate's idea of a ship. A ship has a sophisticated geometry, an elegance of form. It is white and jaunty. It sparkles in the sunshine.

The *Black River* swallowed the light.

She stood looking up at a great black wall of scabbed and pocked and riveted steel, four stories high and as long as a city block. She had to turn her head to take it all in. It was a monstrous tub. A zeppelin, fallen from the sky.

A narrow ladder leaned like a sketch against its hull. She felt it bounce and shake as she climbed, her soles ringing against the metal.

Up top she found a large bearded man coiling ropes. He pointed toward a low white structure weighed down by an enormous black smokestack. She could hear the lunchtime clash of china.

She located the galley by its smell, cooked meat and greasy soup. Inside she was given an apron and a pair of thick blue rubber gloves, steered to two deep sinks by the door, which were piled high with pots and roasting pans. She still wore the clothes she had put on that morning, skinny Daniel Hechter jeans and a lace-up white tank top and cowboy boots. The jeans chafed in the heat. Sweat dripped from her braids into the greasy water.

She would have gone to her room to change but she didn't know where it was. And she was afraid to ask the two fierce women in white who harried each other across the steel-clad galley. She did not bother to try to grasp their argument. Her consciousness was absorbed by the pain that was moving around her body like the hands of a clock. She pretzeled herself over the sinks, trying to relieve the ache that rose up her legs from the steel floor, like water filling postholes. Soon the pain had reached her shoulders, shooting bright flares through her trapezoid muscles.

Kate felt betrayed by her body. She had got soft. She had always been a strong girl, a roamer, a climber of trees. And she was only nineteen; those women, the cooks, they must be at least forty. They casually hefted huge cauldrons off the stove and banged them onto the drainboard at her elbow. They emerged from the pantry with frozen legs of animals and threw them down onto steel counters. They never stopped shouting.

The din was tremendous, like a furious orchestra tuning up: the gonging of pots and pans, the clash of glass and cutlery, the clatter of plates arriving from dining rooms. She scraped away gobbets of pink meat, pale mounds of potato, cigarette butts in mahogany gravy. She had never seen such an abuse of food.

And through it all, a sound that filled the air, a great roar from below her feet, as the boat shuddered out of its berth in the city's west harbour. Kate did not hear it until her body felt it, and then she could hear nothing else.

At one o'clock in the afternoon she glanced through the steam-coated porthole and saw the shore pulling away, the trucks and cranes of the port of Toronto shrinking into toys. It was only then that she realized she had not called Jenna. The ship was carrying her out into the middle of Lake Ontario, and no one in the city knew where she was. But the pain cascading down her spine made the thought inconsequential.

At one-thirty they sent her to do the rooms. As the porter she had six cabins to clean, three mates and three engineers, four before and two after lunch. But she had arrived at lunchtime, so she would have to make up for it now. She did not expect the surge of euphoria that filled her as she walked up the deck. She had entered the galley in the harbour; now she was somewhere else. No city. No land of any kind.

She smoked a cigarette as she walked; it tasted delicious. The water dazzled her eyes. The sheer size of it. Three hundred and sixty degrees of blue, the indigo skin of the great lake under a white dome of sky. A breeze creased the surface and tingled the back of her neck. She watched a lone gull arc across her vision, trailing a silvery cry.

Her pail of cleaning supplies clanked quietly against her thigh. She stopped and listened. There was no engine sound up here, and now her ears picked out the slapping of the waves, the hiss of the spray as the boat parted the water. Her body, eased by movement, had stopped its complaint. She filled her lungs with moist lake air. Only her eyes hurt, squinting against the brightness.

Nothing to it, the union man had said that morning. It seemed impossible that he had said it just three hours ago. Eleven o'clock, summoning her from where she hovered inside the glass doors of the seafarers' hiring hall on King Street East.

She had been about to bolt.

One look at the pacing, smoking, hard-faced crowd and Kate knew she was in the wrong place. It was like a bar without music. Thirty or forty men, throwing dice and slapping cards onto Formica tables, the crack of pool cues like gunshots through the roar of conversation. There wasn't a woman in the place. This fact, and only this fact, was why she had got the job.

'Come here, dear, we don't bite.' A voice like a foghorn and a ruined face to match, a big grey-haired man with a scar across his nose and two missing fingers. 'I'm Bill Stone. I'm the one you gotta be nice to. College student, are ya?'

'Art school. Photography actually.'

Bill Stone's face pleated into a wolfish grin. 'Well then. Planning to take some pictures?'

'A guy I met said there might be jobs. A guy from Montreal.' She had met him at a party and smoked his pot. She could see the obsession in his eyes as he told her about boats that carried grain to Montreal, tankers that ferried fuel to Labrador, past icebergs as tall as mountains, tunafish riding the waves like schools of black angels.

Out there on the water, he said. Out there it all makes sense.

And it was good money, even for girls.

'Runnin' away to sea, are ya?' Bill Stone barked a laugh. 'You're in luck. I got a boat tied up at Victory Soya Mills about to sail without a porter. Got your gear?'

And she had taken a taxi to the foot of Spadina Avenue and stood looking up at the boat called the *Black River*.

Nothing to it, Kate told herself, attacking the third mate's washroom first, scrubbing the toilet with arm extended and eyes squinted. She did not really want to see what she was cleaning, although the sink was all right, she did a good job on the sink, polishing the pitted surface to an opalescent gleam.

Nothing to it, she repeated, pulling apart his bed, holding her breath against the man smell that rose powerfully from the twisted sheets. Nothing to making the second mate's bed, the fourth engineer's bed, the third engineer's bed.

She could do this. Turn a blind eye to the balled-up underwear in the sheets, the stray hairs, the sprinkling of dandruff. One eye closed as she swiped at whisker bits and fingernail clippings, scattered ash and coffee rings, and in the third engineer's cabin, a dried trail of what she knew was and tried to pretend wasn't vomit.

By three o'clock she was in the second engineer's cabin, deep inside the noise again, the rhythmic engine drone that filled the back end of the boat and had already insinuated itself into her system.

The second engineer's cabin was larger than the others and had a double-sized bunk walled in on three sides. She pulled off her boots, shook out the bedding and crawled across the mattress to tuck in the bottom sheet. Backing out on her knees, she saw it had already come loose.

'Fuck,' she shouted. 'Fuck!'

She tore off the sheet and shook it violently. She was panting with fury. She sent it sailing back over the bed, and then bent and raised the mattress, burrowing underneath it, holding it up with her back while her fingers grasped at the far edge of the thin cotton.

Then she yanked it tight from underneath, and hefted the whole thing into place with her back, her feet scrabbling across the floor.

And stayed there, on her knees. If someone came in now they would think she was praying. She knelt with her forehead against the edge of the second engineer's mattress, curving her back against the pain, her eyes pricking. She had one more room to do.

At seven that evening Kate leaned against the railing outside the galley and gazed at the beautiful inky surface in front of her, stretched like a great wrinkled bedsheet in the falling light. The cooks had disappeared into their cabins, leaving her with a bucket of soapy water to wash the floors. They too seemed ill with fatigue, or maybe that was their normal demeanour.

She felt no pain now, just a kind of numbness in her limbs. Breathe, she told herself. Filling her lungs with the cool fishy air.

She stooped to lift the bucket. And then she let out a cry: the steel deck was crawling in front of her eyes, crinkling into waves. Little by little the movement subsided and the red deck was solid once more. She lifted the bucket quickly and dumped a stream of brown water, watched the wind transform it into dirty lace. A posse of gulls appeared out of nowhere, scolding and crying for scraps.

Kate crashed the bucket back to the deck and there it was again, the red paint trembling like the surface of the water. She looked once more at the waves and back to the steel. The effect lasted only seconds. It was an optical illusion: some kind of trick of brain or retina. The thought cheered her somehow. She knew something she had not known before.

By seven forty-five she lay collapsed in her tiny top bunk, wearing the now grubby white tank top and her sweat-soaked underwear. The cook she shared the cabin with muttered something at her as she drifted off, but the words did not make it through the thick green bed curtains.

And anyway it was too late; her body had already shut down, sinking into a sleep so profound that it seemed only seconds till she was ripped awake by a terrible hammering next to her ear.

She bolted up and yelped as her head hit the ceiling. 'Fuck!' she shouted. 'Fuck!' It was morning.

€ 2. Her roommate loathed her.

How else to explain the vicious barrage that the second cook employed as a wake-up call? Her weapon of choice was a giant soup ladle, and she knew exactly the spot on the steel pantry wall that corresponded to the head of Kate's bunk.

It was easier, of course, to pound on the bulkhead than go outside and walk along the companionway to their cabin door. But Kate knew that convenience had nothing to do with it.

'Do you think,' she said after breakfast on the third day, 'do you think you could just call me?'

'You listen me, gel. Is my job to wake you and I wake you, Jesus Chrise!'

The spoon, it was true, was more effective than an alarm clock. The shock of it got Kate out of bed faster than anything in her previous existence.

The second cook was called Pierrette, an appropriate name for someone small and hard and furious. The woman did herself no favours, Kate thought. Dark glasses and cropped hair, a faint moustache, a little man-woman.

The only time Pierrette seemed female was at coffee break in the crew's messroom, when she sat with a pair of Québécois guys, a deckhand and a wheelsman. They were handsome men, quiet and polite, and Kate could see why Pierrette doted on them, addressing them with silly endearments, *mon chou, mon coco* – as if she were their mother, when it was clear she wanted into their pants.

Of the fourteen men Kate had to serve meals to, they were the only ones who said please and thank you. Fourteen men in theory, because she hadn't seen more than eight or nine at a time, and most were gone within minutes, having wolfed their food without conversation, as if they had gone feral out here on open water.

She had thought this part, the serving of meals, would be easy. The party guy from Montreal had said so; the union guy, Bill Stone, had said so. She had waited on rude tourists at Ontario Place the summer before, tourists who stiffed her for tips or sometimes walked out without paying, leaving her to cover the cost from her meagre earnings. How hard could it be, to serve dinner to fourteen men who all sat at the same table?

But they frightened her. The strangest were the ones who emerged from below, from the terrific heat and noise of the engine room. Scowling men with stained overalls and thick, filthy arms that left black ovals of grease on the messroom table. Men who came smelling of alcohol and spilled their tea. None of them called her by name. She was Porter or she was Girly or she was Hey.

On the fourth morning Kate woke at five-thirty with Pierrette's alarm clock. She lay in her bunk in the dark, feeling the boat roll, a long slow rocking that shifted her centre of gravity from her head to her toes and back again.

They were on Lake Superior; she knew this because a watchman had warned her it would be noisy in the night when they went through the lock at Sault Ste. Marie. But she had slept through it. She had slept deeply and dreamlessly and now she was unnaturally awake, listening to the engine drone and the movements in the bunk below, the rasp of a lighter followed by a fit of dry coughing as Pierrette fired up the first smoke of the day. The fumes curled up through the bed curtains, filling Kate's bunk with a bar stink.

She waited till Pierrette had left the cabin and then locked herself in the bathroom and stood under a geyser of lake water, heated to near boiling in the cauldron of the engine room. It went straight back into the lake, according to the chief cook. An unending supply of hot water. She stayed under until she felt her fingertips wrinkling. Her whole body seemed to be smiling.

She was still smiling when she went into the galley and got a cup of coffee from the big aluminum urn that hissed by the stoves, luxuriating in the tidy solitude, the rays of yellow light drilling through the portholes. She went outside and stood with her coffee at the railing, wanting, for the first time since she arrived, to take out her camera.

But she couldn't move. It was a physical thing, this light. It poured across the lake and lit the rough black side of the boat into a precious metal. It stroked her face like a warm hand, making her close her eyes. It dazzled through her eyelids.

Then, as if from a great distance, she heard hammering. Pierrette. She'd forgotten about Pierrette. She laughed out loud. Suddenly Pierrette was irresistibly funny.

'Oh ho, gel, you think you can trick me, uh?'

Pierrette stood in the galley door, the giant soup ladle still in her fist. She was incandescent with anger, her chin up, her scrawny chest puffed out. She was practically levitating with her rage.

'No, no,' Kate said. 'I just woke up –' She tried, but failed, to stop another laugh bursting out like a sneeze.

'You trick me, I know. Very funny. Ve-ry funny. You wan' play games, my gel? Not with me, *moi*. Oh no. *Pas avec Pierrette.*'

Kate ducked past Pierrette and hustled into the messroom to clear the table. It was no good. She was still heaving with laughter. She would have to pay, she knew that. It was the kind of self-sabotage that had sent her to the principal's office in school. It was like a seizure. Maybe she was some kind of mirth epileptic. She laughed again, thinking that.

Pierrette rode her hard through the morning prep, harrying her with orders as she scrambled from the sinks to the toaster to the messroom and back to the sinks. Toward the end of breakfast she sent Kate into the officers' dining room for clean tea towels.

She raced in and stopped short. It was so still in the room she expected it to be empty. But there were four of them at the long table, lingering over coffee, smoke rising leisurely from their cigarettes.

'Got lost, did you?' one of them said. The others chuckled and she turned to see the second mate wink at her.

She blushed furiously, rifling the sideboard for towels. There were linen tablecloths in here too, which she had seen Pierrette flinging over the table for supper. It was astounding to her, not only to discover that a class system was in effect on the Great Lakes, but that everyone seemed to believe in it.

There were twenty-four men on the *Black River*, and ten of them got to sit here, on upholstered chairs at a long oak table with a white cloth. They each had a designated seat, which meant they could linger through the meal hour, sit around and smoke their cigarettes while the fourteen crew men squeezed onto two long benches on either side of a linoleum-topped table. These men got hand-printed menu cards, instead of a chalkboard listing their meal choices – two for lunch and three for supper.

They got exactly the same food, but she had no doubt it tasted better with elbow room.

That idiot second mate, winking as if she was a child or some stupid slut who would roll over. He had a handlebar moustache that made him look like a villain in an old movie. His hair was ridiculous too, puffed up like he had a perm. He probably did have a perm.

She went back to her sinks and laughed into the soapsuds.

Four days on the boat and already she craved the water, her twice-daily escape onto the open deck, the cool spray and constant glittering motion, the applause of the waves. It was more than physical, more than the way her chest expanded, filling up with the clean northern smell of fir and fish.

She had not known till now that she was a water person, even though as a child she was always the last one to come in from the lake, blue-lipped and shaking, long after her sister and the others were wrapped in towels by the campfire. Water seemed to make everything easier, make adults into different people, pink-skinned and light-hearted in their near-nakedness. Even her grandmother would let Kate unlace her oxfords so she could cool her feet in the damp sand at Kitsilano Beach.

They would take the ferry across to Vancouver Island, and the salt spray would make Gram laugh like a girl, standing next to Kate at the bow, her kerchief a tiny sail in the sea wind.

Kate felt that excitement now, feeling the big waves of Superior. The water was darker here, the wind cold enough to steal her breath. Huge white-edged swells rolled under the boat's hull and made her stagger on the steel deck. The air was so clear she could see the sharp curved edge of the horizon, an indigo scimitar.

Feet wide apart, she moved up forward, swaying to compensate for the rolling of the boat. It was like dancing, or climbing. The feeling in a dream of taking big steps and finding the ground had shifted. She was finally going somewhere. She was getting her lake legs.

By the time she entered the second mate's cabin she was grateful for the warmth. She had got used to the idea of cleaning the rooms. She didn't mind the sinks or the beds, except for the second engineer's claustrophobic bunk. Toilets were another matter – she didn't like to think about them. But the rooms got her out of the galley.

What she minded was the way the second mate had looked at her in the dining room. He had already appeared once in his cabin when she was bent over his bunk, flushed with exertion. He said he had forgotten his cigarettes, but she did not miss the satisfaction he took from the fact, not just that his room was being tidied, but that she, Kate, had to do it.

She knew this without anyone telling her. She knew it by the charming Christmas family portrait on his desk, him in his dreadful hairdo and his wife with a feathery bouffant, dressed in a violent red dress with big shoulders. The dress was the same shade as the outfits on a pair of toddlers in the picture, the boy in red overalls and the girl in a jumper. They clutched white teddy bears, which were also dressed in red. The effect was both absurd and oddly touching. She felt sorry for the children.

It reminded her of the vanity card her Vancouver cousin had sent the previous Christmas, her self-satisfied cousin with her dull husband and their two Scottie dogs. Her cousin had taken the dullard's name, even though she claimed to be a feminist, not, she said, because he wanted her to, but because his parents were from the old country and wouldn't understand. What did it matter, really? Susan said. And Kate had said, It matters.

Susan and Bruce, married right out of college, dressed in matching seaweed-coloured chunky sweaters that Susan had knitted herself, apparently out of kelp.

And Kate's parents had never quite said it, but she knew what they were thinking. Why can't you be more like Susan? Why can't you be more like Jenna?

❨ 3. Kate sometimes wondered how she could possibly be related to her little sister Jenna. Maybe Kate had been adopted; maybe she really belonged to some immigrant cleaning lady or a farm girl from the Ottawa Valley, a maid at one of the embassies in the capital. Or maybe Jenna was the one who was adopted, the love child of a senior diplomat. It would explain why she required so much maintenance – except someone had forgotten to send along her staff.

Their differences were as plain as the school portraits displayed side by side on their mother's dresser, beauty Darwinism at its simplest. It was clear where Jenna came from; she had their mother's patrician bones and pale skin, whereas Kate – it was always *whereas Kate* – had a habitual blush and a stubborn jaw and towered over both of them.

Families are the original political body. There are acknowledged and unacknowledged hierarchies. Kate knew she and Jenna were loved equally, but Jenna was also adored.

And who could not adore Jenna? Jenna twirled and pirouetted through life, while Kate crashed through the underbrush. She'd come along sixteen months after Kate, usurping the baby throne, but Kate hadn't minded. She treated her baby sister like a big, tow-headed doll, instructed her and coddled her and occasionally pinched her.

Once Jenna could walk it was Kate she followed everywhere, up and down stairs, into dark garages, crawling under fences into the fields that lay beyond their suburban Ottawa street. Until Jenna got a rusted nail in her foot from one of those fences and had to have a needle.

She became Kate's conscience instead. She would shout till she was hoarse when Kate transgressed, crossing the highway with her friends to invade the abandoned farmlands that awaited development.

The farms were ideal for infiltration. They would be gone for hours, playing spies – she had her own toy pistol – pretending to find dead bodies in haylofts and feed pens, traitors who'd been executed.

In fact nothing would have made them more excited than an actual dead body, but the most dramatic thing they found was the jawbone of an animal.

Jenna never followed, but she never told on Kate.

That was why Kate could not begrudge her her status as Daddy's girl and Mommy's too. And Jenna worked hard to please them. Even in senior high school she would still perch on their father's knee after a boozy holiday meal, while Kate sneaked furious smokes in the back yard.

Love was such a flimsy word for the storm of longing those nights unleashed in her, hearing her sister's happy laugh through the glowing windows of their parents' house.

A day later, in the chilly dank shadow of Thunder Bay's Wheat Pool 7, Kate stood in a phone booth, smoking. Jenna answered on the first ring.

'Yes, yes,' she said. 'I'll accept the charges.' The operator went away. Jenna started shouting. 'Kate, where the hell are you? How could you do that – you didn't even leave a note.'

'I didn't have time. Look, I'm on coffee break –'

'I had to call the *union.*'

'So you know I'm in Thunder Bay, then.'

'No – I didn't know *anything*. The guy didn't know anything either, except that you're on a boat. Told me to call another number, vessel information.'

'Did you call?'

'I didn't have time. Look, I have to go to the seniors' centre. I have a meeting with the director.'

'How's the job?'

'The job? The job is fantastic,' Jenna said, softening. 'I love admin. I think they're going to offer me a promotion. Anyway, Kate, I've been *worried* about you. Are you okay?'

Kate laughed. 'I'm not sure. My roommate hates me.'

'Why?'

'She's a psycho. I think she's jealous. She's got to be at least forty. She looks like a little man.'

Jenna didn't laugh. 'I warned you, didn't I? I said they'd be a bunch of losers. I told you that.'

'Yeah well, I'm going to quit. Satisfied?' In fact she had no intention of quitting; the union man, Bill Stone, had said the job was thirty – at most forty-five – days. She was committed. But Jenna had a way of making her say things she didn't mean.

'You *can't* quit now. You said I could have your apartment till the end of August.'

'You said you hated my place.'

'Your place is fine. It's the neighbourhood I don't like.'

'There you go.'

'No, there you go. We had an agreement. Why can't you ever stick with –'

'Oh fuck off, Jenna.'

Jenna hung up.

Kate slammed out of the phone booth and jogged along the narrow lip between the cliff-like face of the grain elevator and the oily black water of the slip. The *Black River* was tied up behind two other freighters, three boat lengths from the phone. A third of a mile in. which to imagine rats among the wooden palings, grain-fed harbour rats, as big as cats in the gloom.

At the foot of the boat's boarding ladder she felt a gust of wind and looked toward the lake, past the elevator to the little patch of shrubbery at the end of the jetty. It was a ragged square of weeds, bordered by broken slabs of concrete. She could smell the greenness, a smell like clover, and then she was jogging through the shadows toward the sunshine, the white light sparkling on the water.

It was windy here but the sky was hot blue and she had a clear view of a wooded plateau that stretched in the shape of a man across the horizon. She stared hard at its silhouette, feeling a ripple of recognition. She had seen it before, maybe in a book, or maybe on one of the endless road trips her parents had made into the north country when she and Jenna were young.

Five days she had been on the boat, five days and a thousand miles, never sure where one lake stopped and another began, and not until this moment had she felt anything like homesickness. Kate pulled up handfuls of wildflowers, their colours and shapes familiar from Sunday drives, the bright drops that crowded the ditches and meadows of the Ottawa Valley.

Weeds, her mother called them. Her mother grew David Austin

26

roses, the bigger and fatter and pinker the better, and Kate did not think they were half as beautiful as the fragrant stunted blooms of the wild rose. She gathered a bunch of buttercups. These were not weeds at all, she thought. Nature made no such distinction. They were not glamorous but they were stubborn. Hard workers. Survivors.

That was how Kate had seen herself and Jenna: wildflower and prized cultivar. Jenna was a social butterfly, always at the centre of a brilliant fluttering circle. Kate preferred to be outside circles, looking in. That way you could leave when you got bored.

The camera gave her a way to be outside and inside too. At high school dances and football games Kate collected images, officially taking pictures for the school paper, but she knew it was more than that. On weekends in the camera club darkroom she would coax their images out of thick white sheets of paper she held down in the chemical bath, stroking her fingers across the surface to bring up the details. She wanted to make them beautiful, every one of them, even the airhead girls herding for safety at dances, the jocks with destiny in their stupid eyes.

She would find the best angles, the close-ups and moody shots; she would crop out the fat arms or the bad hair. She thought they would be grateful. She thought they would recognize her skill in making them look so good. But mostly people wondered why she had cut off their arm or the top of their head. They weren't the kinds of photos they were used to, the crowd shots at games, the cheerleaders vamping for the camera.

Kate held a buttercup to her palm, watching a tiny yellow spotlight move across her skin. Light moved everywhere here, flitting from the veined surface of the water to the white concrete like a live thing. When had she stopped liking her sister? When her sister got ambition. When the butterfly turned into a pinstriped caterpillar and announced it was going to study business administration, not arts like everyone else; arts was for people who couldn't decide what to do with their lives.

Jenna spent the last two summers of high school doing extra courses, which meant she graduated the same spring as Kate. She got a scholarship to York University, which pleased their parents excessively, Kate thought. She was voted assistant don in her residence and would no doubt become don. She said she was going to get her MBA and run a hospital someday.

Kate tossed handfuls of blooms onto the water that lapped against the jumble of concrete, daisies and wild clover, black-eyed Susans and Queen Anne's lace, other things she didn't know the names of, purple bells on tall stems, flowers with blue fringe like eyelashes. The waves pulled them away, tossed them back, pulled them away again. She watched for a long time, watched them gradually separate and sink.

Now she remembered what that piece of rock was called. It was the Sleeping Giant, Nanna Bijou, the great Ojibwa leader who had brought his people west to the head of the lakes to avoid the white men in tall ships. But it was too late, the voyageurs in their big freight canoes had already infected his tribe.

In history class the voyageurs had always been heroes. They penetrated the continent for their corporate masters, opened the way for commerce and colonization. They sang while they paddled and they paddled like pistons, always in a race for the furs, the pelts that Europe turned into hats. They navigated by eye, by the shape of the rocks and the look of the sky, and they ignored bad weather, because they were always on the clock.

Few could swim. And many drowned.

Kate had seen a show at the National Gallery that told the real story. They were hard partiers, the canoe jockeys, cocky little Frenchmen with massive shoulders who danced around campfires and fought and fucked, took what they could not buy. They plied the native girls with beads and booze, their fathers with booze and knives, and they sowed imperial diseases along with their imperial seed.

They deserved to drown, Kate thought.

₡ 4. 'Where you go, gel? Coffee break is over!' Pierrette glared across the potato bucket. She was seething.

'I was phoning home.'

'You take too long. We got lots to do. We gonna clean the stainless steel today.'

This confused Kate, since the entire galley was stainless steel. 'What do you mean? The counters?'

'Are you stupid, gel? Every-ting.'

'Pierrette, Pierrette, excuse me, what are you saying?' The chief cook appeared in the dining-room doorway, hand on hips and annoyance on her face. Her name was Anna and she was Polish and she did not appear to like Pierrette any more than Pierrette liked Kate.

'We do not clean the stainless when we are loading,' Anna said. 'No no. It will need to be done all over again. We have groceries coming too.'

Pierrette shrugged violently and pulled a large dusty potato from the burlap sack at her feet. Kate could see a muscle twitch in her cheek as she worked her thin, razor-sharp peeling knife with the speed of a machine, parting a thick rind of skin from the pale flesh.

Kate reached into the sack. She had not known how much her hands could ache. The potatoes were old, coated with red earth, stippled with waxy buds. Their flesh resisted her blade, the dirt filling the stinging cracks in her skin like a crosshatch drawing. The tips of her fingers were peeling from constantly being in water and this morning she had burned her wrist on the toaster.

'You so slow, gel!' Pierrette exploded. She had said it every morning and every morning Kate tried to speed up, nicking her fingers in the effort. But not today.

'Yes,' she said pointedly, 'but I do a better job. You peel them too thick. All the vitamins are under the skin.'

'What you try to do?' Pierrette sneered. 'Save money for the company?'

Kate laughed dismissively.

'Oh ho, you think I am funny? You are the worst porter I see! Why I have to share a room wit you? Are you a pig? You think I am gonna make your bed? You gonna clean up your mess or I tell the *capitaine* and he gonna fire you for sure!'

Sweat prickled across Kate's forehead. 'You never said a word about making my bed,' she said. 'I sleep in it in the afternoon. Am I supposed to make it twice a day?'

'Why you ask me? You just make your goddamn bed. You clean your goddamn mess. Or I tell the *capitaine*.'

Kate kept her eyes on the potato. Her face was hot.

The chief cook reappeared, an order pad in her hands. 'What is going on? I am trying to –'

A small scream cut her off. Kate looked up and felt her heart stutter. Pierrette was staring with horror at her left hand, where her index finger was blossoming red like a tiny flower.

Kate thought fast. 'Hold it up,' she yelled. Anna grabbed a wad of paper towels and clamped onto the finger, her other hand firmly grasping the white-faced Pierrette by the elbow, elevating the arm.

But Kate was staring at the bucket. There was a tremendous buzzing in her ears. 'Oh fuck,' she said. 'Where is it, where is it?'

A similar accident had once happened to a neighbour child, which was why she knew what to do. She tottered unsteadily across to the counter, tore off a sheet of plastic wrap and used it to scoop up the tiny white knob of flesh that so resembled a bit of potato it might have ended up in someone's dinner. The tip of Pierrette's finger.

At noon the captain appeared in the pantry and huddled with the chief cook. He was a big baleful Newfoundlander who looked uncomfortable in his beige officer's uniform. Kate hadn't seen him up close before. He did not look pleased.

She kept her head over the sinkful of pots, which had multiplied alarmingly while she set the dining-room table in place of Pierrette. The captain passed by her without comment and went into the messroom, which was uncharacteristically full, no doubt because of the excitement.

The second cook had gone to the hospital in town with the Québécois wheelsman. In her shock Pierrette had lost her English. Kate felt a twinge of sympathy watching her sag white-faced against the wheelsman's arm. He put the fingertip, now packed in ice, in his pocket.

The chief cook warned Kate that the captain would be looking for someone to blame. The company didn't like accidents, she said, accidents cost them higher workers' compensation fees. They had already lost a watchman who had slipped in a puddle of oil and broken his ankle.

But Kate heard laughter from the messroom, hard voices baying in mirth. So when the captain appeared at her elbow on his way back to the dining room she expected to be let in on the joke. He would ask her about her rescue of the finger.

Except what he said was: 'That Frenchie deckhand. He's got his hat on. Don't you know better than to serve a man with his hat on?'

Kate laughed. She held the dripping dishcloth in her hands, teeth parted in a smile.

The captain glowered. 'Didn't your mother teach you better?'

'I'm sorry. I don't understand –'

'What kind of idiot are you?' *Idiot*, he really said that, and for a moment she still thought he was joking. How could he be serious about table manners when she had saved Pierrette's finger?

The captain looked her up and down, his eyes scraping her bare legs below her shorts. 'And for God's sake, put something decent on. Some of these poor buggers haven't seen their wives in months.'

He might as well have slapped her. She stood with eyes smarting as he stalked away. She could hear them listening from the messroom. The laughter, when it came, was nastier. At least she heard it that way. What other way could she hear it?

She did not go back in for the rest of lunch, but stayed bent over the sinks. When the last man had gone and she was clearing away the detritus of plates and cups and overflowing ashtrays, she glanced at the menu board.

It took her a moment to comprehend. Someone had erased her careful script listing chocolate cake and rice pudding and ice cream and had chalked in big awkward letters, HAIR PIE.

❦ 5. The new second cook did not hate Kate. She wanted to save her.

Nancy was a flaxen-haired blonde with small blue eyes and big plastic-framed glasses. She had a teenager's face and the body of a middle-aged woman. She said she was twenty-three. She also said she was a virgin.

She shared that revelation the moment they sat down for tea after supper. What she actually said was, 'You know, I'm not your usual sailor girl type. But I'm glad to be here, Kate, I really am.'

'What do you mean, not your usual sailor girl type?'

Nancy leaned toward Kate and said in an exaggerated whisper, 'Well, for instance, I'm a virgin.'

Kate laughed without humour. She did not think she knew anyone who would be proud of that fact, except possibly her sister. And Lady Diana. But her humiliation by the captain had made it clear there was an older code in operation on the lakes. The captain had succeeded in shaming her, even if she didn't agree with him, even if he was wrong. She was wearing her jeans again and they were sodden with sweat. Nancy had on a pink nylon ensemble of pants and zippered tunic she called her uniform. It looked like a pair of pyjamas.

Nancy frowned. 'Kate, I'm serious.'

Kate shrugged. 'Well, good for you.' A psycho, she was thinking. Another psycho roommate.

But she seemed on the whole to be a benign psycho. They had got through supper in record time; Nancy had none of the hierarchical obsessions of Pierrette but plunged her hands into the dishwater whenever she had a moment. And Kate had been grateful for the buffer of Nancy's chatter, which ranged across her entire employment history and included the galley layout of each of her previous four boats.

Kate lit a cigarette. After a moment she passed the pack across the messroom table. She could hear the screen door to the galley slam; one of the men getting tea.

'Thanks but no thanks,' Nancy said, dipping a cookie into her milky tea. 'I gave them up too.'

'Too? What else did you give up?'

It was Nancy's turn to flush. 'That's what I was trying to get at. Sex.'

'But you just said you're a virgin.'

Nancy was nodding eagerly. 'Actually, when I said I'm a virgin, I didn't mean, you know, physically.'

Kate stared at her. She was resisting a powerful urge to roll her eyes. 'So what do you mean?'

'I've been born again, Kate. In Christ.'

'Oh,' Kate said, smiling, understanding. 'You're a *born* again.'

Nancy heaved herself to her feet and carefully brushed her cookie crumbs into her palm. 'I'm a *Christian*, Kate. An instrument of God. You coming to watch TV? We should get good reception, this close to town.'

'That's okay, I'm going to sit here for a bit.' Thinking she would sit there all night if she had to, to avoid another conversation like this.

And then she felt someone come into the room behind her. She glanced up and away. It was the new wheelsman, the one who had come in place of Pierrette's Québécois boyfriend, who had quit to take her home. The new guy was tall and ruddy and would have been handsome except for the pockmarks peppering his cheeks.

'You watch that one,' the wheelsman said affably, lowering himself onto the bench that Nancy had vacated. He set down a mug and took out a pack of Drum. She watched as he rolled a thin cigarette one-handed, firing it up with a lighter before he put it to his lips. 'Those Bible thumpers are snitches. If they see you having a drink or a toke or anything they'll get you on the black list.'

'The black list?'

'Every company's got one. They aren't supposed to share them, but they do.'

'How do you know?'

He grinned at her wickedly, picking a shred of tobacco from his tongue. The sight of his parted lips sent a jolt through her belly. His lips were pillowy, not something she had noticed before in a man. His teeth were white and perfectly straight.

'I got fired off one boat for toking up, right? Next week I go for another job – totally different company, right – not even based in Ontario, based in Quebec – and the mate refuses me. Just like that. No reason. The union guy was pissed off, but the boat was gone.' The wheelsman shrugged.

'But you're here.'

'They're desperate, right? These guys can't afford to be picky. Their boats are shit. You see the life jackets they got on here? They're so old and rotten they wouldn't float a fucking rubber boot.'

'These boats don't sink, do they?' Kate hadn't considered the possibility.

'What, you never heard of the *Edmund Fitzgerald?*'

'Oh, right. There was a song about it. That was an American boat.'

'What do you think this boat is? It's an American boat, they buy them cheap, all the fittings, paint on a new name. Lakes are full of boats that used to be other boats, other companies. It's like, you know, assumed identities.'

'Really?' Kate lit another cigarette. 'I saw a list on the second mate's desk today. It was called employee selection program, something like that.'

'That's the black list, all right.'

She'd only noticed it because the mate had used it to soak up a coffee spill, which merely succeeded in spreading the coffee further. She was sponging up the brown puddle when she was arrested mid-swipe by the words.

Arlo Davis, possession of narcotics;

James Fisk, refusing to work;

Jeannie Hays, potential suicide.

And on and on, three full pages of offences: using abusive language toward an officer; threatening chief cook with a knife; causing a disturbance; being intoxicated; molesting porter; attempting to jump overboard; being intoxicated on watch; threatening master's life; smashing eggs in the galley.

'There were three down for smashing eggs in the galley,' she told the wheelsman.

'Guess they didn't like the food, eh. Or else they were Cape Bretoners. Those assholes are always going nuts in the galley. I think they got a problem with their mothers.'

'Oh, so you're a shrink, too. Anyway, I haven't had a drink since I got on here.'

'Sounds like you're overdue. I'm heading up for brewskies with the watchman after our shift, if you want to grab a ride.'

The wheelsman's name was Mick and he was studying forestry at Lakehead University. He was from Kenora, a town much smaller and farther north than Thunder Bay. Thunder Bay was the big smoke in this part of the world, Mick said, grinning. 'It's our Toronto, eh.'

What Kate saw of the big smoke through the windows of the cab that evening seemed fixed in another century, narrow cobblestone streets of sepia-toned warehouses, many of them boarded up on the ground floors, the upper windows spider-webbed with cracks. They were built of pale stone and crumbling brick, their sides painted with ancient advertisements that had weathered into abstractions. Ghost signs on ghost buildings. They were beautiful.

Mick directed the driver to a shabby-looking place called the Commodore Lounge, which boasted a separate Ladies and Escorts entrance next to the door to the bar. Once inside, she saw it was all one noisy room, faded red-flocked walls on one side and smoke-brown plaster on the other. There were so many cigarette burns in the carpet they looked like part of the pattern.

Kate sat in a booth with Mick and the watchman, a fat Newfoundlander named Phil. Phil was recently married; he talked about nothing but 'the wife'. It seemed unlikely that he had been in on the chalkboard insult; he talked to her like a normal person. That was why she had come along; Mick seemed normal too. She was desperate for normal.

Mick said she should have a fancy drink; he was buying. She had a Singapore sling, or rather two, since it was Ladies' Night and that meant two for the price of one. After the first drink she felt happy enough to borrow change from Mick to attempt another call to Jenna. Leaning against the pay phone in the hall next to the washroom she left a slightly slurred message saying she was sorry, she was not quitting, everything was fine, fine, fine.

That was their pattern, bitch and back off.

The drinks tasted like Kool-Aid and went down just as easily, and Kate had that sensation that she'd sometimes had at parties in high school, when she drank rum and Coke and felt like she had taken a truth serum.

She would have made a terrible spy, she thought, listening to herself blurt out the conversation with the Christian. But that was nothing, according to Phil the watchman; there were holy rollers all over the lakes, like the newbie oiler from Georgian Bay who waited in vain every Sunday for someone to come to the rec room and join him in prayer.

'Fucking eejit,' Phil said, chuckling as he rolled a joint. 'You want to go outside for a toke?'

Kate looked at Mick, who shrugged and shook his head. 'Nah, man, I don't want to get wasted. We're on deck duty at 7 a.m.'

She watched his face as he watched Phil drift out of the bar. She found his pockmarks strangely alluring. They were like the patterned initiation scars she had seen in photographs of African tribesmen, nicked in rows down their cheeks, rubbed with ash so they would heal in bumps of scar tissue. Manhood scars. Maybe that's what teenage acne really was, nature's way of announcing to the world that you were ready to fuck.

There it was, that word in her head. She was ready, all right. She looked past Mick at the couples crowding the bar. They leaned hard against each other, their paired heads silhouetted against the glow like valentines. It was Ladies' Night at the Commodore and the ladies all seemed extraordinarily happy, their high glassy laughter threading the din.

She smiled easily at Mick and he smiled back, showing his pretty white teeth. 'Let's get a cab,' he said.

They got off at the docks, then walked half a mile farther along the shore, over smooth humped granite seamed with moss and still holding the heat of the day. It was a Tom Thomson landscape, jack pines standing watch on the cliffs above, the sky streaked with stars. They found a shack by the water that someone had built to shelter a picnic table, a frame of two-by-fours covered with layers of clear plastic, which snapped in the wind and gave them light to see each other by.

They lay down on the picnic table with the sound of waves filling their heads and drowning out the noise Kate was making. Afterward she moaned drunkenly on Mick's chest about being stuck on a boat with sexist assholes and psycho roommates. She had come aboard thinking she would take pictures of marine life, but she hadn't had the courage to bring out her camera.

'You can take pictures of me,' Mick said, biting her neck.

¶ 6. She did not want to take pictures of Mick. But she let him into the cabin the next night, when the missionary was proselytizing in the rec room. Nancy had tried to persuade her to come and play cards, but Kate had no desire to spend time in what passed for the common area, a dingy space next to the messroom littered with newspapers and cigarette ash. Surprisingly, it wasn't her job to clean it; it was the job of Phil and the other two watchmen, who could often be found sitting at the beat-up card table, smoking and staring mournfully at the fuzzy television screen.

She wasn't sure what else the watchmen, who were each on a different rotation, were responsible for. They were supposed to burn the paper garbage in an ancient foul-smelling incinerator on the boat deck, but she had seen one of them, a loudmouth named Kenny, dump big black bags clinking with cans and broken glass over the stern railing into Superior. Watching him methodically stab the bags with his jackknife, she imagined a trail of black plastic and rusted metal on the bottom of the lakes, following the shipping channels like a filthy shadow.

Mostly, it seemed to her, the watchmen did tea. They were either drinking tea, or filling the kettles to make tea, or asking the chief cook for more tea bags. The tea was Red Rose orange pekoe, and they liked it tannic and dark, thickened up with condensed milk and two or three spoonfuls of sugar. They made tea for the captain or the first mate, and they collected empty tea mugs wherever they found them, in the engine room or on the stern deck, and returned them to the galley.

They were in the galley a lot, especially Kenny, the one from Cape Breton, who Mick particularly did not like. She knew that Kenny watched her, and she would straighten her spine and arm her thoughts when she felt his eyes.

But last night with Mick had made her vulnerable. It seemed simple at the time, sparked up by booze and moonlight, deafened by the waves. Now she had to calculate the risk of getting caught – not that she knew exactly what that would entail besides more public shaming – against her loneliness.

She locked the cabin door and leaned against Mick's chest. 'No one saw you, did they?'

'No. Hey. Relax.' He nudged her toward the cabin's tiny washroom.

Locked inside with the shower on full, the engines grinding and their hot breath adding to the steam in the room, she tried to forget about Nancy. But that only made her think about Nancy more, which made it difficult to fully enjoy what was happening, the way she had on the picnic table with the lake wind beating against the flimsy walls of their shelter.

Afterward she just felt jumpy. She had nothing to say to him as, later, they sat on the bench on the stern deck, smoking and watching the westering sun above the choppy surface of Superior, the sky filling up with violent pink clouds.

Thirty hours later the boat tied up at an ancient grain elevator in Midland, at the south end of Georgian Bay. It was a hot Saturday morning, and Kate could see the nearby beach gradually fill with encampments of chairs and coolers and striped umbrellas. Walking along the dock to the phone booth, she felt almost festive, like she was on holiday instead of working harder than she had ever thought she was capable of.

Jenna was home. The conversation was brief and contrite. Kate reiterated her apology, and Jenna reciprocated. The apartment was fine, work was fine. Everything was fine.

'So, how's the photography?'

'I haven't done any.'

Jenna huffed impatiently. 'Wasn't that the whole point?'

'You don't understand,' Kate said. 'I'm still trying to get used to things.'

'Okay. Okay. Call me soon, okay? And call Mom. Please.'

The truth was, she felt paralyzed. Maybe she was under too much scrutiny herself to turn the lens the other way. Maybe she was just exhausted. Or maybe she wasn't serious about photography or art school and just wanted to party. Maybe she was completely delusional.

Mick was waiting by the top of the ladder. He said everyone would be heading into town after supper, or at least to the closest bar, which was a roadhouse catering to a local motorcycle gang.

He had heard you could buy beer under the counter there, and proposed that they take a stroll along the shore, which she knew meant they were going to have sex again. Which was, after all, what she wanted.

She and Nancy finished the dishes early and she walked with Mick toward a wooded area beyond the beach. It was still warm at six o'clock and most of the families were now ensconced at picnic tables, where the women tended to children and the men tended to smoking meat.

They found a spot past an old stone mill, hidden by grasses and smelling of fish and clover. There was sand here too, still warm from the day's sun, and they lay companionably for a while, drinking beer and smoking.

'Sand,' she said, running her fingers through it and through it. 'I didn't know they had sandy beaches up here. They must truck it in or something.'

'Nah. The opposite. The Great Lakes were full of sand; they used to be saltwater seas. That's why we've got the salt mines at Goderich. But they trucked most of the sand out years ago. Used it for roads, building, all kinds of shit.'

'That's depressing.'

'Why's it depressing? People need roads.' Mick picked tobacco from his tongue, spat neatly into the water. 'People say that about the forests too, that we shouldn't cut old growth. But you know what happens if you let a forest go? It dies anyway. It reaches its peak and it dies.'

Kate opened another beer and felt a memory skitter through her mind: camping with her family at Sandbanks Provincial Park, filling brown beer bottles with June bugs for her father to use as fish bait.

The memory made her unaccountably angry. 'It's not the way I heard it,' she said to Mick. 'The logging companies are basically raping the north, is what I heard.'

'Hey, hey. Let's not fight, Kate. We were having a nice time.'

Kate glared at him. 'Maybe I feel like fighting.'

'Why is that?'

'Maybe I hate you,' she said, rolling hard against him, pressing her face to his chest.

This time they were quick about it, worried about being stumbled on. Each time, she thought, was less satisfying than the last.

Afterward, Mick built a driftwood fire. 'Listen,' he said. 'I should tell you now, I don't plan to be on the boat much longer. Basically I'm just here for a ride to the Canal, going to try to get a self-unloader. It's saving me the bus fare.'

'Oh,' she said quickly, stung. 'What's a self-unloader?'

'Just what it sounds like. A boat that unloads itself, instead of using the bucket and crane. No waiting, basically. They can dump their cargoes in four hours. It means you're working all the time, lots of OT.'

He was being studiously casual and she knew he was telling her he had a girlfriend there, maybe someone from another boat. She wanted to say something cutting, but instead she reached for another beer, watching the fire, its cheerful destruction. She was grateful that he had told her now instead of two days from now. It was just sex after all.

Nancy was still awake when Kate lurched into the cabin, banging her hip on the doorframe. She followed Kate into the washroom and watched her throw up most of Mick's beer, and then steadied her as she climbed into her bunk and collapsed in her clothes.

In the morning Nancy brought her a cup of tea.

'Thanks, Nance,' Kate said weakly, attempting a look of gratitude. 'Do you have any aspirins?'

Mick didn't come in for breakfast. At lunch he avoided her eyes and by dinner she would not look at him either.

But he reappeared in the galley after everyone else had gone. 'Here,' he said, holding out an accordioned rectangle of pale yellow paper.

'What's this?' she said, shaking it out.

It was a map, tattered at the edges, its creases mended with ambered tape.

'It's a nautical chart,' he said, 'of the seaway system. The mate was throwing it out.' He took it from her and spread it on the table. 'See, there's all the lakes, the Welland Canal, the Montreal locks, the St. Lawrence, all the way to Pointe Noire in the Gulf.' He folded it up and handed it back with an ironic smile. 'I thought you might want to know where you're going.'

That evening she was drifting into sleep when Nancy's voice came floating up from the lower bunk. 'Last night, Kate, when you came in, you smelled like smoke. Like something else too. You better watch yourself. You're going to get a *name*.'

❆ 7. Kate had had a name since she was twelve. Since a boy jumped out of an apple tree, landing on his knees in the scrubby grass in front of her. His name was Bobby and he did it to impress her. She rewarded him by climbing up to his fort in the upper branches, which grew crooked and wormy in an abandoned orchard at the end of their suburban Ottawa street.

Bobby's kisses tasted like apples, the stunted green ones the mothers warned against. His callused fingertips were rough against her skin, but Kate liked being tickled. Because this was just Bobby, after all, big brother to her best friend Wendy. He was fifteen years old.

Bobby was small for his age, inarticulate in front of other kids. He had been kept behind a grade at school. Until the day in the tree, she had laughed along when Wendy made fun of him. But now Kate became furtive, waiting for him in the afternoon heat of the tree fort, a comic book unread in her lap. When she felt the tree shake she knew he would soon raise his crewcut head through the trap door. 'Honey,' he would say, just like a mini husband, 'I sure missed you.'

He built them other hiding places, a nest of dry leaves under the raspberry canes, a cave scooped out of the sand pit across the highway. She felt guilty about deceiving Wendy, who was convinced Kate had found a new best friend. But it was pure pleasure to elude Jenna.

It seemed to her now she had spent a whole summer hiding out with Bobby, but it couldn't have been more than two weeks. Two weeks and then there was a hot late August afternoon when she made him unbutton the back of her madras blouse and then rubbed her pale nipples against his narrow tanned chest. The sunlight beat down on the weathered boards of the tree fort, raising a cat smell. Bobby's eyes darted wildly beneath his lids, teeth bared in what looked like pain.

Kate felt a thickness come into her throat that she could not swallow away. She knew Bobby was too old to be playing with her. And yet when she lay across his wiry body he felt as comfortable as a brother.

It was Wendy who told, told the other kids who ran wild in the orchard, rough kids from the farms down the road. They had grown up around animals, but were no less censorious than the rest when it came to sex. So that when Kate next went to wait for Bobby she could smell the chemical stink of Magic Marker before she read the words: KATE IS A SLUT.

What was a slut? It was a word she had never seen before, yet she knew it was bad and true. So she was relieved when her father announced she would be going by bus to a school in town. The kids around here weren't really her sort, her father said gently. Kate knew he meant Bobby, and that he meant Bobby was dumb. She also knew that dumb was worse than being a slut. The knowledge made her ashamed, of Bobby and herself. She was both betrayer and betrayed.

She was jumped ahead a grade, into an enriched grade nine class that kept her busy with projects. Her parents were relieved when she won second prize in the essay competition for a piece on women's rights. 'I knew you would like it here,' her father said. 'Next year I want it to be first prize.'

Everyone thought she had adjusted and so did she. But the truth was she was drifting. She wanted to be back running with the farm kids through the fields; she wanted to be climbing the sand cliffs across the highway with Bobby, the swallows rocketing from tunnels on either side of their heads, wings beating like tiny dark sails. And when the smart boys, the wisecracking boys with glasses who seemed to get shorter and shorter as she shot up, asked her to dance at the Christmas party she felt nothing but scorn.

She never saw Bobby alone again. In the late summer before she started grade ten her family traded the suburbs for a Victorian house in the Glebe, where the dappled streets were lined with mature maples that no one climbed. Kate walked to school in the mornings with a girl named Ivy, the genius daughter of one of her father's colleagues, who devoted most of her intellect to speculations about the math teacher's marital relations.

Kate knew she was nowhere near as strange as Ivy, but she wasn't as smart either, and she was grateful to have her own tutor when exam time came. She would listen to Ivy's endless analyses of the way the math teacher had looked at her that day, but she never shared her own fantasy, about the French Canadian boy who packed her mother's fruit and vegetables at the local greengrocer, the one called René.

René was tough. This made her strangely excited. She could not be sure of his age, but she was sure he drank beer. In her fantasies she never pictured René at a school dance, holding her close in the sweaty darkness of the streamer-draped gym. She pictured him chasing her through the sun-dappled orchard, holding her hard against the rough trunk of an apple tree, pushing his fingers into her panties. She would spy on him as he took his break by the bike racks, cigarette smoke lazily curling out of his mouth like clouds drifting down a mountainside. If she walked past him a certain way, brazenly, sure of herself, he would smile. One smile, one flash of René's little white animal teeth, and she was good for a week of fantasies.

When she was in grade eleven, Miles arrived. The rumour was he'd been kicked out of a private school in Northumberland County for selling drugs. Her friends were full of the story, but Kate scoffed. She found him annoying, his air of superiority, his habit of saying Brilliant, as if he was some Brit popster. He was tall and considered good-looking, but she found his long fine hair girlish. She thought the bad boy was a poseur.

But then she found herself next to him at the fall formal, where she was taking pictures for the yearbook. He asked about her camera.

'It's a Minolta. I got it second hand. I just bought a new flash.'

Miles looked impressed. He said 'brilliant', and she didn't mind.

They went outside to smoke a joint and watch the first snowfall coat the drifts of dead maple leaves in the gutters of the Glebe and he told her she was the only girl in school who knew how to dress. That made her laugh, hiccuping out the smoke, because she had argued with her mother that night over her all-black ensemble, black fishnets and a black sixties minidress and black suede stilettos from the Salvation Army thrift shop.

'But black is classic.'

'You look like a streetwalker,' her mother had said.

'How would you know?'

'I've been to Paris.'

She told the story to Miles and he laughed too, and then he took her hands and waltzed her out into the empty street, spinning her through the falling snow while they both panted with laughter and finally fell silent, leaning against each other under the streetlamp.

The truth behind inevitable couples is that they aren't. They are a carefully constructed accommodation. Kate knew she needed a boyfriend, and she and Miles were a perfect match in every way that people could see. All through grade eleven they slow-danced at parties, traded novels, finished each other's one-liners. Miles loved her photographs. He loved her style. But the only time he kissed her, really kissed her, was when he was drunk. The rest of the time, it felt like he was performing. She knew it meant he didn't really feel what he claimed to be feeling.

He didn't want her.

He finally admitted it. 'Maybe you can teach me,' he said. 'How to want you the way you need. It's like I live too much in my head.'

One weekend in the fall of grade twelve she took him to bed. Maybe the real thing would unfreeze him. Her parents had gone to the Laurentians with Jenna and she and Miles had the house to themselves for two nights. But grappling with him on the sofabed in the rec room she knew she was as unexcited by Miles as Miles was by her. Pressing her breasts against his face, guiding his fingers to the hungry space between her legs, she could not stop thinking of René.

She didn't really want Miles, even if she wanted him to want her. They panted against each other for half an hour before achieving penetration. Afterward, when he said there was a German movie he wanted to watch, Kate cried but was secretly relieved. She knew that Miles was still waltzing, spinning her under the streetlights in a metaphorical snowfall.

The breakup took until summer, when Kate fucked a football player at a party given by some jock girls she didn't know. Miles was in Quebec on a French immersion course. The football player was amiable, dumb and had powerful arms that kept him propped above her like a bridge. To her shock and chagrin, Kate had what she was sure was an orgasm.

'You mean you broke up with Miles over sex?' Ivy was contemptuous. 'You'll get a name.'

'I've already got one.' Kate talked to Ivy now the way Ivy had once talked to her about the math teacher. Ivy was the only one she could trust, since Ivy didn't have anyone to tell.

But everyone knew. Boys she had been friends with, boys who were friends of Miles, began eying her speculatively. The football player called to ask her out. 'Fuck off,' she screamed into the phone. 'Do you think I'm going to be your party fuck?'

'I can't believe this,' Jenna said. 'My sister is a slut.'

Kate told her parents she wanted to switch schools. 'What the hell is wrong with you?' her father said. 'Glebe is the best school in the city. What did you do, cheat on your exams? Were you smoking pot?'

'I'm not going back there, Dad.'

'You're going back there, Kate.'

She knew she had lost the battle, but she wasn't going to make it easy. On the August long weekend she refused to go to the Laurentians with the family. There was a party at a friend's house but she found she could not gather the optimism required to change out of her sweats. Just before closing time, she walked to the grocery store through the failing light to buy orange juice to mix with her father's vodka. She found René smoking at the bike racks, the smoke curling up, past his ironic smile, into his dark hair. It was as if he had been patiently waiting for her, all these years. She took him home.

¶ 8. It took the *Black River* five days to make its way from the Lakehead down to where the water turns to salt.

Fifteen hundred miles at fifteen knots an hour, twenty-four hours a day. Across Superior and through the Soo locks, one day. Down through Huron and into the St. Clair River, another day. Across the python bulge that is Lake St. Clair and through the Detroit River into Lake Erie and the three-hundred-and-twenty-six-foot drop of the Welland Canal. A third day.

A half day to traverse Lake Ontario, and then into the St. Lawrence River, heading for the first of the six Seaway locks: Iroquois, Eisenhower, Snell, Beauharnois, St. Lambert, Côte St. Catherine. Three American and three Canadian, a stitched seam of international co-operation, descending another two hundred and twenty-six feet down the giant staircase to sea level.

Kate lay tucked in her bunk, a drink in her hand, studying Mick's map. He had given her a parting gift of a half bottle of rum, which she was enjoying immensely. She ran her finger lightly across the stained paper, tracing the intricate contours of bays and inlets, the filigreed rivers, the hundreds of little port towns beading the shores – there must be ten thousand miles of shore – the whole thing stippled with purple exclamation points, marking lights and buoys, beacons to the lost.

Five lakes linked by water and history and blood and commerce. The trinity of Huron, Michigan and Superior in the north, like a gull with wings spread, about to alight. Below the great bird, Erie and Ontario floated like fat clouds toward the east and the St. Lawrence River, a shunt into the heart of the continent.

The river flowed northeast in fact, something she had only learned by studying the map. But she might have guessed from the change in the weather, which had grown steadily colder since they passed Quebec City. Back in the galley, topping up her rum and orange juice, she asked the watchman Kenny for a cigarette. He told her they were in the Gulf of St. Lawrence now, heading for the north shore. They would be in Port Cartier in an hour, in fact, and if they were lucky, they would go straight in, rather than dropping anchor to wait their turn to load ore. He hated being on the hook, he said, everyone did.

It was just the two of them in the galley, the engines shuddering below against the heavy chop on the water, the big kettles steaming on

45

the stove. She could tell he wanted someone to talk to, with no one in the rec room, the television screen hissing static. But then Nancy had burst in, brandishing a tape deck she had borrowed off the engineer.

'Come on, Katie,' she yelled cheerfully. 'Wait till you hear this.'

In the cabin Kate winced as a blast of bass-heavy rock filled the room. 'What the hell is that?'

'It's David and the Goliaths. They're Christian,' Nancy yelled back. 'They're the biggest Christian band around! Aren't they great?'

'You're kidding me, right? David and the Goliaths?' In response Nancy did a little dance in the tiny space in front of the bunks.

Kate climbed up to her bed, holding her drink in one hand. She lay with her eyes squeezed shut, feeling her entire being writhing in distaste at the mournful screed of David and his band. It was like psychological torture. Halfway through the third number she kicked the ceiling.

'Katie! What are you doing up there?'

And she had a wild urge to say 'masturbating,' just to see the look on Nancy's face.

Instead she took the rest of Mick's rum and went up to the boat deck to watch the *Black River*'s approach into the stark wasteland of the Port Cartier ore docks.

Where Boyd Blaikie came aboard.

She had gone to get ice when he came toward her along the companionway, wearing a white tee, light from the portholes strobing across his cheekbones. She would always remember that first sight of him, like a strip of negatives, dark and light, dark and light.

At first she took him for one of the dock workers, but he seemed too sure of his footing for that. In his element. And there was something else – the way he was looking at her, like he knew her, dropping his eyes to her bare legs and raising them back to her face.

Like a stroke.

'You the porter?' His voice was dark leather, black tea boiled on a stove, tannic and throaty. 'Make us a sandwich, would you?'

Kate licked her lips, tasting iron. 'And you are?'

He was grinning, keeping his lips over his teeth. Sweat ran down his forehead and past his ears, dripping from his dark forelock.

'I'm the new oiler, aren't I?'

There was a thickness in his voice. He'd been drinking too. They seemed to understand each other. She pulled her cigarettes out of her back pocket and lit up, cocking her hip against the railing. The tobacco smoke was an improvement on the harbour's heavy air.

'I'm not on shift,' she said, smiling.

'Give us one of them butts, eh?' In the raked light of the galley porthole his eyes were pale green, the colour of river shallows. She could hear the viscous click of his tongue as he mouthed the smoke. 'You gonna make me that sandwich or what?'

'No, but I'll make you a drink.'

He grinned in his closemouthed way. 'Show us the bar.'

Leading him to the ladder, Kate felt his eyes lighting up her body, the cleft where the tops of her legs met the seam of her shorts. On the boat deck bench she filled two coffee mugs with ice and the last of the rum and orange juice and sat next to him. They watched orange flames rise from a molten pool in a black hangar on the other side of the slip, watched the garish reflection in the oily water. She could feel the hot blast of it where she sat.

'I love a good fire,' the oiler said. 'Warms the cockles of me heart.'

Kate snickered and tossed the bottle into the black well of the harbour, where it made a silent splash. Watching the spot where it sank, drinking deep to swallow the thickness that was swelling her throat.

He nudged her with his elbow. 'You forgot to write a note.'

'What would I say?'

'Don't rescue me.'

She laughed for a long time, knowing it was a drunk laugh and not caring. Then he was chuckling with her, and she could see that his teeth didn't quite fit his mouth; they overlapped like a collapsing fence, and when she kissed him the taste of alcohol and smoke and ore dust did not quite obscure the flavour of decay. He closed his eyes, his camel lashes making spiky shadows down his cheeks. It was obscene, how beautiful he was.

She pulled away, feeling her centre of gravity wheel and dip, feeling her body's urge to fall. He hauled her back, steadying her against his hard chest. 'What's your name?' she asked brightly. Only it came out whas.

'Boyd. What's yours?'

'Boy?'

'You deaf or what? Boyd.' His voice was teasing. 'You never met anyone named Boyd before?'

'No.'

'Tell me yours.'

'Guess.'

'Tiffany.'

'Tiffany!' Kate threw her head back and howled, a wild laugh that sounded like an animal. Well, she was an animal. She was a young animal and she wanted another animal's teeth against her throat.

And then his hands were moving down the backs of her bare thighs and wordlessly they descended the ladder to the laundry locker on the stern deck, where he bolted the steel door and pushed her down onto a mattress of linen bags.

'I'm not Tiffany,' she panted as they fumbled at each other's clothing, pushing, unbuckling, unzipping, the combustion of their joined breath like the roar of the flames outside. 'I'm not Tiffany.'

'Who are you?'

'I'm Kate.'

'Come here, Kate.'

She felt oddly calm in the pitch black of the locker. As if in entering it with him she was not just finding pleasure in a stranger's flesh. It was darkness she saw in him, and it was darkness she craved.

In the morning she thought she had dreamed him. But there he was, at the head of the messroom table, giving her a grin and asking for eggs over easy in his dark voice as if he had been there for every other breakfast. When Kenny and the deckhand named Will trudged in, the three clasped hands like long-lost brothers, and it was clear from the way they dominated the talk that not only were they friends but, unlike the solitaries in the crew, they were members of the same clan. The Cape Bretoners. Boyd had taken the job because his friends were on board, and Cape Bretoners liked to sail in gangs.

The loading had started early, a deafening and filthy process that shifted the boat in the water as the holds filled up with the heavy ore pellets. The chief cook told them not to bother cleaning the rooms, but Nancy was not mollified. She complained all morning about the ore dust, a fine pink talc that filmed every conceivable surface, including the insides of the fridges. It speckled the men's cheeks with rusty freckles and filled the cracks in their skin, so that when they came in for coffee break they looked to Kate like etchings of themselves, or old scratched photographs from another era.

Kate was exhilarated. She took her camera up to the boat deck after lunch and shot the cranes and the drifts of ore surrounding the open holds, the pink spirals of dust whipped up by the sea wind. She felt wholly absorbed by the noisy activity of the port, the lines of muddy trucks trundling through the dockyards and the shriek and boom of the huge loading buckets. And there was Boyd, a man she did not know but whose body she had welcomed in the darkness of a steel locker. She wanted more.

❈ 9. But Nancy had had enough. She didn't mind cleaning, she said, she didn't mind doing more than her share of the work, but ore dust defeated her. It was in her sheets. It was in her hair. It was in her tea. She was used to a better class of boat, one with bigger cabins and doors that shut properly. Loading ore here meant they would be unloading ore somewhere else, and it would happen all over again. She put in her notice, and got off two days later, at St. Lambert lock outside Montreal. It was now clear to Kate there was no stigma to quitting, and the knowledge made her want to stay.

In Nancy's place came a woman in a tight jean skirt and a curly blond perm. Carol was from Thunder Bay but she preferred to ship out of Montreal. She liked the men better there. They were sophisticated. You didn't even have to speak French, and they could make you feel beautiful. 'And, of course, they're better in bed,' Carol said, grinning.

Kate laughed. They were sitting at the table below their cabin porthole after supper, drinking Harvey Wallbangers and trying to imagine a breeze. Carol had been in the restaurant business and said she liked the ceremony of a proper mixed drink. She came aboard well supplied.

She had run a place in Thunder Bay with her husband for fifteen years, till he left her for a twenty-five-year-old real estate agent. Carol was forty then.

'He traded me in,' she said. 'So I shipped out.'

But the joke was on him. She was making good money on the boats, and it was her own money. 'It's more than I ever got out of him. Same with the sex. More than I ever got out of him.'

It was just dawning on Kate that Carol was her mother's age. 'Kate, love, I'm in my prime. I had two boys and they're both fine. And guess what? I'm living for myself now. People don't like to admit this – ha! Men don't like to admit this. But women in their forties like sex. A lot.'

She wasn't sure which was more shocking – what Carol was telling her, or the fact that she seemed so pleased with herself. Kate couldn't imagine her mother even talking about sex in such gleeful terms, let alone having it. But Carol was another species entirely.

In Buffalo Kate went ashore with Boyd and Kenny to a sailors' bar where there were two or three others who looked just like them, wiry guys sporting checked lumberjack shirts and long hair. They all seemed to pick up their conversation as if they'd seen each other the night before. They were talking about cars. Cars and dope, the deals they were going to make, the cars they were going to buy with the profits.

Boyd didn't introduce her and no one spoke to her directly.

He called her 'babe', the same way he called them all buddy, as in 'Hey, buddy, how's she going?' As in, 'Babe, you want another?'

The answer was yes, yes every time. She tended to drink too much when she was bored and she was spectacularly bored. She thought about the linen locker, where she had met Boyd every night after dark. On the other hand, she enjoyed having drinks bought for her. Art students have no money and when she went with guys from her class on quasi dates to the Beverley it was always dutch.

Dutch, funny they called it that. The third mate was Dutch. He was the only one who seemed interested in her camera, but the interest seemed to be a pretext to boast about his own experience. Watching her on the boat deck, he wanted to know why she was taking pictures of machinery. She should take pictures of sunsets, he said. She laughed. 'You sound like my father.'

She wished she had her camera now. She would take pictures of Boyd and the buddies in their matching red-and-black checked shirts, eyes narrowed as they puffed smoke rings into the blue air of the bar. Tough boys in matching shirts. She smiled to herself. She was getting tipsy. Rum and Coke was a novelty too. It tasted just like Coke. Sweet. Easy to swallow.

When they took a cab back to the ship Kate reeled across the cindery parking lot and fell hard on her knees. Boyd and Kenny had to half-carry, half-cajole her up the ladder while she complained that they were hurting her. Kenny disappeared into the galley and Boyd put his hands around Kate's waist and marched her back to the locker.

In the morning Carol had to shake her awake. She had scraped knees and no memory of getting back to the cabin.

'I know I'm not one to talk,' Carol said when they were in the galley. 'But I'm forty-five and you are nineteen.'

Kate shrugged, mutinous in her shame.

'Be careful, love. Boyd's all right. And it's a good thing you've got a boyfriend because I see how the others look at you. But I heard you last night. I heard you laughing on the stern. And if I heard you, other people heard you and maybe it'll get back to the Old Man. Boyd ought to know better.'

Kate bent over the sink to hide her blush. Carol was such a hypocrite.

The boat went from Buffalo back to Thunder Bay, where they tied up behind a sister ship run by the same company, the MV *Black Bay*. At the bar up the street it was the same story as Buffalo, only this time Kate tried to engage in the conversation. The place was crowded with dock workers and the sailors were spread along the polished oak bar, the whole place braying and blue with cigarette smoke.

There were only four or five women in the crowd, and she was conscious of eyes on her. She felt like an idiot standing beside Boyd while he ignored her, pounding back beers with Kenny and the guys from the other boat. One of them, a guy with a moustache and an amused look, looked as left out as she felt.

The guy asked her where she lived in Toronto and they talked about Queen Street bars, the chic new ones that had started to appear along with the burgeoning art scene. He knew artists who were moving west, to Parkdale, to find cheaper rents. And then she felt Boyd's arm go around her waist and he was pulling her away to meet someone. He did not let go the rest of the night. He had his hand on her back or her butt or her shoulder.

He did not let go till they were outside. He had to be back at midnight for his watch, and he strode ahead of her under the high yellow lights of the harbour. She ran to catch up, slipping her hand into his. But his hand turned into a fist and he pulled his arm violently away. She stopped and watched him move off. 'Boyd!' she called. 'What are you doing?'

He kept walking. She ran after him again. 'Hey! What are you doing?'

He wheeled around. 'Slut.' He spat the word.

'What did you say?'

'You heard me.' They were circling each other in the shadows of the warehouses lining the dock. His eyes were as black as a seal's, glittering. A sneer twisting his lip.

'No, really. What did you fucking say?' She was shouting now.

'I said you're a slut. Guess that's what Toronto girls are like. Coming on to buddy there. Right in front of the whole fucking crew.'

She stamped her foot. 'Oh my God. We were talking. Heard of that? It's what people do. It's called being polite. You sure as fuck weren't talking to me.'

He turned away again, dismissing her with a backhand wave. It was such a silly, old man gesture she almost laughed. But she wanted to kick him. She sat on a bollard listening to the wet slap of the water and smoked two cigarettes. She couldn't believe these people. What fucking century did they think it was? Fuck him. Fuck him.

❡ 10. In some ways Carol was more like her mother than not. For instance, on the quality of Kate's dishwashing. Carol didn't care in the least about the state of Kate's bunk, but at suppertime the next day she handed back a glass and then a plate and told her to wash it properly. Kate hated it when her mother did it and hated it now.

'What's wrong with it?' Hating the whine in her voice too.

'Grease. You haven't got it hot enough.'

Kate released a geyser of steaming water, straight from the boilers in the engine room. Carol dipped her fingers into the sink they used for rinsing. 'Hotter,' she said. 'As hot as you can stand it.'

'It is as hot as I can stand it!'

'It's not hot enough.'

Kate let go of the pot she was scrubbing and slammed out the galley door. Carol found her on the stern deck, watching the gulls zigzagging across the ship's wake, like girls in a complicated skipping game. They were three hours out of Thunder Bay, moving at a good clip. She watched the birds through a lens of tears. Carol could hurt her feelings the way Boyd could not.

'Look, love, I'm sorry but you can't let things slide just because you have a hangover.'

'I don't have a hangover.'

'All right. You don't have a hangover. You banged into the cabin after midnight. You want to go out and party, that's up to you. But you still have to do your work properly. The bean pot needs to be redone. My frying pan too.'

On the subject of pots Carol was positively obsessive. There was a science to it. She made Kate bleach stains by boiling rhubarb or vinegar. When food was burnt onto the surface, she had to use a paste of baking soda and then scrub with a balled-up chunk of aluminum foil. The worst were the cast iron frying pans, which could never be sullied by soap but had to be scrubbed with oil and seasoned in the oven.

Kate dashed the tears from her eyes and held up her hands to Carol. The wind was whipping her hair into her face and she had to raise her voice over the rattle of the steering gear. 'Look!' she said. 'Look at my hands. They're like an old woman's, and I've only been here three weeks. I've got about five cuts and two burns. I can't stand it.'

'Yes, you can. You can because you have to. Look.' Carol raised her own hands to Kate's, turning them in the bright sunlight to show the thick red knuckles and ridged nails, the knotted veins, the latticework of scars.

'Badge of honour,' she said. 'This is what women's work does to you. And the whole damn world would fall apart if we didn't do it.'

Boyd knocked on her door after supper. They went up to the boat deck and smoked in silence, watching the sunset. She knew he wasn't going to apologize, and after fifteen minutes or so she went to her cabin and climbed into bed with a book, trying not to think of the linen locker and what he did to her in there, his silent intensity, the way he choked and went still when he came, never moaning the way she did.

Carol said women were the ones who patched things up, kept things going. But Kate was not interested in anything that required so much patching. Let it shred, let it tear, let it fall to pieces.

Two days later, when she woke to Carol's shrieks, her first thought was of him. But the crisis was something entirely alien.

'It's the mayflies! The goddamn mayflies!'

Kate looked out the porthole and was frozen by the sight of an enormous pale green cloud. Insects. Thousands and thousands of insects, rising out of the water like mist. They were in Lake St. Clair, the widening in the river halfway between Erie and Huron.

She jumped back as bugs began landing on the glass, two then three then dozens, gossamer fairy wings and little green wormlike bodies, exquisite in their ugliness.

At breakfast, which no one had much stomach for, the Dutch third mate came into the galley to deliver an entomology lecture. He said the mayflies lived for two years as nymphs in the muck of the lake bottom, only to struggle to the surface, learn to fly, mate and die in a single day.

'They come up for sex,' he said, winking at Kate. 'They think it's worth it.'

At coffee break she tiptoed along the companionway to avoid squashing the creatures covering the deck and got her camera. She shot them from inside, close up to the porthole. They had the look of tiny dinosaurs, their closed wings like a dorsal ridge. All perfectly still, ranged in rows, facing into the wind. But by lunchtime dead mayflies lay in greasy drifts on the deck, trampled under the big boots of the deckhands. They spent the afternoon hosing the remains overboard.

The chief cook Anna, who almost never spoke to Kate, preferring to let Carol run the galley while she cooked, invited them into her room before supper.

'I decide I get off in the Canal,' she said, pouring vodka into three delicate liqueur glasses. 'I take my holiday. See my grandkids in Toronto. I'm sick of this crazy life. We had maggots in the pantry in May, now the mayflies. What is going to be next, I wonder?'

'Killer bees,' Carol said.

Anna cackled and raised her glass. '*Na zdrowie*. Your health.'

Kate downed her shot and held out her glass. 'Pretty,' she said.

'Crystal. It is so cheap in Poland I don't mind bringing on the boat. But I'm not going back this summer. Too much troubles. Solidarity will win the election, but people are getting hurt.'

Kate said she wished she could get off in the Canal too. Carol told her not to be foolish. 'You have to finish this relief job, love. Or the union will never give you another.'

'I don't want another boat job,' Kate said, tongue loosened by the vodka. 'I want to go home.'

'No, no, young lady,' Anna chided. 'Is good money for students. My two nephews are on a boat. They study engineering. Is hard work but very good money.'

'It's her boyfriend she's mad at,' Carol said. 'Keep him stewing for another day or two. I always found that worked.'

℄ 11. A day later Carol and Kate waved goodbye as Anna stepped carefully over the deck wires onto the concrete lip of Lock 7 in the Welland Canal, her hair coiffed and her mouth bright with lipstick. She looked much younger than Kate had surmised from the exhausted face she normally displayed. Glamorous, even, in her black pantsuit. Kate wondered which was the real Anna, the tired cook or the elegant émigrée, heading to Toronto to see old friends.

The chief cook's relief was a tall tow-headed man with black-rimmed glasses and a small black bag. Kate was surprised to see a male cook come aboard, but Carol laughed the moment he stepped through the galley door. It was her sailing buddy Jimmy Toivo.

Jimmy Toivo's outfit continued the colour scheme set by his glasses and hair. He wore a white cardigan over a black turtleneck, white pants and patent leather shoes with black socks. It was evening when he showed up, but still hot in the galley, and Kate watched fascinated as the sweat ran down Jimmy's forehead from his pompadour, tinged yellow by nicotine.

It was impossible to guess his age. His yellowed fingers trembled as he took a cigarette from Carol's pack, talking the whole time, about people they had both lost track of, people who had gone broke, gone crazy, gone missing. He'd been on the wagon a month, he said, living with his sister in St. Catharines.

Jimmy and Carol started drinking that night.

For the first few nights Carol came back to her bunk to sleep, after spending the evening in Jimmy's cabin, where Kate could hear them laughing when she got her tea. She resented Jimmy, even though his cooking was better than anything Kate had ever experienced, even in the fancy French restaurant near Parliament Hill her family went to on special occasions.

He would cook in a kind of trance, his skinny middle wrapped in a white cotton apron, stirring and sipping at sauces and what he called 'reductions', turning humble root vegetables into ambrosial soups and stews.

When Kate asked a simple question he delivered a lecture, praising the French way, always the French way, to caramelize onions or make an omelette – airy, melt-on-the-tongue concoctions that were nothing like the rubbery discs Carol had given the men for breakfast.

The division of labour that had existed in the galley was replaced by Jimmy's vision of gastronomic order, with Carol and Kate playing sous to his chef, chopping and stuffing and rolling and kneading, all of them giddy on the fragrance of garlic and herbs, the whole crew barely able to keep away long enough for them to clear the tables between meals.

By the time the ship reached the St. Lawrence, Carol was sleeping in Jimmy's cabin. In Trois-Rivières, flush with her first fat cheque, Kate rode into town with the Dutch third mate to buy supplies, cigarettes and film and beer. She was going to invite Boyd into her cabin for a drink. It was the only way to have a proper talk. She was still waiting for an apology over Thunder Bay. 'Don't hold your breath, love,' was all Carol would say.

As the cab neared the dock on the return trip the Dutch mate asked the driver to stop next to a small red freighter. 'That's a Soviet ship,' he said excitedly. 'Come on, Porter, maybe they'll give us a tour.'

The Russian first mate was happy to oblige. He was young with a breast pocket full of American twenties. He took Kate and the Dutchman through an enormous echoing galley, a sauna strewn with branches that he said with a grin were for whipping and finally to his minuscule cabin, where he lifted his samovar to show off a bucket of silvery fish packed in salt.

'Herring,' he said, pouring glasses of vodka that burned like a poker in Kate's throat. It was much harsher than Anna's vodka, which seemed in retrospect like alcoholic snow melt. The Dutchman talked about pirates in the South Seas. He had sailed out of Singapore until a Belgian friend was killed in a raid on a sister ship. The Russian shook his head sorrowfully and poured more vodka.

As they were leaving he asked Kate if she would trade her Number Sevens for a pack of Russian cigarettes. His turned out to be stubby, unsmokably harsh, with rolled cardboard filters. Back on board the *Black River*, she offered one to Boyd. She was brimming with excitement about her tour.

Boyd knocked the cigarettes out of her hand.

Kate stared at him stupidly, her mouth open. Watched him turn and stalk down the companionway.

'Boyd!' she shouted, pumped on the vodka. 'You come back here!'

Carol hauled her into the cabin. 'Don't let the men hear you fighting, love. It just gets them excited.'

'How can he be jealous of the third mate? He must be fifty.'

'Careful.' Carol laughed. 'Piet's my age. Boyd came looking for you. I think he wanted to invite you ashore. I think he was shocked you'd gone without him.'

'I wanted to surprise him. I got him some beer.'

'In my experience East Coast men don't like surprises. They're a jealous breed. Some women don't mind it. But if you're used to thinking for yourself, it gets old fast.'

'Jimmy's not jealous?'

Carol let out a peal of giggles. 'Oh love. Jim jealous? That man is in love with one thing, and that is Jim Toivo. But he makes me laugh.'

Boyd stayed behind in the messroom after supper. He was pretending to read an auto flyer one of the elevator men had left behind when they came in for coffee. Kate pretended to wash the floor around him. It was no good. He took the dripping mop from her and began to fling it around.

'You're doing a terrible job,' she said. A smile twitched at the corners of her mouth.

'I'm just trying to hurry you up.'

'Why's that?'

'I hear you bought me some beer.'

It was his first time alone with her in the cabin. He did not apologize, and she didn't revisit their arguments. But he talked. He drank the beer and then some rum and he talked about home. Boyd had done an insurance course after graduation. He didn't sell much insurance, but he had amusing stories about driving around Cape Breton in a three-piece suit. He was about to turn twenty-two. She asked how long he was going to stay on the boats.

'I'd like to get my marine engineer's ticket. Buddy down there says he'll put in a word at the school. But I've got other plans too.'

He didn't elaborate, but slid his hand around the back of her neck and drew her toward him. There were waves of gooseflesh running across her skin. They had fierce sex in her shower, Kate with her rear against him, her hands pressed hard against the bulkhead. The drowsiness that followed quelled her thoughts and carried her swiftly into sleep. She did not hear him leave.

In the morning she went down to the little room tucked into the stern where the crew did their laundry. There was a wringer washer chained to the steel bulkhead and lines to dry clothes in the heat that poured up from the engine room. There was nothing but a bare skin of steel between her and the ship's giant propeller, churning the river water the way the washing machine's agitator twisted and punished her clothes.

Leaning over the railing she saw someone moving at the bottom of the great clanging machine that was the engine. She realized then it was Boyd, slipping fluidly between huge gears and pistons, an oilcan in his blackened gloves, shaking his head to fling sweat from his hair.

She watched him bend and duck, tending his machines. He was like a dancer. She could not reconcile the grace of his movements with the noise and stink and heat that filled the air. Hell would be like this, she thought; hell would be loud. She wondered how he could think in such noise. Maybe that explained his habitual silence. He had learned to function in a place where words were meaningless.

❡ 12. She had been on the boat almost four weeks when the *Black River* next tied up in the Lakehead. Boyd had been attentive in the days since Trois-Rivières and she was happy when he asked her if she wanted to come ashore and visit 'buddy'. Buddy turned out to be a

Cape Bretoner named Stan, who was fresh out of jail. Stan had got drunk and broken into a restaurant at three o'clock one morning. 'He was frying up bacon and eggs when the cops came,' Boyd said.

'You're kidding. That was dumb.'

Boyd shrugged. 'He was hungry.'

Stan lived in a walkup flat with a very pregnant and plainly resentful girlfriend named Nicole. Kate knew she was really there to distract Nicole, who was having a hard time with her situation.

It was excruciating. Nicole was on strike from the social niceties and Kate couldn't blame her. She spent the bulk of the evening trying to engage Nicole's eighteen-month-old daughter Shayla while Nicole lay on the couch in a tiny windowless room chainsmoking and watching TV. Nicole was seventeen but moved like an old woman.

Every once in a while she would shuffle into the kitchen and wordlessly replace the empty beers on the table with full ones, and pour herself a cup of treacly tea from the pot simmering on the stove. Boyd ordered in a pizza but Nicole declined a slice; pizza gave her gas. Shayla ate some and got a stomach ache. There didn't seem to be anything else to eat, and Kate thought with regret of all the plates and pots she'd emptied overboard that day for the gulls and fish.

Around nine o'clock Stan and Boyd went out to buy Nicole ice cream. They came back an hour later, staggering and raucous with a bottle of rum from the bootlegger. Kate was by then fuming, pacing alone in the kitchen, calculating how much money she would need for cab fare back to the boat. Boyd put his arms around her and kissed her hard under the harsh kitchen light, pushing his groin against her. 'Come on, babe,' he said thickly. 'Let's have another drink, we're staying the night.'

She was trapped; there was nothing to do but let him fill her glass. Anyway, she liked Stan. His childhood was not the life he wanted for his kid, he said, launching into a story about himself and Boyd as nine-year-olds, jumping freight cars to steal chunks of coal. One kid had run and grabbed the edge of the car but instead of pulling himself up he slipped under and lost his legs. Nicole made a disgusted sound from where she stood at the counter, eating ice cream. Kate wanted to know how Boyd felt.

'Upset?' Boyd said, rolling a joint. 'Fuck, man, I was too young to be upset. Scared. I was scared, 'cause I knew my ma would find out where we'd been getting the coal.' He squinted, sucking in smoke. 'I'll tell you when I was upset. I was fourteen.'

Walking home alone in the early evening, he had seen two cars come out of the fog and crash head on. 'Thirty feet from me, I'm telling you, man. I felt the wind from it.' Two couples, driving drunk. Boyd too shocked to move, the hiss of waves from the sea on the other side of the dunes, the slow silent pooling of blood.

Kate could not get it out of her head. Lying rigid on the pullout couch as Boyd's hands crawled over her, listening to the child grizzling in the crib in the next room, she felt as if she had been abducted. She didn't want to have sex, she didn't want to be there at all, she wanted to be back in her narrow bunk on the boat, feeling the water, the engines below.

She stared hard at the crack of light under the door, hating the tiny windowless room, the humiliation of its banged-together walls, carving up the space of a once-grand kitchen to create another cubby for the landlord to rent.

And then she heard, quite clearly, a shout of pleasure from the next room. It was Nicole, chanting a string of obscenities in a high voice that made Kate press her fingers to her ears. Boyd moved onto her body then and she let him. She craved something, not sex or even love but a feeling of inevitability. Or surrender. Something she didn't want to recognize, even as she opened up to him.

In the morning Stan apologized for being unable to offer them breakfast; Nicole's cheque was late. Riding in the cab back to the *Black River* Kate thought about what people said about welfare mothers, that they were in it for the money. She heard this from other students when they learned she lived in Parkdale. But how could they be in it for the money when the money left their cupboards bare?

She burned to tell Stan off; instead she harangued Boyd. 'He'll get Nicole's benefits cut off if they catch him living with her. Why doesn't he get a job ashore if he can't get a boat? He should take anything. We should take them some food tonight. Carol will give me some steaks, I know she will.'

Boyd said no. He said they would take it the wrong way. Stan would get a boat soon and then they'd be fine. Next trip up they would take something nice for the baby.

Kate wondered why he thought there would be a next trip. She would almost certainly be relieved soon by the regular porter. And then it would be over, and that was, really, a good thing.

❡ 13. From Thunder Bay the boat headed back to Midland, where it dropped anchor in the bay to await a berth at the elevators. It was a hot breezeless Sunday and the deckhands had been knocked off for the day, with no way to get to shore for cold beer. They decided to go swimming.

Kate got her camera. She felt easier around the crew now that it had been established she was Boyd's girl. It was like having a pass. It could be bestowed or revoked, but for the moment she was identified, situated, explained. Sometimes she wondered if that was the real reason she was with him, for the pass. Other times she thought they would get along better alone, in some primitive landscape where his strength and silence would protect them.

Watching Kenny and Will and the deckhands through the viewfinder of her Minolta, watching them shouting and diving from the side like seals, Kate thought they could be from any century. Boys leaping from an English clipper or a Norse longship or a Greek trireme. It was only her presence that kept them from going in naked.

Boyd did not go in. He was on shift, on deck for his coffee break. But Kate longed to, and when Kenny yelled at her to quit taking pictures and try it for herself she went back to the cabin and put on her bikini. Let them have an eyeful. She sensed Boyd wouldn't like it, but she never expected him to tell her, when she walked self-consciously up the deck, that she was an idiot. In front of them all.

What he said was, 'You're an eejit if you go in there.'

'Fuck you,' she said, stepping neatly over the wire and dropping like a rock twenty-five feet into the green water. Thinking as she fell, maybe he was right. She heard them whistling as she hit the surface. And then the force of the water was driving her bikini top up around her neck and pain was stabbing her sinuses and she was too panicked to think anything.

She had descended into a layer of cold so unexpected her limbs seized up. Only her eyes seemed to work, looking up at the green glow of daylight fading above her. All that water between her and the surface. She felt a profound embarrassment. She would die in her bikini. Not even properly in it, since the top was now wrapped around her throat.

And then she thought of that asshole Boyd and her arms and legs began flailing of their own accord, her whole furious body straining up, up out of the green cold and up the side of the submerged black hull to the surface, where the arms reaching for her, pulling her to safety, were Kenny's.

Kenny had jumped in after her. He towed her to the rope ladder and urged her up. 'Wait!' she screamed, pulling her bathing suit back over her breasts. Her humiliation was complete.

The deckhands cheered as she crawled over the wires, and she tried to laugh too, despite the pain spikes reaching past her eyes into her brain, another in her left ear. As soon as she got her breath she knew she would start crying. But Boyd still didn't move toward her.

'She's hurting, man,' Kenny said, helping her limp toward the galley.

'I can see that.'

It was the Dutch third mate who came to her rescue. Carol called him into the officers' dining room, where Kate sat shivering under a blanket.

'She's too cold,' the mate said, tucking the blanket around her shoulders. 'She needs hot tea. Lots of sugar.' He followed Carol into the pantry and was back in a minute with a spoonful of something.

'It's my ear,' she whined.

'I know. You're going to have to lay your head down on the table.' She obeyed, shivering, and felt something warm trickle into her ear. Her whole body relaxed.

'What is that?' she whispered.

'Vegetable oil. An old trick of my mother's. Stay still, now. Let it work.' He patted her shoulder as she snivelled.

When the *Black River* finally docked after supper, the crew fled. Kate watched them scatter from where she stood smoking on the stern. She knew she should go ashore and phone someone, phone Jenna or her mother or her friend Rebecca, to tell her she would be back in Toronto soon. She had been meaning to call Becks for weeks, always finding some excuse, she had no change or the phone booth was occupied or Boyd was waiting in a cab to go into town.

And the longer she put it off the less she wanted to call. Too much had happened, there was too much to explain. She felt as if she had travelled much further than Mick's map of the lakes could show. It would show the route but not the journey.

The bay buzzed with speedboats, young men clutching beer bottles, bare backs burnt red. Across the slip a child holding a fishing rod waved from the dock. Kate waved back.

She thought her wave was why the speedboat guys began to hoot up at the freighter, raising their bottles, their upturned faces carnation pink. But they were not looking at her, they were looking at Carol.

The second cook was sashaying down the deck in her short jean skirt, listing slightly with each step, first to starboard and then to port, as if the ship was on a roll. She leaned against the railing, theatrically wiping sweat from her forehead with the back of her arm. She had an extra button undone, and Kate could see the black lace edge of her bra.

'Girl,' Carol said, waving now at the speedboats like she was the Queen in a cortege, 'I'd do anything to jump into one of those boats, go for a ride. I can't take this heat, not like I used to. Must be the change of life.'

Kate could smell the alcohol. Carol and Jimmy had been sipping at mugs through supper, but it wasn't tea they were drinking. They were getting reckless.

'I'm going to bed, Carol. Maybe you should too. Go cool off.'

'That's a good idea.'

Kate climbed into her bunk and slept immediately, still wearing her skirt, a gathered cotton one she had borrowed from Carol. She slept until Kenny banged on her door at seven-thirty the next morning. She had slept twelve hours.

'Where the hell is the second cook? She hasn't started breakfast.'

'In Jimmy's room, probably.'

She followed him into the dining room where he rapped on the chief cook's door. There was no answer. He pushed it open and looked at her. 'You go in.'

'God, why me?'

Kenny grinned. 'Your department.'

'Carol!' she shouted. 'Carol!'

Kate stood rooted to the threshold as the porthole air conditioner wafted the smell of sex across her face. They looked like a pair of disaster victims, a double suicide, a hit and run. Carol's bare freckled legs wrapped around the skinny naked torso of Jimmy Toivo.

'Come on then,' Kenny said. 'I'll help you do breakfast.'

She was frying eggs when the captain loomed over her right shoulder. 'Carol's not feeling well,' Kate said, blushing furiously.

'Then the chief cook should be doing breakfast, not you.' He surveyed the disorder, the results of her scramble to get the meal started. 'Drunk, are they? Passed out? Well, that's the last time. They won't be staying on my ship.'

Kate sensed that their offence wasn't the drinking, officially banned but necessarily tolerated, or even the sex, shocking as she had personally found it. It was the fact that they had missed a meal, shirked their duty, let their hearth fire go out.

Jimmy didn't see it that way.

Kate found him in the galley after she finished her morning rooms.

'The captain says you have to get off in the Canal,' she said. 'Both of you. I'm sorry. Kenny and I tried to cover for you.'

Jimmy spooned instant coffee into a mug, poured boiling water. 'What's the crew saying?'

'The deckhands are upset. They don't want you to go.'

'Of course they don't,' Jimmy said, hands shaking as he lit a cigarette. His coffee sloshed over the top of his mug as he raised it to his mouth. 'The crew always complains when I get fired. And I always get fired. You know why that is?'

'Because you drink?'

Jimmy hooted. 'My food's too fucking good, that's why! It just won't do, having these lowlifes dining so fine. They might get used to it.'

❦ 14. Four people got off the boat in the Welland Canal. Carol and Jimmy were gone the moment the ladder touched land at Lock 8. Kate waved goodbye and then watched a petite redhead climb up and head along the deck. One of the new cooks, she thought. But she came toward Kate smiling expectantly.

'You the relief porter?' she asked. 'I'm sorry I didn't let you know earlier. I just got a clean bill of health from my doctor.'

'What was wrong?'

'Slipped disc. It's those deep sinks, eh? I'm still not supposed to lift anything heavy.'

Kate went to the cabin and began tossing things into her bag. She

64

had a pain in her stomach that she recognized as anxiety.

She had at least two hours before Lock 7, two hours left to stay out of Boyd's way. She was thinking this when he knocked on the cabin door. He came in unasked and watched her sort through her possessions.

'Buddy dropped my car off,' he said. 'You want a ride into T.O. or what?'

'Don't you have to work?'

He shrugged. 'Quit, didn't I?'

She felt a cold current pour through her. 'Quit?'

'Why not? I've got some business down home.'

She stood and faced him. 'What was that you called me in Midland? An idiot?'

'Come on, babe. You know I was mad.'

She sighed and shook her head. 'Okay. I could use a ride.'

Kate collected her final cheque and her seafarer's discharge book and climbed down the ladder after Boyd, telling herself that it was just a ride, a ride would save her money, it would get her back to her real life that much quicker.

But sitting next to him in a gold leather bucket seat in his low-slung black car – a 1978 Trans Am, he told her – gunning down the highway to Toronto with Meat Loaf cranked in the eight-track, she felt something like vertigo.

She ought to feel relief: she had survived six weeks of work on a freighter and had earned almost half of what she needed for school in September. Forty days on the *Black River* and she had spent almost nothing; all her meals provided, and Boyd had paid for most of the rest, drinks and cabs and sometimes cigarettes too.

But she recognized the same feeling she had had in that tiny room in Thunder Bay. She did not want to be here, among the shiny cars crowding the Lakeshore Road toward Ontario Place, the honking and billboards and stink of exhaust. She was back on land and all she could think of was the water, the empty sky, the iron scent of the ship.

'You're some quiet,' Boyd said, slowing at the lights. 'You all right or what?'

'No. I feel weird. Almost homesick.'

'You're home, aren't you? What exit do I take?'

'Toronto isn't home. I've only been here a year.' But she wasn't homesick for Ottawa, for her parents' gingerbread Victorian in the Glebe. Maybe it was herself she missed.

'What exit?' he repeated, then touched her knee. 'I'm not leaving till tomorrow. You want to go for a beer?'

'Keep going. I'd love a beer.'

They parked at Harbourfront and wandered down to one of the hotel bars that had a patio overlooking the lake. She felt immediately better, and her mood continued to improve as she drank more beer. She wasn't surprised when Boyd disappeared for twenty minutes and came back with a room key. She was glad.

She had been sexually passive on the *Black River*, content to have him grip and fill her, but on the wide bed at the Harbour Castle Hilton she took him into her mouth, licking and sucking hungrily, imagining she could taste the iron in his semen and sweat. She knew she had surprised him too: he pushed her off with a violence that thrilled her, rolled her onto her back and fucked her so hard and fast it felt like the top of her head would explode.

And when she began her chant, his voice joined hers, a guttural counterpoint that she could feel in her chest. And when he came he made a sound like sobbing, an animal cry that made her eyes prickle. She was suddenly flooded with sadness at the thought of leaving him, his strange silences, his fierceness. And then she was crying.

She hadn't cried in front of him before. 'Come on, now,' he said, stroking her hair. 'Come on.'

'I'm okay.'

And then when they were lying spent in the sweaty sheets, drinking beer and smoking cigarettes with their legs twined, he asked if she was getting another boat right away.

'I was going to wait till Monday to go to the union hall. Why?'

'Why don't you drive down home with me? Keep me company. We'd be back by Sunday.' He said it carelessly, in the manner of his tribe.

'I've never been down east.'

'You could take pictures,' he said, pinching her right nipple, making it pop up like a rosy berry, making her excited all over again. 'You'll have a good time.'

❮ 15. 'Kate, what is *wrong* with you?' Jenna hissed the next morning, her arms folded tightly across her fuzzy pink dressing gown, face crabbed with sleep. 'You just got off the boat and you're taking off with this guy? He is drinking a beer at eight in the morning!'

'Shhhh,' she said, watching Boyd over Jenna's shoulder, as he flipped through her record collection. 'He has a hangover.'

'Well, excuse *me*,' Jenna huffed, following Kate into the bedroom, watching her gather her things, her pretty summer dresses, a blanket for the car. It wasn't at all clear why they had to leave so early, but Boyd had been up at 7 a.m., a man on a mission.

'It's just for a few days. And I've never been down east.'

'Yes, but what do you know about this guy?'

She knew what Jenna was really saying. She was saying, what are you doing with this guy?

'I've been sleeping with him for a month, Jenna. I know enough.' She hoisted her bag over her shoulder. 'Look, I'll call you.'

'Sure,' Jenna said. 'Just like you did from the boat.' She plucked at Kate's jacket as they left the apartment. 'Don't be an idiot,' she whispered fiercely. 'It's a stupid idea.'

And Kate knew before they got there that Jenna was right. All the way down, Boyd ignored her, tailgating and passing, stopping only for burgers and bathroom breaks. He would not let her take pictures from a single lookout, not even when they passed the Thousand Islands and could see the freighters moving through the waterway, towering over the cottages. He was on a deadline, he finally said, squeezing her knee absently; he had to meet buddy in Sydney.

'How many fucking buddies do you have?' she snapped, watching the blur of fireworks factories on the outskirts of Montreal. He didn't answer. Down through the Gaspé and through New Brunswick, smoking and drinking truck-stop coffee, eating doughnuts and Big Macs, he never answered. He fiddled with the radio, always looking for big bombastic stadium rock that she hated anyway but was that much more hateful cranked up on Boyd's sound system.

It was raining hard when they crossed the Canso Causeway to Cape Breton Island, but she didn't care; her only thought was that soon she could escape the car and Boyd's growing moodiness. Water blurred the windows, dissolving the sea and shore into streaming bands of grey and blue and taupe. Then they were passing humped green hills, the green so bright it made her briefly cheerful.

'You know it's the water in the air that makes the colours so rich,' she said. 'I learned that in school. Each droplet is like a tiny lens. It's why the best time to photograph landscapes is after a rainstorm.'

Boyd barked a laugh. 'Not much to see down here. All looks the same to me.'

'But we can go to the harbour, can't we – I can get some shots of old boats and things. Maybe we can go out to a pub tonight, hear some fiddle music?'

'Ah Christ, there's no fiddle music any more. What do you think this is, Ireland?'

It was dark when they pulled up to a clapboard house on the outskirts of Sydney.

'Oh, it's you, is it?' a fortyish woman said at the kitchen door. 'How long you down for this time?'

'A few days, Ma.'

His father said nothing at all, simply gave them a look and went into the living room where a television blared a used car commercial.

Boyd's mother ignored Kate till she had the kettle filled and on the stove. Then she turned and dimpled. 'So who's this then? You going to introduce me or what?'

'Kate,' Boyd said. 'From Toronto. I don't want tea, Ma. Give us a beer. I've been driving for a fucking day.'

'Watch your mouth,' his mother said mildly. 'Kate, is it? She's a tall one, ain't she?' Boyd's mother was short, pink and girly. But Kate could see the steel underneath, the intent to slight her.

'Nice to meet you,' Kate said, as sweetly as she could. 'May I use the washroom?'

Upstairs she looked in the mirror, shaking her head in disbelief. The room had no proper door. Just a flimsy plastic sliding thing that latched poorly, leaving a crack. She couldn't understand the poverty of the place, when Boyd had said his parents both had union jobs, she a nurse, he a miner.

She glanced into the three other rooms crowding the landing, all with the same excuse for a door. Three tiny square bedrooms, each containing a double bed and dresser and a very large television. An Eaton's catalogue sat on one bedside table. She could see no books. Boyd had an older sister, gone now to Halifax. She could not blame her. The pink room would be hers.

It was the room Kate woke in late the next morning, to the sounds of hammering. She was alone in the house with Boyd's father, who greeted her in the kitchen with 'Bring in them clothes off the line, would ya? It's starting to rain.' And then instructed her to make him some lunch. 'You're a cook, aren't ya?' he said, grinning sourly, when she asked what he wanted. 'You'll find something.'

She was so stunned she didn't correct him. She had encountered the same casual rudeness on the *Black River*, a deckhand saying to her, 'Can you sew? Then hem these pants for me, would ya?' She had laughed and told him to fuck off, but here she was a guest, even if she was being treated like a servant.

There was nothing to do but what her own mother would do, confronted with bad manners: she got on with it. Found ground beef in the fridge and Hamburger Helper in the cupboard, French fries in the freezer. The only vegetables in the house were onions. In lieu of salad she made devilled eggs, which his father seemed to regard as a waste of breakfast. By the time Boyd came back boozy and stoned in the late afternoon, she was beside herself.

If he had taken her out of the house then, even to park the car down by the shore, it might have been all right. But Boyd ignored her the way his father ignored him, polishing off the devilled eggs and the hamburger and then stretching out on the couch and snoring, while his father hammered away on the laundry room he was building off the kitchen.

Kate put on her jacket and her cowboy boots and left the house by the unused front door, averting her eyes from the cars that slowed, not to offer her a ride but to stare, because around those parts apparently no one walked. Eventually the sounds of children led her to the shore, where she found a gang of grinning dirty-faced feral kids throwing stones at the gulls, their piping voices blending with the birds' cries.

They turned as a group when she raised her camera toward them, and then she saw there were stones still in their hands, stones ready to throw at her, beautiful smooth stones that covered the beach like eggs. Their hard laughter followed as she headed in the other direction.

She arrived back at dusk with pockets full of shells, which she unloaded on the back steps. And his mother, who had come to the

69

kitchen door to let her in, laughed and said, 'Lord, look at those dirty old shells. We'd never bother with shells like that, dear. I'll tell Boyd to take you up to the cabin; there's nice ones there.'

Once she had watched a *National Geographic* documentary about the Masai in Kenya, their treatment of new wives. When they arrived at their husband's village they had to run a gantlet of co-wives and female relatives. Look how ugly she is, they would shout, chasing her with sticks. She is so stupid. And look at her cows! Her cows are undoubtedly sick and will soon die.

It was a useful ritual, getting all the nastiness out in the open. After her hazing the new wife, all of fourteen years old, would be grateful to be left alone. Humiliation as a means to social harmony. And now here was Kate, grateful for the crumb Boyd's mother was offering her.

Late the next morning Kate and Boyd set out on the coast road to Cabot's Landing. It would be cold by the ocean but there was plenty of wood for the stove, and anyway, his mother said, you'll keep each other warm. She said it casually, her eyes somewhere else, but there was a message there just the same. Love my son. A hard boy, yes, but you see where he gets it, don't you?

The drive was pretty, his mother said. She admired Kate's camera and asked about her family. 'I'm not from Toronto, actually,' Kate elaborated. 'I'm from Ottawa. My father works for the government.'

His mother did not miss a beat. 'You hear that, my boy, you better keep this one. She's a catch.'

Once inside the car, alone with him for the first time in thirty-six hours, Kate wasted no time.

'You haven't talked to me since we got here. What did I do? What the fuck did you bring me down here for?'

'Nice talk,' he said. 'Nice talk from a nice Ottawa girl. You never told her how fast you went into that linen locker with me, did you?'

'Fuck you,' Kate said. She felt a wave of cold wash over her. He was a complete stranger.

Twenty minutes north of Sydney the sky opened. Boyd turned down a muddy road and drove a mile or two to a prefab-looking house whose yard was full of vehicles uncannily similar to his. She sat alone in the car listening to the rain drum on the roof and smoked two cigarettes. Then she got out her camera. This was her romantic trip down east. No one would believe it. Taking pictures of rusting cars in a downpour, their greasy parts spread out on the emerald grass.

She shot the house, which looked as if it were melting. Boyd's dashboard, the rearview mirror with the red fuzzy dice, the ashtray full of butts. An hour later she could stand it no longer and ran from the car to pound on the door of the house. A skinny woman took her without a word into a cluttered living room smelling of cannabis and dog. Kate had assumed Boyd had come about his car, but he was sprawled in an old armchair, sharing a joint with a freckled orange-haired guy on the other side of a coffee table heaped with pot.

The guy looked at her appraisingly and turned to Boyd. 'So ya finally managed to drag a lady down here, did ya?'

'Boyd,' Kate said, hating the tremor in her voice. 'I want to go.'

'Go on, have a tea with Cheryl.' His voice was slow, stoned.

There was a case of Labatt's 50 on the floor. 'I'd rather have a beer.'

'Fine. Have it with Cheryl.'

Carrot Top toked hard and squinted through the smoke at Boyd. 'Nah, man,' he croaked. 'Let the lady stay.'

Two beers later she was calm enough to laugh at the guy's jokes. He reminded her of Kenny, sweet beneath the obscenities – a lover, not a fighter.

But when he invited them to stay for dinner, even stay the night, continue the party, Boyd shot to his feet. In the car over the thump of the windshield wipers she said they should at least have had something to eat.

'Why,' he said in a hard voice she didn't recognize, 'did you want to get to know buddy better? I saw the way you were looking at him.'

'Don't be stupid,' she said. 'I'm hungry.'

She saw a gas station with a restaurant up ahead and asked him to stop. When he didn't answer she asked him what the fuck was the matter with him. The beer had made her reckless, she knew that and didn't care. Then she asked what was in the parcel Carrot Top had given him on the way out.

'Shut up, now,' said Boyd, not taking his eyes off the road.

'It's why you came down here, isn't it? You came to buy drugs, and I'm just cover. So your mother still thinks you're her good boy.'

'I said shut up.'

* * *

71

She was asleep when they got to the cabin. She woke when he slammed his door, jerked awake into a cold bright paradise of yellow grasses and the roar of the ocean. She followed him down to a gravel beach where the waves slammed against the rocks, sending spumes of white spray inland. His mother had lied. She could see no shells. Nothing could stay whole in water like this.

Inside the cabin Kate kept her attention on sorting provisions while he built a fire in the woodstove. The sound of the waves had followed them in and she was finding it difficult to hang on to her anger. She felt scoured by the sound, by the salt wind that was pouring through the cracks and the window frames. She put her hand on his shoulder as she handed him a beer. But he didn't want a beer, he had found his father's rum and was opening a can of Coke. She put his jacket on over hers and went back to the beach.

Around six she started drinking out of self-defence. Boyd wolfed down her cheese omelette without comment and sat poking at the fire, his eyes red and glassy. He didn't feel like talking, he said, she could talk enough for both of them. By seven he was passed out in the single bedroom.

She lost count of the beers she drank. She fed the stove, stoking her anger as she stoked the fire. She finished her pack of cigarettes and started on Boyd's. The sea wind roared around the cabin. She wanted to go out and look at the waves but she was held to the spot by her resentment. She needed to know what he was punishing her for.

Around ten she filled a glass with icy well water from the pump beside the sink and went in and poured it on his head.

It was the moment she learned that cartoons were true. Boyd flew up off the bed, water drops spiralling from his hair, and punched her in the face.

She saw stars. Constellations. A night sky wheeling inside her skull. She was falling in slow motion, her ears full of waves. She was on her back on the mattress, kicking and slapping at him, and then he was pinning her and she could not breathe. His hands were around her neck and she could not breathe.

He was yelling something, she could see his open mouth, his loser teeth. She had wanted him to fix his teeth. It took her three or four seconds to register the words he was spitting at her. Slut. He was calling her a fucking slut. Fucking slut had fucked that wheelsman.

Had fucked Kenny. Kate felt a hot fury surge through her body, an electrical force. Popeye after he had swallowed a can of spinach, power shooting from his limbs like fireworks.

She kneed Boyd hard in the stomach and his hands were off her throat and then his fists were in her hair. She was screaming back at him, liar, liar, bastard liar. Then her elbow connected with his groin and he was off her, lying on the floor, doubled over. She got the poker from the stove and brandished it in the doorway.

He looked up at her and shook his head. 'Don't worry. I wouldn't touch you now.'

Afterward they sat in front of the stove wrapped in blankets, Kate weeping between swallows of rum, holding a cold cloth to her face. It came away bloody and Boyd wordlessly rinsed it under the pump. There was blood all over her T-shirt, all over the sheets. But it wasn't much of a cut for all that. A little split between her eyebrows. She found tape and bandages in the first aid kit. She felt better when it was covered.

They smoked a joint, listening to the sea outside, and then Boyd started talking. He would take her to the airport in the morning. He would pay for her plane ticket home. He had never hit a woman in his life before and he fucking well wasn't going to start now.

'I can't believe what you're saying. You're blaming me for this? You actually thought I screwed Kenny. Why would I do that? When would I have done that?'

'I'll tell you when. That night I was working six and six. Buddy saw you on the stern with him. Saw you go in the laundry locker.'

She struggled to remember; it had been in Thunder Bay. 'Kenny spilled a beer in bed. I was getting him clean linen. You knew about that.'

'Fuck that. I saw how you looked at him. When he pulled you out of the lake at Midland. I saw your face.'

She stood and landed a hard slap on Boyd's cheek. She was beyond caring. 'What about you? You would have let me drown. Fuck you.'

He lunged for her. 'Slut.'

'Idiot. Stupid fucking idiot.'

Anger is an unsung pleasure, she thought. It isn't one you admit to. But when he pushed her back into the bedroom she was radiant with it. All the years of pretending to behave, and this was her dirty secret.

She felt the rosy heat of it spreading up her thighs, across her belly, over her breasts, as she fucked Boyd in the cold bedroom, on the bloody sheets, the pale dawn reflecting from the surface of the Atlantic, filling her head with white light. She would carry the shame and revelation of that pleasure long after the bruises were gone. Her stigmata.

PART TWO

❦ 1. 'You can't go back to the boats,' Jenna shouted that morning, taking up her refrain from the night before. 'I swear to God, Kate, I'll call Mom.'

'What's Mom going to do? Anyway, Jenna, you don't want me here. The apartment is yours for the summer.'

'I could move back into residence.'

'Don't be ridiculous,' Kate said. 'It would take you hours to get to work from North Toronto. Go on, you're going to be late.'

'Kate!' Jenna in her Lady Di haircut and Laura Ashley sundress, her arms crossed like their mother. For a moment Kate felt laughter tickle her throat, the way it always did when Jenna tried to boss her. She had been trying to boss Kate since she was five and Kate was six, and it had never worked.

But what Jenna said next wasn't funny. 'Look at yourself, Kate. You still have a black eye.'

Kate turned deliberately to the mirror by the door and appraised her reflection.

'It's green, actually. Green with a bit of lavender. It looks like eyeshadow.'

Jenna slammed the door. She would be sorry later, Kate thought, stuffing the last bits into her canvas bag, a couple of extra paperbacks, a half-filled box of Tampax, rolls of film.

Almost a week she had spent holed up in the apartment, sleeping on the couch because the bedroom belonged for the summer to Jenna. She had insisted on the couch; Jenna was upset enough at the circumstances of Kate's return without having her sleep disturbed.

Besides, the couch meant Kate never really had to get up, could stay squirrelled in her nest of pillows and quilts, watching reruns of *Green Acres* and *Gilligan's Island* all afternoon and late into the night, keeping her head so full of noise she didn't have to think about what had happened. A week of watching TV and leafing through Jenna's copies of *People* and *Time* and *Glamour*, because her head hurt too much to read anything real.

The magazines were full of the royal wedding, an event apparently on the scale of world peace. Jug-eared Charles was to wed Diana Spencer, almost a commoner! Of course she wasn't. She was Lady

Diana, daughter of an earl, as Kate told her sister repeatedly. The fact that she actually had a job and didn't know how to dress made her a better story.

Imagine, Diana worked at a daycare! She was nineteen years old, just like Kate. And had the same shaggy bowl cut that Jenna had, as Jenna never tired of pointing out.

It was a story girls the world over learned at their mother's knee. Some day my prince will come. It made girls like Jenna giddy. It made Kate want to spit.

But wanting to spit was better than wanting to die. After Kate exhausted the magazines she turned to the newspaper. The postal union was threatening to strike. Mortgage rates were through the roof. The miners in Poland were marching. Children were starving in Africa. The children made her cry. But chocolate could improve your mood; it had to do with brain hormones, endorphins. She sent Jenna out for Mars bars after reading that. Mars bars and aspirins and cigarettes and Canada Dry.

And on the afternoon of the third day, the pain and self-loathing having subsided enough for boredom to surface, she set up the Minolta and the tripod next to the window and started photographing her face.

The fingerprints were the worst; a full set on the left side of her neck. Like the ghost of a necklace. She hadn't noticed them until that morning, when she forced herself to look into the bathroom mirror.

It helped to be documentary about it. Over the next two days she recorded the transformation: grape to plum to puce to a jaundiced yellow. All the colours of the violence rainbow.

'It's amazing,' she told Rebecca on the phone. 'The different shades your skin can turn. It's like watching a print develop. Things appear out of nowhere.'

'Sounds like they would make a kick-ass series. I'm serious. I could organize a show in the fall.'

'No.'

'Violence against women is super hot right now,' Becks said, deadpan. 'We could probably get a grant.'

Kate burst out laughing. It was a relief to laugh. 'God, you are bad.'

One year in art school and Rebecca had already decided she was going to be a gallery owner. She was going to be the next Peggy

Guggenheim, was how she put it. Kate didn't think Becks would be so breezy if she had seen the damage first hand.

But Kate wouldn't let her visit.

'I'll let you see the photos,' she told Rebecca. 'But that's it. And they aren't going to be in any show.'

'So why are you taking them?'

'I'm trying to teach myself a lesson.'

And then yesterday afternoon the man from the seafarers' union had called about a job. It had never occurred to her that she would take another boat job. But Bill Stone was hard to refuse. He seemed to think she was one of them now. He needed her.

'I'll be honest with you, dear,' Bill said. 'I'm not supposed to call anyone at home. You're not even up on the job board. But no one in the hall is going to take this relief. It's the *Huron Queen*. She's an old scow and the galley's hot as Hades. The company's cheap to boot. Lord knows why she's still running, she'll be heading for scrap soon enough. Have I sold ya yet?' His chainsaw laugh buzzed through the receiver. 'Why I'm calling is I know the cook on there. Hazel. Sailed with my mother. She's a good egg and she needs a good girl. You're it, Katie my love. It's a cakewalk compared to the *Black River*.'

❲ 2. Kate's heart was thrumming as the cab hung a sharp left and drove halfway up the length of the SS *Huron Queen*, stopping at the ladder. The boat was brick-coloured, tidier than the *Black River*, with a sparkling white forward house that rose in layers like a wedding cake.

It was tied up below the gates of Lock 1, a black cliff guarding the entrance to the Welland Canal. A deep roar filled the air, the sound of pent-up water, twenty million gallons to be emptied before the boat could enter. Tiny white spumes of water spurted from fissures in the doors. A flock of gulls dipped and wheeled above the Canal.

The *Huron Queen* was early. The cabbie had radioed his dispatcher on the drive from the St. Catharines bus terminal and asked him to check with vessel information. It would be another hour before it went into the lock, he said; July was high shipping season and the Canal was stacked up with traffic.

There were five or six cars parked by the ladder. Wife cars. Five or six women waiting and chatting, smoking cigarettes in the front seats with their feet in the pale dust of the parking lot. The Welland Canal was their only opportunity for conjugal visits. Boyd said sailors' wives would make good cops, sitting at home with radio scanners tuned to the shipping channel, tracking their husbands' vessels whenever they approached the Canal.

It was all about timing: it took twelve or fifteen hours to traverse the twenty-seven-mile channel, its eight locks climbing the three-hundred-odd feet from Lake Ontario to Lake Erie, bypassing the sharp drop of Niagara Falls. That was plenty of time to collect your husband between watches, pick him up at one lock and drop him off at another, time for a lightning raid on the marital bed, an argument over bills, a couple of drinks at a maritimers' bar.

But the wives' happy conversation stopped when Kate stepped out of her cab. Boyd had told her there was nothing a sailor's wife hated more than a young porter. He said this laughing at her, on a day when the first mate's wife had been on board and snubbed her offer of coffee. Kate had been angry then and felt angry now. She said the last thing she wanted was some ship's mate twice her age after her ass.

She paid the cabbie and craned her neck to see the top of the ladder. The rain had paused but clearly wasn't finished, the air still heavy with storm. She felt a wobble in her legs as she climbed, awkwardly hefting her canvas bag and big leather purse, a flicker of panic as the ground dropped away. But then a work-gloved hand reached down and lifted the bag.

'All right there?' The voice was pure Cape Breton, sour and amused.

The hand reached down again and gripped her elbow as she stepped over the thick wires. 'Easy now. I've got ya.'

Then she was on board, at the centre of the *Huron Queen*'s long red deck, its flat hatch covers ranged in either direction. She stood reeling for a moment, fighting vertigo, feeling the canted steel surface under her feet. Then he came into focus, a skinny kid with amused blue eyes and ratty blond curls, half the age of his voice. Which, she figured, made him about fifteen.

'You must be the porter,' he said with a poor attempt at a leer. 'Hazel's expecting ya.'

* * *

Hazel didn't appear to be expecting anyone, the way she banged open the door of the cabin marked Chief Cook, a short broad woman with bottle-red hair done up in pincurls. She was dressed in a man's green plaid dressing gown and yellow rubber gloves.

'I was in bed,' she said peevishly. 'It's after eight.'

'Sorry.' Kate's eyes wandered to the rubber gloves.

'For my arthritis,' Hazel said. Behind her a TV hissed like a lake. 'Well, ya managed to miss the groceries. You sail before?'

Kate nodded. 'What's in the gloves?'

The cook gave her a shrewd look. 'Castor oil. What happened to your forehead?'

'Fell off my bike.'

'Lord, I haven't rode a bike in years. What boats you been on?'

'One boat. The *Black River*.'

Hazel crossed her arms over her belly. 'I heard about the *Black River*. Couldn't keep a chief cook on there. This here ain't a party boat, you know.'

Kate looked down the long dining room to the steel door screwed shut at the stern. No molecule of ore dust could possibly filter in here, but the deck was covered in sheets of cardboard just the same. There was a whiff of camphor and onions, a hotel smell of soup.

'I know,' she said, shrugging. 'That's what Bill said.'

There was a chuckle behind her and she remembered the skinny watchman. Hazel's broad face broke into a grin. She had spaces between her big front teeth. 'Bill, eh? Did Bill Stone send you? Well then. You do a good job on pots?'

Kate smiled. 'I do a great job on pots.'

The cook patted her hairnet and laughed. 'Well, I never heard anyone say that before. I guess you'll do. Your cabin's on the starboard side. Calvin here can show you.'

In the little cabin marked Two Cooks she kicked off her boots and went to the porthole. The parking lot was empty now; she could see the last of the cars pulling out past the poplars that lined the town side of the Canal. Heat rose from the engine room through her stockinged soles, the vibration of gears below. Noise was such a constant at the back end of a freighter you only noticed when it changed.

Bill had said the *Huron Queen* was a steamboat built in the twenties, one of the last steamers on the lakes. 'Maybe even the last,' he said. 'But I don't know about the American side.' The words hadn't meant anything to her, steam or diesel, they were part of the language that men talked. But now she could feel a powerful shudder moving through the boat, a rattling that brought a tinkle of glass from the washroom and made the striped curtains around the porthole sway. There hadn't been sounds like this on the *Black River*. There might be animals below, the way the boat groaned as it came awake.

Kate turned and surveyed the cabin: narrow and panelled in dark oak, almost luxurious after the acid-green steel of the *Black River*. Nail holes speckled the walls. The baseboards were stained black by years of mopping.

The green linoleum deck, on the other hand, looked new. A pair of metal lockers had been bolted into the corner next to a scarred oak desk, above which a grimy fan coughed out a faint breeze next to a red alarm bell.

She pushed the room's single chair, a chrome and leatherette job with rust-scabbed legs, over to the bunks. Clean bedding was folded in a tidy square on the top mattress, a bar of soap tucked in like a party favour. She rubbed the thin, wash-softened cotton against her face before launching the sheet across the striped mattress ticking. Another cheap company, Bill had said. But good people. She laid out the two thin pillows, a grey wool blanket that she would need once they were out on the lakes and a green plaid bedspread with a handsewn patch.

She liked the patch. In the glow of the brass reading lamp her bed looked like something from a fairy tale, the cinder girl's cot before she meets the prince. The bottom bunk was a slattern's nest: dog-eared magazines and pilly crocheted afghans and cushions, paperbacks and cigarette packs. A squat blonde with a grubby child on her hip grinned from a snapshot taped to the wall. May, the watchman had said her roommate's name was. And he was Calvin, an old man's name. May always got off in the Canal, Calvin said. She wouldn't be back on board till the bars had closed.

The washroom was a hemorrhage of pink. Sitting on the high lidless toilet, Kate touched the fuchsia ruffles of the shower curtain with aghast admiration. Not May's handiwork, Kate decided, but that of the porter she was replacing, who had got off in Montreal.

A sign was stuck to the mirror above a pink chrome ashtray full of butts: a sixties-style cartoon of a woman with a cigarette in her pink mouth and her hair on fire. DANGER: Never Light Up While Using Hairspray. Who would use hairspray on a boat? There were slashes at the edges, as if someone had tried to remove it with a nail file. That would be May, too, she thought.

Cigarettes made Kate think of the bottle in her bag. She would have one drink.

She could hear the galley before she found it, a thousand pieces of china rattling in their berths. The room was tiny, barely space to swing a mop, the air hot and dense as a forge. Two big kettles steamed on the black stove; a tarnished coffee urn muttered on the counter. Above her head the caged safety lights dimmed and glowed in time with the stuttering engines.

Kate paced through the pantry, past the padlocked doors of the food locker and walk-in fridges, into the high-ceilinged officers' dining room, then back through the galley to the tiny crew's mess. She picked up a white china mug left from someone's coffee break. Thinking as she did it, I've turned into one of those women. The ones who are always tidying.

It was odd how comfortable it felt.

She carried the mug to the sinks, where dishes juddered in tepid water like clams in a tide pool. She yanked open a tap, releasing a geyser of steam. Her hands trawled through the hot water for a dishcloth, breaking up the little waves that marched across the surface. It was like this in rivers and canals, waves in your coffee cup, a tiny lake ruffled by a breeze. Water always behaved like water, that was the beauty of it.

There was a single deafening blast of the boat's whistle; she felt it in her bones. They were letting go the lines. She dried her hands and went out to watch another laker emerge slowly from the canyon of empty lock, its bulk sending diagonal waves out to rock against the *Huron Queen*'s hull.

She thought of getting her camera, but something held her there at the railing. It was the casual majesty of the scene, no one watching but her and a couple of tiny figures at the top of the lock.

'Hey man, get us some of that smoked meat, would ya?'

She whipped around frowning to see the teenage watchman, Calvin, not quite focusing on her face.

'I'm not working yet,' she said. 'Anyway I don't know where it is.'

'C'mon, man.'

Kate pushed past him into the galley. She threw open the door of the crew's fridge.

'There's a tray of ham in here.' She felt herself blushing now, the cold air billowing up and cooling her face as she bent to fill two Styrofoam cups with orange juice.

He came up and watched her fit their plastic lids on. 'I hate that cheap ham Hazel puts out,' he said. 'You gotta get the key to the walk-in. Hey, you having a party?'

'No. I'm just thirsty.' Up close she could see his pupils were pinpoints, the whites of his eyes bloodshot. She caught the peaty smell of pot rising from his plaid lumberjack shirt. 'Anyway, I can't get the key now. We already got the chief cook out of bed once. Good night, now.'

Now. That extra word she had picked on the boats, formality or familiarity, depending. There was a way of talking on water just like there was a way of walking. She could already feel it working in her tongue, like rough poetry, the cadence of Boyd's tribe.

❆ 3. Locked inside Two Cooks, Kate fished the vodka from the bottom of her bag and drank a screwdriver where she stood. She poured a second and took out her Minolta, framing shots by habit: the oak-panelled bunk with its glowing lamp, the framed station bill mounted on the door – 'in the event of emergency, galley staff required to provide (4) blankets' – herself in the mirror above the bolted-down desk, her freckles blending in with the spots of tarnish, eyes shadowed with fatigue and fading bruises and the other thing that always hit her in the evening, before she could muster herself to go to bed, the melancholy that she had learned to manage with TV or phone calls to friends when she was home but otherwise seemed to require a certain number of drinks.

Here is Kate McLeod, relief porter on the SS *Huron Queen*, July second, 1981. The lowest-paid person on the boat, but well paid for all that.

Buck up, she told herself.

She had loaded up with fast film, meant for low light or

movement, meant for the gulls she would try to catch tomorrow, floating on the wind above the stern, meowing like cats for scraps. But for now she lowered the camera to just below her chin and held her body still as she released the shutter. 'Buck up,' she said out loud this time. It was something her father used to say, and it used to make her think fondly of campfires and pine woods. But now she thought of her father and was glad that she hadn't called home.

The cabin grew dark; they were in the lock now. She went to the porthole and lifted the heavy scratched circle of glass, hooking it to the metal eye above her head. The lock wall was close enough to touch, its dripping concrete and steel grid like a massive abstract canvas sliding past. The engines began a violent backward thrusting, bringing the boat to rest, and then a deafening roar of water rose up. She had been waiting for the sound, the great rushing of those twenty million gallons through underwater valves, propelled by gravity, water craving its level, always hungry for the sea. It took only ten minutes to fill the lock, float the boat up to the level of the town and civilization, if you could call it that.

Kate unhooked the porthole and let it fall heavily into place, gravity again. She screwed it shut against the shrieks of the winches pulling the cables back on board. The boat would be noisy all night, stopping and starting, and she needed sleep for her first day.

She rifled through her bag for her books. Three Agatha Christies she had raided from Jenna's cache, her collected works of Gogol, her Everyman copy of *Tess of the D'Urbervilles*. She tucked them by her pillow, then kicked off her jeans and climbed up past the swaying bed curtains and into her bunk, the half-finished drink balanced carefully between fingers and thumb.

She loved this moment, her head on a fresh pillowcase, the sweet smell of the bleached cotton, white sheets flapping on a line. Eau de mother. Then her body was rocking along with the ship and she was reaching up to set the drink on the narrow shelf. Eyes closed now, feeling her breathing slow, thinking of the drink she had not yet finished, it might slide, it might spill, and she couldn't move, could not move, even to reach up a hand to douse the light.

The light was still on when she woke to the sound of retching. The second cook must be pregnant, she thought languidly. She'll have to quit sailing. No good for a child to grow up away from its mother. No good for the mother.

Then the room was filled with grey light and her bladder was urging her up. She shimmied down from the foot of the bunk and slipped into the bathroom, which had a new sour smell. Coming out it was worse and she remembered the noises in the night. She glanced at the bottom bunk.

And stopped short, holding her breath. The face, half buried in the pillow, had one surprised eye open. It stared unmoving at Kate, a fixed blue marble, a little world.

She put out a hand to steady herself but her legs had gone rubbery. Someone had got on the wrong ship and died in the bunk below her. Then, oh fuck, the head lifted. A little creased face with one eye that stared and one that darted wildly.

'Lord Jesus girl, you gave me the fright of me life,' said the little crone. 'You must be our new porter. I'm May.'

C 4. 'It ain't glass, you know.'

There was a lull in the breakfast, and the second cook wanted to set Kate straight about her eye. Outside the open galley door Kate could see grassy green banks, willows and wildflowers. The last leg of the Canal, heading south to Port Colborne and Lake Erie. 'They make them out of whadyacallit – silicone. That's why it looks so real. Warms up, like. I had to go to Toronto to get it.'

'You had to go twice,' Hazel said heavily. 'You went and lost one in Port Cartier.'

'That's right, I did. I was cleaning it, and I threw the damn thing out with the water.'

The chief cook shook her head, catching Kate's eye. Kate smiled politely. It felt like listening in on one of her parents' arguments, more about habit than anything else.

'What time did ya get back on last night?' Hazel demanded.

'Oh, I don't know, I guess around midnight?' May looked at Kate, who shrugged helplessly. 'Calvin would know. He was on deck.'

'Well, what lock was it?'

'Lock 3. Frank brought me back.' May's voice was casual but she hugged herself fiercely around the middle of her navy blue uniform, one hand cupped over her fake eye. The same hand held a cigarette between two fingers, giving the impression of a tiny debauched child.

'I didn't know Frank's boat was gonna be in.'

'Neither did I,' May said shortly.

Kate wondered whether Frank was responsible for the state May had been in when she came aboard. May had told her the eye only misbehaved when she'd had a few, 'a couple-three cocktails' is how she put it, although it was clear she had come in seriously inebriated. May said even her daughter in Cape Breton – the blonde in the snapshots, holding the grubby little girl – even her daughter who had been there when the doctor pulled off the dressing and said the whole mess had to come out before the infection went to her brain – even her daughter sometimes forgot the eye wasn't real.

'Not a penny of workman's comp, neither,' May said now, her voice darkening with sorrow. That was because the cook on the cement boat she was on – her first boat, mind – had told her not to bother with the captain's room that day – they were loading in a wind. Except the cook hadn't bothered to tell her how cement dust could burn holes in your flesh. 'As if I was going to leave the captain without no fresh towels,' May said scornfully, 'with everything so filthy that day.'

She had got a load of caustic dust in her right eye in the morning and hadn't told anyone till the ship was in the middle of Lake Erie and she was nearly unconscious from the pain. They took her off in a helicopter.

'That's unbelievable,' Kate said. 'The workman's comp thing. It doesn't matter what the cook told you, you were doing your job.'

'Well, it's water under the bridge now,' Hazel said warningly. She was filling a pot with some kind of bloody organs that Kate guessed were kidneys. She was right; she could smell the ammonia as Hazel slammed the pot into the sink next to her, to fill with water from the drinking tap. The chief cook grinned. 'I'm soaking the piss out of them,' she said.

Behind them May's voice trilled. 'Good morning, Swede.' A mountain of a man with massive tattooed arms and a grey beard like a biker Santa shambled in from the crew's mess. 'Swede is the eight-to-twelve wheelsman,' May announced to the room. 'This here is Kate.'

'Whole wheat toast, Kate,' Swede rumbled. 'Easy on the butter.'

Swede poured himself a coffee from the urn steaming next to the crew's fridge. Everyone she had served so far had got their own coffee, the three deckhands and the fireman and the oiler. The heady smells of breakfast, bacon and butter and home fries, steam from the kettles and grease sizzling in the frying pans, made it feel like someone's kitchen. May read her thoughts. 'Swede's been on here ten years. He's like family.'

May said the *Queen* was a homesteader boat. Most of the men returned every spring when the ice broke up, staying to the end of the season in December. Kate imagined their children, teenaged girls in St. Catharines or St. John's, having pleasant breakfasts in quiet father-less houses. Nine months of the year the men lived on board, taking a month off in the summer, which meant temporary work for less dedicated sailors. Like Kenny and Boyd.

But they were an unhealthy-looking group, these men, as if they belonged in a sanitarium instead of a ship. Most of them, according to May, were on special diets – for cholesterol, gall bladder, blood pressure. Ailments of a sedentary life, the boat always on the move but its crew in no particular hurry. Unlike the feral young men on the *Black River*, these seemed like a boatful of pensioners, paunchy grey men with sleep-puffed eyes, shoulders rounded with decades of labour.

A sanitarium would have an exercise room; it would have a sauna like the one she'd seen on the Soviet grainboat in Trois-Rivières. There would be a recreational director leading her charges through their morning exercises, patriotic music piped over the loudspeakers. Here they had May doling out stewed prunes and dry toast, cruel treatment for men whose only relief from boredom was food.

The four-to-eight crew seemed more cheerful, bound for their bunks instead of having just been rousted from them. The first mate, a short plump Quebecker with a brush of white hair, loitered by the coffee urn till May had gone back to her frying pan.

'Four toast,' he told Kate quickly, his ruddy face blushing redder. 'Wit butter.'

'Marcel, you bugger!' Hazel cried, appearing behind Kate as she handed him his order. 'You're gonna have another heart attack.'

Marcel backed away grinning, shielding the plate in meaty hands. 'No, no, Hazel, I lost five pound.'

'You're the one's going to give him a heart attack, Hazel, yelling at the poor man like that.' Kate looked up at the source of the voice, a wiry man with a lantern jaw and deep-set blue eyes, leaning in the doorway. He must be the wheelsman: too clean to be engine crew. 'I'll have two slices of rye,' he said. 'No butter.'

His accent, she realized, was Irish. His cologne mixed nauseatingly with the smell of frying bacon. He must have spritzed himself before coming down the deck.

May hustled up with a plate of bacon and three eggs, perfect yellow yolks in ovals of white. 'I thought I'd have them ready,' she said. 'This here's Kate.'

The Irishman made a moue. 'No eggs today, Maeve. Got to get back in shape.'

May stood uncertainly, the plate still in her hand. 'You're going to start it up again? You'd better watch yourself, Kate, Brian'll be getting you out there jogging around the deck.'

'God no,' she said. 'Not me.' She halved his toast with a thwack of her knife and put it on a plate.

'You call that toasted?' he said, smiling unpleasantly, looking her up and down. 'That's barely brown. Put it in again, there's a good girl. And tell Maeve I'll have a couple of eggs after all. Soft boiled.'

She turned away abruptly, the hair on her arms standing up like bristle. Maeve, she thought. Had to put his own stamp on a little wrinkled woman from Cape Breton. Asshole, she thought.

Well, fuck the Irishman. She'd just read something about Ireland. The country that still banned the Pill. Where girls would rather bury their newborns than admit they'd had sex.

At eight-thirty a smiling sandy-haired man in a beige uniform came in from the officers' dining room. He winked at Kate. 'What's a fellow got to do for service around here?'

But May was already scurrying toward him, mug in one hand and porridge bowl in the other.

'You might as well get back to them dishes,' Hazel told Kate. 'May likes to do the captain's toast herself.'

Two hours she'd been at it. Grease ringed Kate's wrists as her hands paddled through the cooling water, capturing the plates and cups that rocked in the sink's swell. She craned toward the circle of light, the porthole eighteen inches to her left, placed where its view was of zero use.

Obstacles came with the territory, the bunks too narrow, the ceilings too low, everywhere steel sills to trip over, doors bolted shut, porthole covers seized up. She winced as she tipped the heavy porridge pot onto the draining board. The aluminum was at least a quarter-inch thick, pitted from thousands of stirrings.

Where had she read that aluminum pots caused senility? The same place she'd read about the Irish girls. One of Jenna's magazines. She shrugged to release her cramped vertebrae and took a mug over to the coffee pot. Hazel looked up from her notebook, scraps of paper spilling from the pages: her recipe book. She put down her pencil and frowned. 'You got back trouble?'

'No, it's the sinks. They're too low.'

'Ha,' Hazel said. 'They're okay for me. You're too tall.'

'Whoever designed this galley never washed dishes for five hours a day.'

'Probably never washed dishes at all.'

'Wash a dish?' said May, sailing by with a load of dirty plates. 'My Tommy never touched china to water in his life.'

'He must've, before he married you,' Hazel objected. 'He was twice your age.'

'Before who married May?' The captain had brought in his coffee mug for a refill, a toothpick jaunty between his thin lips. This time Kate heard the Newfoundland accent, buried under years of Ontario living. 'I thought she was saving herself for me.'

'Go 'way with you, now,' said May gaily, her wrinkled cheeks the colour of roses.

On the boats the captain was known as the Old Man. Up close Kate could see that this Old Man was fiftyish, freckled, eyes pale blue under blond brows. He looked like a cruise ship captain, a pheasant among farmyard geese, a vain man who would strut even here, on a third-rate laker. 'So you got yourself a tall one, Hazel. Get those ceilings washed for you.'

'Oh, I got plenty of plans for her.'

The captain twinkled at Kate, rocking on his heels. 'You're a good-looking girl, Kate – is it? Your boyfriend must be a trusting fellow, to let you go off to sea.'

'No, I've had enough of boyfriends for a while.'

The captain chuckled softly: it was the right answer. 'Come on up to the wheelhouse after you've signed the articles, Kate.'

❡ 5. '*Black River*, May fifteen to June twenty-four, nineteen eighty one.' The first mate, Marcel, sat across from Kate at a battered oak desk, examining her discharge book. She liked the way he let his accent loose on the date. But Hazel was right, he was cheating on his diet: a Coffee Crisp wrapper sat next to a studio portrait of a pretty woman and three lardy boys. He shook his head and grinned.

'I hear she's a bad boat, that *Black River*. Lots of drinking.'

Kate shrugged, smiled.

'Birthday?'

'September fourteenth, 1961.'

'So, you'll be –' He hesitated. 'Twenty soon. Me, I'm married in '61.' He smiled and went back to his laborious printing in the big bound registry. She wondered if he always printed this slowly, or whether it was a function of operating in a language not his own. It made sense to go slow, when you didn't know what was coming next.

'Health insurance number?'

She recited it.

The mate grinned broadly, showing a silver cap. 'You are the first person I meet who knows their number. You are a student?'

'Yes.'

He stopped printing and nodded at the photograph. 'My oldest son is at Laval. In Quebec City. Gonna be *engineur*, but not on a boat.'

'That's great.'

'And you, you are studying –'

'Photography.'

'Very nice. Okay, sign here. You are on the payroll now.' She took the pen, jumping at the buzz of the heavy black phone on his desk. He picked it up and nodded vigorously. 'Captain want you in the wheelhouse now.'

Her footsteps clinked up steel steps to the top deck. She could hear laughter through one of the windows that ringed the room. The captain looked past the third mate to motion her in.

'Ever been up to the bridge before, Kate?'

In fact she hadn't. The captain on the *Black River* was not the type to invite social calls. The wheelhouse, the bridge, the brains of the boat. It was a room full of light and machinery, dials and gauges and humming screens. But her eyes skipped over them and went to the windows.

From here she could see the whole improbable length of the ship, like a landing strip in red steel, the rectangular hatch covers shrinking in the distance like railway ties, the deckhands like labouring ants. She stared, held by the drama of it, the sheer opulence of the view.

The captain smiled out over his boat. 'Six hundred feet. Not so big by today's standards, but she was the queen of the lakes when she had her maiden voyage. That's almost sixty years ago.'

At the opposite end of the deck the tiered white aft house shone beneath the huge black stack. But it couldn't hold her interest against the burnished surface of Erie, filling the horizon in every direction like the grainy hide of an animal. Sooty clouds built themselves into cliffs above.

She felt herself holding her breath.

'Not bad, is it?'

'I wish I'd brought my camera.' He ignored her remark; maybe he thought she was fishing for another invitation. It was far too quiet up here, away from the wind and the engines, the creak of the wheelsman's high stool blending with the low hiss of the marine radio. Swede, he was called. The three men gazed off in different directions, rapt. Then a cloud cracked open and sunlight lit the room like a lantern.

'That's better,' said the captain. He motioned her over to a screen. 'Now, here's a camera you probably haven't seen before. Do you know what radar stands for, Kate?'

'I didn't know it stood for anything.' She stared at the arm sweeping silently, painting streaks of phosphorescence.

The third mate, an elderly little man with a broad British accent, jumped in. 'Radio detecting and ranging.' He had ignored them till now, staring out the starboard windows, and looked embarrassed at having answered so eagerly.

The captain nodded. 'There you go, Kate. Ronnie's been reading radar for fifty years. Works with radio waves. Now sonar, that's newer. Works with sound waves. Ultrasound. Amazing tools we've got these days. Ever thought about mate school?'

She laughed. 'Not really.' Thinking Ronnie was a perfect name for the mate. He was like a little old schoolboy, spit-slicked hair and jug-handle ears. They were like Prince Charles's ears. She wondered what evolutionary advantage there was to ears like that. Perhaps to convince women they were listening.

'We've had a couple of girls come through here. Cadets. It's a fine career, lots of travel, eh, Swede?'

Swede, one hand on the ship's wood and brass wheel, rumbled with amusement. 'That's what you keep telling me, Cap.'

Kate knew there were a couple of female officers on the Great Lakes; they had made the news. But the men on the *Black River* had just scoffed. 'I'd like to see them handle this fucking crew,' Boyd had said.

As if reading her thoughts, the captain said, 'You were on the MV *Black River*. Diesel. Fifteen thousand tons. The *Huron Queen*'s a different kind of boat. This is the last working steamship in the Canadian fleet.'

'What happened to the rest of them?'

'The rest of them? Oh, they retired. Steam used to be all there was, Kate. It's efficient. You got your coal down in the stoke hole, and the fireman keeping it going. The fire makes steam, the steam turns the turbine. You ought to get the chief engineer to give you a tour. Let's see, there must have been three hundred freighters on the Canadian side when I started – that was thirty-five years ago. All steam. Some of those were converted to diesel. Most were scrapped. But not us. We're going for the record now. Isn't that right, Swede?'

His smile was so dazzling she had to look away. She glanced toward the big chart table, where the third mate was making notes. 'Where are we headed?'

'We've got a load of ore for Toledo, then we'll pick up durum at the Lakehead.'

'If we don't lose an engine,' Ronnie said, turning abruptly to glare at the horizon.

The captain ignored him. 'Did you know durum semolina is the finest wheat in the world? Half the pasta in Italy is made of Manitoba wheat.' He was smiling her out the door. 'Better get back now or Hazel will be after me.'

'Thanks for the tour.'

'Come again, Kate. Bring your camera.' He winked at her through the glass.

Calvin was leaning against the rail at the foot of the first stairway, his dirty blond ringlets falling loose from a rubber band. She'd forgotten him till now; he'd missed breakfast.

Close up in daylight, she saw how pretty he was, the soft boy stubble blooming on his chin like fuzz on a peach. He'd been toking again, she could smell it on him. Or maybe his clothing was permanently imbued with pot.

'Come *again*, Kate,' he mocked in a breaking falsetto as she pushed past. His work boots rang dully behind her as she descended the second flight. 'Was it good for you too?'

She stopped and turned. A damp wind twisted across the white gangway and up the nape of her neck. 'Was there something you wanted?'

The merriment rose up his narrow face like beer filling a glass. Then he was gripping the railing with ragged work gloves, hoisting his body into the air. He launched himself toward her, feet first like a sarcastic gymnast, but she turned to hide her laugh before he could land.

❧ 6. In the third mate's quarters she attacked the washroom first, polishing the sink, buffing the mirrored door of the medicine cabinet. The shelves inside were a mini pharmacy, crammed with jumbo packages of painkillers, heartburn tablets, remedies for constipation and its opposite, prescription bottles filled with pills large and small. There was no room for the boxes of new soap May had given her, so she stacked them tidily on the edge of the sink. Thinking, poor man.

She thought it again looking at his bunk, at the blankets wadded into a damp lump, pulled from their moorings. She would have to remake it. Shaking out the bedding she watched a cascade of frayed toothpicks fall to the floor. The bed was walled in on three sides, which meant she had to heft the mattress out from the wall to secure the bottom sheet. Then she had to sit on the edge of the bunk with her back arched until the kinks eased out. She had forgotten how brutal the first few days on the *Black River* had been. Her week of enforced idleness had left her feeling geriatric.

'Having a break, are we?' Ronnie stood at his cabin door, toothpick busy.

She stood quickly. 'Just my back.'

'You're too bloody young to have back trouble, my girl.' He went to his locker and took out a pair of binoculars with a worn leather strap. Kate waited, stung, till he had cleared the room. She bent to pick up her bucket and the knotted bag of garbage.

But he was still there, standing in the doorway, casting his eye over her handiwork. 'Not going to wash the floor, then? It's not been done in three days.' His voice was heavy with disapproval.

'I'm a bit rushed today. I'll do it tomorrow.'

He nodded abruptly and turned, and she thought, fuck you. She sat back down on the bed, feeling a familiar bitterness seep into her stomach. Not good enough. You can clean the shit off their toilets but it would never be good enough.

She stood again guiltily at the sound of boots down the corridor. It would be the second mate, she thought, looking for coffee before his watch started at noon. She could do his room next.

But it was only Calvin again, a wreath of coiled rope looped over his shoulder. He leered comically as he passed the doorway. 'You can do my room now if you want.'

'You fucking wish.'

His laughter echoed down the hallway.

They all did, though; why wouldn't they wish to be serviced? Why should it just be the officers who got their beds made every day, their sinks cleaned? Well, it was simple, according to Carol. If the officers weren't treated differently, how could you tell who the assholes were?

In the second mate's washroom, Kate studied her reflection in the mirror, her mutinous hair, her breasts under the tight V-neck tee. There was no mystery to Ronnie's disapproval. He was a buttoned-down man, an old-school man. In his world women undoubtedly would not be allowed on ships at all, let alone sashaying around the wheelhouse in a T-shirt and jean skirt.

The captain was a different fish. Maybe he had daughters. Some fathers did dote on their daughters. Or so she had heard.

'Don't pay no attention to either of them,' Hazel said dismissively.

'Ronnie can't get over the fact that he's been demoted to third mate and the Old Man can't get over that Ronnie thinks he's a fool.'

They were drinking tea in the pantry, refuelling before lunch. Kate and May sat knee to knee on overturned milk crates, for which some industrious cook had sewn cushions of flour sacks. They were half-assed cushions, lumpy with rag stuffing, but they served the purpose. Naked potatoes plopped rudely into the bucket between them, sending drops of cold water onto their legs.

'The captain is not a fool. He has never been anything but a gentleman to me,' May said passionately. She had stopped peeling and had gone dusty pink.

'Oh, go on, May. You know what I mean.' Hazel was warming her big red hands on her mug after rooting in the walk-in freezer, emerging like a prehistoric hunter with an ice-furred chunk of meat. 'You'd think you were in love with him.'

'Hazel, you know I'm married to Frank.'

Kate kept her eyes on the potatoes, scraping at the pocked skins with slow hands. Her fingers had begun to sting.

May's voice rose a little. 'Frank, he ain't a patch on my Tommy, rest his soul. But I never met anyone could be.'

It had the ring of an old refrain. 'So,' Kate interrupted, 'what's wrong with the engines? Ronnie seems to think we might lose one.'

'He said that, did he? What'd the Old Man say?'

'Actually, he hustled me out of the wheelhouse.'

'It's nothing,' Hazel said. 'It's fixed. We flooded an engine in the Soo lock and hit the wall. Hit it pretty hard. May here fell right out of bed.'

Kate grinned at May, who was hiding her eye as she tittered. 'Lord Jesus, girl, I thought we were done for. What time was it, Hazel, about ten? I couldn't remember where we were. Could of been the middle of Superior for all I knew.'

Hazel swallowed the last of her tea. 'I was watching the news. I like to watch when we're near shore. I was hearing all kinds of sirens down below and then boom! Everything went flying. My damn TV too, but guess where it landed?'

Kate shook her head.

'In a carton of paper towels. Makes you think, though, just one little bump against a lock wall, and the whole boat feels like it's gonna buckle like a tin can. You gotta wonder about the *Edmund Fitzgerald*. The chief engineer said that boat hit the same lock wall we did. And they lost an engine too.'

'What about our engine?'

Hazel slid off her stool and brushed crumbs from her apron. 'The chief says it's fixed, but Ronnie's always after him. It's like I said. Ronnie thinks he should be running this ship, but his heart can't take it. He used to be first mate, but he's had two heart attacks in the past two years. So he makes everybody's life miserable.'

Kate nodded, feeling fatigue wash over her. It was nearly eleven. Two hours till she could climb back into her bunk for the afternoon. Two more hours at the sinks.

May set down her mug and snapped her yellow rubber gloves higher on her wrists, like a surgeon about to operate. She looked at Kate with concern. 'Your poor hands, dear. You sure you don't want a pair?'

'I'm faster without them.'

'Ha. You're not very fast anyway,' Hazel said. 'So you might as well.'

C 7. On the lakes she slept like the drowned.

Day or night, it was the sudden sleep of a narcolept, a sleep seizure that was like slipping from a rock into a black well of water, sinking to rest in the silent plush mud.

In Toronto, a passing car stereo could send her skidding wide-eyed into the cavernous post-midnight hours, but on a boat she could sleep through the clatter of steering gear, the blast of the horn, the call and refrain of the men on deck. She could sleep through it all.

Surfacing was another matter. It was like coming up out of an anaesthetic. You could get the bends.

'It's time, my dear.' May's voice, the colour of old leaves. 'It's six-thirty.'

Kate groaned. 'In the morning?'

May laughed. 'Of course in the morning. Kate? You've got to get up, dear. Hazel don't like no one to be late. I've brought your tea.'

This time she got her head off the pillow. May's eyes, the real and the fake, peered over the edge of the bunk. 'I raised five kids,' she said, handing up the mug. 'I think they slept more in their teens than when they were newborns. Hazel don't understand that.'

The tea was milky and sweet on top, bitterly tannic underneath, the way they liked it down east. Kate drank greedily, wiping her mouth on her wrist. 'Hazel doesn't have children?'

'No, never married. She has a nephew she's close to. Well, used to be. They've been having some troubles, but Hazel don't like to talk about it.'

Kate swung her legs over the edge of the bunk and stalled there, her head pressed against the cabin ceiling. She felt like drowned wood, the blackened trees they sometimes saw tangled in the shallows, swagged with acid-green weeds. Sleeplogged. Then a spasm of yawning shook her and she slid to the floor, shivering. 'God, I'm freezing. Where are we?'

'We're in the river. Toledo. You'll be able to go ashore this afternoon. That's if you want to go. I don't always go, and Hazel hardly ever goes, but I could use a few more balls of yarn.'

'Right.'

'Maybe we'll find a craft store.'

'By the harbour?'

'Well, if we don't we could always have a drink.'

May was crocheting a poncho for her granddaughter in three different shades of pink – fuchsia, rose and bubblegum – which reminded Kate of some twisted internal organ. The poncho had a fringe along its bottom edge and bits of fringe were migrating out from May's bunk, sticking to the bottom of Kate's feet. May had shown Kate her 'gift cupboard', a violently colourful cache of plant holders and wall hangings and slippers and afghans, all made of the finest polyester, that May kept stashed in anticipation of Christmas.

'But you know,' she'd said in a confiding voice. 'I'd be happy to make you something, my dear. I made my niece a real nice purse. She's your age.'

Standing under the shower Kate imagined what May's idea of a real nice crocheted purse would look like and felt a mix of irritation and gratitude. She resented having a roommate, the lack of privacy and forced camaraderie, but a roommate came with the territory. And May made her feel safe. She should say a prayer of thanks for May, for a roommate who would bring her tea and wake her more gently than her mother ever had. Not like Pierrette. She still got a stomach ache thinking about Pierrette.

It was no wonder, Kate told herself, stepping out of the shower into the steaming pink bathroom – it was May, of course, who had crocheted the ruffle on the shower curtain and the poodle toilet paper cozies, which, since the toilet paper was stacked in piles of five or six, resembled toques on skinny snowmen – it was no wonder she had been desperate for someone to be nice to her.

To talk to her. To hold her. It would have been better if it had been Mick, someone amiable and not jealous, but Mick had left and Boyd had arrived, and she hadn't been able to help herself.

She drank the last of her tea and rubbed away the condensation from a circle of mirror. Her face, pinked up by the heat, showed a faint green shadow still filling the hollow of her right eye.

Then it was no use, she was crying.

She was almost twenty years old, but she was suddenly back in her childhood, the time she had got locked out of the house in the rain, her mother upstairs with Jenna, not hearing her panicked hammering. Only a matter of minutes, according to her mother, but Kate still remembered it as hours. And then shaking with cold as her mother swaddled her in a towel and carried her into the kitchen and gave her tea. Milky, sweet tea. The taste of rescue.

The steelcased galley clock was nudging past one p.m. when Kate followed the cooks down the wooden gangway to the dock in Toledo. They'd been giddy all morning, the old women. It was the port effect, the measurable rise in the level of cheer whenever a boat reaches land. Even a grubby Lake Erie steel town. It must be part of a sailor's genetic code, she thought, that relief at arriving, one more passage achieved without disaster.

Hazel and May descended eagerly, the wind kiting their kerchiefs. They had traded their uniforms for slacks and blouses and looked much younger, possibly because of the rouge smeared rakishly across their cheeks.

The Irishman – Brian – was lounging on a lawn chair at the bottom. So that was his idea of getting in shape. 'Ah, ladies,' he said with a smirk. 'Going to town, are you? Those American fellas better watch out.'

'You better believe it,' Hazel laughed.

Kate could smell his cologne follow her as she passed, feel his eyes on the backs of her bare legs below her short denim skirt. She wished she had worn something longer, jeans or her Indian cotton dress. She wished it again, climbing the road up from the harbour. The air tasted of rust. She squinted against the reddish dust raised by the pickups roaring by, horns blasting, hard-hatted men whistling.

'I guess they don't get too many women down here,' Hazel said. She was breathing hard.

'Not your age anyway,' Kate said.

Hazel grinned and pretended to take a swipe. 'Watch out, missy, or I'll leave ya here.'

The first mate, Marcel, had told them how to find the drug store, a cramped independent under a sign coated purple with ore. Inside, only the condoms and candy bars looked new. Kate ran her finger along rows of gritty shampoo bottles as she followed Hazel and May back to the pharmacist, a balding man hunched behind a little barred window.

'I need some diet pills,' Hazel announced.

The pharmacist scratched nervously at his comb-over. 'You haven't had any heart trouble, have you?'

Hazel shot a look at Kate, who steered May into the far aisle. 'Don't know who she's dieting for anyway,' May muttered. 'She's over sixty.'

'How old are you, May?'

'Not a day over fifty-nine.'

The aisle was a treasure chest of beauty supplies: tarnished gold compacts and lipsticks, rhinestone combs on silkscreened cards.

Kate ran her fingers across packages of hair rollers, leaving streaks in the dust. She had a sudden memory of her mother before a party, unspooling the prickly wire sausages in front of the bathroom mirror. The curls were never more perfect than at that moment, bouncing and shining like rolls of new pennies. Then she would take a big hairbrush to them, flattening them into a dull alloy.

At the back of a display of dusty cologne bottles Kate found a little flacon of familiar blue. 'Evening in Paris,' she said.

'Oh my. My kids got me that.'

Together they inhaled the acrid contents. 'What a hum,' said May.

'It must've been here for twenty years.'

Kate sorted through a basket of lipsticks, twisting one open to show May the bright greasepaint tongue, a slash of flame in the gloom of the store. It too smelled like her mother, her pale pretty mother blowing kisses at her and Jenna when they went off to school, her mouth so improbably red it might have been a pair of wax lips.

She felt a stab of guilt; she had meant to call Jenna. Maybe she could call from the dock.

'You girls off one of them boats?' A woman's voice floated from the front of the store.

'We sure are,' May said politely, looking for the source of the voice. 'They got you in a cage too?'

'I'm around here.' A hand waved from behind a stack of Coke cases. 'How many women on those things anyway?'

'Only us,' said Hazel, bringing up the rear. 'Three women and twenty-four men.'

'My. That must be something.' The cashier was laughing, but Kate could read her look: what kind of female needs odds like that?

⁋ 8. 'Whores,' Hazel said, picking up the subject in the bar down the road. 'That's what little boys used to yell at the women cooks, oh this was years ago, when we were going through the Canal.'

'God,' Kate said, thinking of the gangs of boys who still roamed the green banks, their piping voices magnified by water as they shouted up to foreign ships for coins. 'That's unbelievable.'

Hazel smirked. 'Believe it.'

'I don't think it's very nice,' May muttered. She was scribbling on a postcard of a baby giraffe. Greetings from the Toledo Zoo.

'Hell, May, of course it's not nice,' Hazel said. 'Especially since they got it from their mothers, and half their mothers used to sail too.'

They were sitting by the front window of a faux half-timbered establishment called the Angry Sea Inn. They were the only customers. Hazel nodded at a display of sloganed T-shirts pinned above the bottles. 'Sailors Get Blown ... Ashore,' she read out. 'There must be some hidden meaning,' she added with a wink.

Kate burst out laughing.

'My lord, Frank would never let me wear something like that,'

May muttered, looking around the bar. 'He'd knock my block off.' Then she let out a little shriek.

'What's the matter now?' Hazel said.

May was staring toward the shadows at the back of the bar. A rogues' gallery of heads, life-size and garishly painted, was displayed on shelves: earringed pirates, raven-haired gypsy girls, Moors with nose rings. 'They're wax,' the waitress said, setting down their drinks, rum and Cokes for the cooks, a screwdriver for Kate. 'An artist made them for us.'

'You should see some of the guys in our crew,' Hazel said.

They watched the waitress wobble back on platform high heels to the bar, where a dark man with a pointed beard had appeared like a genie. He was reading a newspaper and drinking from a teacup, his pinky raised.

'She's kinda old to be wearing a skirt that short, don't you think?' Hazel said.

'I bet he makes her,' Kate said. 'They made everyone wear hot pants at a place I worked last summer. Some of the older women faked it with Bermuda shorts.'

'I'd like to see that.'

'It was the House of Monte Cristo. Everyone called it the Monte Crisco. It's in the business district. I only stayed a week.'

Hazel barked a laugh and then shook her head. 'It makes me so mad what they make women do,' she said. 'You ever see a man have to wear hot pants to work?'

Kate snickered.

But Hazel was frowning. 'Like when I bought my house. I had to get a co-signer cause I was a single woman. And the boats were the same. When I started, I got ten bucks less a week than the messman even though I did the same job. You know what ten bucks was worth in those days?'

'We get the same now, don't we?' May asked.

'Of course we do,' Hazel snapped. 'Don't you read your damn contract?' She looked at Kate. 'You know there were women working out of this port a hundred years ago? There were women all over the lakes. But the captains' wives put a stop to it.'

'How?'

'Wrote to the newspapers saying women cooks were no good.

Said they were loose. They started up petitions till the companies stopped hiring them. I've got a book, if you want to read up on it.' She waved at the waitress. 'Might as well have another round.'

'I think a boat needs women,' May said. 'Makes it more home-like.'

'Yeah,' Hazel said, raising her glass. 'You know something else? We're better cooks, too.'

But they were cheap drunks. Halfway through the second round Kate emerged from the ladies' room to hear bickering.

She had felt buoyant redoing her lipstick in the pink light of the old-fashioned vanity. She felt like she did when she was a little girl, carrying a balloon on a string around a backyard party. It was a beautiful balloon, but you had to keep it out of the way of the adults. She sat down smiling.

Hazel ignored her. 'You gotta stop doing this, May. I can't bail you out every time you blow your pay. You didn't need them drapes, and now you're gonna have him on your back and you owe me a thousand dollars.'

'I want nice things,' May said fiercely. 'I want nice things when I'm home.'

'A thousand dollars?' said Kate. 'For *drapes?*'

'He's going to knock my block off,' May said. Kate felt a chill cross her shoulders. She wondered if May's husband really hit her, or just threatened to.

'He ain't gonna touch you. It's your money, hell, now it's my money. But you go and spend it all on curtains and then you tell me you're gonna lose your land.'

May had shrunk back into her seat, cupping her eye. 'It's too late for that. I already give Frank the money for that. Anyway, you done the same thing with Jamie. Where's that car he was gonna get for you?' She lurched out of her chair. 'Where's the ladies'?'

Hazel watched May weave toward the back of the room. 'She's as thick as they come, I tell ya.'

'What land?'

The chief cook waved at the waitress. 'Can we get the bill?' She lowered her voice. 'May gave Frank eight hundred dollars when he went home to Cape Breton for a visit. It was to pay the back taxes on a piece of land. This was land from her first husband. It's why she started sailing, so she could save up to put a cabin there.'

'But he didn't pay the taxes?'

'Gambled it away. May never knew till her daughter went back for a wedding. Can you believe that?'

'She lost the land?'

Hazel downed the last of her drink. 'Oh, the land's still there. Nobody else wants it. But why would she stay with him after he did a thing like that?'

Kate shook her head and lit a Pall Mall, inhaling the woodsy smoke. 'Who's Jamie?'

'Why? What did May tell ya?'

'Nothing. Just a minute ago, she said something about – sorry, it's none of my business.'

'My nephew,' Hazel said shortly. 'He's having some trouble, but it ain't all his fault.' She hauled her handbag into her lap. 'The drinks are on me. You wanna see what's taking May?'

Kate found the second cook in the foyer by the washrooms, staring at a display of dusty floats and a fishnet that had never seen water. Its centrepiece was the wax head of a buccaneer with jet black curls, a steak knife wedged between his teeth.

'It's the spitting image,' May muttered close to her ear. She smelled of rum and old roses, and swayed slightly. 'Kate. I seen you bring your camera, didn't I? Can you take a picture?'

'The spitting image of who?'

'Of my Tommy. Back when we got married.' She lowered her voice, slurring her words. 'I never loved Frank. I never loved that cheap bastard.'

Kate pulled the Minolta out of her bag and checked the light meter. She would have to back the shutter speed down and brace her elbows against something. Even so it likely wouldn't turn out.

'Miss, miss! You can't do that; you can't take a picture in here.'

Kate hunched her shoulders and took two quick shots, looking up to see the bearded bartender hurrying toward her. 'Who sent you?' he demanded.

'What do you mean?'

'Who sent you? Was it the *Blade*? I told them if they want to do an article they must arrange with me.'

'The blade?'

'He means the newspaper.' Hazel spoke up behind her. 'She ain't from the paper, she's off a boat.'

The man wheeled on her. 'A boat?' he sneered. 'What kind of boat?'

'A real boat,' Hazel said. 'Not like all this fake crap ya got decoratin' the place here.'

'Now you insult me?'

'You better believe it,' Hazel said.

Outside in the road the wind had picked up, sending shards of sunlight bouncing off the chrome of passing cars. Hazel was wheezing with laughter, bent over with her arms braced against her knees. May danced back and forth on the pavement.

'You told him, Hazel,' she said. 'You sure told him!'

Hazel shoved her purse strap higher on her arm. She turned toward the harbour and sniffed the wind. 'C'mon, girls,' she said gaily, launching herself down the gritty road.

Kate skipped after them, laughter bubbling out of her chest. Below her the *Huron Queen*, emptied of Canadian ore, towered above the dock. A short whistle blast tore the air. 'The captain's calling for ya, May,' Hazel shouted as they rounded the gatehouse.

'Yeah,' May said, panting behind her. 'And I'm comin'!'

Kate heard their hoots float back as she felt her camera thump against her hipbone. 'Wait,' she yelled, stopping and raising the viewfinder to her eye. 'Wait a minute!'

They turned back together, full of good humour, waiting for the next joke, and she caught them like that, rebellious and ribald, pink with booze and wind and exertion, two old women on a toot, grinning at her. And she thought she had never been so happy to get a picture.

¶ 9. Curled in her bunk with a pencil between her teeth, Kate traced her progress on the map. From the Canal to Toledo; from Toledo north through the Detroit River, Motor City on the west and Windsor on the east; through tiny Lake St. Clair and the St. Clair River, past Sarnia and into the clean open water of Huron.

She had slept well after leaving Toledo, waking fresh and energetic before May's morning call, feeling the swell of Huron's big waves. She had gone to the glowing porthole and looked out at the shining empty surface of the lake, aquamarine veined with gold, the sun pressing a bar of heat across her face. The sight buoyed her like nothing else could.

Tonight she had crawled into bed with Agatha Christie after supper and fallen asleep in her clothes. She'd have slept through until morning, but they had hit the Soo at eleven and she always woke when the motion stopped. She had gone to the galley for tea and then changed her mind and got a Styrofoam cup of orange juice instead, spiking it with the vodka she kept between her mattress and the bulkhead.

She took a sip of her drink and circled Toledo with her pencil, surveying the collection of other ports she had marked, turning them into a souvenir charm bracelet.

The rust ports: Cleveland, Toledo, Port Cartier. Iron ore.

The dust ports: Midland, Thunder Bay, Trois-Rivières. Soybeans. Corn. Wheat.

The good thing about the rust ports was that you were out fast, barely time to wash the sulphur from your tongue with a watery American draft. It was different in the dust ports. She thought of Midland, a sleepy town where they loaded down the road from the beach and she could taste grilled fish on the air. Midland had felt like a holiday, and she had circled it twice, for the day when she might go back like a real tourist, drink beer on a blanket with her shoulders burning.

Kate folded up the chart and tucked it between her books. She checked her watch: eleven-thirty and she was fully awake. She lay making an inventory of sounds, May snoring below, the shriek and rumble of the winches, the shouts of the deckhands manning the lines.

The boat was in the lock now, slowly being winched to the wall. She could hear Ronnie on the stern just beyond her cabin, calling the numbers into the walkie-talkie, a running report to the wheelhouse of the shrinking distance between steel and concrete. *Fifteen feet aft. Ten feet aft. Five feet aft.*

And then sudden quiet as millions of gallons of northern water filled the lock, floating the ship up twenty-one feet to the level of the biggest lake in the world.

The locks were on the American side; it meant that even though Sault Ste. Marie, Ontario, was only a few miles from Sault Ste. Marie,

Michigan, a Canadian sailor couldn't be paid off there, would have to wait to quit in Thunder Bay or the Canal.

It had never occurred to her before studying her chart that the Great Lakes were half American, in fact more than half. The U.S. claimed not only all of Lake Michigan, but more than half of Superior too, including Isle Royale, which lay just a few miles off Thunder Bay, and whose name signalled its ancient roots in the French, fur-trading past. Before the United States or Canada existed.

But there had been no mention of the Americans, or of the Indians for that matter, when they had learned about the lakes in high-school geography – only of the vast resources the area had offered up for plunder. The trees and the fish and the silver and the copper, and now that that was gone, the pre-Cambrian rock itself, the two-billion-year-old face of the Canadian Shield, was being quarried and dynamited for roads and buildings in eastern cities.

It would be the water next, still pure in the upper lakes despite centuries of abuse, the biggest resource of all.

Kate took the Minolta and another shot of vodka to the galley, where she topped it up with orange juice. They were out on the lake now, the mates and deckhands gone to their bunks up forward. Outside on the deck she glanced up and went still.

The sky above Superior was an overturned colander leaking light. It was the kind of sky that made people invent gods. City people never saw this many stars, not a tenth of them, not a twentieth. She had seen stars like this in Algonquin Park, camping with her parents, had tried to describe them to someone in the darkroom at school, attempting to explain the inarticulate mass of white that had swum up out of the developer when she was printing night shots. You could take years learning how to photograph a sky like this.

The guy hadn't believed her. He'd seen stars. Starlight didn't make shadows. Kate smiled at the memory and raised her hand, watching its shadow wave back at her. Even the rivets in the steel were making little shadows, changing shape as the ship swayed.

Kate climbed the ladder to the boat deck one-handed, holding her drink high. The wind whipped her hair, obscuring her vision, and she felt a little thrill of fear as she crested the top. She sniffed the air, smelling smoke. Not wood smoke: They were too far from land. She turned. No land in any direction.

A shape unfolded from the bench by the starboard lifeboat.

'Hey man, want a toke?' It was Calvin, scuffing his big boots on the deck as he leaned back against the railing.

She hadn't been offered a toke since the trip down east with Boyd. She edged closer so she wouldn't have to yell. 'No thanks.'

'Shit,' Calvin said. 'I'm still the only one.'

'More for you, then.'

'Fucking A.' He coughed wetly, spat. 'Nice camera.'

'Yeah.'

'What're you gonna take pictures of, the northern lights?'

'I don't see any.'

Calvin laughed and pointed toward her. 'Turn around.'

Kate looked to the northwest, the direction the boat was headed. They were faint, pale green, not the huge curtains of lurid colour she had seen pictures of. But she set down her cup and raised her camera anyway. She had never seen them before.

She framed her shot and leaned hard against the rail, wedging her elbows against her ribs. She would open her shutter for five, and then ten and then fifteen seconds, see how much light the film could collect. Hopeless without a tripod. Like filling a cup of water to represent a waterfall.

Her tripod, her swimsuit, her rain slicker, forgotten. She could look in Thunder Bay for a second-hand one, maybe, except what good would a tripod do when the boat itself was swaying like a drunk?

She turned back to Calvin. 'Are we heading into a storm?'

'Nah. Won't get any real storms till fall. We're just rolling till we get turned into the wind. It's hitting us on the side.'

Kate sat on the bench and bent to light a cigarette, cradling her camera in her lap, watching the wind whip long tresses of foam from the tops of the waves. She thought of the fields outside Ottawa where she had first started taking photos, the landlocked seas of grass. The moon was rising, laying a road of silver across the chop, so bright it was like day on a different planet. She looked at her hands, pale blue.

'I always come up here when we pass this spot, man,' Calvin said. 'It's where the *Fitz* went down.' He gestured to the west. 'Twenty-nine guys, just like that. Gone.' He sat beside her and relit his joint. 'That's the fucked-up thing, though. They're still down there. Trapped in their cabins like the night they drowned.'

'Why would they be in their cabins? Wouldn't they have all been on deck?'

'Fuck no, man. Happened too fast. Been down there for five years. Too deep to get them out.'

She thought there was something pathetic about the way the sailors talked about it, as if it somehow legitimized them, proved what they did was dangerous or romantic. They were proud of it.

Calvin was doing it too. 'You know how many wrecks are at the bottom of this lake? Five thousand. Five *thousand*, man. Two-masted schooners, steamers, passenger ships. Probably still Indians down there from the fur-trading days. Perfectly preserved. Like zombies. Waiting for someone to bring them back to life.'

Kate flicked her butt over the railing, watching its little red eye wink out. 'Oh, come on,' she said, her tone more scornful than she'd meant. 'What about the fish? I read they found sturgeon down there as big as lifeboats.'

'Fish can't get into cabins, man.'

She shook her head. Why were they having this ridiculous argument? 'That's not what I meant. It's only that song, you know. If Lightfoot hadn't written that song, no one would remember the *Fitzgerald* except the people who are supposed to.'

Calvin swivelled his body to look at her directly. His eyes were wide with affront and she almost laughed at the picture he made, his blond ringlets pulled from the ponytail, whipping around his face. But his voice was hard. 'What do you know? You're just a tourist.'

❲ 10. Kate's back rebelled over the breakfast dishes. The *Huron Queen* had tied up at the Thunder Bay grain elevators at eleven the night before, almost twenty-four hours after leaving the Soo. She had lain in the warm darkness of her bunk feeling the ship heave against the timbers of the dock and felt a familiar relief settle through her. And then something else.

Her sadness.

She wondered when she had begun to think of it as her own particular sadness. It was not a new sadness, but in the year since she left home it had become harder to fend off. She didn't feel it when she was taking pictures, that was the thing. Or drinking with Becks. And she didn't feel it on water the way she felt it in the city, riding the streetcar, on land. Alone on the deck in the middle of a vast empty lake, eye against the viewfinder under a faultless sky, she felt charged with a kind of power.

And then Boyd had come along.

Kate stretched toward the porthole to catch a glimpse of the dock, hungry for distraction from the ache that was snaking up both sides of her spine. She could see wildflowers growing from a lip of crumbling concrete, a slash of sunlight on water, a cement wall.

'Captain says we'll be here till tomorrow morning,' Hazel said, banging a pot into the sink beside her. 'You'll be able get off and visit your friend from your other boat. What was her name?'

'Carol.'

'What's wrong with you? Back sore?'

'Yeah.' Kate arched like a cat, grunting with pain.

'It's hurtin' because we're tied up,' Hazel said. 'When we're on the run you gotta shift around, keep your balance. Keeps the blood flowing.'

It was true: her legs felt strangely boneless, like hitting pavement after a long fluid train ride in the bar car. That feeling of arriving too soon.

'Maybe you ought to get some better shoes,' May said, bending over to peer at Kate's Docs. 'What kind of boots are those, anyway? I've been meaning to ask you.'

'Doc Martens,' said Kate. 'They're from England.'

'Comfy, are they?'

'No, actually.' Kate laughed. She had been seduced by the purple boots, the sure grip, the grommets and long laces. But they were no good for standing still.

'Mine sure are comfortable,' May said.

'Jeez, May, you've had those old nurse's shoes ever since I've known you. What's that, ten years? Here, Kate.' Hazel nudged her elbow and shook two aspirins into her palm. 'I gotta take these every day myself. If it isn't my hands it's my damn knees.'

'God, Hazel, every day? Maybe it's time you retired.'

Hazel snapped the pill bottle shut in her fist. Kate could see the colour flood into the old woman's cheeks, just as she felt it rising in her own. 'Retire, huh? Easy for you to say, you're just here long enough to get your money for school. I got the whole rest of my life to save up for.'

Kate could think of nothing to say. She exchanged a look with May, who was twisting her dish towel around in her hands. 'This friend of yours, Carol,' May said brightly, 'is she a heavy woman?' She held out her skinny arms to demonstrate, flourishing the towel.

'Carol? No. Actually she's kind of flat-chested.'

'Well, there's another Carol on the lakes, she was out to *here*. Like a couple of honeydews, the watchman used to say.'

'No, more like fried eggs. Sunny side up.' They were both laughing now. May broke off suddenly. 'Hello, stranger,' she said. 'Coffee's fresh.'

Kate turned to see a white-helmeted man in spotless white coveralls, with a bushy red beard.

'Malcolm's a manager at the elevator. This here's our new porter. Kate.'

'Hello, Kate. You talking about Carol Goulais? I heard she's driving a school bus now.'

'Do you know her?'

Malcolm chuckled. 'Oh yeah. Everyone knows Carol.'

Calvin was on ladder watch, another term for doing nothing. Seeing him at the bottom, slouching on a lawn chair with a coffee, she nearly turned back. But it was too late; he was smirking up at her.

It was a long climb down. The boat was still high in the water, its deep holds waiting to be filled with wheat. She hated the thought of him sitting there, looking up at her ass.

She felt his hand on her elbow as she descended the last few rungs. He was still holding on when she hit the ground. She shook him off.

'Hey, man,' he said. 'No hard feelings, right?'

'About what, exactly?'

'You know. What I said.'

'Oh, you mean about me being a tourist? Not actually working my ass off? Anyway, what's wrong with being a tourist?'

Calvin shook his head. 'Aw, fuck. Whatever.'

She found Carol easily in the phone book, but there was no answer and no machine. She hung up and called her own number in Toronto and left a brief but cheerful message for Jenna. The cooks were nice, she said. Everything was fine. She would call tonight after supper. Then she tried Carol again.

'Yes?' She sounded breathless.

'Carol, it's Kate.'

'Who?'

She hesitated, embarrassed. 'You know, Kate from the *Black River*. Your roommate?'

'Oh. Oh, Kate. I'm sorry, love. My memory's not what it used to be. Are you in town?'

'Yes. I'm on the *Huron Queen*.'

'The *Queen*? Good Lord. I thought they scrapped it.'

Carol said she'd be happy to see Kate, but she'd rather have her come over than meet in a bar. She had just moved into a new apartment and she wanted to show it off. 'It's nice; you'll like it,' she said. 'I feel like I'm a student.'

Kate stopped on her way back to the ladder to pull up a fat bunch of wild snapdragons. Hazel was in the pantry when she went looking for something to put them in. The chief cook's hair had come loose from her hairnet and surrounded her face in a grey-streaked halo. She was kneading her hands in her lap. A cup of tea sat beside her menu pad, a little island of coagulated milk on the surface of the liquid.

Hazel pretended to ignore the jar of yellow blooms that Kate set in front of her. She took off her glasses and rubbed her eyes with her roughened knuckles. Without the hardware her face had a blind, vulnerable look that made Kate think of her grandmother. The same red gouge on either side of her nose where the glasses had rested for fifty years, the same unguarded apprehension.

'Hazel?'

The glasses went back on and Hazel was all business. 'Yeah?'

'Anything you need right away?'

'You're a student, you must have good handwritin'.' Hazel shoved the menu pad, leaved with carbons, across the counter. 'My hands are paining me something fierce. You can write up the menu.'

Tuesday, July 13, 1981

Luncheon Menu
Home-made Cream of Barley Soup
Hot Turkey Sandwich
Shaved Beef on a Bun with Horse Radish

Chef's Salad
Mashed or Boiled Potatoes
Mixed Carrots and Peas
Apple Pie à la mode
Banana Creme Pudding and Whipped Cream
Tea or Coffee

Bon Appetit!

'Oh for pity's sake, this ain't a cruise,' Hazel said, looking over her shoulder. 'You don't gotta say coffee and tea, they always have that. You don't gotta say home-made either – they know I make my soups from scratch.'

But she was grinning. Kate added a little soup bowl at the top with wavy lines for steam. She stopped short of embellishing the corners. She felt absurdly pleased.

'Well, ain't that pretty,' May said, bustling in from cleaning the captain's quarters. 'My, you have a nice hand, Kate. Doesn't she, Hazel? And look at them flowers. I wish I'd known, I'd have picked some for the dining room.'

'You can take these ones, May. I don't think Hazel wants them.'

Hazel snorted. 'Make sure there's no bugs in 'em.'

¶ 11. Malcolm drove Kate into town after supper, which he had eaten along with the crew in the messroom. But first he made her wait outside the elevator office, mostly, she suspected, because he wanted the men on shift change to see he had a girl with him.

She was wearing sunglasses, her lace-up sandals, shoulders bare under the spaghetti straps of her navy Indian cotton dress. It was the kind of dress that was wasted unless you wore it out with a guy, but there was no guy and she hadn't felt like a girl in days. She kept her eyes straight ahead as she leaned against Malcolm's shiny new pickup truck, ignoring the comments as the men passed her in groups, scattering to their vehicles. Only once did she lift her glasses to stare back, at an Indian guy with knife-edge cheekbones and skinny blue-black braids. She thought about what that would feel like, a man's braids. Like silk whips across her breasts.

Then Malcolm was there with his fat cheeks and red beard, driving too fast up a gravel road with the radio blasting country. 'So how'd a nice girl like you end up on a freighter?' he shouted over the din.

Kate laughed and reached over to turn down the music. 'You're assuming I'm nice.'

There was always a Malcolm, she thought. The hard-working guy who'd paid cash for his new truck. At night he studied management books. Malcolm the plodder. The beard, no doubt grown to make him look older, didn't quite hide the acne scars.

But there was no sense in leaving him with a bad taste. 'I met a first mate at a party.' She shrugged. 'How'd a nice guy like you end up as a dock foreman?' The answer got them all the way to the liquor store, where Kate immediately forgot what he had said. She bought two bottles of chardonnay, happy to be earning money again, feeling she could splurge. Climbing back into the truck, she ignored the hungry way Malcolm looked at her breasts. 'Is it much farther? I said I'd be there at eight.'

The house, when they found it, looked like downtown Toronto, litter spread across a weedy patch of grass, bloated black garbage bags spilling onto the curb. There was a rusting baby buggy balanced on top.

'I guess Carol's not doing too well,' Malcolm said, looking doubtfully across at Kate. 'I have to drive back down to the elevator for the night shift. Want me to pick you up?'

'No, no. I'll be okay.'

'Look, it's no problem. There's a lot of, you know, Indians in this part of town.'

'That's okay,' she said, slamming the truck door. 'I like Indians.'

Carol's front hall was carpeted with what looked like soil. Dead leaves and flyers left from another season, composting between the muddy tires of the bicycles barricading the stairs.

'It keeps the B and Es down.' Carol's drawl floated from somewhere above her. 'They figure we have nothing worth stealing.'

'God! How many people live here? There must be ten bikes.'

Carol laughed. 'Yeah, but only a couple work.' Kate remembered the laugh. Warm. Melodious.

Inside the apartment Kate sank into a low leather sofa upholstered in cushions and women's magazines. Now that she was horizontal she realized she was exhausted. She could be in her bunk, asleep.

'Cheers, love.' Carol shoved an oversized goblet of wine into her hand. 'This should perk you up.'

Kate drank greedily. It was strange to see Carol without an audience of cups and saucers, a stove to fuss over, vegetables to peel. 'So you've quit sailing?'

'Ha. Sailing quit me.'

'What about Jimmy?'

'I'm surprised you don't know. Everybody here does. We both got blacklisted. We didn't find out till we tried to ship out together, out of Montreal. But Jim's fine. He's gone deep sea. Signed onto a Limey boat. No jobs for women deep sea.'

'God, you can't go back ever?'

'Oh, I think it's five years, then they let you back. But I'll be fifty in five years. I don't think I want to be cleaning anybody's toilet when I'm fifty, love. Except my own.' Carol chortled, refilling her glass. 'I don't think we ever thanked you properly. We'd have been caught with our pants down if it wasn't for you. Literally.'

The chortle turned into a belly laugh, and all at once Kate was back in the crew's mess on the *Black River*, listening to Carol's big laugh, egging on the men with double entendres, jokes about carrots, how many wieners it took to properly fill a hotdog bun.

They had all laughed when Carol was on the *Black River*, even the filthy-mouthed crew from the engine room, the old Brit who always scuttled away at the sight of Kate. It didn't have to be a good joke, sailors would laugh at anything, they were desperate to laugh.

Kate studied her wineglass. 'So you and Jimmy,' she said. 'Is it over?'

'Oh, love.' Carol laughed. 'Jim's a friend. Good in bed, too, though you'd never know looking at him.'

'No,' Kate said, grinning. 'You wouldn't.'

Carol was trying to salvage the scraps of her former life. 'My fake life,' she said dismissively, tipping back her glass. 'What was I doing? Letting myself be sucked dry by my children, wanting to be sucked dry by my children. Opening my legs to my husband every time he said the word. I thought I had him. I thought it was that simple.'

She had got a job driving a school bus. Now that her boys were grown she missed being around little kids. They were therapeutic, she said. She was trying to drink less and was also, Kate remarked, doing her nails.

'Yeah. Manicure therapy. All kinds of therapy. I'm doing yoga too.' Her toenails and fingernails were painted a shiny deep red. She held her hands up to the light. 'This is new,' she said. 'Shiseido.'

Kate sloshed back wine and listened to Carol justify her refusal to go to a lawyer over the shabby way her husband was treating her. The lawyers all knew her ex, they went to his restaurant. But he was going to give her a down payment to buy a house. If she was good.

'What do you mean by good?' Kate sat back. She hadn't meant to shout.

But Carol just laughed. 'Oh, you know. Curb my behaviour. Refrain from walking into the restaurant after drinking two bottles of wine. I did that.' She trailed off for a moment. 'I still get the idea sometimes, that I could just walk in after closing and unzip his pants and he'd take me into the back room and fuck me.'

'Carol!' Kate couldn't keep the shock from her voice. 'You don't really want him back, do you?'

'Kate, love. It's not as simple as you'd like. Sometimes I think, if one of the kids was in an accident? Then my ex would have to talk to me. He'd have to talk to me at the hospital. He would be sad and he'd let me hold him. And then we'd go home together, back to the house.' She emptied the second bottle into Kate's wineglass and held up her hand. 'Finish that. I've got another bottle.'

She walked unsteadily to her tiny kitchen, scattering ash. 'Christ, enough about that. How's Boyd?'

Kate followed and leaned against the counter. Her heart had begun to hammer. 'I have no idea,' she said as Carol worked the corkscrew into a jumbo bottle of chardonnay. She ran her finger down the red line between her eyebrows. 'Boyd did this. He hit me.'

The bottle slammed onto the counter. 'Oh, wow.'

'A couple of weeks ago. In Cape Breton.' She felt her throat tighten and swallowed more wine. That was better. She didn't want to cry. Carol might try to hug her.

She patted Carol's shoulder, smiled at her stricken face. A

mother's face, after all. But Kate could never tell her own mother about this. 'I'm okay. Really. It was all the clichés. Everything slowed down. It was like I was watching a movie.'

She stroked her forehead. 'I should have had stitches, but we were in the middle of nowhere. It bled a lot.'

Carol nodded. 'Head wounds bleed the most. I learned that with my boys.'

'I'm going to have a scar. A permanent frown line. I've been wondering. If you look pissed off, does it actually make you feel pissed off?'

'Why not? If people think you're mad, they get mad back. So then you get mad at them, because it isn't fair. Like when I came to this town. People thought I was a snob, so they didn't talk to me. I wasn't a snob; I was from Ear Falls, for God's sake. I was scared shitless.'

'From *where*?'

'North of nowhere. Anyway, love, Boyd did you a favour.' Carol sank into the couch, her bare legs stretched out on the floor. 'If Ted had hit me instead of calling me a stupid cunt for half our marriage, I'd have left when I was still young. And I'd have got the kids and the house and half the restaurant.'

Kate flinched as a blast of amplified sound came up through the floor.

'My neighbours,' said Carol, reaching for the heavy ashtray and casually crashing it against the hardwood. 'Don't get me wrong, I liked Boyd, but you should have turned him in.'

'Come on, Carol. Then he'd really have something to come after me for.'

'Oh Kate, love.'

'What?'

'When I first saw you, I thought, that girl's a fish out of water. It isn't a life for a girl like you. God, when I was nineteen –'

'Don't say it.' Kate could feel herself getting cranky. She was also very drunk. She bent to gather her things.

'I was only going to say – no, listen to me – you're a smart girl, Kate. Don't hide your light. Don't be like the rest of us.'

'Carol. I have to go. How far are we from downtown?'

Carol got up in one sinuous movement. She was laughing again.

'There *is* no downtown in Thunder Bay.'

'Come on, Carol.'

'You could walk from here. Why?'

'Let's go out for a drink.'

She knew Carol wouldn't come. They hugged at the door. 'You aren't going to see Boyd again, are you? That wouldn't be wise.'

'I'm okay, Mom,' Kate joked. 'Really. He's on another ship or he's still down east. I just need to use my legs.'

'I'm sorry, love.'

'For what?'

'For being no goddamn help to you.'

Clattering down the stairs Kate thought no one had been much help to her, including herself. She stood on the porch sniffing the air, and launched herself toward the bar strip. It was almost eleven and just getting dark, and she remembered how far north they were.

It felt good to walk, feel the stretch and pull of her wine-fuelled muscles, the brush of her skirt against her thighs. Boyd hated walking. Where he came from it meant you were too poor to own a car. Boyd and his muscle car and his bad teeth. She was sorry about his teeth. She had told him he should go see a dentist and he had been furious. Now he would never go. He would be like the homesteaders on the boats who had false teeth by forty.

It gave her no satisfaction to think of him that way. She couldn't think of Boyd at all without a flood of shame in her belly. She had lied to Carol. She had lied to her sister and Rebecca and she would lie to anyone else.

Because on the fourth night she spent holed up in her misery there had been a knock on the apartment door. And she had known it would be him. And she had let him in. Because Jenna was out with friends, and no one would know. Because she was curious. Because she craved comfort more than revenge.

There was comfort in watching him cry his boozy traitorous tears as he stroked her bruised eyes with trembling fingers. There was power too, letting him unbutton her shirt and push his face between her breasts. Thinking, just this once.

Was that why women let them back in? To hear them beg forgiveness? Let them pull off your jeans and have to bite your lip to keep from shouting your pleasure? Kate wondered at the taint in her, that she could enjoy it so much when it was so wrong. But she wasn't going to let him in again.

She caught a tendril of smoke in the air and walked faster. It was cool for July, but too warm, surely, for a fire. She thought of the woodstove in the cabin on the Cape Breton coast, the smell of smoke in her bloody hair.

It was stronger now. She had come out of Carol's street onto Simpson, its lights hazy with smoke. Then she turned south toward the water and saw a tall narrow building with an orange fright wig of flame.

❡ 12. A grain elevator was on fire, an impossibly narrow structure of four or five stories with a little peaked attic that hemorrhaged flame. Only now did Kate notice the wind against her bare legs, as she watched it catch the flickering mass and shake it, pulling it east toward the thickening darkness over the lake, where tiny feathers of yellow broke off and scattered. The flames licked silently at a column of grey smoke that poured itself into the sky. It was so quiet she could hear herself breathing.

But she wasn't alone. All along Simpson Street traffic had slowed and then stopped altogether, as people piled out of their beaters and pickup trucks and hippie vans to come and watch a part of their heritage burn down. Thunder Bay was still a frontier town, she thought, a boiled dinner of cultures, full of Eastern European grandmas and Ojibway teenagers pushing baby carriages. And looming on the edges, everywhere you looked, water and rock and bush, the same implacable landscape that had greeted the voyageurs.

She moved among the groups gathering on the sidewalks, waitresses in pastel uniforms, native men with braids and lumberjack shirts, geezers in baseball caps. They seemed stunned into silence by the beautiful destruction in front of them.

The sirens broke the spell. The crowd woke, shifted and stretched, began talking all at once. It was an old elevator, a man next to her said, unused now for years. They used to burn down a lot, he said, when the dust inside them ignited. Kate was jostled to the side by a phalanx of emergency personnel, who seemed irritated at having been beaten so badly to the scene. Camera flashes strobed through the air and she felt a surge of anger at herself for not having her Minolta.

Then a nasal voice behind her detached itself from the pandemonium. 'Got a light?'

Boyd's voice. Or not quite. She whirled around, ice snaking down her chest, and bumped into a woman in a kerchief who hissed at her. She turned again and felt a hand on her shoulder.

'God, Calvin,' she spat. 'You fucking scared me!'

'Now why would I scare you?' He was grinning broadly, an unlit cigarette clamped between his teeth.

'What the fuck,' she said. 'Now you're following me?'

He removed the cigarette. 'Nice talk. Saw you from the bar, didn't I? Saw everyone heading for the fire. I love a good fire. Reminds me of home.'

'Burned your parents' house down, did you?'

'Tell ya the truth, it's more fun burning cars. You get to crash them first.'

'Uh huh.' Kate stood back from him, arms crossed, her eyes sliding around the buzzing crowd, now burnished red and blue by the lights of the emergency vehicles. She was looking for a silhouette, someone standing still, looking for her.

Calvin jockeyed closer, past a pair of lank-haired teenage girls who were eyeing them both. She caught the sharp punk of rum. 'Yeah, buddy and me, we burned three cars last winter,' he said, his words going soft at the edges. 'Made the cops mental.'

Kate turned her gaze on the black hoses pumping water into the elevator's lower levels with no discernible effect.

'Yeah, right,' she said. 'Three cars.'

'They were just junkers, man. Cops had a reward out –' Calvin's voice was drowned out by the crowd, groaning as one when the little peaked house on top of the elevator suddenly leaned to the side like the head of a quizzical giant. In quick succession, the roof collapsed inward in chunks and a slice of metal siding fell onto the power lines, which crackled and sparked. The black rafters were a charcoal sketch in the glittering flames.

Calvin tucked the cigarette behind his ear. 'I'm getting some thirsty. You coming up to the bar?'

'I don't think so.'

He smiled slyly, his eyes sliding down her chest. 'Be a shame to waste that getup you're wearing.'

She could smell his sweat, a boy's sweet sweat mixed with aftershave. The deliciousness of it assailed her. Her eyes went to his tanned biceps straining the rolled-up sleeves of his check cowboy shirt. It surprised her how easy it was to picture his arms around her.

'Calvin, I'm surprised you can even get into the bar. What are you, seventeen?'

'I got good fake ID, man.'

He went, laughing, the lank-haired girls looking on in frank interest. She watched him thread his way through the last knots of onlookers, bumping into someone and making a joke, handing over a cigarette, saluting. The booze had turned the skinny kid into a man about town, the way it had transformed the males of his ancestry, all those men trading lies in the local while their women sat home drinking bitter tea.

Kate watched till Calvin had turned the corner, then headed in the same direction. She'd lost her nerve. She wanted to be back on the ship, safe in her bunk, but she would have to walk along Simpson to flag a cab.

Bitter tea and Simpson Street made her think of Nicole, the grim, pregnant girlfriend of Boyd's friend Stan, chain-smoking at the table in her shabby spotless kitchen like someone in an airport waiting for a flight out.

Kate still felt shame remembering it, the way they had imposed on a girl preparing for a new child in a windowless flat with nothing in her cupboards but tea and cereal. Her baby's father just out of jail. She wondered if Nicole had had a boy or a girl, if Boyd had brought a baby gift as he said he would.

Boyd could be here now, she thought, could have got a new boat in Quebec City or Montreal and beat her to the Lakehead. She thought of them circling each other as they circled through the lakes, tiny dots on the surface of her map. The thought made her slow her steps. She needed to know where he was. She wouldn't feel safe until she could track him.

Taking her to meet Stan, she thought, was taking her to meet one of his real family, the gang of boys he had grown up with, cousins and friends and brothers of friends, who would teach each other how to fight and drive and punish each other with casual beatings they liked to recount over drinks. Their mothers always away at the fish plant, their fathers in the mine. Boys raised by boys.

Kate thought of the terrible story Boyd had told, the head-on crash on the sea road, the hiss of waves, the pooling blood. She had since imagined the scene so often it was as if she had seen it. In a movie maybe. A horror flick, when you realize that one body is missing a head. Then you see another's legs jerk and suddenly you are running for help, face wet with tears or fog, not hearing yourself crying.

But she had heard Boyd crying. The night he had knocked on her door after Cape Breton, the night he had kissed her bruised eyes and begged absolution. Not knowing she had let him in so she could erase him. Exorcise him.

And when he called the next night, she had said no. That was it, they were done. And he said, 'You used me. You can't do this to me. Please, babe.' His voice breaking up like a bad radio signal.

She crashed the receiver down as if it had burned her.

❰ 13. At seven the next morning Kate watched sooty clouds roll over Superior like tumbleweed in a black-and-white western, a scene of silent desolation played above the empty theatre of the lake. To the east the sky was a roof of indigo pierced by a cone of white light. She held her camera against her face, despairing at the beauty. This was Lawren Harris country, distilled sixty years ago into his transcendental north shore paintings. She could capture only a fraction of it, a suggestion. But suggestion could be more potent than fact.

What was it she wanted to show? Sometimes she thought there was meaning enough in the simple act of bearing witness: a roll of film, a pair of eyes and hands. She believed this when she came across snapshots in junk shops, scratched photos tucked in books or half-filled albums, of bungalows and swing sets, women in sunglasses and kerchiefs. The images always seemed provisional to her, as if they were studies for some better picture, some bigger work. And yet they had the glow of truth.

I was here. I have proof.

I am here, she thought, framing her shots, ignoring the cold wind whipping her hair across the lens. I have proof. The huge sky, the tumbleweed clouds, the little white tugboats towing them out past the breakwater. Out on the lake, too distant to capture, whitecaps rose and rose. Then the tugs peeled away and the boat wallowed briefly before levelling out.

Kate felt a flicker of disappointment. She knew it was bad luck to wish for bad weather, but she remembered a fast and furious squall on Lake Ontario on the *Black River*, how it had cheered everyone up. The storm effect, she thought. A break from routine.

Just after morning coffee break it appeared she would get her wish. The portholes grew dark and Kate felt the deck fall away from her feet. The sky was coppery black now, a tarnished negative cracked by streaks of light. She watched the water in her sink brim up and then recede, the ridges of soapsuds mirroring the foaming waves outside. There was a weight behind her eyes, as if she were one of those dolls who go to sleep as they're tipped backward. Each time the ship swayed she felt the urge to lie down.

'We're rolling,' May announced.

'I noticed.' Hazel had emerged from the walk-in freezer with her right hand swaddled in her apron. She was not cheerful. 'I cut my goddamn thumb in there.'

'How did you do that?' Kate asked.

'Trying to cut open a box. Kate, I need you to go in there. Get me a couple dozen of them veal cutlets. And make sure none of them cases are loose.'

Kate hated going into the freezer. A tiny chamber of slaughtered meat, so cold it was like blades being drawn across her cheeks. She had never seen so much dead flesh in her life, haunches and ribs and legs of creatures with the bones poking out, stacks of staring fish, veiny hearts, buckets of bloody offal.

'It's just meat,' Hazel had said. 'We're the same as them animals we eat.'

Kate found the case of cutlets and pulled the whole thing off the shelf. She had stopped eating veal in high school, after seeing a documentary on the fattening pens. Crates really, like the freezing crate she was in now, only the crate was tipping and she had to put her whole weight against the steel door to get out.

'You okay?' It was Calvin, a cup of coffee in hand, laughing as she burst out of the freezer. She dropped the box on the floor and bent over, her hands braced against her knees, panting. She had got scared at the last moment.

'What are you doing in here?' She didn't look at him as she spoke.

'The storm, man. Captain sent me back to help. It's gonna be a big one. There's already waves coming over the side.' He was grinning gleefully. 'You know what they say about boats, eh? The only difference between a freighter and jail is you can't drown in jail.'

'Goddammit, Calvin!' Hazel was glaring at him as she held on to the counter. 'You can get the hell out of my galley if you're gonna talk that way.'

She took big clown steps over to Kate and looked at the box of veal. 'Don't know if there's any point now. I can't have the oven on till it calms down. Get out of my way, Calvin. Make yourself useful. Start packing up the messroom. Everything's gonna fly. And do the dining room too.'

The old women had a system: one box for the messroom condiments, one for the dining room, to be stored on the deck underneath the tables. Every counter cleared, every cupboard latched. The kettles penned inside their fences, the mugs and teabags and thermoses of coffee stowed in one of the sinks.

Calvin was talking nonstop, holding the box as Kate quickly emptied the crew's table of its jars and bottles, salt and pepper and ketchup, toothpicks and napkin dispensers. 'We aren't supposed to get storms this time of year, but you know what? They've clocked eighty-fucking-mile winds in July. Superior's so fucking big it makes its own *weather*. And the waves, man, on Superior they're *square*, they're killer.'

He followed her into the officers' dining room, both of them angling their bodies against the pull of inertia. A chair had fallen over, and the others were sliding in and out from under the table, like old people shuffling to music. She could hear Hazel and May calling to each other in the galley. But Calvin was still talking. 'My buddy on the *Meaford* last summer? Thirty-foot waves, man, I'm telling you. Out of nowhere. Waves like that can break a boat in half.'

Kate glanced at the portholes. They seemed to be filling with water. She turned to him, teeth gritted. There were waves of nausea rising up her chest, a cold tide of gooseflesh pouring over her skin. 'Calvin. *Shut the fuck up.*'

'You're seasick, aren't you? You're white as a fucking sheet.'

She shook her head. 'Help me lay these chairs down, otherwise they're going to hit the walls.'

'It's better outside, you know,' Calvin said. 'In the fresh air.'

She watched him tipping the chairs, shoving them under the long table, wedging the box of jars in the centre. He was happy, she realized. In his element.

There would be no hot lunch. Hazel and May made up plates of sandwiches, which they left bolstered in one of the sinks. They were heading for their cabins when the phone buzzed in the pantry. It was the wheelhouse, asking for toast. Calvin would take it up. He could make it, too, Hazel said.

'You can't go up the deck,' Kate said.

Calvin laughed. 'Sure, why not. I do it all the time.'

'You can't, you'll get washed over.'

'He's pulling your leg,' May said. 'He'll take the tunnel.'

Kate had forgotten about the tunnel that ran the length of the cargo holds, a dank claustrophobic catwalk that May had shown her once. 'Does that mean I have to go up and do my rooms?'

'No, my girl,' May said. 'The Old Man said he wants us in our bunks. It's gonna get worse before it gets better.'

Hazel stopped in the doorway of the dining room and looked back. Her face was ashen. 'Jesus Christ. He ain't going straight across the lake, is he? If it's this bad he should be taking the north shore.'

'Nah,' Calvin said. 'He won't go across. He'll turn for sure.'

Following May into the dim cabin, Kate stopped on the threshold, riveted by what she saw in the porthole, a circle of hissing lakewater as the ship rolled to starboard, a half-circle of purple sky as it slid back to port. Rainwater mixed with lake water on the surface of the heavy glass, making aquarium patterns across the walls. But it was the colour of the lake that mesmerized her, a colour she could only dream of capturing on film: foamy green, pale jade, lit from within. It moved against the ship in beautiful jagged green waves that shook the hull and shattered like exploding glass.

She reached up past the already snoring May, past the swinging bed curtains, and felt for her camera. May could sleep through anything, she was like a soldier, always conserving her resources.

It was dark in the cabin, but it was only the porthole Kate wanted, the pale eye of the lake. She leaned her elbows hard against the wooden windowsill and took three shots before she realized her lens was wet. The big brass screws holding the porthole closed were not quite watertight.

Kate retreated to her bunk and propped herself against her pillows. In the darkness she could see her breath, a tiny damp cloud. She was like the lake, she could make her own weather too, she was a regular weather girl. Her eyelids were heavy with invisible coins. There were weights on her wrists and ankles.

She felt herself go under, and startled herself awake. She had always slept well in storms, she was like her father that way. It was as if the rain were a narcotic sluicing through her brain, revealing all the anxious bits, the rocks and the wrecks, and then washing them away. She was like him in temperament too, she thought. Stormy. *Storming around the house*, her mother called it.

Kate closed her eyes, remembering how she imagined herself when her mother said that – her hair blowing back like a shampoo commercial, her sleeves puffy black cumulus clouds, her skirt a black tornado. Everything would be torn from its moorings as she stormed her way through the rooms, books and papers, china and silver, the flowers from the vases. Her skirt of destruction growing bigger and bigger, raising her up to the ceiling, lightning in her eyes.

❆ 14. Bells jerked her awake.

Bells shrilling in the engine room, engines grinding and stuttering as the *Huron Queen* slowed, wallowing in the waves. Kate shook her head violently and checked the clock. She had been asleep only minutes. It was just past noon, but outside looked like midnight.

She closed her eyes and sorted through the sounds: deep thump on the lifeboat deck above, something loose. Something banging next door in the galley, something she had forgotten to stow. A rumble like thunder from below, shaking her bunk. The captain would be turning now. It would be very bad and then it would be better, Calvin said, once they reached the shelter of the north shore.

And then she heard the unmistakable patter of water splashing, rain falling through the vent of the wind scoop that funnelled in fresh air from the deck above.

She raised herself on an elbow and scanned the cabin in the half-light. Outside the porthole the sky had turned the colour of weathered copper. There was a puddle spreading on the floor, streaks of water sketching dark lines on the linoleum. The wind scoops should have been battened down. That was Calvin's job. Where was Calvin?

Something hit her back and she gasped in fear – just the alarm clock. She was wide awake now, watching the cabin pitch from side to side, tilting her head to fight the dizziness. And then she was scrambling out of her bunk, looping her camera strap over her neck, grabbing her jacket from the hook beside the door.

Outside on the stern she pulled up her hood and inched along to the ladder. The air was full of water, but she was out of the driving rain here. She felt her camera hit her chest and released her hands for a moment to zip it into her jacket. It was not till she had raised her head and was climbing onto the boat deck that she could see the storm for what it was.

They were heading for a black wall. No more green waves, but ink-black water meeting ink-black sky, and the wheelhouse glowing white against it. She slid her way across slippery steel to the lee of the smokestack and along in its shelter to the front of it, where she could see the whole ship below her. Glassy waves curled over the long narrow deck, huge cartoonish waves edged in ragged yellow lace that lingered caressingly over the red hatch covers.

There were lights shining from the wheelhouse. She braced her back against the stack and pulled out her camera, holding her breath against the wind that wanted to pull it out of her lungs.

She was shooting blind. The water had filled the lens and the viewfinder and yet the film advanced. She had taken a dozen shots and had stopped to wipe her face and then she let the camera fall back against her chest as she rubbed her eyes hard and squinted into the squall, her mouth opening in shock.

The boat was twisting.

Undulating through the waves like a heifer swaying through a field of tall grass. She had heard about steel towers flexing in the wind; anything this big had to have some give. But she could see it; there it was again, a slight torque to starboard beneath the slow-motion waves, waves like the Hokusai print she had had on her wall in high school. Rising and then curling and crashing onto the narrow deck.

And then, as if her hearing had shut down when she entered the storm and now decided to turn itself back on, she became aware that the air was full of noise. The deafening barrage of the rain itself, the percussion of steel on steel, all of it made terrible by the shrieking of the wind, a banshee chorus. But below it all there was another dreadful sound, a deep groaning that welled up through her feet and belly. The boat, moaning like an old person in pain.

She was deaf with listening, her body rigid against the stack, when she saw a blurred scrap of red in her periphery and realized it was Calvin, hair streaming water, teeth bared with the effort of yelling. She was still listening for the groaning. He had to grab her to make her hear him, even though he was shouting.

'Get below, you fucking idiot! Get below!' He pulled her after him, skating across the wet steel plates of the deck toward the ladder, and shoved her down behind the bench. 'Wait here!'

Kate watched him slide over to the lifeboat, which was swinging wildly with one rope loose, and she thought, he'll be hit. But he had the rope now. They were safe. She watched him tie down the boat through the curtain of rain, then turn and shout at her again, jabbing his finger toward the ladder.

She nodded, watched him disappear down the ladder, and stayed where she was. Her hood was full of water, she was breathing water, but she didn't feel particularly cold. The waves were coming directly toward her now, and the boat seemed to have stalled, swinging back and forth like a metronome. She pulled out her camera – it might be working yet.

Out of the darkness a green wall was rising, a wave like a building of glass. She wedged her legs under the bench and pushed her back hard against the bulkhead. She didn't bother to hold the camera against her face, but braced it against the bench, both of her arms laced through the steel armrest. She wouldn't get another chance like this. She watched the wave come and knew she was smiling. But she hadn't counted on the boat tipping at that moment, putting her face to face with a curtain of water that seemed to shout her name.

On the sea, Calvin said, sailors sometimes came to believe the waves were grass. They would jump overboard, craving a foothold, the smell of green, the fields of home.

'That's what I thought you were doing, man. Getting ready to jump. A lot of people do, you know. There was a guy on my last ship, disappeared in the middle of the night.'

'I never heard about that.'

'There's lots you don't hear about. If that fucking wave had washed you over, think it would have made the six o'clock news? No way. No one gives a shit about sailors.'

'That wave wasn't going to wash me over. I was halfway under the bench.'

'Yeah, well, the fucking bench might have blown off. It's been known to happen.' He cawed with laughter. 'I hope you got some good pictures at least.'

She was still shaking. The wave had washed over her and left her clinging like a limpet to the steel bench. Then the boat had tipped back and she had crawled to the ladder to find Calvin reaching for her. He pulled her down through the hatch and pushed her bodily into her cabin. She shivered violently as she stripped off her clothes in the dark, swaddling her wet body with May's afghans, making a nest of them in her bunk. She no longer cared if the boat sank. She just wanted to get warm.

Sitting on the stern after supper, in the lowering rays of the sun, on a swing that someone had welded out of steel rods and caging, she began to feel herself unclench. Hazel and May had both gone back to bed after serving a minimal evening meal of hot beef sandwiches and baked beans. The captain had gone to bed, too, exhausted by five straight hours of piloting the boat through the storm. Only Calvin knew she'd been up on the deck.

He had got some beers from his stash and they were drinking out of coffee mugs, watching the western sky, its regattas of clouds cruising the sunset. The stern was shaking with the effort of the engines, trying to make up lost time to the Soo. It was hard to believe this was still the same body of water, so smooth was the surface now.

She hadn't seen the boat twisting, Calvin said. There was no way. Of course the hull had some give, but not enough to see with the human eye. It was her imagination. He said he hadn't heard any noises he hadn't heard before. The *Huron Queen* was a tough old girl. Lakers were long and flat, built of steel plates riveted together, plates that could shift, could expand and contract. It was what they did.

'And the rivets, man. You can hear them pop out in storms. Like gunshots. We probably lost hundreds.'

'What do you mean, hundreds? You mean the plates would have gaps?'

'Nah, there's a million rivets on a boat like this. A few don't matter.'

'You didn't tell anyone, did you? That I was up there?'

'You kidding? The Old Man would fire you if he knew. But I don't blame you. I love a good storm.'

Calvin was a born-again sailor. He lived for seawater, the smell of salt, the uncharted skies of the ocean. His best job had been a coastal tanker with a regular run to Goose Bay. The trip up to Labrador was nothing like the lakes, he said. On the Atlantic you felt like part of something great. There were icebergs, schools of tuna sailing by with their big pointed fins.

'And the whales, man! They belly right up to the side of the boat. I'm smoking a joint one morning and I think it's starting to rain and it's a whale spraying me.'

Kate had seen a pod of pilot whales, their spumes like tiny jaunty geysers against the dark water, when the *Black River* was heading for Port Cartier. The deckhands called them blackfish. They reminded her of a family on vacation, playing tag in the waves, rather than creatures in danger of extinction.

Calvin said that on his last trip in to Goose Bay, he had bought rounds of drinks at the bar for a pair of pilots from the NATO base there. The next morning, when the boat was headed east through Hamilton Inlet to the sea, two jets had torn out of the sky, making a beeline for the wheelhouse, veering apart at the last moment to pass on either side of the mast. It was the pilots, saluting him for the drinks.

'The captain was shitting himself, man. He said he was going to call the fucking prime minister, he was that mad. Fucking pilots, man. What a fucking life.'

'It would have been really exciting if they'd hit the boat,' Kate said drily. She'd heard about the air force base in Labrador, the test flights driving the caribou and the Innu hunters into the bush. The military considered the area uninhabited, and for the flyboys it was just a game.

Calvin had lost the tanker job when the mate caught him toking up. 'It was a frog boat anyway, man. They were just looking for an excuse to get rid of me.' His ambition was to go deep sea for real, sail across to Europe or down to South America, where the drugs and anything else you wanted were cheap. He had an uncle who'd been a bosun on an English ship. 'It was perfect, man. Regular run to Rotterdam. They have bars there where they sell you hash. It's legal there.'

Kate held up her cup for a refill. She was feeling better now. 'So why don't you sail deep sea? Go to Rotterdam and sign on to a salty? Get on your uncle's boat. Go to the tropics.'

She thought about going ashore to take pictures in Hong Kong or New Orleans. Being a real sailor. She told Calvin about the Soviet ship she had gone aboard in Trois-Rivières, about the Russian first mate's steel bucket of salted herring. 'Just like the Newfies jigging for cod. Everybody wants a chance to pretend they're having fun.'

Calvin listened, producing a joint from somewhere inside his jacket and taking her cigarette from between her fingers to light it. The familiarity of the gesture sent a little current up her arm. She had felt the current in Thunder Bay, but she had had a lot of wine. Maybe it was the storm, the way he had pulled her down the ladder. Maybe it was the smell of him. Boy sweat.

'Deep sea, man,' he said, toking hard. 'It's over. There's no Canadian ships left. Well, there's a couple CSL boats, but where are the fucking things registered? Singapore, man. Fucking Canada Steamship Lines. They don't deserve the name. Canadian-built, Canadian-owned ships, man, and they're crewed by Chinks.'

'Chinese.'

'Chinese, Filipino, whatever. Guys who work for ten bucks a day. Ever see those guys in port? They don't let them off their ships, man. Even if they did they don't have any money. They don't get paid till the end of the trip. If they get paid.'

The Dutchman had said much the same thing. But it was better for officers. He had taken her aside and given her a little crystal dolphin in a jeweller's box when he paid off the *Black River* in Montreal. Boyd had been right, he was sweet on her. Piet said he was going back to the East. He missed the salt.

She smiled now, thinking about it. He was better off. He would get a pretty dark-eyed girlfriend in a tropical port, one who appreciated crystal dolphins and courtly manners. Unlike her. The beer was working; she felt the knots in her stomach loosening. From the corner of her eye she watched Calvin tip his cup to his lips, lower it and belch extravagantly.

'Charming,' she said.

Calvin wiped his mouth with the back of his hand and grinned. He was a boy, she thought, a teenager.

She said, suddenly seeing it, 'You're Kenny's brother, aren't you?'

He sat back, frowning.

'You *are*,' she said. 'I can see the resemblance. You have the same ringlets.'

'Ringlets! They aren't fucking ringlets.'

'They look like ringlets to me.' She was laughing. 'I always liked Kenny. Kenny was a gentleman.' A lover not a fighter, Kenny would say, making calf eyes at the waitresses wherever they went ashore for a drink.

'Yeah well,' said Calvin. 'Kenny's an asshole.'

'So you must know Boyd.'

'Fucking right I know Boyd. They're both assholes.'

'Why's that?'

'Why's that! Boyd lost a thousand fucking dollars of my money on the loser dope deal he fucked up in Toronto. Never paid me back, either, and Kenny says he isn't going to, because we all lost our money. We were partners. It was a business risk.'

'What happened?'

'Ambush, man. Boyd got jumped. All right. Not his fault, except he was an asshole. But now they fucking aren't cutting me in on the next deal,' he said bitterly, crushing the tip of his joint between thumb and finger, letting the wind take the ash away. 'Fucking *part*ners.'

'I think you're lucky to be out of it,' Kate said, remembering the package Boyd had got from Carrot Top the night he punched her at Cabot's Landing. She stood up, slapping grit from her jeans. 'So what boat are they on now?'

'Last I heard they were in the Canal. Trying to get a self-destroyer.'

'A what?'

'A self-unloader.' He glanced up. 'Why, you worried?'

'Why would I be worried?'

'I heard what Boyd did to ya down home. Kenny told me. He wasn't impressed.' A blast of the boat whistle erased what he said next.

'What?'

'I said neither was I.' Calvin looked past her at the water. She turned and saw a freighter heading west, a huge ship with a black crane folded along the length of its deck like an extra limb. Or a giant prick.

'Maybe they're on that one,' Calvin said behind her. 'Fucking filthy, those things. Good place for the pair of them.'

'Have you ever been on one?'

'Nah.' He was silent for a bit. Then he touched her shoulder. 'Don't worry about Boyd, man. Kenny'll keep him in line.'

Kate laughed. 'No one can keep Boyd in line. Except maybe his mother.'

'His mother? She thinks the sun shines out of his arse.'

❦ 15. Friday was fish day all over the Great Lakes, clam chowder and baked whitefish and fried cod. Saturday they looked forward to their weekly T-bone and baked potato, Sunday their roast turkey and all the trimmings. But on Sunday the *Huron Queen* had been in the grip of a freak gale, and Hazel was making up for it on Monday, filling the galley with the smell of a holiday feast.

Kate craned toward the porthole and its circle of Lake Huron, her hands paddling through warm soapy water. She had half a sink of dishes to do, evidence of mid-afternoon snacking, as if the men had felt the need to replenish yesterday's missed calories. The sky was a robin's egg, cloudless and serene above an empty curve of dark blue.

The *Huron Queen* had been named for this lake, back in the twenties, when vessels of every size worked the waterways from Ontario to Superior. Now it was leisure craft that covered the southern bays and inlets like confetti, armadas of motorboats and sailing yachts crewed by sunburned men who drank too much and sometimes managed to drown their families.

Scents were memory triggers, she had read that somewhere. Smell more than any other sense could wake chemical receptors in your brain, take you back to your childhood. That must be why her eyes were suddenly welling up. It was chemistry. The galley smelled like Christmas. Parsley, sage, rosemary and thyme, just like the song, like all the Decembers she could remember.

She had not talked to her parents in two months, since she had called from the dock in Cleveland to tell her mother she was okay, the boat was fine, everything was good. She was lying, but she had been lying to her parents for a long time.

It was funny how telling lies felt like love.

Yesterday, Sunday, they would have been out for a drive. They had started exploring the countryside when Kate was sixteen, when her father had bought a new car and her mother spontaneously developed a passion for china, specifically locally made ceramics from the potteries that were now a lost industry in Ontario.

Her mother was devoted to these excursions. It was their family time, she said, the Sunday drive, lunch and antiquing. Kate knew other people visited relatives on Sundays, or went to church. But her parents' extended families were out west, and church, in her mother's opinion, had very little to do with faith. Her father just quoted Marx: religion was the opiate of the masses. Et cetera.

Kate wished family time didn't involve current affairs lectures. Even classical music would have been better than her father's driving soundtrack, the Sunday morning news programs on the CBC, which were always turned up too loud, like some kind of psychological torture. The news was her father's setup; once a week he liked to parse world events for his daughters' edification.

But Kate and Jenna, who battled over little things at home, were firmly allied in their loathing of the drives. In fact the drives became Kate and Jenna's family time, stifling giggles in the backseat, poking each other like ten-year-olds when their father said something particularly pompous, rolling their eyes in unison and then going off in silent hysterics again.

It was always a delicious relief to escape the car. They would stop for lunch at one of the antiques barns along the old highway south of Ottawa, some place with a tea room selling local preserves, peach chutney and tomato relish. Jenna would sort through grimy pottery with their mother while their father, who claimed he hated to shop, would find a gummy horse brass or a musty copy of Dickens, *Christmas Books* or *Nicholas Nickleby*. The books were never any good, according to their mother. Foxed, she called them. The specks of decay on their pages could spread to their own books. It wasn't worth the risk.

How many times had Kate heard her father say, as he turned the car back toward the city, 'That was a real find. I won't see another edition like that.' Taking a kind of pleasure in his own regret, turning it on his daughters. 'You're missing the scenery. We might never take this road again.'

And then one Sunday when she was sixteen she had found the Minolta.

It was a barely used thirty-five millimetre in a stiff leather case, buried in a jumble of equipment unloaded by the family of a deceased camera buff. She hadn't been looking for a camera. She was perfectly happy with the little Kodak she had got for Christmas, which took surprisingly good shots of her friends, but the Minolta was of a different order entirely. It felt serious. She held it carefully in her hands, enjoying the weight of it as she raised it to her eye. Looking through the viewfinder, she saw a black needle suddenly pulse upward. The light meter. It was as if the camera were alive.

In that moment, Kate saw her future. She felt charged, humming with ideas. Her heart was pounding as she panned the chaotic interior of the shop. She saw order. She saw art.

Kate had learned from her father's regrets. She didn't know much about cameras, but she knew fifty dollars was a deal she wouldn't see again. A friend in the school camera club confirmed the fact with envy.

Now she had something real to do on the Sunday drives, making her father pull onto the shoulder while she got her shots, turkey vultures ranged on lightning-blasted pines, rutted gravel roads curving secretively into the lush green of woodlots. She began to turn her lens more and more toward the ruins dotting the countryside, the crumbling foundations and destroyed machinery, the smashed fences, the rusted silos.

Her mother and sister would wait in the car, Jenna with her nose in a mystery, her mother tuned to a classical music program, while her father paced and smoked, calling out annoying suggestions. Why didn't she get a picture of those wildflowers? The horses in the field? Why was she taking so many shots of wrecked things?

She couldn't explain it. It felt right. She had always liked ruined things. Her father's books, her mother's old handbags, the musty smell of her grandmother's house in Vancouver, where as a child she would beg to be allowed to look through the trunks in the basement. They were full of yellowing movie magazines, souvenir towels, tarnished hand mirrors. It was all junk, Gram said. But just the same she would not part with any of it.

Kate's father never followed her into the fields or buildings, even when she found subjects farther and farther from the road, first to get away from his voice and then because she loved the idea that no one had been here for years, no one had passed through this cabin doorway, or seen the way that blown-out window framed a piece of sky.

It was like salvage, she thought. She felt as if she was saving something.

The images, when they swam up from the tray of developer in the school darkroom, never fully achieved the vision she held in her mind. But she had learned to look for a detail, a grimy preserving jar or a twisted spike, a shadow falling across a doorless threshold. A single element that she knew would telegraph the utter loneliness of the whole. She wasn't sure how she knew it, but she knew it.

In her final year of high school, a new teacher took over camera club. He said she should try submitting some shots to a photography magazine. She sent her best ruined silo, along with a black and white study of weeds in a ditch and a moody shot of Shetland ponies huddled in the rain. The magazine bought the ponies and she was both thrilled at her success and disappointed that her father had been right about the wrecked things. It was her ambivalence that made her agree to go out with the camera club teacher for coffee.

The teacher was from Toronto and tall and good-looking, and the girls in camera club had speculated graphically about what he would be like in bed. Kate knew most of them had never actually been in bed with a guy, petting in a car was probably the height of their transgressions. But Kate had, and it made her feel powerful and ashamed when she listened to their prattle. The teacher seemed old but not intolerably so – twenty-eight, in fact, Kate learned at the café, a little place in the market where no one was likely to see them. Later, drinking beer and taking wet drags off his cigarette in the front seat of his car, she let him kiss her. She liked the voracious way he covered her mouth with his, the way he ran his tongue over her teeth and gums, the way his eyes rolled back in his head. But when he wanted more, she was firm.

No, she wasn't a virgin – it was a ridiculous concept anyway, she told him. What kind of meaning could it have, when your first time was likely to be terrible? What she really craved from the teacher was praise. She was drunk on more than beer, she was drunk on the idea that he had put into her head that she had talent. Editing was the most important thing in photography, he said. Her decision to focus on old things, ruined things, imperfect things – it showed she had ideas. He said she was an unusual girl.

Part of her knew he was just hoping she was unusual enough to change her mind and fuck him. But another part knew he meant it. Just like knowing that any twenty-eight-year-old who fooled around with a student was a loser, but also knowing he was right about her pictures.

The teacher said she should do a photography course at the York School in Toronto. It was a new school, like the Art Students League in New York, very passionate and anarchic. He knew people there.

But the York School wasn't accredited. She told her father photographers didn't need a diploma, just a good portfolio. And he said fine, she could pay for it herself.

'Photography is a perfectly fine hobby,' he said. 'It's not a career. Especially for a smart girl like you. What do you want to do, take wedding pictures for the rest of your life?'

'Of course not.'

'Well, that's the only way you'll make a living. Who's going to buy pictures of old machinery? You need a degree that will give you options.'

'What options?' she demanded, voice rising, losing it. She was always losing it with him now, he was always setting her off. 'An option to work in the civil service like you? Are you happy? Are you satisfied with your life?'

He said what he always said. 'Of course I'm happy. We are lucky, Kate. If you'd grown up the way I did you might appreciate that fact.'

She walked away like she always did. Instead of saying what she wanted to say. If you're so happy why are you disappointed all the time?

As far as she could tell, the only time her father was happy was when he'd had four or five vodkas or when he was fishing on some remote lake in Algonquin Park. He was like a boy at summer camp then, only he had never gone to summer camp, he had grown up in a logging camp in Northern Ontario. He was never more at ease than when he was chopping wood and frying his pickerel or bass over the fire, or foraging under logs for chanterelles. Though their mother would never let the girls eat the mushrooms, just in case.

The last time the family had driven to Algonquin – the previous summer – it had rained torrentially. They were staying in a cabin, her mother having finally put her foot down over sleeping in a tent. And her father had refused to come in from the storm.

Kate and Jenna and her mother watching from the window as he stood grinning in the deluge, a vodka-and-rainwater in his hand, shouting, 'I love a good storm! Liz, get your rain gear!'

Her mother shouting uselessly back: 'John, for God's sake! You'll be struck by lightning!'

But Kate had been glad that he stood his ground, even as the ground was melting into muck.

¶ 16. She felt a poke in her side.

'You all right?' Hazel said. 'You seem kinda slow today. Can you do me this roaster next?' She banged a big rectangular pan onto the drainboard.

'I'm okay. Just tired.'

Hazel chuckled. 'Wait till you're my age.' The smell of turkey rose up as Kate lifted the pan, and she was instantly ravenous, suppressing the urge to tear off the bits of shiny brown skin cooked onto the surface. She plunged the pan into the water, sending puffs of soapsuds into the air.

The shaking in her legs had stopped; now she merely ached. The truth was, she had frightened herself in the storm. She had been carried away, transported by the power of it. Now she felt embarrassed by her recklessness. If she could call her mother right now she would, but ship-to-shore calls were reserved for emergencies, and anyway, what would she say up there in the wheelhouse, with all of them listening? Tell Dad we had a kick-ass storm?

The men were coming in now, a gabble of voices as they crowded the messroom. Kate dried her hands and went to take the orders; smiling along with their jokes. Garrulous in the aftermath of the storm, they had a new story to tell. They would chew on it for days, just as on the *Black River* they had passed around the story of Carol and Jimmy's disgrace like an old canvas sailor's sampler, each of them embroidering a new bit. Yarning.

Kate delivered their dinners and retreated to the sinks. At six-fifteen the cooks downed tools.

May bustled over. 'Everyone's been in, my dear. Come sit down. Can I make you up a plate?'

She had been famished, but now the thought of food made her queasy. And she wanted to be alone. She thought with intense longing of her bunk, her blankets, her bottle of vodka tucked beside the mattress. One drink and she would be oblivious. 'I'd like to keep going, May. I'll get something later.'

'Well, if you're sure, my dear.' She hated the way May could make her little face collapse in disappointment. 'I could make you up a plate for later. Is it white meat you like?'

'May! Kate!' Hazel was calling. Their presence was not only desired, but required. She thought of home again. They didn't sit down together for dinner every evening, but when they did, they all did.

'Okay,' Kate said, wiping her hands on her sodden apron. 'I'm coming.'

The messroom had been taken over by Hazel's coterie, the men who lingered after the evening meal instead of playing cards in what passed for a rec room or retreating to the solitude of their cabins. They missed their wives, Kate thought, or maybe it was their mothers. Except for Calvin, it was all old men today, Ronnie the third mate and Swede the wheelsman and a scrawny, ancient Newfoundlander named Charlie, who was the four-to-eight watchman.

Swede was showing Hazel a photo of a girl in a gown and mortarboard. 'Yup, she did it,' he said. 'I never expected her to do it but she got the degree.'

'What'd she go in for?' Hazel asked.

'She's in pharmacy. She has to drive thirty miles each way to her job, but she's got the car now too. Pharmacy. Never expected that.'

Kate picked at her mashed potatoes and looked at Swede, his massive tattooed arms folded on the green table. He looked like a biker, and he had a pharmacist for a daughter. It was oddly appropriate.

'So I guess she's on your case now,' Hazel said.

'Eh? Oh, you mean the blood pressure.' Swede laughed. 'My cholesterol too.'

'Well, good on her.'

May was nodding eagerly. 'Kate here,' she said, 'she goes to school for photography.'

Kate glanced at Calvin, rolled her eyes. His grin was appreciatively ironic.

'Photography, eh?' Ronnie jumped in, his Limey accent nasal with skepticism. 'I suppose you got some good shots of the storm yesterday.'

Kate shook her head, hoping her face wouldn't give her away. But Ronnie was looking meaningfully at Swede, and she realized he had only been waiting for his turn to speak. He had some opinion he was burning to share.

'Oh, she wouldn't take a chance in weather like that,' Hazel said.

'It's a bloody shame the captain doesn't have that kind of sense,' Ronnie said, his cheeks now pink, looking from Hazel to Swede and back. He was furious, Kate realized. She remembered what Hazel had said about his heart condition. He took things hard, Ronnie did. He got worked up. As the mate on watch last night he'd have been in the wheelhouse for the brunt of the gale, watching the captain take charge.

Watching the captain take chances, apparently.

But Swede wouldn't play along. He tipped back his mug and finished his tea. Then he dabbed delicately at his beard with a paper napkin and rose with effort from the table. 'He did his best, Ronnie. None of the forecasts said it would turn that nasty. And it wasn't his fault the engine cut out again when we hove to. We'd have been all right otherwise.'

Ronnie was stone-faced, staring off through the porthole, his bleak expression almost comically offset by his protruding ears.

Charlie caught Kate's eye and winked. 'Well, guess I got to go check on the Old Man. He'll be wanting his cuppa.'

Hazel watched the two of them leave, the mountainous bulk of Swede making a midget of Charlie. Then, lowering her voice, she spoke coaxingly to the third mate. 'Now, Ronnie. You shouldn't have said that about the captain, it could get back to him, and then all that nonsense will start up again. You gotta admit, Felix is a good pilot. He's one of the best on the lakes.'

Kate moved down the bench closer to Calvin, who was now making a show of reading a newspaper at the end of the long table. 'Got a cigarette?' she asked.

He slid her his pack of Export A, jerking his eyebrows toward Ronnie and Hazel. If he was listening any harder, she thought, he would pop an eardrum.

Ronnie looked mutinous. 'Haroun says the captain knows all about that bloody engine,' he told Hazel. 'The chief told him he couldn't count on it in a storm.'

Haroun was the fourth engineer, on the same watch as Ronnie, a tall young Pakistani who had told her he held a master's degree in engineering. He would sometimes lean in the messroom doorway after meals, not quite a full member of Hazel's family, but conferred a certain protection nonetheless.

Kate thought of his cabin, which she cleaned each day before lunch. Tidied, really, since it was always spotless, the bed tucked up with military precision. In Haroun's room she did nothing, in fact, except wipe the sink and pick up a towel from the floor. Always a single white bath towel, spread neatly in the centre of the green cabin floor.

Ronnie stood up, brushing imaginary crumbs from his uniform. 'You ask Haroun. I went to sea when I was fourteen. That's fifty years, Hazel. Fifty years. I think I know what I'm talking about.'

¶ 17. The rain clattered on the roof of the cab like popping corn.

It poured down the windows, dissolving the trees between the Welland Canal and Government Road into streaks of green. Kate felt lulled, listening to the windshield wipers squeak and thunk, squeak and thunk. She always felt sleepy in a car in the rain when someone else was driving, but it was more than that. Hazel's comforting bulk on the seat beside her made her feel like a child.

'We're gettin' close, driver,' said the chief cook, straining forward and squinting. 'I think it's the next left. I can't see a thing in this rain.'

Hazel had been ready to abandon her excursion when she saw the weather, but timing like this was too good to waste. How often did they arrive at Lock 8 with the afternoon break in front of them? The trip through the Canal could take a day, but the captain said traffic was light. The boat would be halfway through by the time they were ready to pick it up at four o'clock.

It was a twenty-mile cab ride to Lock 7, but they had shared with Calvin and Swede, who insisted on paying for it when they got off at a sailors' bar in Thorold. Kate had felt a pang watching them shoulder their way through the heavy doors of the Canal House. She would much rather be having a drink in the comforting twilight of a bar than trailing around after Hazel as she stopped at her drug store and then her bank, fussing the whole while about the rain and how little time they had.

But the boat was going to Toronto; they had got the orders that morning. Kate could go home and see Jenna. She could call Rebecca.

The cab driver glanced over his shoulder. 'We getting warm?'

'About half a block,' Hazel said.

The cab crept past emerald green lawns humped like sleeping cats. Kate knew the reason for the trip wasn't really Hazel's banking or her arthritis prescription. She wanted Kate to see her house.

There was no point telling Hazel she wasn't interested in houses. A cheap apartment with a balcony, an attic flat with a rooftop deck in a gingerbread Victorian, preferably among the clubs and galleries of Queen Street West, was the height of her ambition.

The houses on Hazel's street were of a different era, postwar bungalows like her grandparents' old place in Vancouver, the rain like Vancouver too.

Hazel opened her purse and pulled out her wallet. 'You can slow down. It's the brown one, right here.'

Kate looked at a wide low house, more red than brown, with a long sloping roof, two fat shrubs bracketing the front door. She grabbed Hazel's carryall and got out of the cab, hooding her jacket as she headed up the walk.

'Hey!' the cook called behind her. 'Where you going?' She stood frowning on the sidewalk, her drugstore bag tented over her head. 'I said the brown one.'

'Oh. Sorry.' Kate followed Hazel to the drab little house next door. It was half the width, with dormer windows poking out of the roof, set back from the street behind a rose garden overgrown with weeds. It had a derelict air, the kind of house neighbourhood children would populate with ghosts or killers.

She tried to keep the surprise from her face, but she could tell she had failed by the way Hazel was marching up the narrow walk. The house that Hazel talked about with such pride looked like someone's cabin, not even brick but some kind of siding meant to resemble it. Kate wondered which of her own dreams would look this mingy to an outsider.

'It ain't much,' Hazel said heavily as she unlocked the door. 'But it's mine.'

They were in a hallway wallpapered in roses and smelling of earth. And something more surprising, the peaty smell of pot. Kate took off her wet jacket and shoes and walked into a tiny, tidy living room with a bricked-up fireplace and a plaid couch and chairs. There were crocheted afghans heaped everywhere.

'It's nice. It's so cozy.'

'You think so?' Hazel bent slowly to take off her shoes. She stepped into a pair of men's leather slippers that were sitting under an oak coat tree. They were the same kind she wore on the *Huron Queen*. Women's shoes were too narrow now, she said.

Hazel moved around the living room turning on lamps. 'Those afghans on the chesterfield, they're all from May. Can you believe it? She must spend half her pay on wool.'

'And the other half on drapes.'

Hazel let out a bark of laughter. 'Make yourself at home. We got at least an hour. Want some tea?'

'I could make it.'

'The pot's in the cupboard over the toaster.'

The kitchen was right out of the 1940s, walls and cupboards painted yellow enamel, the counter a speckled green Formica. The toaster was a fat, stainless-steel model like the one Kate's grandparents had before they sold their house and moved into an apartment. There was an old food processor, a sleek glass container on a round enamelled base. The smell too was like her grandparents' kitchen, shoe polish and sugar cookies, a note of mustiness. Her grandmother had loved that house, had worked thirty-five years at the Hudson's Bay store in Vancouver to help pay for it.

Waiting for the water to boil she wondered why she hadn't seen it before, the way Hazel reminded her of Gram, the same habit of easing criticism with a joke, the same impatience with sloth. The same stoicism, even when she knew she was dying, still sending Kate and Jenna a Christmas parcel, the traditional flannelette pyjamas and fuzzy slippers they'd been complaining about every year for as long as they could remember.

Kate still had her last pair of slippers. All the years of pink and turquoise and the last had been fire-engine red, as if some final bit of wildness had seized Gram in the Bay's sleepwear department, and she had wanted to give her granddaughters a laugh. Or maybe, like her mother said, Gram had got Auntie El to shop that year. Kate had never asked her. Oh God, now she was going to cry, and no fucking Kleenex in sight.

She unplugged the kettle and rinsed her face at the sink. She could hear floorboards creaking above, Hazel collecting things to take back to the boat. Inside the cupboard Kate found a box of teabags and a brown ceramic teapot. The sugar bowl had been turned on its side, a trail of coffee granules leading from the crystalline white pile to a crack in the corner.

Kate looked more closely and saw that the granules were two wavering lines of tiny ants, one convoy marching toward the windfall, one marching away, each ant with a single grain in its jaws. She watched them till she heard the toilet flush and then quickly brushed ants and sugar into her palm, turning on the faucet to wash them down the sink, eyes averted so she wouldn't see them struggle.

Hazel was coming downstairs, lugging something by the sounds of it. Kate put teapot and mugs on the table along with the sugar bowl. She knew there would be no milk in the ancient rounded Frigidaire but looked anyway. Coffee Mate: it would do. There was a reek of garlic coming from a pizza box jammed into the second shelf, on top of a couple of overturned jars of preserves. Pickle juice had dribbled through the racks onto the bottom shelf.

The nephew.

'Thought ya might like this.' Hazel was wheezing, plastic shopping bags hanging from her arms, a small leather case in one hand. She sat down heavily.

'What is it?' Kate took the case and opened a rusted latch. Inside was a black box camera with three lenses on the front, a big one and two smaller. She read the name on the strap. 'A Brownie!' she said with delight, peering down into the viewfinder. There was Hazel, upside down at her kitchen table. 'I've seen these in antique shops. This might be worth money, Hazel. You should hang on to it.'

'I got no use for it,' Hazel said, stirring her tea. 'Left by one of my lodgers. I had three of them at one time.'

'Cameras?'

'Lodgers. Three bedrooms upstairs. I slept in the dining room.' She waved toward the dark room off the kitchen. 'Them glass doors lock. But I couldn't make enough to pay the mortgage. Plus they kept getting work and leaving. And I didn't allow no drinking, so it was hard to find people.'

Kate ran her fingers across the camera. It had a black art deco design on its silver face. 'How long ago?'

'Oh, it was the late sixties, just after I bought the house. I was trying to quit sailing.' She slurped her tea. 'Don't know why I saved the camera. You probably can't get film for those things now.'

'Someone at the school will know. Hazel? Do you think when we get to Toronto I can get a meal off?'

Hazel chuckled indulgently. 'I was waitin' for you to ask. I figure I can give you supper and breakfast off, anyway. There's no telling how long we're gonna be there, after the inspectors come.'

'What inspectors?'

Hazel waved her hand like she was batting at a fly. 'Company inspectors. They're gonna take a look at the hull.'

'What happened to the hull?'

'That storm. The chief and the captain've been arguing about it ever since. Waves like that can put cracks in a boat.'

Hazel laughed at the look on her face. 'Go call vessel information, honey. I need to set here a minute.'

The phone was an old black model that weighed a couple of pounds, wedged along with the phone book into a tiny windowsill in the hall. There was an oak dining room chair set against the wall below it. It had been installed in the days when a home had only one phone and every room had a door, leaving the hall a relatively private place. Listening to a recorded request to please stay on the line, Kate stared out the small window at the diminishing rain. Cars hissed up the street, spraying water. She could hear birds, the bass note of a boat horn, close enough to make her anxious. But she was with the chief cook, and a boat couldn't sail without one.

It felt odd to be on shore, especially in a town like this, where everything looked straight out of an old movie. She knew it was an illusion. Tidy bungalows are perfect cover for human degradation, no shared walls to listen through. She knew from Boyd that there was a dank underside to the towns along the American border, a taste for crime cultivated during Prohibition and kept alive by newer hungers, drugs and guns and who knew what else. It made her think of Love Canal, all the toxic sludge seeping in to taint their foundations.

But in daylight the illusion held, and when she sailed past the green lawns of the Canal, it was happy homes she imagined. Happy mothers with happy children, bills paid, freezers full.

'What vessel, please?' The woman's voice was bored.

'The *Huron Queen*.'

'Hang on.' She heard the static blasts of the marine radio in the background, the scratchy voices of skippers reporting in. 'Just coming out of the narrows. Lock 7 at three-thirty.' They still had half an hour.

Kate went upstairs to pee, lingering to glance into tiny, dim bedrooms as she headed back down. Two rooms with beds, the third stacked with boxes and leather suitcases, steamer trunks with wood strapping. Hazel was a packrat like Gram. All the rooms had slanted ceilings, light filtering in from the dormer windows. They seemed bereft.

Hazel was washing the cups. The zippered bag was on a chair, packed. 'You want to call a cab? It's in the Yellow Pages – I use the outfit called Seaway.' Kate went back to the hall and leafed through the book. The dispatcher said five minutes and she hung up. Hazel was calling her.

'Hon, can you run down to the basement and check the water heater? My knees can't take them steep stairs.'

'What am I checking?'

'It's that tall round tank in the corner. Look at the bottom; make sure the flame is blue. I'll watch for the cab.'

In the dirt-floored basement she found the source of the other smell. On a square of carpet in the corner an old-fashioned stand ashtray was piled high with ash and roaches. It sat next to a threadbare easy chair behind a wall of stacked cardboard boxes. Very cozy. Some well-thumbed copies of porn magazines lay on the carpet, open to pictures of women with their legs spread. The title on a page read

'Beaver Hunt'. A pilly grey wool blanket with shipping company insignia was wadded on the seat of the chair. A candle stub protruded from an ash-coated beer bottle.

There was something tubular sticking out from under the chair; she nudged it with her toe and felt a shock in her chest when it rolled. A baseball bat.

What did Hazel's nephew need with a hidden baseball bat?

The scene reminded Kate of the dope dens of boys in high school, the back corner of an unused garage, a storage locker in an apartment building. Sometimes there had been sleeping bags and foam mattresses too, not for overnight accommodation but for whatever girl could be enticed to lie down. But there was no mattress here; it looked like the nephew – what had she called him? Jamie? – partied alone.

She headed for the heater and found the little blue flame in order. There were more boxes behind the furnace. They looked new. She stared until the black markings printed on the cardboard resolved into a symbol she recognized. Stereos, two dozen boxes at least. Hazel's nephew was a thief, but Hazel couldn't know that, or she'd never have sent Kate downstairs.

A car horn was honking. The cab.

Hazel stood in the front hall, the pizza box in her hand. 'Hold this, would ya? I gotta lock the door.' Anxiety made her brusque. Kate took the overnight bag too and walked down to hold open the cab door.

'We gotta find a garbage can on the way,' Hazel said, sinking into the back seat. 'It's my damn nephew. I told him he couldn't stay in the house, he's just supposed to mow the lawn and take in the mail. Driver, we're going to Lock 7. Geez. And he used the damn bathtub too. Thinks he owns the place.'

¶ 18. Toronto was no longer a port town. No one paid any attention to the black-and-white freighters nosing the quays at the foot of Bathurst and Spadina and Jarvis. Commuters drove indifferently past the massive grain elevators that stood between the Gardiner Expressway and Lake Ontario, their ranked silos like the columned fortifications of an older civilization.

It was as if the business of the port had nothing to do with the city.

Hogtown had spewed out its filth for a couple of centuries and then built a complex barrier of roads to hide its dirty work. In summer, Torontonions took the ferry across the oily water to Centre Island or drove east to the Beaches or the Scarborough Bluffs. The harbour was strictly for tourists, tourists who would take a boat tour around the waterfront and then eat Nova Scotia lobster at Captain John's.

But Kate was still a tourist in this city. She liked being a tourist. Leaning against the *Huron Queen's* portside railing, she smoked a cigarette and watched Ronnie shout at Calvin as the boat nudged into its berth. There was a warm wind blowing across the water. A few hundred yards to the north the Gardiner was choked with morning traffic. Watching the trucks stop and start, stop and start, she felt a stab of anticipation. Beyond the Gardiner was King Street, the distinctive rumble of its streetcars audible even from here. In a few hours she would climb down the ladder and get a westbound car to her other life. Her real life.

Hazel called her into the pantry after lunch. She pointed to a tinfoil-wrapped package on the counter. 'You got a proper kitchen at your place?'

'Not proper. But I have a kitchen.'

'I got a couple steaks here. You can have them tonight or freeze them for later. Take a couple of them baking potatoes too. And I got some nice tomatoes, if you and your sister want to make a meal of it.'

'Hazel, that's so sweet. You don't have to do this.'

'I wouldn't want you to go hungry. Anyway, I don't think I'll have much of a crowd for dinner tonight, except for the inspectors maybe. The crew's all got shore fever.' She patted Kate's arm. 'Go on, get going.'

Calvin was at the payphone at the top of the slip. 'I'm fixed up for tonight,' he said gleefully as she headed past. 'Buddy knows some ladies who work at Starvin' Marvin's.'

'Yeah, right,' she said, 'the cleaning ladies?'

'You jealous?'

'Oh sure,' she said. 'I'm really jealous of someone who takes her clothes off for a room full of losers.'

'Yup, thought so. Jealous.'

'Fuck off, Calvin,' she called over her shoulder. Yelling at him made her feel better. The truth was, she was anxious about going home. She was in some kind of bubble, and she was reluctant to pop it. And she didn't like to dwell on the circumstances of her last stay there.

The city noise, the stink, the traffic felt like an assault. By the time Kate had threaded her way through the maze of underpasses to King Street she felt sick and disoriented. She couldn't bear to look at the faces of the other people crowding the streetcar stop, men in suits checking their watches, women in summer dresses impatiently flicking ash from their cigarettes. Bits of litter blew against her legs, newspaper and chip bags, and she wondered for possibly the thousandth time why Toronto claimed it was a clean city.

On the 504 King streetcar she dived for a single seat and turned her face to the window, watching the streetscape shift like a time-lapse film, from limestone warehouses to the glass bank towers of downtown to the grimy red brick factories of Parkdale, relics of the industrial age now claimed by artists and drug dealers.

According to Jerry, her building super, it had been a nice neighbourhood once upon a time – maybe a little down on its luck, but decent. Jerry called himself an original Parkdalian, which meant he had been born and raised there, before the city bulldozed a good chunk of it, his family home included, to build highrise apartment buildings. Now the Dumpsters between the highrises overflowed with stained mattresses and crushed baby carriages, spoor of the transient and marginal.

But not Jerry's building. It was a low-rise on a side street, small enough for him to maintain to perfection, as if he was still the sergeant he had been in his former career. There was no litter on the sidewalk in front of Jerry's building, no dandelions on the lawn. No spilling Dumpsters, only a row of tidy garbage cans. Jerry would get along well with Hazel, Kate decided.

Kate got off by the liquor store and bought a bottle of domestic white wine, jaywalking across King to the top of her street, a dead end that might have once gone all the way down to the shore of Lake Ontario but now stopped at a chain link fence overlooking the expressway.

Even Boyd had claimed the area scared him, mostly because of the Jamaican and Vietnamese gangs that warred over the local drug trade. True, they came from cultures more practised at gunplay, but after her trip to Cape Breton she realized he was afraid of the place because he had no clan there. He came from an island that was really a village, where even at the airport ticket counter one of his distant female cousins had come up and asked why his girlfriend was going back to Toronto before he'd introduced her around.

Boyd had given Kate his aviator sunglasses to hide the bruises and he looked defenceless against the woman's affectionate scolding. On the plane flying back she realized what it was about Boyd and his friends, what made them such boys. It was the women. The doting mothers and grannies and aunties who smiled indulgently on their rebellion, because they believed their rebellion would protect them. It was a hard and unforgiving world out there; it was better to be hard and unforgiving than to show you cared. But then how would you ever learn to care?

The apartment was silent and dark, the curtains closed, but the city stink was here too, the sweet rot of ripening garbage. Kate went into the tiny kitchen and hauled out the offending bag, along with a couple of mildewed dishcloths and a can of Ajax, which she used to clean the sink and counter.

She remembered the steaks in her bag and shoved them into the fridge after wiping up the worst of Jenna's spillage. In the bathroom she pushed aside a crowd of hairspray and conditioner bottles and scrubbed the sink. She wouldn't do the tub, she didn't plan to lie down in it. It amazed her that Jenna could spend two hours in the bathroom waxing her legs and never notice the mildew coating the shower curtain; she could spot a chip in her nail polish instantly but remain utterly blind to the flyspecks on the mirror even when Kate pointed them out. It was the perfect secret vice for the pretty girl: filth.

They had fought about it the week Kate came home to lick her wounds. Everything she looked at seemed soiled and damaged, as if the damage she saw in the mirror had imprinted itself on her vision. She scoured the kitchen one morning when Jenna was at work, washed every wall, polished the glasses in the cupboards, scraped the gunge from the seams of the stove. When Jenna came home she gave her an inventory of what she had found and eradicated.

Jenna just laughed. Kate had clearly lost her memory, she said. Not only had she been a packrat growing up, she'd always been the worst at washing dishes. But that wasn't true any more. It was Carol who had opened Kate's eyes to the world of grime. And once your eyes were open, they stayed open.

Kate found her corkscrew under a pile of newspapers on the floor next to the couch and uncorked the bottle, carrying her glass to the big drafting table in the corner. She was proud of the table: fifteen bucks at the Sally Ann. Now Jenna's junk covered it like flotsam on a beach: wineglasses and pizza boxes, bills and magazines and stray lipsticks. Lady Diana smiled up from the cover of the weekend paper; the wedding juggernaut was about to be launched, and cheerleaders all over the world were going to set their alarm clocks and watch it broadcast live on TV.

She needed music. She moved to the stereo and flipped through her records, past the Pretenders and Patti Smith and the Police, settling on Van Morrison, because it had been a long time since she'd listened to anything and she wanted to ease into it.

She pulled open the curtains and gazed at the tree outside the window, its leaves limp in the heat. Her mother had made the curtains, driven down last fall from Ottawa with her sewing machine in the back of the station wagon. It was just after Gram died and her mother had spoken to an old woman in the hallway, a frail thing who cried talking about her son and how he never came to see her. 'He's so busy,' she said plaintively. Kate didn't care if her mother wanted to talk to the old lady, until she said, 'I have a daughter right next door. If you feel lonely you can always call on her.'

Later that night, gulping the Chardonnay her mother had bought, she wanted to shout, what do you know about loneliness?

Kate lit a cigarette now, leafing through her little pile of mail, mostly charity pleas and envelopes from school. At the bottom were three postcards, port scenes, and her pulse quickened when she recognized the awkward handwriting. Montreal, Quebec City, Thunder Bay. The inscriptions were strikingly short on creativity. Bitch. Tramp. Slut. Why not Jezebel? She could feel the blood rise up her cheeks.

'God, Kate, you scared me half to death!' Jenna slammed the door and kicked off a pair of white slingbacks. She was wearing a pale blue suit. 'Mom and Dad are majorly pissed off. You never called them. Is that wine?'

'It's wine. I brought steak too.'

'Oh yuck, red meat. I'm off that.' Jenna went into the kitchen and came back with a glass. She looked at the label. 'Yuck. Ontario wine?'

Kate hid her irritation in a shrug. 'Don't drink it, then. Is that suit new?'

'Yeah. It's my board meeting suit.'

Kate laughed. 'I can't believe you just said that.'

Despite the wine's shortcomings, Jenna filled her glass to the top. She wandered over to the couch. 'I got it at Holt Renfrew.'

'You already have a good suit. Your job interview suit.'

'That doesn't mean I can't get a better one, does it?' She laughed at Kate's face. 'Oh, relax. It was on sale. I'm glad you're here, actually. He's been calling. I never pick up, so he leaves messages. There's mail too. Though I thought of throwing it out.'

'I saw it.'

Jenna leaned forward, her patrician features screwed into an attempt at empathy. 'Look, Kate, I haven't told Mom and Dad anything, but I'm worried about you. You need to call someone. Let someone know this is happening. It's harassment.'

'Call who? You think the cops care if someone calls me a slut?'

Jenna looked away. 'Come on,' she said quietly. 'He assaulted you. He could do it again.'

Kate had to give her points, her little sister. She hadn't said what she must desperately want to say: I told you so. But there was no sense giving her a big head. 'He's not going to do it again, Jenna. I started it, remember? Anyway, he doesn't even know where I am.'

'Rebecca said the postcards are an escalation.'

'Rebecca said? Why were you talking to Becks?'

'She called to get your address. I told her about the phone messages, too. She told me not to erase the tape.'

'Why not?'

'It's evidence.'

'Oh, for God's sake.' Kate wasn't going to talk about it. She took her wine into the bathroom and turned on the shower. She stood a long time under the hot spray, rubbing her stomach, which was signalling the arrival of her period. She closed her eyes, imagining she was a rock in a stream, currents flowing over, fish slipping by. An ancient crustacean, dreaming calcate dreams. She would stay under; she would eat plankton and krill.

Okay, she could get her phone number changed. She would tell Jenna to get an extra lock, the double-key kind they advertised on TV. Jerry the super would install it. Jerry owed her a favour, in fact, over that thing with his little girl.

He had practically accosted her once in the foyer. He said he had his seven-year-old daughter Brittney visiting, and little girls were beyond his ken. In fact she was making his life hell. Maybe because Brittney's mother, his ex, was in Las Vegas. On her honeymoon.

Kate responded to the desperation in his voice and suggested Brittney come up for a girls' tea party. They had Sara Lee frozen chocolate cake and then Brittney demanded to see her jewellery, which Kate had a lot of, having relieved her mother of all her fifties bangles and rhinestone combs, clip-on earrings and fake pearl necklaces. Brittney had put on about ten pounds of the stuff, plus some of Kate's bright red vintage lipstick, and she had run downstairs to see her father looking like a very small drag queen. Naturally, she was loath to give up her finery, and clung so fiercely to a particular pink cut-glass necklace that it broke when Jerry tried to remove it.

'It's okay,' Kate told Jerry. 'Really.'

Afterwards, feeling ashamed that she hadn't let the child pick something out in the first place, she painstakingly put the pink necklace back together and took it down to Brittney. Her little face, sticky with candy juice, had opened like a flower.

Jenna was lying on the couch watching TV when Kate emerged damp from the bathroom. 'That's my robe,' Jenna said.

'That's my wine.'

'Was your wine.' Jenna laughed. 'I can go get us another bottle.'

Kate perched on the arm of the couch. 'Jen, I'm going out. I'm meeting Rebecca.'

Jenna sat up. 'Are you coming back?'

'I don't know.'

'God, Kate.'

'What? I might stay with Becks.'

She watched Jenna stalk into the tiny kitchen and fling open the fridge door. 'So why'd you bring the steaks? Did you ever think of having dinner with your sister?'

'You just said you've stopped eating meat.'

'That's not the point. I didn't have to take this place for the summer, you know. I did it as a *favour*.'

'It's closer to your job.'

'I did it as a favour. And you have to call home.'

❆ 19. Kate wore her royal blue Chinese shift, the one she had bought at the Salvation Army thrift shop, enchanted by its intricate embroidery of birds and flowers, the rich feel of the heavy satin. The dress had talismanic properties: it had given her Rebecca.

After class on a wet October Friday last fall, the slim tanned blonde who never talked to anyone came booting after Kate onto Spadina, wanting to know where she had found *that fabulous dress*. Kate considered lying, not about where she had got it, but about how much it had cost.

But it was too delicious to resist.

Rebecca actually shoved her. She put an elegantly gloved hand against Kate's shoulder and pushed hard, shrieking happily. 'Get *out*. One dollar? *One?*'

They were off then, bent double in helpless laughter, Kate's voice rising to helium pitch as she panted out her punchline. 'Well, it was half-price day. Normally it would have been *two dollars*.'

To make her prove it Rebecca drove her home, to deepest Parkdale, along the western barrens of Queen and King streets, passing the Sally Ann and the IODE shop – the Imperial Order of the Daughters of the Empire, Kate explained, which explained nothing – and finally stopping at the Crippled Civilians thrift store on Roncesvalles, because it had a parking lot.

Rebecca gamely tried to see beyond the grime and the junk to what Kate could see, not just the Italian cashmere sweaters or English porcelain teacups, which, hailing from a place called Forest Hill, she was actually very good at spotting. No, there was something else. A purity of spirit, maybe. An essentialness. She was amused when Kate bought a pair of handknit wool socks for fifty cents just because they were handknit wool socks.

'It's like a kind of attention to making,' she told Rebecca over beers at a Polish restaurant up the street. 'I don't know why, it's just what I notice. A pair of socks can be beautiful. I think about who made them and when and where. And who they made them for.'

'You're talking about provenance,' Rebecca said, nodding. 'It's the biggest thing in valuing art, really, the history behind a piece, the documentation.'

'But there is no documentation to handknit socks. They're anonymous. It's why I like them.'

Rebecca's uncle was a gallery owner. She was doing courses as research. 'I'm going to take over the business at some point, but right now I'm his art scout. He wants me to be out there, on the edges. In the trenches.'

Kate was irritated on two counts. One, that Rebecca should have such a smug certainty of what she was going to do with her life, and two, that she could be so sure she was operating in any trenches. She had a brand new car, for God's sake.

But then Rebecca disarmed her completely. 'It's why I like you, Kate. You're the real deal.'

'Hello, sweetie,' Rebecca said, bending down to offer her cheek. Kate had missed her smell, Paco Rabanne and Pall Malls. 'Been waiting long?'

'Long enough to drink a carafe.'

'Oh, goody. Then I get to catch up. White, right?'

It was one of the things they had in common, the drinking thing. Bad girls from bourgeois families had plenty of opportunities to give in to temptation – wine with dinner, champagne on New Year's, G and Ts at friends' cottages. Becks's family had money, that was the difference. Kate had to camouflage the extent of her drinking; Becks had open-bar holidays at Club Med.

A pretty waiter was hovering. 'A carafe of the Chablis, James, please. And a plate of spring rolls. And some of those little puff pastries, spanakopita?' Rebecca grinned at Kate. 'So. How is it? Tell me everything.'

Kate shook her head. 'So. You called my sister.'

'I was going to write you. Then she said you were coming to Toronto. Also that Boyd was leaving scary messages. You need to get an unlisted number.'

'I can't afford unlisted.'

'You probably could get it for free, you know, if you had a restraining order against him.'

'A restraining order? That would make him mental. Anyway, it's ridiculous. It's not going to happen again.'

'Sweetie, sweetie, listen to me. If it was over he wouldn't be leaving nasty messages. He's mad that he let you get away. He's thinking about it. He's stewing. He's escalating.'

'God, Rebecca, how do you know so much about it?'

Rebecca laughed. 'Don't ask.'

'No, really, how do you know?'

Rebecca looked up as James arrived with their order. 'Thank you, darling.' She waited as he filled their glasses, then rummaged in her bag and pulled out her Pall Malls.

'I've never told anyone this, okay? This is cone of silence. People think I'm in control of my life. I am in control of my life. But in high school? Totally fucked up.' Rebecca crooked her fingers in air quotes. 'A nympho. My mother put me on the Pill, but my father wanted to have me committed. I'm not kidding you. I went to my graduation stoned on MDA. I don't know how many guys I was with at the after party.'

Kate reached across the table, touched Rebecca's hand. 'But there was one particular guy. The one I woke up with. Smart guy, cute, good family. We became a couple. My parents were happy. No one asked me what I wanted. It was like he won me in a poker game. So when I got tired of it, when I broke it off, he broke my nose.'

'Fuck. But you have an adorable nose.'

'Sweetie, I love you, you are such an innocent. It was the best excuse for a nose job ever.'

Kate sat back. 'Oh. So they fixed your nose. What about the guy?'

'That's the fucked-up part. My parents blamed *me*. They didn't want me to report him. And then my uncle saved me.'

'Saved you?'

'Do you know what a mensch is? It means a good man, a great guy. My uncle called the cops. In the end we didn't proceed with charges, because we probably would have lost, and I was sick of the whole thing. But we got a restraining order. Eventually I realized it wasn't about my nose or my fucking around. My uncle helped me see that. And he helped my parents see it too.'

'So what was it about?'

'I was angry.'

Kate shrugged. 'Yeah, well, been there.' She lit a cigarette. 'Who were you angry at?'

'It's weird, I know, but it wasn't my parents. It was everything. The bullshit. The culture. All that girls-have-to-be-good and screw having a good time. Oh, and forget about having an opinion. The *guy* has an opinion, the guy is going to be a doctor, the guy gets his dad's car, the guy decides you're going steady, the guy bores you shitless and everyone expects you to say how fucking great he is.'

Kate was grinning, enjoying the tirade. It was merely a difference of detail; it could be her speech. 'Any woman with a brain is angry. How could you not be?'

Becks laughed. 'I know that. But you have to channel it. Dr. Freud knew what he was talking about. Nihilism is fun, but it's not terribly productive.' She paused, took a breath. 'People use their anger in different ways.'

Kate looked at her, waiting.

'Like you, Kate. You use it to punish yourself.'

She felt it as a body blow. She felt it in her belly, which was bloated and crampy, ready to expel another month's wasted preparations. 'What do you mean?' Knowing as she said it, that Rebecca was right.

'Maybe what you really need to think about is why you would get involved with someone like Boyd. I mean, look at you: you're smart, you're talented, you're beautiful –'

'I'm not beautiful.'

'Ladies.' It was the waiter, exchanging ashtrays, whisking away the empty carafe, refilling water glasses. He produced a lighter from his apron and illuminated a pair of tea lights that Kate hadn't noticed before. 'Would you like me to heat up the spring rolls, Rebecca?'

'No, but we'll have another carafe.'

Kate averted her face and lit another cigarette. She had chosen this brand, Number Seven, for luck. How could you tell if you were lucky? You could never know what worse thing you had avoided.

'Now, him, Rebecca, him.' She stabbed her cigarette furiously in the direction of the retreating James. '*He* is beautiful.'

'I'm not going to fight with you.'

'That's good.'

'But you are fucking beautiful.'

Kate laughed. She couldn't help it. 'Fuck off,' she said. 'Fuck off, fuck off.' Thinking of her mother, what she had said once during grade eight, when Kate wore a yellow dress and her classmates called her Big Bird. Her mother said they were jealous. She said that other girls might be pretty, but prettiness wasn't interesting and what Kate really was was beautiful. She said Kate would know this when she grew up, and Kate asked why her mother would lie to her as if she was an idiot on top of everything else.

'Okay, enough about you,' Rebecca said. 'Let's talk about me. I'm organizing a show. I'm going to have a show by hookers.'

'Yeah, right.'

'I'm serious. I'm getting them cameras. They're going to document each other.'

'So you're teaching them skills? Rehabilitating them?'

Becks guffawed. 'Are you kidding? These are sex trade workers. They have their own PR woman. I'm in it for the ink. The media love stuff like that.'

'You're going to be a star, Rebecca.'

'I know. I told you, I'm going to be the next fucking Peggy Guggen-heim. So how's the portfolio going? Shoot any cute sailor boys?'

'I shot a storm. I thought I'd wrecked my camera. I almost got washed overboard.'

Rebecca leaned forward. 'Really? You have to let me do a show in the fall.'

Kate laughed. 'What, pictures of weather?'

'Everything. Boat life. You just need to sell it.'

Kate looked around the bar. It seemed brighter now, like a Renoir painting, one of those sparkling, *fin-de-siècle* It spots where everyone was clever and well-dressed. Her anxiety had evaporated in the warmth of the tea lights. A tumult of voices rose jubilantly to the frescoed ceiling. It occurred to her she might be a happier person if she went more often to places like this, with people like Rebecca, smart people who could make you laugh.

Even the solitary diners looked content. They smiled up at their waiters; the waiters smiled down and made jokes. That big guy with the brushcut and the black bowling shirt. He didn't look rich. He came here to eat because it's better to eat in a happy restaurant than home in front of the TV. He had a friendly face. He was smiling at her.

'That guy in black,' Kate said. 'No, don't turn around yet. Do you think he's an artist or an accountant trying to look like an artist?'

Rebecca turned and laughed. 'No, he's a poet. Henry! Henry! Come join us.'

Henry came and hulked over the table, grinning. He had beautiful teeth.

'Henry, sit. This is my friend Kate. Henry's just got a book of poems out.'

Henry sat. 'Are you a writer?'

'No,' Kate said, smiling easily now. 'I'm a sailor.'

€ 20. It was a good line.

She had caught the poet's attention and she held it by letting him interrogate her for the next twenty minutes. A sailor on a steamboat? Do steamboats still exist? She could tell he was both excited by the idea and annoyed at his own ignorance. Becks teased him: 'You're such a *guy* guy, Henry. I bet you want to go down and take a look at that boat right now.'

He looked at Kate and Kate shook her head. 'No way,' she said. 'The cook'll put you to work.'

That set the poet off on his own stories, about a terrible summer spent tree planting in Northern Ontario. Rebecca made her excuses then; she had an early meeting. Henry moved into Becks's chair, describing the plagues of black flies and mosquitoes, the rain, the lost wages when the tiny spruce seedlings were flooded out.

'This whole tree-planting thing is a scam,' he said. 'If it isn't floods, it's drought. Most of those seedlings don't survive. It's the logging companies that pay for it – it's the law, they have to replant. But they've gotta be paying off the inspectors. I mean, you can't even call it planting, you're shoving a little spike into the ground, sometimes you're shoving it into gravel or scree, there's no topsoil at all.'

The worst, he said, was the food. The camp was advertised as being vegetarian-friendly, but the cook was an old-school lumberjack type. 'I swear to God, he had never heard of tofu.' Henry would go out into the woods and pick morels and berries. Watching his full mouth forming the words Kate imagined the taste of his lip blood, like salty berry juice running down his chin. And then she realized she had stopped listening and now he had stopped talking. Their smiles were complicit.

'I've got a bottle of wine at my place,' he said. 'It's just down the street.'

They drank the wine and she talked. She talked about her photographic aspirations, about the storm and the colour of the water and the inkblot skies.

But the poet had run out of words. After the wine things progressed in short scenes. Bedroom. Futon. Sex. Crying. Someone snoring. At seven in the morning he gave her tea with brown sugar before she lurched into her Chinese satin. In the daylight she could see that his place was full of scraps of paper covered with writing. There was grit stuck to her bare feet and the air smelled of socks. She noticed a blood-stained tampon sitting on one of the scraps and remembered him pulling it out of her, like a cork out of a bottle.

Henry neither offered his phone number nor asked when she would be in town again. Everything about his behaviour told her it would have been better if she had left when it was still dark.

Riding west on the Queen streetcar, last night's wine and nicotine coating her mouth like soot, she hoped that the tampon had ruined a good poem. There was a taste of sulphur on her tongue. It was like the stink of the ore docks, only it was her own polluted system, spreading its familiar poisons.

Not a Renoir painting after all, but that drab Degas, Absinthe Drinkers. Absent drinkers. The lost woman in her sad coquettish hat, the vacant surrendered face.

The thing was, a line could work too well. In the boozy glow of the bar you could conjure up an adventurer, a sexual buccaneer. But if you suddenly wanted to wipe off the lipstick and confess the loneliness that weighed down your blankets in the morning, they would snap shut like clams. They would do what Henry had done, crinkle their eyes and give you a quizzical smile. 'A sexy girl like you,' he had said, 'you must have a guy in every port.'

She felt shame for crying. He had turned away from her after coming, quietly and quickly, without inquiring after her own satisfaction. She had wept against his back, wanting, needing, more. Angry that he seemed to have exhausted desire with talking, whereas in her it had built and built. It made her think of her old boyfriend Miles. Guys who could only feel things in words – who only had so many words, and therefore only so much feeling. Miles felt in full sentences, always careful of punctuation. Henry – Henry the poet – seemed to feel things in haiku.

Or maybe he just knew. There was a sinkhole in her, a treacherous, unchartable space that no amount of language could fill. Like a hole in the water.

At eight-thirty she bought her usual hangover supplies, aspirins and ginger ale, at her usual corner store. She tried but could not muster a smile to return to the cheerful Asian woman who handed her the change. Chugging the ginger ale as she walked, she regretted her churlishness. The woman had been a doctor in Korea, never imagining she would still be unable to practise five years after emigrating to Canada. There were exams, she said. Courses to upgrade her. She was unfailingly, stupidly optimistic. Like May.

Kate hurried now. She had to retrieve her things and be back to the boat by ten. Past the playground, the creak, creak, of swings whining through her head. There was a dark man with a ponytail leaning against the chain link, watching the children. Thinking bad thoughts, Kate decided. She looked him in the face as she passed, so he would know someone had seen him. And then he smiled, revealing a gold tooth.

Kate smiled back, mentally revising. He was just missing home, another country, childhood. She had done the same thing, arrested by the happy shrieks, had stopped to remember herself and Jenna, how they used to dare each other to pump harder, swing higher, back when they still played together, when life required nothing but showing up.

She missed home. Not home now. Home *then*.

There were men loitering everywhere this morning. Two smoking outside her building, wearing uniforms she didn't recognize. Then she noticed the ambulance and felt gooseflesh flare up the back of her neck.

But she found the apartment quiet and empty. She took three aspirins and stood under a hot shower till her headache had dulled. Pulled on her jeans and a white tee of Jenna's that smelled comfortingly of laundry soap, and lay down on the unmade bed. Just for a minute. She was so tired.

It was a good mattress, this mattress. Her parents' first bed. It was part of a Danish modern suite they bought the year they were married, all round edges and blond wood. Her parents had driven it down with a dresser after she found the apartment. Her father had been like a salesman. You just can't get quality like this any more, he said. Look at the drawers! Like satin. Sliding them in and out, the wood whisper-smooth.

She came awake panicked, drooling slightly. She had been asleep ten minutes. There were thumps from the apartment next door, men's deep voices. She should go now. But she couldn't move, not yet. The bed was so soft.

She hadn't wanted the bed. Hadn't wanted to be lumbered with heavy furniture, the weight of home. But they had insisted on driving it down to Toronto, to see the apartment and the sketchy neighbourhood she had found to live in, see how determined she was to live on her own.

Her parents were doing what they were trained to do, what good middle-class parents always did. They were hedging their bets. They didn't want to alienate her. They weren't going to finance the photography course but that didn't mean they wouldn't stay *involved*.

Kate had taken the dresser too because it would store everything she owned, clothes and bedding and papers, and she liked the big mirror. It had been her mother's shrine to beauty, crowded with satin-lined boxes that had drawn Kate and Jenna like magpies. She could still see Jenna's little face in the mirror, barely clearing the top of the dresser, both of them wearing big clip-on earrings, their lipsticked clown mouths and gappy grins.

Eighteen months apart and it might as well be a generation. Jenna's crap covered the dresser now: a college mug filled with pens and pennants, a pair of bikini panties emblazoned with the word 'Tuesday', snapshots of the residence girls with their Diana haircuts.

The furniture had been free but it had cost her. It was built for a different era, when middle-class girls could count on real homes, on husbands to shift things for them. Kate stared up at the square glass shade suspended below the ceiling light, at the husks of dead insects forming a bracelet of shadow.

She thought with longing of her narrow bunk on the *Huron Queen*, which she faithfully made every morning, for May's sake, if not her own. Her single bag of belongings, a half-dozen books on her bedside shelf. Maybe she could stay on the boat, work through till lay-up in December, when the waterways froze over. Have enough money saved for once to stop her incessant calculations. But even if she gave up her place what would she do with the furniture? She laughed out loud. She would have to stay for the furniture.

The phone jolted her up from the bed in one electric movement. She grabbed at the receiver and listened, heart pounding. A male voice, not Boyd's. Harsh and obsequious at the same time, a wolf-in-sheep's-clothing voice. 'Hello? Hey man, somebody there?'

'Yes?'

'Hey, all ri-ight. Is that Boyd's chick? What's your name, babe?'

'I'm sorry, who are you looking for?'

'Oh, you're sorry are ya? You tell the Boyd man he's gonna be sorry too, okay? Tell the Boyd he's fucking dead meat. You got that?'

'I don't know what you're talking about. I just rented this apartment.'

Kate clattered the receiver down onto his laughter and flew to the worktable. It took three sheets of paper before she had a legible note to Jenna. Talk to Jerry, she wrote. Ask him to put in a security lock. Today. She triple-underlined 'today'. Then she added: Give him the steaks.

She was late now. Hazel would be cranky. Outside her apartment door she collided with a stocky man manoeuvring boxes. 'Steady there,' he said with a Caribbean lilt. He had a kind face.

She had an irrational urge to ask him for help. Instead she said, 'Who's moving out?'

'More like moving up, dear.' He jerked his chin at her neighbour's door and then shook his head.

'Mrs Greer?'

'Yes, that's de one. The old lady. She died not two hours ago. The day we come to move her t'ings.'

Kate stood speechless, the fear knocked out of her.

'Her son's gone with the body. He was here this morning, telling her what she could take to the home. She was sitting in the chair waiting and she just fall over. I saw her go. Damn.' He scrubbed at his face and then glanced down the hall as the elevator chimed. 'I got to go.'

Kate nodded dumbly. She told herself to move. Pick up her canvas bag and walk toward the stairs. Feeling the gravity pull harder as she descended, the heaviness move into her shoulders and neck, the oily cloud darkening her vision. She remembered Mrs Greer weeping frailly at her mother's kindness, at her mother's promise that her daughter, her responsible and mature daughter, would be 'just next door'.

That had been the day they found her on her knees in the hall, peering through Kate's mail slot. She claimed she had lost her glasses and couldn't read the apartment numbers. But Kate knew she was just lost. She wondered how you could stand to live with that feeling all the time, knowing that you are close, that it's right behind you maybe, you'd know it if you saw it, if only you could find it.

She'd gone over once. Tea in Royal Doulton cups and the smell of pee. The old woman lived in the circle of her reading lamp, the way a cave woman would have lived by her fire, gathering close the tools of survival: cookie tin, pilly afghan, *Reader's Digest*, reading glasses.

And also: a lifetime's meagre treasures, the silver cream and sugar set, the worn albums piled stickily on the coffee table. Full of photos of a little tow-headed boy, the boy who might be looking at those pictures right now, two hours after he watched his mother die before he could warehouse her.

Kate had never gone back to see Mrs Greer. She had promised to, knowing even as she spoke it was a lie.

❨ 21. Kate leaned against the stern railing after lunch the next day, watching the *Huron Queen*'s wake slap against the rocky margins of little islands, some so close she could probably hit one with her apple. They were in the St. Lawrence River again, heading for Pointe Noire. She could see birds hopping around in the branches of the evergreens, hear them chirping and warbling. There was a smell of pine in the air.

She'd been through the Thousand Islands half a dozen times, never without what felt like homesickness. She liked the smallest islands best, their improbability, their tenacity. Owning one seemed absurdly luxurious, and yet ordinary people apparently managed it. Like the woman who had waved to her one morning from a sunlit front lawn the size of a beach towel. Dressed in a bright red robe, a fuzz of white hair like a dandelion gone to seed. She held something in her hands, a mug of coffee probably, and even from a distance Kate could see her happiness, her tiny smile, opening like a pore.

Hazel should be having mornings like that, savouring a hot mug of tea on a dewy green lawn instead of battling a cranky stove and wearing rubber gloves full of castor oil to bed because her hands ached so badly. She'd been as cranky as the stove when Kate arrived back on board in Toronto, sweaty and apologetic and an hour late.

It wasn't until after lunch, when Kate found Hazel in the pantry and apologized again, that the chief cook told her the news.

The news was bad.

'Basically, the engine's had it,' Hazel said. She was stuffing a turkey, shoving in handfuls of bread cubes and herbs and chopped onion, tears running down her red cheeks. 'It's old. Like me.'

She turned away abruptly and pulled off her glasses, wiped her face with the back of her arm. 'Don't mind me, honey. It's just these damn cooking onions. I asked for Spanish onions. Why can't they ever send me Spanish onions?'

'Are they going to fix it?'

'Fix the engine? No one's saying. But the chief doesn't think so. He figures they're just gonna scrap the boat.'

Kate remembered what Bill Stone had told her over the phone. The company wouldn't put a penny more than was necessary into the *Huron Queen*. 'What does the captain say?'

'He says we're gonna finish out the season just like always.'

'Is it up to him?'

'He told me not to worry. He's got friends at the company. But I don't know. What am I gonna do, if I have to get another boat? I've been here fifteen years. I'm used to it.'

'Hazel, you're a good cook. You can work anywhere.'

Hazel shoved the turkey pan hard against the counter wall and tore off her apron. 'I don't want to work anywhere! I want to stay here!' Then she stalked out of the pantry, almost colliding with May, leaving Kate with her mouth open.

May took her by the arm. 'You look like you could do with a cup of tea.'

Sitting in the messroom, May spelled it out. Losing your ship was losing your home. What would Kate feel like if her parents announced, for instance, that they were selling up, moving to a new town? Kate shrugged; it had already happened. She couldn't understand Hazel's reaction. It was just a job, wasn't it?

'Oh, my dear,' May said. 'No. It's a job, but it's her life, too.'

Kate took a last bite of the apple, an early, tart McIntosh, and raised her arm.

'Give us that.' Calvin came up behind her. 'I'll plant you a tree.' He took the core and hurled it toward the closest island, sending gulls shrieking. It fell short by a good thirty feet. Kate laughed, lifting her camera to scan the river.

'Watch you don't drop that in the drink.'

Blue-green in shadow and bright green in the sun, the islands were like blobs of paint flung from a loaded brush. Most had tiny houses, meant to blend in: granite pink, dove grey, bloodstone red. In between the islands floated little boats, people fishing from their sides.

The fisherfolk ignored the *Huron Queen* as it towered past them, never changing position even as their small craft rocked violently in its wake. They were apparently used to the big boats the way people next to a highway were used to eighteen-wheelers. But trucks didn't produce whistle blasts that could burst your eardrums.

'Fuck!' Kate jumped at the sound. It came from another Inland Shipping boat, saluting as it passed upbound. Two cooks in whites waved furiously from its deck. Kate raised her camera and tracked them through the lens, catching them at the moment when they lowered their arms, disappointed.

'It's fucking ridiculous,' she said, 'that they would blast the people who live here just to say hello to another boat.'

'It's this company, man. Think they're the navy.'

'The Old Man likes his uniform all right.'

Calvin spat over the railing. 'The Old Man's an idiot.'

'Hazel says he's trying to save the boat.' Kate had turned her lens on him and was watching him smoke, eyes hooded against the sunlight. He was choirboy beautiful, with his hollow cheeks and beige freckles, the sun lighting his curls in a halo of gold.

'Fuck that. This company's too cheap for an overhaul. They'll scrap it. You watch – we'll get paid off in October.'

Kate shrugged. 'I won't be here in October.' She tightened the focus, closed down the aperture to reduce the depth of field, make everything behind him blur into soft browns and greens. 'Look at me,' she said.

He swung his eyes toward her and froze.

'Fuck off, man. My hair's all fucked up.'

'Come on, Calvin, you look like you always do.'

He pulled a face and then began to mug and she took four or five tight shots, watching his eyes search for hers through the viewfinder.

She kept the camera raised. 'So this deal.'

'What deal?'

'Kenny and Boyd.'

'I don't know anything about it, man. They cut me out.'

'You know something about it. Why'd they cut you out?'

'They were paranoid. After the last time. Like it was me who fucked it up.' Calvin put his hand over the lens. 'Why do you want to know? You gonna turn them in?'

She slapped his hand away. 'I want to know because some asshole called my apartment yesterday looking for Boyd. My apartment, where my sister is living by herself.'

'What'd he say?'

'He said Boyd is dead meat. Boyd must have ripped the guy off or something.'

Calvin shrugged. 'It's his funeral.'

'Calvin, would you pay attention here? I'm serious. The last time Boyd tried to do a deal, you told me he got his head bashed in. These are not nice people he is involved with. And now he's given someone my number and maybe my address too. Okay? I want you to tell Kenny. Kenny will know who the guy is.'

'All right! I'll call the old lady. She always knows where Ken is.'

'When?'

'At Iroquois Lock, okay? If it isn't too late. She'll skin me if I wake her up.'

At eight o'clock that evening Kate watched a copper-skinned sailor walk to a solitary phone booth on the cement holding wall at Iroquois Lock. He had ambled along the pavement from a salty tied up behind the *Huron Queen*, stopping to light a cigarette and kick a pebble toward the water. Savouring the feel of land under his feet.

She was watching for Calvin, wondering whether he would have time to call his mother, but the occupation of the phone made the question irrelevant. The booth glowed golden in the *Huron Queen's* long shadow, lit up like a shrine to the god of communication. It stood in the centre of a carpet of graffiti, names and dates in four or five alphabets: I was here in a dozen national colours. Calling cards of the exiles who passed through here, always on their way to somewhere else, to the American rust belt or back to the dark Atlantic, where their ship might crack in half before they saw home again.

She heard footsteps behind her, the crackle of a walkie-talkie, and turned to see the third mate in his white overalls, toothpick working, a Styrofoam cup in his hand. Ronnie's creased face wore its customary melancholy. She thought of his medicine cabinet, filled with pill bottles. He was a hypochondriac, Hazel said. She said he had given himself a heart attack with his worrying.

'Are we going into the lock soon?'

'Very shortly,' he said. 'You can wave to the tourists.'

He jerked his head at the viewing stands at the top of the lock, where three or four knots of people brandished cameras and binoculars. 'Bloody tourists,' Ronnie said. 'You know what it means, don't you?' He fixed Kate with a furious squint. There were years – decades – of bad weather mapped in the creases of Ronnie's face. She would like to photograph him, but it wasn't something she could imagine asking.

'What what means?'

'When an industry becomes a tourist attraction, it's the beginning of the end. It's a dying trade we're in, my girl. We are becoming quaint.'

There were visitor viewing stands in the Welland Canal too, which Kate had not realized till the afternoon when she was smoking on the deck of the *Black River* and looked up to see dozens of people watching her.

But now she shook her head. 'How could it be dying?'

'Dead simple. Bigger ships.' Ronnie chewed furiously on his toothpick. 'Back when it was just the Lachine Canal, the big ships couldn't get through, you see. This was before the Seaway was built. Do you realize it was only built in '59? There's been a Welland Canal for a hundred and fifty years, but this lot couldn't get the Yanks to agree on the Quebec bit until the fifties.'

Kate shook her head, not following. 'Before that, the foreign ships couldn't get any closer than Montreal. The lakers would have to bring the wheat down to them. There were hundreds of lakers then, you see.

But now the salties are all over the lakes. Just like the bloody lampreys, and whatever else they've got living in their ballast tanks. They are fouling the lakes just as surely as they are killing the Canadian lakers, you mark my words.'

She followed his glare down to the phone booth. The copper-skinned man was walking away quickly. Was that a skip? Was he whistling? Who had made him whistle? The woman at home, woken from sleep, her words made awkward by the overseas delay? Or the woman in Montreal he had just arranged to have sex with?

Ronnie was still talking. 'The Yanks have it sorted. They've got three times as many boats as we do on the upper lakes. Domestic trade. Ore from Wisconsin goes down to Toledo, Buffalo, Cleveland. There are boats that never leave Superior and Michigan, they're that busy.' He paused for effect. 'And why do you think that is?'

Kate shook her head again.

'History,' he said triumphantly. 'Yanks are obsessed with it. They keep their lake trade alive because they understand its place, you see. It's the single most efficient way to move goods ever devised. Look at the Greeks! Look at the English! But what do Canadians do? Bloody trucks.'

'You could go back,' she said.

'Where? Deep sea? No, my girl. Oh no.'

'Why not?'

'There were twelve to a room when I went to sea. I was fourteen years old. We slept in hammocks. In shifts, mind. It was the tropics. The walls were black with cockroaches. Black.'

Ronnie tipped back his cup and swallowed carefully, producing a folded white handkerchief to dab his mouth. She felt suddenly sorry for him. Only a person carrying a painful cargo would attempt to unload so regularly. Fourteen when he went to sea. A skinny little Cockney kid.

'But I got lucky, you see. Got on with a Dutch outfit. Registered in Rotterdam. Seventeen years with that company. Wonderful food. Of course, in the tropics, they'll sell you anything. They come out in little boats, with fish and trinkets and fruit and so on. Everything fresh. Marvellous.'

'What happened?'

Ronnie glanced at her sharply. 'What d'you mean?'

'Why'd you leave?'

'The company was sold. And the new owners decided they would save a few guilders and register their ships in Singapore. A flag of convenience. Paid most of us off and hired Malaysians.'

Ronnie gazed off toward the horizon, wreathed now in haze. 'You can never tell with those crews. They don't have the same credentials as Europeans. But my friend stayed on, you see. As master. A promotion. And that ship was lost in a typhoon the first trip out. All hands. Never found.'

❡ 22. It was supper hour on Thursday when the *Huron Queen* anchored off Pointe Noire, a grim mining town on the rocky north coast of the Gulf of St. Lawrence. She heard the big hook's chain rattle down below and a general complaint from the crew in the messroom. The boat would not go in to the ore docks for hours; they would miss their drinking time.

'You know what this means, don't ya?' Hazel said sourly. 'They're gonna go fishing.'

They started jigging before the meal ended, the deckhands and Swede the wheelsman and Calvin, their raucous laughter drifting in through the stern door. May hovered by the screen with her arms wrapped around her little body, tittering with excitement. 'Fresh cod for lunch tomorrow, Hazel, won't that be a treat?'

'Don't count on it,' Hazel said. 'They'll be frying it up at midnight. We'll have a goddamn mess in the morning. I hate them using my stove.'

'Don't you worry, Hazel,' May said gaily. 'I'll keep an eye on them. What about you, young lady, you ever had fresh cod?'

'It ain't all it's cracked up to be, codfish,' Hazel interrupted. 'The last time we were here they got one with a big ugly worm coming out of it.'

'Oh that's nothing,' May said.

'Oh, please.' Kate rolled her eyes.

'Don't bother washing the floor tonight, neither,' Hazel told Kate as she was drying the last pot. 'There'll be fish guts all over it.'

Her bunk was no escape from the shouts carrying on the wind from the stern. She got a mug of tea and sat in the rec room, where

Charlie, the little Newfie watchman, was standing on a chair, twisting the dials of the television bolted to a high wooden shelf. The screen hissed and crackled, ghostly figures appearing and disappearing into pointillistic static.

'It'll all be in French, won't it, Charlie?' Kate said. 'You speak French?'

'Nah, just Newfenese.'

'I thought you'd be out there fishing.'

'Oh, not me,' he said with an embarrassed laugh. 'Can't stand the sight of blood, not even fish blood.' Kate looked at him with interest. It wasn't normal to admit to sensitivity on a boat, but then Charlie seemed more leprechaun than man.

'So I guess you don't go seal hunting either.'

Charlie squeezed his eyes shut and shook his head vigorously. 'Oh, my lord, no. I couldn't do that.'

'I don't know how anyone can,' she said.

'Well, why shouldn't they, earn a little extra when they've got the chance?' It was the Irishman, leaning in the doorway with a mug in his hand. 'Life's hard in these parts, isn't it, Charlie? It's hand to mouth for a lot of folks. But I suppose Toronto people wouldn't know much about that.'

'So Brian,' she said, knowing he wouldn't like to hear her use his name, 'So Brian. How would you know what Toronto people know?'

He smiled a cat's smile but his voice remained studiously mild. 'I know you, don't I?'

'Fuck you,' she said evenly.

'Sorry, miss,' he laughed, pretending to tug a forelock. 'Forgot my place, miss, and you being a photographer and all. Only, why aren't you back there taking pictures? You won't get any pictures like that in Toronto, now, the boys jiggin' for cod. Very colourful, I'm sure.'

Then he was gone. Kate fixed her eyes on the snowy TV screen, stung. Charlie still vainly fiddled with the dials, giving no sign of having heard the exchange. Then he switched it off and climbed down from the chair. 'You got to steer clear of that one,' he said quietly. 'He'd stick a knife in his own brudder's back.'

'Yeah, I know.'

'Well, guess I'll go make myself a cuppa, since there's nutting on the TV. You coming?'

'No thanks, Charlie, I'm fine.'

Kate headed back to her room and poured a shot of vodka into her water glass and drank it straight. Brian was right; she would never see anything like this in Toronto. She got the Minolta and took the forward ladder up to the lifeboat deck, above the commotion.

She could hear them as she approached the railing, and she did not like the way they sounded. Men laughing like little boys, unguarded and verging on wilder emotions. As if they all might suddenly burst into tears.

Then Calvin's wire-tight voice. 'Fuck! Fuck! Grab that one, buddy!'

Looking down she saw carnage. The deckhands and Calvin and even mountainous Swede moving balletically as they worked their nylon lines, jerking them back and forth, back and forth over the ship's stern railing. Like threshers in a field, hauling in their bleeding harvest. Around their feet shiny bodies thrashing, their mouths opening and closing as they suffocated.

She'd had it explained to her once. Jigging was brutal but efficient: thick nylon lines tied at intervals with vicious triple-pronged hooks five or six inches long. The hooks danced in the dark sea below, drawing the fish close, luring them, till the sharp points got them in belly or mouth or side.

It was worse than anything she'd seen as a child, when her father and his friends would fish on the little lakes north of Ottawa for rainbow trout. Beautiful sleek creatures that took her breath away when she glimpsed them in the green shallows. And then reduced to desperate dust-covered muscles convulsing on the rocks, until one of the wives went over and beat them senseless with a husband's moccasin. Kate would walk up and down the wet sand, burying every dead minnow she could find.

The ship, buoyant in the salt water of the Gulf, was pitching as she made her way back to her cabin. She put away the camera; she had not taken a single shot. In her bunk she tried to interest herself in Thomas Hardy. But she kept hearing Calvin's voice though her porthole, and soon she was climbing back down and pulling on her jacket. A cold brackish wind scoured the companionway. She imagined it blowing in from the Atlantic, in past Newfoundland and Cape Breton and Prince Edward Island. For half the crew on the *Huron Queen*, it was a wind from home, the kind of wind that unleashed tongues. She could hear May holding forth in the galley.

'Oh, but they weren't all bad, the Mounties,' she was telling Calvin, who was frying something on the stove. 'The first time I drove in my life was after Tommy died and I was desperate to see my sister. The Mountie pulled me over and he said, 'My dear, you were fishtailing all over the road. You are not fit to be alone right now. Just promise me you'll get some lessons and I'll drive you where you gotta go.'

Kate dropped a teabag into a mug and filled it with water from the kettle, averting her eyes from the pile of gutted fish on the draining board. Bad enough that she couldn't help thinking of it alive, just minutes ago, twisting on a hook. Worse was that the aroma of butter-fried fish was making her weak with hunger.

'You're just in time,' Calvin said, holding out a frying pan full of small browned pastilles of delicate-looking flesh. She swallowed against the saliva that was filling her mouth.

'No thanks. I saw how you caught them.'

Calvin laughed, his eyes bright with bloodlust. 'Some fun, man. You should try it sometime.'

'Fuck off.'

'Now now, that's no way to talk.'

May disappeared into the messroom and came out with a wedding cake of white plates piled in her arms. She was followed by a grinning Charlie, bearing a white tower of mugs. It was clear they had been drinking more than tea. 'Oh, my girl,' May trilled. 'That there's an East Coast delicacy. You got to try it.'

'Cod's tongues,' Charlie said. 'Calvin must be sweet on you, if he's sharing his cod's tongues.'

Kate blushed. 'Charlie, I thought you said you hated fishing.'

'Well, I hates the fishing, but I loves the eating.' He was grinning, his freckles and missing front tooth making him look like a demonic child.

May tittered and reeled slightly. 'Whoops. Well, I'm to bed.'

'Sleep tight, girl,' Charlie said.

'Tight all right,' Calvin said.

Kate looked at him. 'Tongues? Really?'

'Yeah. Cheeks are good too.' He was nodding, encouraging. 'Boat's going in now. You comin' up to the bar after?'

'Maybe. Okay, Calvin. Give me one of those.'

He watched her face as she chewed, first tentatively and then with gusto, tasting the rich buttery juice as it collected under her tongue. It was ambrosial, rich and subtle, melt-in-the-mouth tender.

She couldn't help it. 'Give me another.'

Calvin nodded with satisfaction.

Like most mining towns, Pointe Noire was a place you only went by choice if you thought you were going to make a lot of money. It was a man's town. Even at eleven at night, the harbour roared with jostling vehicles, pickup trucks, transports, dump trucks and forklifts, their lights like angry monster eyes. From the taxi driving through the denuded black moonscape of the port, she saw that the vehicles were entirely occupied by men, men in hard hats and plaid jackets, men in ball caps and windbreakers, men in suits in the back seats of dark cars.

Men swarmed around the doorways of the bars on the tiny main street, six or seven luridly signed establishments in a row, CLUB SEXY, CLUB KITTY, CLUB 69. Only one of them, according to the taxi driver, was suitable for a young woman, which was how Calvin and Kate ended up sitting in Club Lucky, a big square prefab room with a linoleum floor and a stage at the back. Like a high school auditorium, except that the ceiling was too low and there was a runway projecting from the stage.

'I don't know what the guy was talking about,' Kate said. 'I'm the only female here who isn't working.' A scrawny girl who looked like she was in grade nine tottered over to their table on platform heels.

'You got those quart bottles here?' asked Calvin, sketching one with his hands. '*Grandes bouteilles?*'

'Sure. You wan' two?'

'I didn't know you spoke French, Calvin.'

'Lots you don't know about me.'

Kate laughed and lit a smoke. 'You've got to phone your mother in the morning,' she said. 'Don't forget.'

'You worry too much.'

'I don't fucking worry enough.'

'Ca'm down, for fuck's sake. Have a drink.' He pronounced it *cam.*

'Where'd the deckhands go?'

'The tavern. You can get takeout beer there.'

They were into their second bottles when the jukebox volume cranked higher and garish orange light flooded the stage. There was no perceptible change in the bar's conversational flow; whatever the show was, they had seen it before. Kate watched the teenage waitress walk toward the back of the room with a tray. Bringing the stripper a drink. But no, the girl set the tray on a table, wobbled up the three steps to the stage and, in a gesture so intimate and casual it caught Kate's breath, pulled her sweater over her head.

Kate felt sick watching the girl stumble out of her skirt and face the crowd. In her bra and panties, dancing stiffly on her thin legs and high, chunky platform shoes, she might have been any gawky adolescent watching herself in her bedroom mirror: half hopeful, half resigned. And then, without changing her rhythm she reached behind her back and undid the bra, dropping it onto the pile of clothes, her small pale breasts bobbing in the light.

Her body was dancing but her head barely moved. She had her eyes fixed somewhere else, on the lights of the city, any city, somewhere free of the stink of ore and men's beery breath, men who might have been her father and were probably her father's friends. The music seemed to grow louder as she slid her hands down her narrow hips and hooked her thumbs into her panties, inching the thin fabric down. Someone whistled. Kate turned to Calvin, about to speak.

But he was already picking up his smokes. 'You want to head back?'

C 23. By morning the ore dust covered everything. Even the captain looked like he was wearing mascara, which gave him the air of a rock star or an eighteenth-century rake.

He came into the galley after breakfast, hands in pockets, lips pursed in a soundless whistle. 'You've got some fresh cod, I hear, Hazel,' he said.

'Don't you worry,' she said. 'It'll be on the lunch menu.'

'That's fine, that's fine. What about you, young lady?' He sidled over to where Kate was drying mugs. Then he pinched her on the cheek, hard. She jerked away, shocked, but Hazel and May were already laughing, anticipating a joke.

'You're looking a little tired this morning,' he said. 'Up at a strip club, I hear.'

Hazel stopped laughing. 'At a strip club? When?'

'Last night. With young Calvin is what I hear,' said the captain. He winked but there was no humour in his face. 'Got to watch that fella.'

Hazel saved her anger until he was out the door. 'You know what kind of day we got ahead of us?' she shrilled. 'I need you to get those cardboard boxes out of the storeroom and cut them up for the hallway before the boys are back in for coffee break. They're gonna be tracking ore from one end of this boat to the other. You're gonna need cardboard for your rooms too. I don't know what you were thinking, going ashore with Calvin. It must have been midnight.'

Kate couldn't believe what she was hearing. 'Hazel. The captain just *pinched* me. You saw him. He can't do that.' She rubbed her cheek, just in case they missed the point.

'It was just a little pinch,' said Hazel. 'It wasn't your rear end.'

May was turning pink with the effort to speak. 'If you ask me, Calvin's a nice lad. Look how much he helps out in the galley, Hazel, always getting us the vegetables from the locker.'

'He just helps us so's he can get out of work on deck,' Hazel said peevishly.

May shook her head, banging mugs onto her tray as Kate dried. 'I got a soft spot for Calvin,' she said. 'There ain't a mean bone in his body.'

'You got a soft spot, all right,' Hazel said. 'In the head.' The old women glared at each other for a moment, like old cats too tired to brawl. They broke away when Kate burst out laughing.

'God, I can't believe this,' she said. 'What am I missing? It's not as if we're doing anything.'

'You're not?' May said.

'Calvin's just a kid. I mean, he's what, seventeen? I just needed someone to share a cab with.'

'Why didn't you say so?' Hazel said, swatting playfully at Kate with a dishrag. 'I been thinking. Whyn't you go out with someone who's educated? Whyn't you go out with Haroun? He's nice-looking, too.'

Kate knew the fourth engineer would be only too willing to take her out. He had told her so after the trip to Toronto. He had been to a new discotheque. 'You would like it, I think. It is called Heaven.'

What was Haroun's picture of heaven? A virtuous wife who gave him many sons? She was sure Haroun would be very happy to have her between the fastidiously clean sheets of his bunk some night. But anything beyond that was highly unlikely.

The fact that she had so little to do in his room had led her to sometimes linger over the books on his desk. They were marine engineering texts, mostly, but there were also novels, collections of short stories, Margaret Atwood and Morley Callaghan and Leonard Cohen. He was educating himself in Canadian culture. She imagined herself as part of his field study, his bit of indigenous wildlife. It made her feel attracted to him, and repulsed at the same time. He reminded her of the camera club teacher. He had too much history. She would feel swamped.

He was also taken, maybe even married. One morning there had been a half-finished letter, full of crossed-out words, on graph paper.

Now is the time to ask you on what grounds you want me to go to the US with you and start over. You say we are in love but what kind of love is it? If we are in love why did we fall apart? Do we trust? I have to say I do not trust you any longer.

Go out with Haroun? No, she didn't need another person who had a problem with trust. But she had borrowed some of his books. He had novels on his desk she had never heard of.

Kate put a towel over her head before she went down the deck to the ladder. Ronnie stood guard in a filthy helmet and overalls next to a black deluge of iron ore. He was shouting at the hungover-looking deckhands, who were shovelling drifts of the heavy, marble-sized ore pellets. Like a hailstorm from Hades. She had saved a jar of them on the *Black River* to take back to Toronto, but when it came time to pack they were too heavy and she dumped them out her porthole.

The footing was treacherous and she had a moment of panic as she stepped over the side. It didn't do to be afraid of ladders on a ship. You could freeze and that could be dangerous. Like the time in Port Cartier with Boyd and Kenny, cabbing back just before sailing after drinking too many Singapore slings. The ladder, which had been at a forty-five-degree angle when they left, had been pulled almost horizontal, suspended across the water like a flimsy bridge, and she stalled in the middle on her hands and knees, wailing. Boyd had almost pissed himself laughing.

In the phone booth she marshalled her pile of change. She had told Jenna not to answer the phone, so she knew there was no point trying to reverse the charges. She fed the machine and let it ring once, then hung up and dialled again. Jenna picked up the third time.

'I thought it would be you,' she sniffed.

'What's wrong? Do you have a cold?'

'Don't you know what day this is?'

'No,' Kate said. 'What day is it?'

'It's the *wedding*.'

'What wedding?'

'Charles and Diana. Oh God, it's so beautiful. I got up to watch it at three a.m.'

'And it's still on?'

'No no, they're showing it again. They're showing it all day. Maybe you could get it there.'

'I don't think so.'

'You should try, Kate, really. I don't think Charles is ugly at all. I think he's sweet. When he said his vows he was crying.'

'Look, Jenna, I don't have much change. Have you had any more calls?'

'You mean from Boyd?'

'From Boyd or anyone else, um, weird.'

'No. But Mom phoned. She's freaking. You need to call her. What are you trying to prove? I gave her your address.' Kate was silent. 'Oh God, they're showing Diana from above. They're in the nave. Her train is about a mile long. She looks like a queen bee in a hive.' Jenna was sobbing. 'One of those giant queen bees.'

'Jenna. Jen, listen to me. Did you get the new lock on?'

'What? Oh, the lock. Yeah. Jerry did it.'

'Did he take a key?'

'I don't know. Kate?'

'What?'

'Why am I crying?'

'I don't know, Jen. Make sure Jerry has a key.'

* * *

Calvin showed up late for coffee break, his face almost black with dust. He looked like a child coal miner, scrubbing at his eyes with the back of his hand. 'I got a fuckin' load of ore in the face when I went to phone home. Ken and Boyd are on the *Hurontario,* lucky fucks. It's a self-unloader. Ken called the old lady on Sunday.'

'How long are they going to stay?'

'That's all she wrote, man.'

'What did you tell your mother?'

'I told her they won the lottery.'

'You did not.'

'No, I did not,' he said in a singsong voice, mimicking her. 'I told her they owed me money. That'll keep them away from me better than anything else I can think of.'

'Fuck, Calvin. You weren't supposed to do that.'

'What was I supposed to do? I thought you were worried about Boyd.' He lit a cigarette and grinned. 'I heard the captain grabbed your ass.'

'No, he pinched my other cheek. He came back to tell Hazel I was at the bar with you. Who told him we were at the bar?'

Calvin shrugged. 'You're lucky it wasn't your ass. That's what he did to the last porter.'

'You're kidding. Did she complain?'

'Nah. She told him she'd tell his wife. That put a scare into him.'

'Do Hazel and May know about that?'

'I doubt it. She thought they were idiots.'

Hazel called Kate into the pantry after lunch. She had that grin on her face, the kind she put on when she was going to say something critical. 'I need to talk to ya. Here, sit down. You got your tea?'

'What did I do now?'

Hazel raised a hand. 'You're turning into a good little worker, hon. The best porter we've had on here. Ronnie was saying you've been doing a real good job on his room.' She slurped at her tea. 'But I wish you'd stay away from Calvin.'

'Hazel –'

'Listen. The regular porter called the boat this morning. She ain't coming back. The job's yours if you want it. You can stay on till your school starts up, when's that, September? That'd give you what, five more weeks?'

Feeling relief mixed with resentment, Kate swallowed the last of her tepid tea. 'Thanks. But I don't know.'

'What don't you know?'

Kate sighed pointedly. 'I don't know if I want to stay, if you're always going to be telling me who I can go ashore with.'

Hazel regarded her stonily.

'If I want to have a drink with someone it's nobody else's business.'

'It is if you're bringing it back to the boat.'

'God, Hazel, it's 1981! The officers can bring their wives on board every time we go through the Canal, but the crew aren't even supposed to have a beer in their room. They're grown men!'

'Yeah? Whatcha saying, you want to have a drink in your room? Go ahead. But if you get caught fooling around with Calvin the captain's gonna fire you both.'

Kate shook her head impatiently. What was it about Calvin and the old women? He was just a kid. Maybe they thought he had a crush on her, and they were trying to protect him. They had nothing to worry about. She wasn't interested in Kenny's baby brother, or anyone else from that godforsaken island. Not even slightly.

❨ 24. A river as big as this one, Kate thought, deserved a better name. Jacques Cartier had taken the usual explorer's way out, christening it according to whatever saint's day he happened to arrive on. Saint Lawrence was a Roman martyr of no particular distinction, a poor namesake for a highway to the centre of the continent.

Much better, Kate thought, was what the natives called it, Kaniatarowanenneh, which according to her high-school history meant 'the road that walks'. A stilted translation. Why walks? Why not moves? The moving road.

The Québécois sailors just called it *le fleuve*, but on her marine chart it had other names, too: Lac St. Francis, Lac St. Louis, Lac St. Pierre, swellings in the stream like sausage links, lambs swallowed by a boa. At the downstream end of the swelling called Lac St. Pierre came the port of Trois-Rivières, named according to geography instead of catechism.

Trois-Rivières was the site of Laviolette Bridge, an elegant arc between the north and south shores of the St. Lawrence. Kate had begun a collection of bridge shots, but the grander they looked in reality the worse they looked in photos. The Mackinac, for instance, that absurd spidery link across the top of Lake Michigan, like a floating road to a distant future world – it looked like nothing in her pictures. Best so far was the rusting little bridge over the St. Lawrence near Cornwall, smeared with dripping red graffiti: *This is Indian land.*

Kate lay on the boat deck bench, pointing her lens up at the sky. Laviolette stretched diagonally across her viewfinder, a filigreed necklace against gilded clouds, growing and then shrinking as the boat moved below it. She released the shutter at the last possible moment, just as it was passing out of the frame. Then she felt dizzy and sat up and lit a cigarette, watching the bridge recede into a sketch, a scrawl, a smudge.

Somewhere were people who would pay money for pictures of bridges, she thought, just like there were boat buffs who collected shots of the freighters that went through the Canal; she had seen them standing on the shore, canvas bucket hats, camera bags weighing down one shoulder. You could order pictures of individual boats at the tuck shop in Lock 5, ten bucks for an eight-by-ten, the ships looking so clean and generic they might have been toys on the river.

She wasn't any better. She thought she wanted to document boat life, but she was happier taking pictures of bridges and clouds and the scabbed walls of grain elevators. Empty docks and empty water. Storms.

It was growing colder on the river. She had watched the western sky turn pink; she had watched the south shore darken from green to grey to black. Lights had begun to twinkle from the farmhouses perched atop the cliffs in their ancient seigneurial divisions, each claiming its piece of shore, its long narrow acreage spooling out behind. She threw her cigarette butt overboard and lit another. It was lonelier on a river than in the middle of a lake, passing through people's lives, knowing it was really people's lives passing you by. And then, as if in answer to her thoughts, she heard a blast of sound from the high dark cliff on the south side, which after a moment she recognized as a scratchy rendition of 'O Canada'.

An old-fashioned loudspeaker was playing the national anthem, and it was happening here in Quebec, where nation meant independence from the *maudits anglais*. Kate stood and squinted hard, but there was nothing to see except a scatter of lights. And then, just as the broadcast ended, an ear-shattering salute from the ship's horn above her made her bash her knee against the railing. Fucking horn! Fucking ships!

She didn't realize she had said it out loud, until Calvin's answering laugh came floating up from the ladder. His head followed shortly and then she could hear the clink of bottles as he loped over to the bench. She could have kissed him.

'Scared you, eh?' He handed her a beer.

'What the hell was that?'

'You never heard the music man before? Some geezer plays the national anthem for every boat that goes by. Russian, Dutch, whatever. He's got 'em all.'

She thought about what kind of personality would make this his life's work. A completist. 'Does he have Singaporean? Ronnie says the Canadian trade is dying.'

'Yeah well, he would, wouldn't he? He's always gotta know better than anybody else.' Calvin sat forward, jiggling his knees in sudden agitation. 'But I'll tell you something. He's right about this tub. Somebody should tell the coast guard. Shouldn't be going up on Superior any more. Shouldn't be heading for the Gulf either. Want to know what I think?'

'Do I have a choice?'

'Salt.' He said it with satisfaction, hunkering down to roll a joint in the shelter of his jacket. 'It'll be where they send us next.'

'Salt water?'

'Nah. You kidding? Goderich. Biggest salt mine in Canada. They'll put us on the salt run and that'll be the end of this fucking thing. It's where they send old boats to die. It'll rust the guts right out of her.'

'Where's Goderich?'

'Lake Huron.' He paused to take a couple of hard tokes and then held it out to her, eyes squinting comically. She shook her head. 'South end,' he said. 'Good beaches.'

He toked again and looked at his watch, then stood and crumbled the roach into the wind. 'Gotta check in with the wheelhouse.'

'Got another beer?'

'Sure, go ahead. Take my last beer.'

❦ 25. Four days later, there was a parcel in the Canal. Kate had a flicker of anxiety watching Calvin collect the mail at the wicket in Lock 5. He held up a white envelope and a small brown package and mimed excitement, but she didn't smile back. She thought of what Boyd might send her. Balled-up dirty panties? A used condom?

She knew what the white envelope was. Next to the Marine Post Office was what Calvin called the rip-off store, the tuck shop that sold overpriced cigarettes and toiletries and pornography to the sailors. The shop sent film out for developing, also overpriced, but Kate didn't care. Her films had come back. She plucked the envelope out of Calvin's gloved hand the moment he stepped over the railing.

'Hey! You owe me ten bucks.'

Taking photographs is an act of faith. You try to capture a moment, but you do not see what you've caught for hours or days. In her mind the storm had taken on demonic proportions; she could now imagine she heard the boat cracking beneath the roar of the rain. She had pictured the twisting over and over, until it seemed miraculous that the *Huron Queen* was not lying in two pieces at the bottom of Superior, a consort to the *Edmund Fitzgerald*.

In her cabin, sliding the images out of their folders in the porthole light she knew she expected to be disappointed. Yet by the third or fourth print she allowed herself to breathe. The dark swollen clouds she had photographed leaving the Lakehead were perfectly etched, moody above a glittering lake.

The storm shots were more chaotic. They wouldn't win any awards for composition, yet even in these flat, four-by-six-inch rectangles she could feel the force of the gale again, the dark water raising its fist to knock her down. She swallowed against a rising excitement: they were good. With careful darkroom work, they might even be publishable – yes, she could send these to one of the photo magazines. 'Storm on Superior', she could call them; they were *reportage*.

She would show them to Calvin.

In her excitement she forgot the other parcel until she was back in her room after lunch. It was from her mother. A book, by the shape of it. Which was good, since despite her habit of falling asleep within minutes of hitting the pillow she'd still managed to work through everything she'd brought with her.

Tearing open her mother's careful wrapping, she inhaled the smell of her father's bookshelves, musty leather and antique dust. But she could tell he had bought this book for her. It was a 1927 hardcover edition of *Two Years before the Mast*. World Famous Literature, it said on the spine. She had never heard of it.

Inside the front cover was a single sheet of stationery, covered with her mother's perfect, tiny script. *Dad thought you might like this. He found it at that antiques place outside Perth. We drove up with the Fieldings, remember them? There was a set of photography books, very new, though Dad thought they were a bit high. He thought he might be able to get them to drop it a bit …*

She shoved the letter between the pages of the book, knowing she shouldn't be angry. Books were how her father showed his love. Never a hug, but he would pick her up something when he went down to the antiquarian shops. Edifying books. Proust, for instance. Books even he found unreadable.

Kate had no memory of the Fieldings. The bridge players, possibly. The ones with the lawyer daughter. Her mother said the daughter was getting married. Her parents were going to the Laurentians for the wedding. She wondered why she was expected to be interested in people who'd never shown the slightest interest in her.

She wondered why her mother didn't ask about the people she shared her life with, slept in rooms with, worked side by side with seven days a week. Her mother knew nothing about Hazel or May or Carol. Kate thought this was because her mother was in denial about what Kate was doing, even though it would be like her to tell friends over dinner how brave she was. Isn't it marvellous, her mother would say, Kate's making loads of money on a *cargo* boat.

It was what they liked to think she was doing, having a lark. Two Years Before the Sink, all right as long as it wasn't her real life. Real life was career-track education, marrying your own kind. A house and a station wagon, for when the children come. Not pretending to be a photographer. Not a crap job on a freighter, sleeping with sailors.

'Somewhere you got a rebel gene,' Becks had told her.

'It's got nothing to do with rebelling. I do it for the money.'

'You could make the same money in a bar.'

'Maybe, but I'd have to talk to people.'

The money wasn't enough, though. Hazel did it for the money, how else could a woman with a grade ten education buy her own house? But look what it cost her. Not a day passed that Hazel didn't think about quitting. When it got cold, she said, her hands would ache so bad that she sometimes cried in the morning. And now this screw-up with the bank.

After the mail arrived Hazel had burst into the galley, holding up a letter. It shook in her fist. 'No, I don't want to sit. I'm too mad.' She had phoned the loan officer about her mortgage the last trip through, but now they had written to say the quote had been in error.

'Because I'm a woman on my own. Do you believe this goddamn bullshit after the women's libbers and all that bra burning, and here I am, never missed a goddamn mortgage payment and I'm supposed to pay one and a half per cent higher than if I was a man?' She was flushed, her voice rising raggedly.

'Are you sure?' Kate asked.

'Of course I'm sure! It was the captain who told me the rate I should ask for. It's what he just got.'

'How can that be legal?'

'Oh, honey, you have no idea the kinds of things that are legal in this country. When my cousin got divorced she got to keep the house and that was all she got. Thirty years she cooked his meals and washed his clothes and then he starts up with this girl in his office and cleans out the savings accounts too and there's nothing she can do about it.'

Watching the colour deepen in Hazel's face, Kate felt afraid for her. She tried a joke. 'Well, good thing you never got married, Hazel.'

The cook looked at her sharply before deciding to laugh. 'It ain't like no one *asked*. I figured they were after someone to take care of them. If anyone asked now I'd figure he was after my house. May was smart about one thing. She signed her farm over to her kids before she married Frank.'

'Women have many faults,' May intoned. 'Men but two. Everything they say and everything they do.'

The old women cackled like maniacs. 'Well, I feel better now,'

Hazel said, wiping her eyes. 'But I'm gonna phone them from Cleveland and give them a piece of my mind.'

Stretched out in her bunk for her afternoon break, Kate reread her mother's letter. Characteristically, she had waited until the end to say what she had to say.

What I don't understand, Kate, is why you've decided to boycott us. If it's about the money for school, I thought we had been through all that. Please don't blame your father for standing by what he believes. He's a good man, Kate. He loves you more than you know.

⟪ 26. In Cleveland the captain came into the galley after breakfast to tell Hazel they were going to be there for a while. 'The chief and I are going uptown, if you girls need anything. There's only one dock running that can handle straightbacks; we're going to have to wait.'

'That's okay,' Hazel said. 'Just bring us back a couple air conditioners, would ya?'

The heat in the galley was fierce. May was in a trance, making circles on the counter with her dishcloth.

'It's the humidity,' Hazel said. 'It's worse every summer. I can't take it like I used to.'

She eased off her stool and went over to the fan that was wheezing from its bracket on the wall. 'This goddamn fan. It's got no juice. I asked the chief twice to fix it.' Then she screamed and clutched at her hand.

Kate sat like an idiot. It was May who jumped up and tore off her apron, wrapping it around Hazel's hand. 'Quick,' she said. 'Get it under cold water.'

Hazel's voice had risen to a shriek. 'Those goddamn assholes! The fan blade's right by the switch! I thought it was covered!'

Kate followed them to the sink, where May held Hazel's hand under the Drinking Water Only tap. 'You'll be all right, Hazel,' she said soothingly. 'It's a clean cut. I'll wrap it up nice and tight.'

Hazel sat miserably as May fussed. They were both flushed and perspiring. 'Why don't you and May go take a break?' Kate said, as diplomatically as she could. 'You can't serve soup on a day like this. I can make a big potato salad.'

'I don't know,' said Hazel.

'Trust me. It'll be good.'

She found Calvin smoking on the stern, staring across the water at a self-unloader. 'That's where the money is,' he said dolefully. 'The mate said this dock used to be able to unload half a dozen straightbacks. But now they've taken out all the old cranes except the one we're waiting for. We're on a dinosaur, you know that? A fucking dinosaur.'

'I thought you said self-unloaders are disgusting. Could you get me a bag of potatoes from the bin?'

'What did your last slave die of?'

'Hunger.'

She stationed the bucket in front of the bench, where a suggestion of breeze was coming off the river, and sat with a cigarette and a knife, bending rhythmically to the burlap sack, turning the scarred, lumpy, dirt-thick tubers into smooth white ovals. They were old potatoes, their stripped flesh giving slightly to the touch, like a firm thigh. They felt good in her hand.

She had grown deft with the knife, almost as fast as May, and felt pleasure at her skill, at the soft plash that each potato made as it dropped into the chilled water of the white plastic bucket. She would make her mother's potato salad, she thought, running through the ingredients in her mind: eggs, apples, celery, Dijon mustard – but Hazel didn't have Dijon. Shallots, chopped very fine. Sour cream ...

Calvin was back with his tea. He was still on about self-unloaders. It was the money. His overtime on his last cheque had been down. Self-unloaders were the way of the future. The crews could triple their wages with overtime, but they never got ashore to spend it. 'You know why they say ugly women like self-unloaders?'

'Don't tell me.'

'The crew's so desperate they'll screw anything.'

'God, you have a sad pathetic little mind, Calvin,' Kate said, cutting rot from a potato. 'Go away.'

He went away. He didn't bring in his dishes after lunch, but Kate was too pleased with herself to care. Hazel had suggested Kate make the salads from then on. 'Since you like salad so much,' she said. 'The problem with May is she don't eat anything raw, so she don't know how they're supposed to taste.'

The ship was still tied to the holding dock by the time Kate dumped the floor water after supper. She caught a whiff of grass drifting down from the lifeboat deck and climbed up the ladder. Calvin was on the bench, shirtless.

'You're an idiot to smoke that inside an American plant,' she said. 'I could smell it down below.'

Calvin shrugged. 'Never seen cops at this dock. Seen them in Indiana Harbour though. Had a whole SWAT team in my room, three guys in sunglasses and a German shepherd. I was shitting myself, man.'

'That's hardly a SWAT team.'

'Whatever. They didn't find what they were looking for.'

Kate had read about drug seizures on ships coming from overseas. Why not lakers?

She wheeled on Calvin. 'It's what Boyd and Kenny are doing, isn't it?' she demanded. 'They're bringing dope across. A self-unloader's so dirty it would be easier to hide.'

'How would I know that, since I'm not involved in whatever the fuck they're doing?' His tone was so self-pitying she almost laughed. It made her want to reach over and grab the mass of gold ringlets brushing the top of his sunburned shoulders. She would twist it around in her fist and pull his head back.

'Calvin. What was the deal before? Sell it down east? That doesn't make sense, there must be tons of it coming into Halifax. I mean literally.'

Calvin was shaking his head. 'No man, you don't get it. It comes in and then it goes out, to Montreal or Maine. The good stuff never gets up to us. You should see the crap they're selling in the bars in Sydney. Now this –' he paused to suck in smoke, filling his lungs with the last little sips, a reverse image of her father blowing up balloons, till he was red in the face, till the balloon popped – 'this shit is *good*.'

'Yeah, well. I think you are all fucking idiots. Anyway, I'd rather have a cold beer.'

He shrugged. 'Go up to the bar, then.'

'I'm not walking through this plant alone.'

It was a mile at least to the gates. From where the ship sat tethered to a back dock, the view might have been of a deserted city, everywhere crumbling concrete and weedy trees, umbrellas of foliage not quite hiding piles of rusting machinery. In the distance she could hear the faint roar of trucks and backhoes, like hungry zoo animals left behind by a fleeing population. 'Anyway, there's no one to go up with.'

He grinned. 'I might go up when my watch is done. Things'll still be hopping at midnight.'

She lit a cigarette and sat down beside him, stretching out her legs. 'No. Someone'll tell the Old Man on us again.' The captain had winked at her that evening, as if they were sharing a joke.

'Fucking Irish.'

'Brian?'

'He's always after me about you, man.'

'Really.'

'Yeah.' Calvin laughed humourlessly. 'Are ya gettin' any yet, Calvin? Do ya even know what to do with it? Are ya queer or what, Calvin?'

'Brian's an asshole.'

Calvin looked at her face and held out the roach. 'Come on, have a toke. It'll ca'm you down.'

'What makes you think I'm not calm?'

'You're all red. I can see steam coming out your fucking ears. Anyway, this shit about Kenny and them. They couldn't organize something like that if they took all fucking year. They're strictly one-deal wonders, man.'

'I don't believe you.'

Calvin widened his eyes, all innocence. 'You're a hard woman, aren't ya?'

She hadn't registered the colour before. His eyes were like Boyd's, like shallow green water on a breezy day, sunlight sparking on the points of the wavelets. Breathing in the sweet skunky smell of his sweat, she felt a pang so sharp she winced.

He saw it. 'The fuck did I do now?'

'What did you tell Brian when he said those things about me?'

Calvin laughed. 'I told him you're too old for me.'

The thing about beautiful girls is that even the halfway beautiful are beautiful enough. Carol said girls never learn this until it's too late, until they are forty and would take it all back, not just the high breasts and the glossy hair but the baby fat and spots too. The way a girl of twenty sucks on her cigarette, the way she blushes too hard, if only she knew what Carol knew at forty, that she is as beautiful as she will ever be in her life.

But Kate was nineteen and still learning, she knew even as she was getting up and walking away that she was being stupid. What would she want with Calvin, all of seventeen? Which was like twelve in female years. Anyway, what would he want from her? Where Calvin came from, you had to play the man, and to do that you needed a girl you could break in.

If Carol were here she would laugh at Kate now, laugh at her probing her face in the locked washroom, the sweat running between her breasts. Her cheeks were too pink, her jaw too strong. She pinched the softness under her chin. She must have gained ten pounds on the boats. She could see lines under her eyes. Don't be silly, love, you call those lines? What are you using, a magnifying glass? You call that fat? Oh love, you're too young to be an old woman.

Calvin brought in his tray after breakfast, the way he always did, but she knew the way he banged it down he was still annoyed. 'What got into you last night?'

'Nothing.'

'Fucking right, nothing.'

She laughed.

'Made ya laugh,' he said, turning on his heel.

She was still smiling when she noticed Hazel watching her. 'You finished them dishes yet? I need some carrots done.'

'Just about.'

The cook was slamming a meat cleaver into a hunk of beef and tossing the pieces into a pot. It made Kate queasy to watch.

'So there *is* something going on between you and Calvin,' she said.

'Yes, there is. We're friends.'

'Men and women can't be friends on boats. Those deckhands went ashore without you last night. See? They don't want you along when they're trying to pick up girls.'

'I don't care about the deckhands,' Kate said impatiently. 'But I need someone to go out for a drink with. There aren't any girls my age. What am I supposed to do?'

Hazel fixed her with a glare. 'Whyn't you try not drinking?'

But Hazel had a better idea after supper, when the boat was in the

Detroit River, a valley of light on the American side, darkness on the Canadian. 'You want to come over and watch *Love Boat*? Seeing as you say you need company.'

Hazel had an old black-and-white television perched on her dresser, tucked between boxes of napkins and paper aprons.

'Is it any good?'

'I wouldn't call it good. But it's comin' in real clear.'

'I'll come, Hazel,' May said. 'I can bring my crochet.'

'I'll be there in a minute,' Kate said.

She didn't want to go. She was so hungry for privacy she felt it like an ache. She lay in her bunk in the dark cabin with a mug of tea balanced on her chest, listening to May's transistor radio, the dark chocolate tones of an American deejay spinning Motown tunes. She would like to listen all night to the voices coming from the lit-up side of the river.

Kate climbed down and went to the open porthole, looking across the oily waves of the river to the golden skyscrapers of Detroit, the glittering box of the Renaissance Center. Only sailors saw a city this beautiful, she thought. A galaxy of lit confetti sharpening to a liquid string of jewels, a Vegas of colour. A lightshow for the marginal.

There was a knock and Calvin stuck his head into the cabin. 'Hey man, you got the room to yourself? Got anything to drink?'

'No.'

'You're not still mad, are ya?'

'Of course I'm not mad. I was never mad.'

'It's nothing personal, right?'

Kate huffed in exasperation. 'Calvin, what's nothing personal?'

'Just what I said. That you're too old. You know, mature. For someone like me.'

'Oh, for God's sake. You're too young for me.'

ℂ 27. The Missions to Seamen was a trailer parked at a dusty crossroads on the outskirts of Thunder Bay. There was a sign above the window in the tiny living room. Keep These Drapes Open At All Times. It was meant to discourage sailors from using the place the way Kate was using it now.

She was drinking wine. Calvin had snuck a glass out of the bar at the Holiday Inn and kept it from spilling all the way back in the cab. He had traded a shift and invited her to town. She knew she was asking for trouble going, but she didn't care. She wanted to be drunk. It felt fucking great to be drunk, to not have to think about her sister and her father and Boyd and Hazel and how nineteen could feel too late for anything good to happen.

She told Calvin that. She told him more than once, interrupting his recitation about bad boats and bad behaviour, watching his mouth as he laughed and smoked. The crew thought Calvin was after her ass but she knew it was another part of her he wanted. He was the little brother, the kid no one ever listened to. Calvin wanted an audience.

He had his own stories to tell, even if they were no different from the others she'd heard around bar tables. The time when. The guy who. The place where.

He was telling one now, about the time the Mounties were after the guy who had a stash of dope in the woods, and they found his blow-up sex doll instead. She knew he was flirting with her then. But she hoped the story was true. It was only truth she found interesting.

They had two bottles of wine and some shooters and she let Calvin pay for it all. On the way to the dock she leaned lightly against his shoulder in the back seat, feeling his voice through his bones as he detailed to the cab driver the relative risk of muggings in various U.S. ports.

'That's okay, buddy,' said the guy, an Eastern European type who was going bald. 'I used to sail.'

She felt the floor shift as she swayed over to the shabby brown couch. That was the trailer, not her, although she had succeeded in getting as drunk as she wanted to. She knelt on the couch to close the curtains and then lay back to watch Calvin roll a joint at the coffee table. It was so quiet she could hear crickets through the trailer walls. Males. Males calling to females, she had learned in high school biology. She suddenly felt the bareness of her legs under her jean skirt.

The fridge hummed in the little kitchen. A sign said Soft Drinks 50 Cents, Leave Money In Box. There was a pay phone by the door. You had to have the right coins. A notice in a wobbly hand gave the times the chaplain would be in. Kate could imagine the foreign sailors pretending faith just for the chance to walk a quarter mile from the

Liberian-registered hellholes they sailed in. It was true you never saw those guys in port. But some of them were allowed this far, to phone home and buy a Coke.

And pick up a Christian tract or two. They were the only thing free in the place, dozens of little illustrated booklets displayed in a wire rack, in all different colours and alphabets. The Bible as comic book. *Are You Saved?* In English, Greek, Cyrillic, Arabic.

'Are you saved?' Kate asked Calvin.

He laughed. 'No fucking way.'

Below the tracts was a rack of scarred paperbacks, the edges yellowed and stained. Books, 25 Cents, in the same wavering hand. She lurched off the couch and went over to scan the spines. Bodice-rippers, bestsellers, no-sellers. She picked four that looked readable, along with a couple of old pocket-sized hardcovers that felt good in her hand, a Dickens and a Thomas Hardy. Her father would be pleased.

Calvin filled his lungs with a hiss and croaked at her. 'Toke?'

'No. Do you have any change? I want a couple of these.'

'Fuck, just take 'em, man.'

'Come on, got a buck fifty?'

'Gave it all to the cab driver.'

'Fuck it.' She crammed the books into her bag.

Calvin laughed. 'Leave an IOU.'

There was an eye pencil in her makeup bag. She tore a cover from one of the tracts and scribbled a note: IOU 1.50. Thank you for providing. The Porter, SS *Huron Queen*.

She heard the room fill up with static. Calvin had switched on the old record player and was inexpertly fitting a record onto the spindle. The needle ripped across the vinyl, catching on the deep bass notes of 'Smoke Gets in Your Eyes.'

It was like listening to campfire songs, the way the disc popped and crackled. Kate was laughing, vamping with her wineglass in one hand, a cigarette in the other. She closed her eyes and swayed to the music and then she felt Calvin's arms go around her waist and his groin push against hers and she shoved him away. But she could feel the current going through her, lighting up her nipples and jolting her between her legs. She was breathing hard.

'C'mon now.' His eyes were half closed. 'You never danced with me at the bar.'

'Okay,' she said. 'Put it back to the beginning.'

She heard the needle pop and then the trailer filled again with the crackly organ music and Calvin took away her glass and cigarette. She stood still and let him do it because she had decided she couldn't stop it. She could feel saliva filling her mouth before he even kissed her, and when he did the kiss was dry, tentative, so she put her arms around his neck and her tongue into his mouth.

His hands went up under her shirt and pulled up her bra and then she leaned back to let him undo the buttons. They were still kissing, kneeling now on the hard carpeting, and then he was pushing her down, sucking on one breast and then the other, his eyes closed. She heard someone moaning and realized it was her. She bit her lip to keep herself quiet.

The song ended and she pulled down her bra and pushed him away. Her voice was wobbly. 'This is as far as it can go, Calvin.'

Watching his unsteady gaze, she knew he was drunker than she was. He had been drinking doubles at the end. How much would he remember? He levered himself to his knees and held out a hand. 'You're gonna be that way, are ya? C'mon then.'

Outside the trailer it was pitch black, moonless, but she felt like she could see through her skin. Then with a whoop she was running down the dirt road toward the elevator, feeling the wind lift her hair. The crickets went silent as she flew past, her ears filled with the rustle of grasses.

Calvin caught up near the dock. She stopped and looked into his face, bluish under the lights. He moved in and out of focus, as if he was underwater.

'What?' he said raggedly. 'Fuckin' sorry, okay?'

She kissed him hard and laughed. 'I'm not.' Then she ran across the lighted yard to the ladder, not looking back.

After breakfast the next morning Ronnie told Hazel the Missions to Seamen chaplain was aboard. 'He's here for a reason,' he said ominously. Kate was scrubbing the morning pots with her head down. Wretched, wretched, wretched.

Calvin was nowhere. She had told May they'd been out together but she hadn't told Hazel anything. Hazel already knew. Hazel said she'd been around plenty of drunks in her lifetime. 'You smell like a bar,' she told Kate before breakfast. 'How much did you drink, anyway?'

The galley phone rang while Kate was watching the chaplain walk back up the road. He was a small man, dressed in green work pants and a sweater.

'Captain wants ya,' Hazel said stonily.

The captain wanted her to understand. 'There's nothing wrong with having a drink. But not in the Mission trailer. There were records all over the floor. You were drinking wine in there. I don't like my crew to get in trouble. It gets back to the company. Look.' He pulled out a sheaf of pages and slapped them on his desk. 'The black list. If you get on there they tell every other company.'

Kate said nothing. She wondered if Calvin was going to get a lecture too.

'The security guards saw you.' The captain lowered his voice. 'They thought you were looking for a place to make love.'

'No,' she whispered, ashamed, hating herself for feeling ashamed. 'I'm sorry.'

He put out an awkward hand, patted her shoulder. 'I asked the chaplain if he wanted me to do anything and he said no. But you've got to watch yourself. Don't mix with bad company.'

She looked up. 'What do you mean, bad company?'

'You know who I mean. Go on, now.'

Kate went to the door and stopped. 'Are you telling me I can't go ashore with Calvin?'

The captain waved an impatient hand. 'I'm telling you to watch yourself, young lady.'

Hazel didn't talk to her for the rest of the morning, even when they were both sitting in the messroom listening to the union patrolman, who'd come on board to tell them there was going to be a strike vote. He was a summer intern, probably some official's son who'd never been on the water, clearly intimidated by the skeptical faces around the table, the Irishman and Swede and Charlie.

He was too young, she thought, to be telling middle-aged men they should be prepared to go on strike, even if it was true that the shipping companies were stonewalling on safety. 'We've been talking to the companies about this for a couple years now,' the union guy said.

'We got the report from the government over the fire two years ago on the Hall boat. Seven men died. But there's still no sprinkler systems on these boats. We wanted the hatch covers closed when a boat's on the run and they said okay, but you know as well as I do those hatch covers aren't always on.'

There were nods around the table. She had heard them talk about hatch covers; if they were open in rough weather they could take on water, swamp the boat.

'We asked for boarding ramps in the Canal, and they said they'd think about it and there's still no ramps. I don't know if any of you knew Brother Beecher? Brother Beecher who died in April, fell between the ship and the lock? Three kids and a wife back in Newfoundland – a boarding ramp would have saved him.'

'I heard Bill Beecher was drunk,' Hazel said. There were mutterings at that, but Hazel ignored them, looking more stubborn than Kate had ever seen her.

'Ah yes, well, Brother Beecher had a couple of drinks ashore. That's his right. Plenty of others have fallen who were stone cold sober. What I'm saying, brothers and sisters, is that we have lost too many good people in the past few years who would be here today if the companies had acted like decent, responsible citizens. These aren't expensive changes. Boarding ramps are cheap. The time it takes to put one across the wires? Two minutes.'

Kate put up her hand. 'What about survival suits?'

'That's a great question, Kate, is it? Survival suits would've saved those men off Labrador last year. Twelve men, not our men, but twelve good Canadians. Survival suits would have saved twenty-nine men on the *Edmund Fitzgerald*. Only survival suits are four hundred bucks apiece, and a company that won't pay for a boarding ramp isn't going to shell out for a survival suit for everybody, now, is it?'

He had them now. 'Which is why we're asking for a strike mandate,' he said, leaning forward. 'I've got the ballots here. You can mail them in or I can make it easy, take them back with me today.'

'Just as long as you don't steam 'em open,' Calvin said, not much of a joke but everyone laughed anyway.

Except Hazel. 'What about this boat?' she demanded. 'The company came and inspected and we haven't heard a thing.'

'Yeah, I heard about that. I'll see what I can find out,' the patrolman said. 'I can come back later.'

'Yeah, come back for lunch, that's what they all do.'

There was more laughter as the men got up, handing in their ballots and dropping their Styrofoam cups in the garbage, until it was just Calvin and Kate and the union guy.

'Damn, I forgot,' he said, pulling a little camera out of his briefcase. 'I was supposed to get some pictures for the paper. Can I get you guys?'

She could feel herself blush as she held up her mug of tea, sitting at the table shoulder to shoulder with Calvin. Thinking too late that Boyd would see the picture in the union paper and know where she was, and then thinking, surprised, that he probably already knew and she didn't care.

'Hey buddy,' said Calvin suddenly. 'You wanna see some great pictures, you should see hers. Storm shots, man.'

'Really?' He raise his eyebrows at Kate. 'I'd like to see those.'

She stood quickly. 'I'll get them.'

Hazel didn't talk to her until four-fifteen, when she went in to yell at her for sleeping into her supper shift. 'You getting up or what?' Her voice was high with anger. 'You think you're on a cruise?'

'Wish to hell I was,' Kate muttered.

'What did you say?'

'Nothing.'

'It ain't my fault you were out making a fool of yourself. I know what happened. I hear them talking.'

'Hazel?'

'What?'

'Were you ever young?'

It caught her off guard and Kate saw the smile, quickly snuffed out. 'Think you're smart, don't you?'

'Yes.' Kate laughed.

¶ 28. It was amazing to Kate that on a boat with unlimited hot water there were men who never washed. It was Wednesday, linen change, and she was holding her breath as she bent to count the dirty sheets of the unlicensed personnel, strewn across the red steel deck outside the linen locker.

May got to hand out the clean things, trading fresh for soiled as each man emptied his pillowcase. Someone had decreed long ago that they each got two bars of soap a week, though May said most of the soap went home in their bags at the end of the season. It was Kate's job to sort and count the dirty things, which she did resentfully – all day she'd been changing officers' beds, Ronnie's and Haroun's and the second mate's and the third engineer's, and her back ached.

Twenty-eight sheets. It should be thirty-two, but Calvin hadn't come, and they were down one deckhand. Twenty-three towels, twenty facecloths – they were supposed to get clean linen only for what they handed in dirty, but May wasn't strict.

'The company can afford a few extra towels, my dear,' she said. Except the company couldn't afford much of anything, judging by the letter they had sent Hazel in Thunder Bay, telling her she had to cut back on her food costs. That hadn't helped her mood.

The smell of dirty feet rose up like a fog. Kate stuffed sheets into one canvas bag, towels into another, separating out the irredeemables, the shredded bedspreads, the pillowcases so black with oil they would contaminate anything they were washed with. Holding her breath as she bent to the piles, turning her face to the wind gusting across Lake Huron, the sweet smell of green coming from a shore she couldn't see. It blew a pillowcase across the deck toward the scuppers and she chased it down, yelping as a handful of moths flew out. Then she smiled: not moths but feathers, hundreds of feathers. Someone's pillow had a leak; she would have to tell May.

Emptying the pillowcase over the side, watching a cloud of white feathers fly silently over the dark water, she thought of the mayflies and Carol and Boyd. She thought of him again in the stifling laundry locker, piling up the white canvas bags that made such good mattresses, thinking of the nights in the locker on the *Black River* and now her own dirty linen being hung out to dry.

I hear them talking, Hazel had said. Kate knew how it went. Talk was precious on the boat. It was currency you could use over and over. Talk about motives and troubles and mistakes. Sex, violence and gall bladder operations.

Talk was what they did best, she thought. Certainly not work, certainly not *listen*, they talked like they dressed, the same clothes over and over till they were full of holes. In the old days, she'd read, they would patch the holes, embellish them with embroidery, they would haul out their stories while they mended their socks, yarning to pass the time in the doldrums, waiting for a big wind to take them somewhere.

Like Calvin. Where was Calvin? He had been avoiding the galley – only the occasional whiff of pot from the stern deck, but she hadn't gone looking. May asked if they had had a fight, but Hazel remained pointedly silent on the subject. Well, fuck him if he thought it had meant anything.

And she had new books. The chaplain had said nothing about the books. Maybe he was hanging on to her IOU, maybe he was going to appear at the dock on their next trip to the Lakehead and send it up to her like a secret summons. Make her come to his trailer and Be Saved.

May put Calvin's clean linen aside; she said she would make him take it in the morning. But Kate said she shouldn't bother if he wasn't going to make the effort. She climbed into her bunk with an Agatha Christie and a cup of tea. She was going through books too fast. Her father used to joke about their shared addiction: if there were an Olympics of reading, they wouldn't make the team, they'd be too tired from staying up all night to finish a book. She had laughed sometimes at the posters on the subway promoting literacy. Reading could be a bad habit just like gambling and TV. Kate consumed books the way she drank. Binge reading, whole lost weekends when she didn't get out of bed except to pee and make tea and toast.

'What're ya reading this time?' May called up.

May had taken to complimenting Kate on her reading prowess. That was because May herself had always been a reader, she said.

'Agatha Christie. What about you?'

'Just a minute, dear. I can't remember.' There was the sound of pages being flipped. 'Oh, here it is: *Five Minute Marriage*. It's more or less a romance.'

Kate lay back in her bunk, laughing soundlessly. She imagined May and her cronies sitting around drinking tea and comparing sex scenes at the bodice-rippers' book club. She smelled the smoke from May's cigarette and called down, 'May? Got anything to drink?'

There was rummaging in a drawer, a happy laugh. 'I do so.'

The captain had given May a bottle of screech for her birthday. It was sort of a joke, she said, concerning who drank the more potent liquor, Newfies or Cape Bretoners. But it would do. She could use a nip, what with the way things were going.

Kate climbed down. 'What do you mean, the way things are going?'

'You know, are we gonna be scrapped or aren't we, will I need to get me another boat or won't I?' She said it casually, shrugging all the while, but the hand holding her Export A trembled.

'You wait here, May. I'm going to make you a real drink.'

Kate went into the galley and came back with pineapple juice and ice and strawberry syrup. She added the syrup last, pouring it over an overturned spoon, the way the bartender at the House of Monte Cristo had done for the occasional lady having lunch with one of the business guys. But he had used Galliano.

'I don't care much for screech,' May said, sipping gingerly. 'But you've mixed it up nice. What do you call this, now?'

Kate looked out the porthole. 'Let's call it Huron Sunset.'

'Pretty good,' said May, lighting a cigarette. 'This sure would have improved the taste of the brew they used to drink down home.'

Now May would tell her a story, something about drinking or death. May's stories all had the same happy ending: May living to tell the tale. She had told Kate about her first husband dying in a field in a rainstorm, about getting a rusty spike through her foot and being kicked in the head by a birthing cow, all with the same sense of wonder. She was a little old Scheherazade, fending off eternity with words.

'Lord,' she said now, 'that stuff they made was powerful strong. We had a neighbour, he had his brew barrel in a hole in the floor. Built his own coffin and kept painting it to cover the smell.'

'Who was he hiding it from?'

'The Mounties, my dear. He used to test his brew by settin' a spoonful on fire, pouring it on the floor and seeing how far the fire went.'

'What did it taste like?'

'I wouldn't know. I never drank till I come up to Ontario, after Tommy died.' She tittered into her hand. 'Lord, I didn't know anything then. I was second cook, and the chief cook and porter were just girls. There was nothing them girls wouldn't do. I opened the cook's door one night and there were naked men and bottles all over.'

May emptied her glass and held it for a refill. 'I'll have another. Yes, they were wild girls but I got along good with them. They weren't hurting anybody. As long as you're enjoying yourself, there's nothing wrong with it.'

'I don't think Hazel would agree with that.' Kate was feeling the drinks now, the heat moving through her blood like a tropical current. The evening sun had ignited the porthole as if it were a lighthouse lens. Huron sunset.

'Well, Hazel's had a hard life.'

May would say that. It was Hazel's arthritis. Or her mortgage. Or her nephew. May said Hazel had called him when they were in Thunder Bay and she'd been simmering ever since, her swallowed anger like a pot left on the stove, building a head of steam. If you open a pot like that, you can get a painful blast.

'Did she tell you what she's mad at him about?'

'No, but it's likely her house. Why she gets so fussed about that house, I just don't know. She's the same about the boat. She loves this old boat. That union kid in Thunder Bay didn't know nothing. And what the captain knows he won't tell her.'

'If the boat's unsafe why are we still going up to Superior? Calvin says if they get a bad report they have to stay down below.'

May was shaking her head. 'My dear, they never tell the women anything.'

⟨ 29. It was dark when the *Huron Queen* reached the Canal, a hot humid darkness flavoured with fish. Kate filled a mug with iced tea and looked at the calendar on the pantry wall. August tenth. She counted: she had been on board just over six weeks, four trips upbound, now four trips down, and she had got off here only once, with Hazel. All summer she had been engaged in circling through and around and back through the Canal, as if she were tying a knot at the centre of a big loose bow.

And every time she looked at the calendar she felt the same tug of anxiety, the thought that Boyd was making the same circuit, tightening the knot. She took her tea out to the deck, where Charlie stood smoking at number 2 winch, waiting for the boat to go into the lock.

Together they watched the lights of Port Weller glow in the damp air, watched the bright bow lights of a freighter passing upbound, sending waves slapping against their hull.

'She's brand new, that Upper Lakes boat,' Charlie said. 'Seven hundred and thirty feet. That's the biggest these locks'll take.' They gazed after it in companionable silence. 'But they're building thousand-footers up above. Never go through the Canal, stay on Superior and Huron.'

'Calvin told me it's got a fake union, Upper Lakes.'

Charlie shrugged. 'It's a company union. They aren't all bad. Upper Lakes was the only company that stood up to Hal Banks and his gang when he come up in the fifties.'

'Came up from where?'

'From the States. Canadian government invited him up. Wanted him to break up the Canadian Seaman's Union, and by Jesus he did. He did it with baseball bats.'

'Why'd the government want them out?'

Charlie shrugged and tossed his butt over the side. 'Said they were Commies. But the men in that union were the men who went to sea in the war. The merchant marine. A lot of those fellows died, and there was never no compensation. You know why I think the government wanted that union broke up?'

She thought he would make a joke now. It wasn't like Charlie to be serious this long. But his voice was sorrowful. 'They wanted it gone so's they couldn't go after the veterans' benefits. That's the truth.'

'God. Were you in that union?'

Charlie chuckled. 'I ain't as old as I look. No, I had an uncle. Hal Banks's men come aboard his boat and told him he was blacklisted. Just like that.' He stopped for a moment and tilted his head toward the galley. 'Oh by Jesus, now what's she want?'

May was calling from the galley door, wanting help with her bag. Kate could smell her from yards away, the perfume and hairspray she always piled on when she was going ashore in the Canal. She swallowed the last of her iced tea. May had promised to get her a bottle of vodka from the bootlegger – a very reasonable markup, and he delivered. But May wouldn't be back for hours.

The *Huron Queen* slid slowly into Lock 8 and Kate moved away from the winch, blocking her ears against its shriek as it reeled in the braided steel cable. It was a big ugly machine, the size of two refrigerators, powered by steam and prone to breakdowns. It was also a dangerous machine, the single greatest cause of lost fingers on boats, according to Calvin.

May scrambled over the deck fence and onto land the moment the ship was made fast. Charlie handed her bag across. 'What you got in here?' he said. 'Rocks?'

'Wool,' May snapped.

Charlie winked at Kate. 'She's going to her knitting club. They hold meetings up at the bar.'

Kate hugged herself, watching the wet black walls rise up as the lock emptied, the water unseen as it surged downstream, toward Lake Ontario and the St. Lawrence. The whole system powered by gravity, water seeking its true level, the sea. It was like descending into a valley of cold, a trough at the bottom of the ocean.

There was someone walking back from midships, a tall, lean figure she didn't recognize, a ball cap obscuring his face. She wondered if a new crew member had just come aboard, but the figure carried no baggage, and she had a sudden choking sensation, as if one of the swallows circling the high spotlights had flown into her throat.

But then he walked into the pool of light spilling from the afthouse and she saw it wasn't him. It wasn't Boyd.

'Where's Hazel at?' The guy addressed himself to Charlie, ignoring her. He was dressed in scuffed denim, smelling of booze. She could see a muscle pulse in his cheek.

'Back in her room, I imagine,' Charlie said. 'Not bad news?'

'No, no. Nothing like that. I need to talk to her. Family business.'

Charlie nodded toward Kate, standing in the shadows by the port companionway. 'The porter here can show you.'

He gave her a dismissive glance. 'I know where it is.'

Yes, she thought, and I know you. The nephew. She felt the hairs lift on the back of her neck. He would be here to hit Hazel up for money. He was taking an opportunity where he saw an opportunity; he was seeking his natural level.

Kate's fists clenched as she watched him head down the passageway. She had said nothing to Hazel when she had her own opportunity. She had rationalized. So what if he smoked dope in his aunt's cellar? You had to smoke it somewhere. It was obvious that the stacked boxes had once held stereo equipment, but she hadn't actually looked in them. Maybe they were empty. Hazel didn't trust him, and she was right not to trust him. But she still let him into her house. Why is it always so hard to say the thing you need to say?

She waited ten minutes and then headed for her own cabin. There was shouting coming through the chief cook's door, Hazel shouting, punctuated by guttural male curses. Kate hovered in an agony of indecision, her heart pounding painfully. She could make out the words now.

'It ain't your house!'

She tapped on Hazel's door.

It opened immediately, Hazel glaring up at her, pink-faced and damp. 'Yeah?'

'I just –'

'You just what? It ain't your business, my girl. It ain't your concern.'

€ 30. Kate was counting the days now. She was counting her money, too, making columns of figures in her notebook and then starting over, trying to see how she would make it stretch to next spring. Two more weeks till she would be leaving with her cheque, heading back to school.

Three days from the Canal they tied up in Quebec City. Kate took her camera after supper and walked up the gravel road next to the elevators in the Old Port, counting thirty or forty silos on her left, a half-dozen ships moored on her right. She kept her eyes straight ahead as she passed a group of boys lounging in the warm dusk by a tied-up salty. They were sunburned and stocky, English judging by their accents when they called to her. But she wasn't interested in sailors. She had on her dress, the red Indian cotton with the spaghetti straps. She was going to be a tourist.

Calvin could fuck himself. Twice since the Canal she had offered him a drink and he had found a sudden need to check his laundry in the dunnage room, or go talk to the mate. Fuck them all.

She came into an open area and looked up. The old city hung above her, the beautiful decayed buildings ranged up the cliffside to the citadel. Flocks of gulls and pigeons circled over the tiled roofs. She wondered if living in a place this beautiful made people happier.

A car's tires crunched behind her and she turned in the billowing dust. It was a little red convertible with a cream interior. The driver spoke to her in French. She gestured at the hill. 'I'm going to town.'

He switched to English. 'Do you come from Quebec?' He was handsome, sandy hair, in his thirties maybe.

'No, I'm off a boat back there.'

He smiled, showing white teeth. 'I'm off a boat too.'

She had noticed the dark green uniform. 'The coast guard boat?'

'Yes, but I'm off duty until tomorrow. Can I give you a lift?'

Driving up into the cobblestone streets he slowed to let crowds pass. The sidewalks were full of couples, couples with maps, couples holding hands, couples studying menus in restaurant windows. It was a couple zone.

'I'm Gerard,' he said. His accent appeared with his name: Gerar. 'I see you are a photographer.'

She shrugged. 'A student.'

'Does the student have a name?'

'Kate.'

'And what are you planning to photograph, Kate?'

'I haven't decided.'

'Then you must let me show you something.'

They were stopped at an intersection behind a car with New York plates. It was like being in a parade, she thought, she should be waving. She felt a delicious languor, being driven through the narrow streets in Gerard's little car.

He parked at the edge of a square. 'The mariners' church,' Gerard said.

It was a pretty building of pale stone, baskets of petunias hanging from brass hooks. In front of it a massive anchor was embedded in a cairn. But through her viewfinder it was pure kitsch. She lowered her camera and put it in her bag. She felt foolish now. She should have stayed down at the docks, shot the elevators, the English sailors.

'There's a nice terrace on the other side of the church,' Gerard said. 'May I offer you a glass of wine?'

Gerard was forty, she revised. Maybe forty-five. She could see it in his lined face as he leaned back in his chair, seeking a last blast of evening sun. All those years of squinting at water and smiling at women. His smile was dazzling. There was stubble gilding his cheeks like red gold.

They clinked glasses and drank. A sweet pink smell of petunias drifted down from the hanging baskets. She sighed luxuriously. 'I feel like I'm in another country.'

'But you are, mademoiselle.'

He soon got to the point. 'I am surprised, a pretty girl like you being allowed to go to town alone. You don't have a friend on your boat?'

She laughed, finishing her glass. She was drinking fast. 'No, no friend. Not really.'

'That's good for me, I think.'

They talked about the river. Gerard said there were more and more tour boats out whale watching, which meant work for the coast guard. They'd been called to the waters off Tadoussac, when one boat had sideswiped another jockeying for a closer look. 'It's the best spot for belugas,' he said. 'The waters there are rich with little creatures they like to eat. But unfortunately the whales are dying.'

Gerard knew a marine biologist who said the belugas were taking in much more than seafood. They were also swallowing decades worth of industrial poisons, chemicals and heavy metals pumped into the river by the pulp mills and the mines along the seaway. They were so contaminated, no one knew how to safely dispose of the carcasses.

And yet most people didn't know they lived in the river. The first time a deckhand had pointed them out to her, she'd been sure he was mistaken. They looked like fat white life rafts in the distance, children's beach toys blown offshore. She had seen belugas up close only once, when her mother had taken her out to Vancouver to see Gram before she died. It was near the end, and there was a day Gram didn't want Kate and her cousin Susan in the room. They went to the Aquarium to watch the killer whales do tricks.

The belugas were the lesser attraction, viewed through an underwater window while a guide explained how they'd had to be put on a diet. Captivity had made them fat. Kate was furious at his patronizing tone. It was obvious that any intelligent creature would overeat when it had nothing to do. And then she saw that the whales were playing: taking turns blowing and chasing rings of air bubbles toward the surface of their featureless tank. Like jaded drinkers blowing smoke rings in a bar.

She thought of Gram cracking jokes in her hospital bed the day before the cancer won. The white whales' comical faces, smiling in their prison. Gallows humour was universal.

Gerard looked at her face and chuckled. 'Don't be sad. The belugas used to have it much worse. They built processing plants all along the river to grind them up for oil. When I was a child my uncles hunted them for sport.'

He refilled her glass. 'So you see, mademoiselle, slow poison is not so bad.'

Gerard ordered another bottle of wine after a discussion in French with a man in a pale blue silk shirt. The owner, he said. All the voices murmuring at the tables were French. A girl in a flowered dress came by with a tray of tiny lit candles, like a fairy bestowing wishes. In the thickening darkness the fragrance of the flowers intensified. A musical clatter of dishes came through the windows of the old stone building, lit up yellow like oil lamps, and she wondered what it would be like to be the one washing those dishes, sharing cigarettes with the cook, learning French from the busboys. Well, she had a marketable trade now. She could wash dishes.

She shivered, suddenly cold. He put his arm around her and she leaned into his shoulder. With one fluid movement he tightened his grip around her neck and forced her face toward his. The kiss was rough, his stubble scraping her chin. She fought it for a moment and then let her curiosity take over. Gerard's tongue filled her mouth. It was not particularly erotic, and she was relieved when the girl in the flowered dress appeared with the bottle and fresh glasses.

'Ah,' said Gerard, smoothly leaning forward to taste the offering. 'A nice Chablis. Monsieur le patron chose well.'

Kate moved forward too, shrugging off his arm. She'd seen something in the girl's eyes, judgment or pity, something Gerard wouldn't be able to read. She was much too young for Gerard, and the girl wanted her to know she wasn't the first. But Kate was feeling the wine now, and she wanted to feel it more.

She was unsteady on her feet when she excused herself to find the washroom. Inside she went up some stairs to a hallway of wooden doors. The washroom was in a converted bedroom, with a toilet in one corner and a sink in another. When she came out Gerard was waiting in the hall.

'Mademoiselle,' he said, brandishing the bottle. 'This is a marvellous building. Three hundred years old. Would you like a tour?'

She laughed. 'Yeah, right. A tour of your room?'

He laughed too, and then she was laughing with him and following him into a pretty bedroom, with stone walls and pine furniture and bright rag rugs scattered on the plank floor. The bed frame was shaped like a sleigh. Gerard threw himself down and patted the woven bedspread.

Kate shook her head. 'I'm going to look for glasses.'

She came out of the little bathroom to find him shirtless, fondling himself through his pants. God. Maybe it was what older guys had to do. She walked quickly past him, not sure where to look, and poured herself a tumbler of wine.

She could hear him panting now, his mouth open. 'Take off your clothes, mademoiselle Kate.'

She took a gulp of wine and picked up her bag. 'I have to go.'

'In a moment. I want to see your body. Please.'

'No.'

'Shhh,' Gerard said, rising and putting his back against the door. He took her head in his hands and forced her lips open with his tongue, filling her mouth with the sour taste of used wine. She wrenched her face away. 'Let me out.' Sober now.

He was undoing his pants. Reaching inside. His face was grim.

'Gerard,' she said. 'Open the fucking door, or I will scream. Now!'

Kate screamed. He leapt away from the door as if it had given him a shock. She heard a woman's voice in the hall and screamed again.

'*Assez.* You can stop now,' he said. He was putting on his jacket. 'Come, I'll take you back to your ship.'

'Fuck you,' she said. 'Keep your fucking hands off me or I'll call the police. I'll call the fucking coast guard.'

Her fingers were shaking so badly it took her two attempts to get the chain off the door. She slammed it behind her and stood trembling in the hallway. At the far end was another stairway that went down to the front of the building. She leaned hard on the banister as she descended, trying to control her legs.

No one was at the desk in the foyer. She passed a breakfast room on her right, clean linen folded in a neat pile on a table. She went in. A moment later she went out into the street, not caring if anyone saw that she wore a white tablecloth wrapped around her bare shoulders, like a shawl.

¶ 31. On the rue St. Jacques she stuck out her thumb at the cruising cars. She felt toxic. She could feel herself sinking into the sludge, down with the wrecks and the bones and the muck. She had taken in everybody's crap, all their sad, stinking crap and it had concentrated in her tissues like the poisons in the belugas.

She got a ride down to the docks in a van smelling of patchouli oil. There was a chain across the entrance of the road to the elevators.

'Sorry, I can't pass troo.' The driver gave her a sad smile. He was a scrawny man with a van dyke beard. She thought he must fancy himself an artist. 'You want me to walk wit' you?'

'No, thanks, I'll be okay.' She reached out quickly and squeezed his hand. '*Merci.*'

Then she was out and running, feeling the heat flowing down her arms and legs, the cool river air filling her chest. Gravel from the road pelting her ankles as she hurtled past the red-and-white coast guard boat. It had a flower's name: *Marguerite.* She was panting now, the air hurting her throat. But there was no convertible parked there.

She slowed when she reached the bow of the *Huron Queen* rising solidly on her left. The boat was heavy with grain, low enough in the water that she could see the deck, the hatch covers off, waiting for unloading to start in the morning.

Calvin was sitting on a lawn chair at the foot of the gangway, smoking as he watched her stumble up through the yellow dock lights. 'Christ, I could hear you running from a mile away. You look like you seen a ghost.'

She bent over and locked her arms against her knees, still panting.

'What the hell are you wearing, a tablecloth?'

'I was cold.'

'You all right or what?'

She looked up. 'Why won't you talk to me?' Running had made her drunker; that much was clear. She sank into a patch of grass by the ladder and hunched over, letting the tears drip into her lap.

Calvin's boots crunched toward her. His voice was worried.

'What the fuck's got into you?'

'I don't know.'

'Wait a second,' he said. 'Don't move.'

She heard his boots pound up the ladder. Then there was no sound but the sound of her sniffling and the waves lapping and the crickets in the greenery by the edge of the dock. There were daisies growing here and she had meant to pick some for the messroom. Marguerites, they were called. The boots came back down. 'Here.'

Calvin draped a blanket over the tablecloth. 'Drink this.' He handed her a mug. It was tea laced liberally with rum. She coughed and he reached down and slapped her on the back. 'You gonna live?'

'Yeah. Thanks.'

'So what happened?'

She shrugged.

'You don't have to tell me, man,' Calvin said.

'What do you care? You haven't talked to me since Thunder Bay.'

Calvin lit a cigarette. 'I'm out of weed, man. I gotta score tomorrow.' He coughed and looked at her. 'Yeah well. I was some mad at you.'

'At me? I'm the one who got called up to the captain's office.'

'Is that when you told him I trashed the trailer?'

'I *didn't*. I wouldn't.'

'Keep it down, man. Irish is wandering around up there. Look, I'm off in five. Hang tight, okay?'

Ten minutes later they took the blanket and the rum and walked to a grassy patch behind the grain elevators. They sat in silence, watching the lights on the far shore.

'Fucking Brian and Hazel,' Calvin said. 'They told me the Old Man was gonna fire me if he saw me talking to you again.'

'Brian and Hazel?'

'Yeah, Hazel. She told me not to come around the galley any more.'

'When was this?'

'The day you slept in. She was that mad.'

'Well, now I*'m* mad.' Hazel was a meddler, whether she thought it was for Kate's sake or not. 'Hazel's scared,' she said. 'She's an old woman. May told me about a porter they had ten years ago, an Indian girl who was sleeping with the deckhands. Hazel fired her. The deckhands went after Hazel with a fire axe. They had to call the police to get them off.'

'Fucking serves her right.'

Kate was silent, thinking of the hotel room, the bed. Gerard would be out looking for someone else now, because he hadn't gotten it into her.

'Nah, fuck that,' Calvin amended. 'I hate a lazy porter. Food's cold, table's always sticky. So Hazel, she thinks I'm gonna come after her with a fire axe?'

'No.' Kate lit a cigarette and handed Calvin back his lighter. 'She just doesn't want me to get in trouble with the Old Man. She doesn't want to lose me.'

'Oh, so you're that good.'

'I am.' She smiled. 'She said she's never seen pots so clean since she was a porter. Anyway, I don't think you're the fire axe type. Firebug, maybe.'

'I never set a fire in my life. On purpose, anyway.'

'That's not what you told me in Thunder Bay.'

Calvin laughed. 'You believed that shit?'

'So you never stole a car?'

'I did, once. I was fifteen. Wanted to go to a party and no one would take me. Cracked her up on the way back. Man, that was the best part.'

Kate looked across the dark water and wrapped the blanket tighter. She saw a car turn over and over on a dark gravel road, silently crashing and burning. Boyd's nightmare. She had imagined it so often it had become her own.

'It's cold out here.'

'C'mere, I'll warm ya up.'

Then she was curled into his chest and he had his face in her hair, and he was laying little kisses all over her head. Kate watched the lights of the ferry moving across the river to Levis. And then she felt him harden against her, felt the ridge of his zipper through the cotton of her dress, fitting into the cleft of her rear.

They lay still, as if listening, waiting to see what their bodies would do. Her body moaned; she couldn't stop it now. She pushed back hard against Calvin. His breathing faltered.

'You okay?' he choked, his voice damp in her ear.

'I'm okay now.' She peeled away her panties so she was bare against him on the rough wool blanket, feeling a thickening in her throat. 'Undo your pants, Calvin. Please.'

'You sure? I don't have any rubbers on me.'

'It's okay,' she panted. 'I'm not ovulating.'

'You're not what? Oh fuck.' He groaned as Kate backed herself onto him, sliding herself down. She was so wet she had to work her buttocks to hold him. Calvin whimpered against her back, his arms a steel band around her midriff. It sounded like he was praying.

She knew he wouldn't last and it didn't matter. Afterwards they lay spooned on the thin blanket until the cold crept up from the ground and then she kicked her underpants all the way off and climbed on top of him, straddling his thighs with the tablecloth tented over her head.

Calvin took her braids in his hands. His kiss was hard, his tongue hard in her mouth. She felt his chin scrape hers and realized with surprise it was stubble. He was hard again and she reared up and slid herself on.

'Docking completed,' Calvin said, his laugh snuffed out as she began to ride him, lazily at first, her fingertips resting on his chest. Then she couldn't help herself and started bucking.

'You are some ruffian,' Calvin said. He was panting raggedly, like a man in pain. 'Oh my Christ go slower, woman. I can't hold it much longer.'

'That's okay,' she said, her face aching with the smile she couldn't control. 'I'm ready now.'

¶ 32. A hangover has its uses. An inoculation against worse things, a moat of self-inflicted misery between you and the real world. It was her hangover that made it easier to pretend it wasn't really happening when Kate walked into the pantry at seven-thirty and found Hazel and the captain like a pair of mismatched gargoyles, outrage carved into their stony features. But how could they know already? Calvin wouldn't have let it slip. Anyway, Calvin wouldn't even be up yet.

She stood looking from one to the other, words uselessly circuiting her brain. The boat had left Quebec in the night and was rocking now on the salt water of the Gulf, making her shift her feet.

Hazel was shaking something at her, shaking it in front of her face. It was the union newspaper. There were more papers in a stack on the counter, and the same image was on the front page – her photograph of the *Huron Queen* in the storm, the lace-edged waves poised over the deck like the Hokusai print. It filled the page, grainy but beautiful, beautiful.

She read the headline: Serious About Safety? Not On Your Life.

It was the captain's turn to shake the paper. 'The patrolman in Quebec left these. What in God's name have you been playing at? You trying to put dis whole crew out of work?' Dis, he said. In his anger his Newfie accent had come back.

'I didn't know –'

'It says right here, you gave this picture to the union. After you disobeyed my orders to go on deck during that gale – do you have any goddamn idea how this makes me look? Do you?'

Hazel's voice took up the refrain. 'What's she care? She's going back to school. This is just a cruise to her.'

Kate turned away, but the cook moved around to block her. 'Oh no, you ain't going anywhere. You're gonna serve the crew same as you always do. You can explain to them why you decided to screw them out of their jobs.'

In fact no one said a word to her. Not please, not thank you, not fuck you. She brought their regular orders and scuttled out of the messroom back to the sinks. May made the toast. She brought over a load of dirty dishes and patted Kate on the shoulder, which made her start snivelling all over again.

By nine o'clock she had numbed herself enough to go up forward. She spent a long time doing Ronnie's room, scrubbing the bathroom walls, polishing the mirrors and portholes, washing the deck even though they were heading to an ore port; maybe he would tell Hazel.

Where was Calvin? It had been his idea to tell the union guy about her pictures. And she had leapt at the chance to show her work, flattered by the interest, never realizing what the union might see in them. Evidence.

What good would it do to tell Hazel she never meant it to happen? I thought you were a smart girl. You never saw that coming?

In Haroun's cabin back aft she picked up the white towel from the centre of the deck and folded it neatly over the back of his chair. The union paper was spread out on the engineer's desk. She had the words nearly memorized now: 'A sixty-year-old ship with a dicey engine, a storm on Superior clocking 50-mph winds, and what do you have? A recipe for potential disaster. Sister Kate McLeod took these pictures on the *Huron Queen* in July, during one of Superior's legendary nor'easters. Union officials have subsequently learned that the company was aware of the cracks in the *Huron Queen*'s hull, yet did not restrict its orders to the lower lakes until repairs could be made.'

She didn't remember telling the guy exactly where she had taken the shots, or when. But she didn't need to; she'd had it drummed into her at school to put her name, date and description on the back of every print she made. She had done the same with the four-by-six shots of the storm.

'It was I who told the union about the cracks,' a soft voice said behind her. She whirled around to see Haroun, smiling apologetically. 'So you see, it isn't just you. Everyone knows the captain made an error. But there is the old boys' club, you know. Skippers are like physicians; they close ranks. Please, you must not take it to heart.'

She released a sigh. 'Thank you.'

'Ah, I see you have rescued my prayer mat again.'

'Your what?'

'My prayer mat.' He pointed to the white towel.

'Oh. I thought you were just giving me something to do.'

Haroun laughed, a hearty belly laugh, joined after a moment by Kate. She felt they understood each other, watching his laughter mirror hers, watching him wipe his eyes, waving a hand helplessly as he left, still chortling, to go below. She felt like she had swallowed bubbles.

She still wore a smile when she went in to start on the mid-morning pots. But a smile was powerless against Hazel, who filled the galley with the black cloud of her anger. There was no ladle, saucepan, cutting board or rolling pin available that was not slammed onto the counter, banged into the sink, beaten against a pot.

When Hazel finally went into her cabin to lie down, Kate prayed she would have a drink. She had never seen an old woman furious before, not in real life, not even in a movie. Old women were supposed to make jokes and knit sweaters. They weren't supposed to frighten you.

Kate felt herself sinking again, the effects of Haroun's sympathy flattened like a burst balloon. She got out a box of baking soda and started polishing the backsplash, the stainless steel cupboard doors below the sinks. It was best to keep moving, let the poison make its way through your system, last night's booze and today's humiliation, work your body so hard there would be no energy left to feel depressed.

That was one thing about the boats that no one on shore understood, the consolation of work. All those weekends she had spent holed up in her apartment during the school year, too blue to call anyone or get dressed, burying herself in books. But there were no pyjama days on a boat; it was seven days a week, hung over or healthy, in the doghouse or out.

Now she could see those weekends for the waste of freedom they had been, all the days she might have had lunch with Becks, trekked through unfamiliar streets, loitered in bookstores. Here it was down to fifteen minutes here, a half hour there, two hours of unconsciousness in the afternoon, her body by then so grateful for respite that it felt like a kind of happiness.

May came into the galley and watched Kate work, eyes narrowed appreciatively, puffing on her cigarette. Then she was hauling the stepstool from the corner and peering under the range hood.

'It's got to be done anyway,' she muttered. 'Might as well get a start. My lord, Kate, just look at it. It's as black as Satan's heart.'

She was kneeling on the stove with a box of steel wool when Hazel came in with her mug. 'What the hell you doing?' she barked at May. 'We're gonna be loading ore tomorrow.'

'Well then, we'll clean it again. Won't we, Kate?'

Hazel looked at them both. Maybe she would say something kind now, forgiving. But she set her jaw. 'Well, don't be expecting no overtime pay.'

May laughed. 'No, no, Hazel. We're doing this for the good of our souls. Ain't we, Kate?'

Yes. May knew. It was penance. Ten Hail Marys, twenty pots, polish the stains from the stainless. She thought of the girl in the folk tale whose task was to weave shirts of thistledown, to free her brothers from their bewitching, turn them from geese back into young men. That girl picked and spun and wove for years, her fingers always bleeding, and still it wasn't enough; at the end, one unfinished shirt and a brother forever stuck with a wing instead of an arm.

Kate moved her cloth rhythmically across the ridged steel of the drain board, feeling the grainy resistance of the baking soda, the way it would suddenly soften and give way. Resist, dissolve. Dissolution.

There was a whole world of companionship women had, of making things clean together. She thought of Carol and her eradication campaigns. May was cut of the same cloth: she was a poet of dirt.

'Now, iron ore dust,' May said with relish. 'That's a bastard, excuse my French. Ever hold one of those pellets in your hand? It's like a drop of hell. Heavier than it should be. Makes me think of this old mine shaft up by the schoolyard when I was a girl. All the kids used to think it went down to Hades. Oh, I was some scared of that hole.'

After the galley they moved on to the messroom, Kate wiping the ceilings, May doing the walls as far as she could reach. Kate finished first and started on the condiments, refilling and polishing the absurdly large collection of bottles that sat on the messroom table, HP sauce and Worcestershire and mint jelly and Tabasco, things she had never tasted and rarely saw the men use, but which accrued a film of dust and grease by proximity.

May was still talking about cleaning. 'Sand, now. Ever do floors with sand? My floors at home were pure white, never varnished 'em. Scrubbed 'em with sand.'

'In some parts of Africa, in the desert,' Kate said, 'they wash their dishes in sand. I read that in National Geographic.'

'You don't say? I wish I'd've known that when we had our lobster boils up the beach.'

'You can use ashes too. From the fire. They use ashes to make soap.' Suddenly remembering her father, that fount of arcane knowledge, directing her and Jenna to scrub the frying pans with the remains of their campfire. It was in Algonquin. Think of it as an experiment, he said. Where's your scientific curiosity?

'Ashes?'

'Yes. It works amazingly well.'

'My lord,' May said. 'The things you know.'

Calvin found her on the stern after lunch, throwing scraps to a scrum of seabirds coasting above the wake.

He said he was sorry. He said it had never occurred to him that the pictures might be used to make a point. He said he just thought they were really fucking great pictures. He said it wasn't her fault, if it was anyone's fault it was the companies' for keeping scows like the *Queen* on the water. He said fuck them. He said the crew knew it was coming anyway; her pictures had nothing to do with it.

He said Charlie was going to do his watch so they could go into town in Pointe Noire. He said – she didn't want to think about what else he said. It was better not to talk about what had happened between them in Quebec. If they didn't talk about it, maybe it could go on for a while.

But she still couldn't look Hazel in the eye. After they had docked she hovered in the dining room, hoping to get her alone, finally realizing Hazel had gone down the ladder. From the railing she watched the cook pick her way through a sea of viscous pink mud, heading for the phone booth, a white plastic bag knotted over each shoe. She lost her footing halfway across, arms windmilling like a comedian signalling a pratfall, and sank to her knees.

Kate saw her opening. She scrambled down the gangway and sprinted across the mud, offering her arm. But Hazel slapped it away. 'Leave me alone,' she said. 'Ain't you done enough?'

Anger gave the old woman strength; in a moment she was up again, labouring across the yard in her filthy trousers, not looking back. Kate stood, blinking back tears. 'I'm sorry,' she called, hating herself, hating her own weakness. 'Hazel, I'm sorry!'

At seven-thirty, riding in one of the town's two cabs past red mountains of ore, she told herself to buck up. She was wearing her Indian cotton dress and her Doc Martens. Her outfit made Calvin laugh.

She and Calvin were going to town, just like all the freshly scrubbed miners heading up in trucks, pale faces and shower-damp hair. Town was about anticipation. Town was about having fun. Even in a town like Pointe Noire, an armpit of a town, a town where apparently there wasn't a single free hotel room.

'No room at the inn,' Calvin joked. 'Maybe there's a stable.' They were sitting over drinks in the main floor bar of the Hotel St. Laurent, watching tables of paunchy company men in suits, all comb-overs and crooked ties, trying to make the middle-aged big-haired waitress laugh.

It was Calvin who suggested that they get a room, muttering into her ear in the cab as if the whole thing embarrassed him. He said he just wanted a chance to do it right. His romanticism touched her.

But the woman at the front desk looked them up and down and said the hotel was booked for a conference.

'A conference of assholes?' Calvin said now.

'I bet that waitress makes serious tips.'

'I bet she makes more selling something else.'

Kate shook her head in irritation.

'We could try the other place,' Calvin said.

The desk woman had said the hotel down the street would have rooms, but walking into the place Kate felt her cheeks go hot. The posse of raccoon-eyed girls lining the bar made it clear what the woman had meant.

'Fuck,' she said. 'They're all prostitutes.'

'We're here now. Might as well get a drink.'

She was into her third Singapore sling when Calvin jerked his head at the bar. Brian was leaning against a stool, watching the stripper onstage.

'That asshole. What's he doing, spying on us for the Old Man?'

'Come on now,' Calvin said. 'Keep it down.'

'I don't give a shit,' Kate said, her voice rising. 'He's an asshole. They're all assholes. I have a life, you know. This is my fucking life, too.'

'Come on,' Calvin said warningly. 'Let's go.'

There is always a moment when the night threatens to go aground. A closing-time moment, when the bar lights go bright and you can see who you've been drinking with, yelling your personal details to over the noise of the band. It could go either way: go home or find a bootlegger, a speakeasy, a bed to fall into. Kate felt it now, felt eyes on her as she got up to leave, felt them saying the words under their breath. Every woman knew the words, had had the guilty pleasure of hearing them said about someone else. But Kate had heard them used on herself.

Outside on the empty sidewalk she lit a cigarette. 'Let's go somewhere else. Let's have another drink.'

'In a minute. I want to smoke a joint.' Calvin pulled her against him and hugged her hard. She could feel his erection, insistent against her belly. She laughed and let him take her hand, tow her through the parking lot, her boots crumbling the ridges of dried mud, toward the back of the building.

And then she caught her breath, because there was nothing but bush behind the hotel, the stunted pines of Quebec's north shore, a sweet-smelling meadow grown up around a half-dozen derelict sheds. Beyond the furthest shed she kicked off her panties and went down on her hands and knees in the moonlight, the scent of grass and wild roses filling her throat.

She closed her eyes as he kneeled behind her, pushing the skirt up over her back. The wind was cool against her skin. 'Lord Jesus,' Calvin said.

Kate reached behind her and tugged at his jeans. 'Now.'

She left her panties in the long grass, a souvenir for the crows. They circled slowly back to the ship like a pair of escaped dogs, wordlessly stopping to taste each other's faces, coming together and moving apart, staying in the shadows as they crossed the ore docks, where under yellow lights the huge loading chutes were filling the hatches with sooty pellets, conjuring a sooty wind.

Climbing the ladder behind her he slid his hand under her dress, stroking her bare skin, and she realized they had crossed over into foolhardiness. They were swaggering, not caring that someone might see them and know from their faces what they had been up to. Not caring who might still be up when they went into the pantry, who might notice that half an hour later they still hadn't come out. Because she just didn't care any more.

She didn't care that there was no bolt on the inside of the food locker. She pulled him hard against her, laughing soundlessly into his neck. Laughing as he pushed a stack of cases against the door like a throne and positioned her there, his fingers sending little waves up the insides of her thighs. Then he went down on his knees. 'I'm going to worship you now, baby,' he said.

'I'm not your baby,' she said. 'Call me queen.'

¶ 33. Pleasure is seditious.

A boy with an artful tongue can upset the social order. When he can make your body flare up like a constellation, who cares about prospects? It was the kind of thing that fathers and husbands all over the planet stamped out at the first whiff. Drown it, stone it, bury it. Never let your wives and daughters smell it.

But it was more dangerous than that. Calvin had made her vulnerable. It had been good with him in Quebec City, but last night in the pantry had been wholly unexpected. He had made her nearly pass out with pleasure, holding one hand hard against her teeth to dampen her noise. She wondered where he had learned it. Not from his tribe. It was something that Boyd had always refused to do, give her pleasure while deferring his own.

And she thought: there is no future in pleasure.

She would pay off and go back to Toronto and Calvin would go home and find a pretty fifteen-year-old to spoil. He would spoil her with pleasure; he would make her think all men were as generous.

The mistake with Boyd was letting him see where she lived. She needed to be like the girl in the fairy tale, the one who only came to her lover's bed in darkness. You couldn't let them see your true nature.

You couldn't let them into your real life.

In the morning she was sure Hazel would be able to smell the sex on her, the way she could always smell the booze. She showered for a good twenty minutes, soaping herself lavishly and then having to stop and lean against the wall with her eyes closed, going over it.

But it didn't matter what Hazel thought; Kate had decided to quit in the Canal. It would be a relief to go. She hated the way the old women deferred, the way May scurried anxiously in and out of the dining room, bringing the Chief his cream of wheat, the Old Man his stewed prunes, two blowhards blowing wind from opposite ends of the table. Now they would be talking about Kate, saying she had no business on a boat, going around pretending to be a photographer, and wasn't she up in the bar again last night with young Calvin? But she was kidding herself. They would say be saying worse things.

Calvin was there at breakfast; just a wink and she had to shake her head to stop the swoon that bloomed behind her eyes. It was like a post-hypnotic suggestion. She spent the morning in a trance, taking her coffee out to the railing to let the wind whip her hair, taking big gulps of the briny air.

In the distance she could see a pod of pilot whales, the ones the Newfies called blackfish, their spumes tiny geysers against the dark water. If they were closer she would get her camera. The thought comforted her. She wasn't going to stop taking pictures. She was just getting started.

And then she saw a burst of spray rise in front of her face, and looked down to see a huge dorsal fin, black and rubbery and pitted with scars, turning like a wheel. She saw the blowhole and heard the hiss, like a secret being whispered. Then it puckered like a kiss and the whale disappeared, leaving her damp and laughing.

Calvin found her like that. He let his shoulder nudge hers and she felt the side of her body erupt in gooseflesh, the hairs lifting on her neck. But then he stepped away. He had news. 'Phone call for ya. In the wheelhouse.'

'Kate, you have to come back.' It was her sister.

She leaned a hand against the chart table for support. Fear filled her chest. 'What's wrong? What's happened?' Gripping the heavy black receiver, aware of the captain and mate in her periphery, listening.

'Someone broke in. Everything's in a mess. All the books, your jewellery. I can't tell what's missing.'

'But I thought you changed the lock.'

'I did. It was *unlocked*. Everything's all over the floor. It's got to be him. It's Boyd.'

'Jenna, listen. You could've left it unlocked. Someone walked in. Someone from the building. Did you give a key to anyone? Did you leave it in the door?'

'No. No.'

'Where's Jerry? Have you told Jerry?'

'He's not home. I'm calling the police.'

'Don't call the police.' She was shouting now. 'What are the police going to do?' Wishing the Old Man was not standing there on the other side of the phone.

'Kate –'

'Please, just get out of there. Get Jerry to put a padlock on it. I'll deal with this. Okay? It's my problem.'

Adrenalin would make it easier to do what she had to do. She was shaking with anger. She would kill Boyd when she saw him, because even if it wasn't him, it was someone he knew, the asshole who'd called her or one of his asshole buddies.

But then the captain had to go and ask if everything was all right at home. It was better when they stayed mean; she could cope with that. Now she couldn't hold the tears in. She stood in front of him, sobbing, the wheelsman and the second mate taking it all in, telling him she was sorry. He nodded, reaching into his pocket and handing her a folded white hanky.

'I'm so sorry,' she repeated. 'For everything.'

'You'll be all right. Maybe you learned something. I'll tell the mate to make out your time for Montreal. You can get off in Côte-Sainte-Catherine Lock. We'll be there tonight.'

She was packing when Hazel barged into the cabin, banging the door against the wall. 'What in hell do you think you're doing now?' she shrilled. 'You're quitting on me? Ain't you caused enough trouble?'

Kate dropped her duffel bag and crossed her arms. 'My place got broken into. I have to go home.'

'I asked you a question. You quitting on me?'

'I thought you'd be glad to get rid of me.'

'Listen. You quit now and I won't get another girl. Not in August. Not with the rumours going around about this boat.'

'But Hazel –'

'No. You listen. You've caused more trouble than you're worth already. But I ain't working shorthanded down in Indiana Harbour in August. I'm too old. You can't quit. I'll fire ya first.'

'What for?'

Hazel lowered her voice to a furious whisper. 'For fooling around with Calvin in the food locker, that's what for. You didn't think I'd notice the mess? You think the union's gonna back you over that?'

'But my *apartment*, Hazel. I don't know what's missing. I have to go sort it out.'

'So get off in Montreal and meet us back in the Canal. That would be the day after tomorrow. Ask May. It was her idea.'

Kate looked past Hazel to see May hovering by the door, nodding fiercely through her cigarette smoke. They were giving her another chance.

❦ 34. At the Kingston rest stop she followed a skinny guy with a greasy blond ponytail out behind the restaurant to smoke a joint. She felt driven to it; she'd chugged two beers at the Montreal bus station but was still rigidly awake at 4 a.m.

In the lineup at the cash the guy seemed eager to make conversation with anyone who would catch his eye. He seemed familiar, or maybe that was just his desperation.

Lighting the joint he told her he was going to Toronto for a trial. To plead or testify, he didn't say, and she didn't ask. She asked about his tattoos.

He made a fist. 'Honest to God, I got no idea what they mean. I asked for skulls, he gives me these freakin' stars. I think it was the only thing he was good at.' He said when he had the cash he'd get them redone. But Kate doubted he would get anything better. The stars on his knuckles were prison tattoos: she knew because Boyd's friend Stan had one. Crude symbols, made with safety pins and the ash from the incinerated liners of cigarette packs. She smiled to herself: every crowd has a silver liner.

Three or four tokes and she was drifting outside her body, seeing herself and the ponytail guy and all the sleeping people on the parked bus, the young francophone couple spooned in the seat across from hers. She felt strangely at peace, like a prisoner on a day pass, someone looking through the glass. Like a bubble in a bloodstream, drifting till she crashed.

'Whoops,' he said. 'There's the driver. Where you from anyway, down east?'

Kate laughed, feeling clever and weightless. 'No. From nowhere.'

At 8 a.m. she called Rebecca from the Bay Street bus terminal.

'You're back just in time.' Becks said. 'You're getting an accent.'

'I'm not back.'

Rebecca interrupted Kate before she finished her story. 'You have to get out of the apartment. It's gone too far now. You have to put your stuff in storage.'

'What do you mean, give up my apartment? How can I do it in a day? I'd have to give notice.'

'Extenuating circumstances. Talk to your super. He likes you, right? I don't think he wants another break-in. Listen, I can meet you there in an hour. I'll help you pack.'

Even Jenna agreed. 'I'll take the bookcase,' she said, handing Kate a coffee from a Tim Hortons bag. She had taken the morning off work and come straight from the university, where she was staying with a friend.

They sat on the couch, surveying the chaos. The books lay in drifts, clothes were scattered by the dresser. She had a day to pack up her life.

'Good. Great. You can take the encyclopedias too.'

'You sure?'

'Yeah. You want the bed and dresser?'

Jenna frowned. 'You can't get rid of Mom and Dad's bed.'

'I'm not. I'm offering it to you.'

'Come on, Kate. You know I can't have my own furniture in residence.'

'Well, I can't take it with me, can I?'

The truth was, she felt exhilarated. It was like a shopping spree in reverse. You ran around filling bags with everything you never wanted to see again. The too-tight shirts, the shoes that pinched, everything she had ever worn in high school. Likewise her record collection – the Eagles and the Bee Gees and Fleetwood Mac – none of it meaning anything any more, or meaning things she'd rather forget.

Books she had loved, books she had never read, jettisoned. Binders of school notes, souvenirs of places she couldn't remember, tossed. The absurdly large collection of flowered sheets that had come with the bed, along with tablecloths and aprons and linen napkins, all the lovely embellishments of middle-class married life, into a big green garbage bag and dumped at the door.

People did this all the time, for all kinds of reasons. Eviction, boredom, death. They did it for fun. They did it more in Toronto than Ottawa, especially in Parkdale. Every week she would walk past three or four lawns piled high with a life's haul, abandoned or thrown out by a landlord: fake leather loungers with ripped seams, three-wheeled strollers, shoes missing heels, broken guitars.

Sometimes she took things. Once there was an old wicker sewing basket that reminded her of Gram, sitting just inside a box in front of a Sold sign. At home she sifted through ribbons and zippers, little tins of buttons and cards of needles and fasteners, savouring their patina and garish typefaces. And then at the bottom a small soiled linen bag, heavy with treasure: a dozen 1950s silver dollars, delicately tarnished and embossed with buffalo and teepees and Indians in canoes.

Someone had been careless, that was all. Even if they'd made a bundle selling the house, no one threw out silver coins. Her mother had taught her well enough that she felt compelled to walk back and knock on the door. But not well enough that she didn't feel bitter when the woman said offhandedly, 'Oh, yeah. I forgot about those. Those belonged to my girls. You say you got them out of my garbage?' And no Thank you or Here, why don't you keep one for your trouble?

Her mother would have taken one look and offered them all. She had always found it easier to be kind to strangers.

Listening to Jenna banging through the kitchen cupboards Kate thought it wasn't such a bad thing she'd only had three hours' sleep. It made it easier to do what she had to do. She was beyond considered decisions or guilt for not calling her mother. And she wasn't going to call her mother today, she told her sister calmly, each of the three times she asked. Not today. There wasn't time, was there?

Maybe there would never be time. She was getting used to not calling, now. Not calling seemed like the right thing to do.

When Becks arrived at noon there were a dozen boxes and bags ready to ferry to the Sally Ann. 'Where in Christ did you keep all this stuff?'

Kate laughed. 'I'm a good packrat.' She helped Becks load the car and then knocked on Jerry's door.

Jerry was freshly shaved, hair snaking across his scalp like an oiled animal, the citrus scent of aftershave mixing with sweat and coffee. Behind him a television blared sports scores.

'How's Brittney?'

'Fine. Just went home to her mom's yesterday.' Jerry rolled his eyes. 'Not a moment too soon. She was pestering all the tenants. I was ready to call in Children's Aid.'

'How old is she now?'

'Eleven. Going on thirty. And a mouth on her just like her mother.'

'Look, Jerry, I'm sorry about this. But I have to get out of here.' Kate's mouth trembled.

He nodded gravely, patting his hair. 'I understand, dear. You gotta do what you gotta do. I might have somebody interested in the place.

You could get some of your deposit money back. I just can't figure the bugger out. The lock looks fine.' He lowered his voice and leaned toward her. 'Unless it was a pro. You in trouble, dear?'

'I don't know.'

He gave her a sharp look. 'You better come in. Tell Jerry all about it.'

At the super's kitchen table she smoked one of his Export As and watched him fill the kettle. He was light on his feet for a big man. The kitchen was as clean as her mother's, with flowered tea towels folded over the oven door handle. He opened a cupboard for mugs and she saw rows of keys on hooks, apartment numbers written above them. The fridge was papered with paintings of princesses and flowers. On one, BRITTNEY dripped in lurid pink letters.

'Are those pictures new?'

'From a couple years back.' He laughed. 'She don't paint much now. Except her nails. You take your coffee regular?'

'Yeah, thanks.'

'Listen, I got a friend who's a cop. You ever get a name when that guy called and threatened you?'

'No. It wasn't me he was threatening anyway. It was Boyd. Do you really think someone could open a lock like that without damaging it?'

'No doubt, dear, no doubt. But do I think a professional might be involved? That depends.' He laughed. 'If you had a stash of coke in there, maybe.'

Kate was shaking her head. 'Jerry, I have no idea if Boyd was using my place for drugs. I didn't think he would do that. But now –' She shrugged and put down her cup. 'I have to go.'

Jenna had finished packing up the dishes and was sweeping the kitchen. Jerry said he could drive her bookcase up to the university in his truck, but he'd need to get someone to help him move it downstairs.

'Okay, I'm off,' Jenna said. 'Did you figure out what's missing?'

'Nothing that I can see. Nothing.'

'I'm taking the popcorn maker. There are some boxes of books to come up with the bookcase. Why's Jerry being so nice?'

'I think he feels guilty. For not watching out for us.'

They walked together to the stairs. When they hugged Kate could feel her sister's anger. Her shoulders were rigid with it.

'For God's sake, you have to call Mom and Dad,' Jenna said,

pulling away. 'You know what Jerry said to me? "I think this was a professional job."'

'He was just trying to impress you.'

'What am I supposed to do if something happens to you? What will I say to them?'

'Jenna,' she called after her sister. 'This is my problem, okay? My life. Nothing to do with you or Mom or Dad.'

Jenna stopped mid-step and looked up the stairs. 'Oh, because it's your life it has nothing to do with us? You should get off that boat. It's making you stupid.'

Jerry was still in her apartment, flaked out on the bare mattress. He sighed gustily and opened one eye. 'Sorry, dear. It's my back. Been years since I've seen a Beautyrest. Best mattress in the world.'

'That's what my father says.'

He opened the other eye. 'This is a real nice bed. They don't make quality like this any more. Your sister taking this too?'

'She can't.'

'I guess I could try and stick it in a storage locker. Mrs. M's down the end is empty.'

'I was going to ask you about that. If you let me keep my locker for a while you can have the bed. And the dresser.'

'Oh, I couldn't. This is worth money, dear.'

'You have to, or I'm leaving it here. Just don't tell my sister.'

A smile lit Jerry's face. 'My lips are sealed.'

It hit her after he'd gone, a Mack truck of fatigue with a trailer of panic. She was on her knees hauling Ilford photo paper boxes out from under the bed. RUINS was scrawled in big block letters across three of them, the stuff from high school. She pulled out another, HOME, and a fifth labelled TORONTO MISC. There were pictures of Brittney in there; she would give them to Jerry.

She laid her head on the hardwood floor, her cheek in the film of dust that had been unleashed by their activity. She felt the Mack truck roll over her and leave her flat.

'Kate, sweetie. Don't go to sleep on me. We've got work to do.'

It was Rebecca, squatting beside her, wafting perfume and coffee. 'I've got bagels. Cream cheese.'

They ate sitting on the bed, watching the maples nod their

branches outside the window. Trees were what she missed most on the boat, the green smell of them, the shushing of their leaves. Was that why they had planted poplars and oaks all along the Canal, the lacy barrier between the waterway and the real world? She was drifting now, hearing the tiny slaps of wavelets against the bow.

'Hey, Kate. Hey. You've got to focus, sweetie.'

'That's funny. I can't even see straight.'

'You know what I was thinking? I could drive you. To the Canal. I could see the boat.'

Kate leaned down and set her coffee carefully on the floor. Wordlessly, she put an arm around her friend. Becks patted her arm. 'I know, sweetie.'

Kate closed her eyes and smiled. 'Rebecca, will you marry me?'

'Come on, let's get this show on the road. What are you doing with the futon couch?'

'Jerry's letting me keep some stuff down in my locker. It'll be my bed when I come back.'

'What, you're going to live in the storage locker?'

Kate laughed. 'It's an idea.'

People did it, after all. Went underground. Into caves, church cellars. Anchorites and exiles. She considered this, dragging the futon with Becks along the perfectly swept corridor between the wood-slat storage lockers. Jerry really was the cleanest man she had ever met. The basement was deliciously cool and dry, lit sparsely by bare bulbs and the pale streamers of daylight falling through window bars. It was as quiet as she imagined a monastery would be: only the sounds of their breathing as they laboured to manoeuvre the futon into the wooden cage. It lay invitingly on the cool grey floor, a white canvas monk's pallet. If Rebecca hadn't been there she'd have lain down and slept till morning.

This was what a life could be distilled into: a two-foot pile of photos, a four-foot pile of books. Three suitcases of clothes and letters. A box of shoes, a box of bedding. A table and two chairs. A half dozen second-hand lamps: lamps could make any room liveable.

'No dishes?' Rebecca asked.

'Jenna took them up to York. There's a kitchen there.'

'You'll never get them back.'

'I don't care.'

'You can move in with me, you know.'

'Be careful. I might.'

Rebecca bent over the pile of Ilford boxes. 'You can't leave your photos down here. What if there's a flood?'

'Oh, Becks. Jerry wouldn't stand for it.'

'I'm serious. Let me keep them at my place. Where are the self-portraits?'

'Here.' Kate held up a baggie. There were six rolls of film. 'They aren't processed yet.'

'Let me get them processed. Seriously. I won't show them to anyone.'

'Promise.'

'Promise.' Rebecca was piling boxes into her arms. 'But I mean it, I could get you a show. Just you. The portraits and the storm pictures. I think they go together.'

'No.'

'Why not? Why not get something back?'

¶ 35. She tried to explain on the way to the Canal the next morning. It was five in the morning, barely light, and they had takeout coffees and Danishes. 'You don't understand, Becks, it isn't over yet. I still live with these people. Because of me, their livelihood is going to be affected. I feel sick about it.'

Rebecca accelerated as she turned onto the highway, heading west. Trucks towered past them, more than Kate remembered on this stretch. The first rays of sunlight were almost horizontal, raking the surface of the road with molten gold.

'God, sweetie, sometimes I wonder what hick town you came from. You've been used. Just like your boat is being used. There have to be other boats with cracks, with fucked-up engines, but some great photos fell into their laps and they're using them to make a case. A union would be stupid not to. I mean, it's what they do. Light me a cigarette, would you?'

Kate put two cigarettes between her lips and fired them up, like a lover in an old movie. She passed Rebecca her Pall Mall.

'Anyway, you did the right thing. I mean, it's like these trucks.' Rebecca gestured with her cigarette. 'There are way more of them coming up from the States now; they don't get inspected, they lose wheels, people get killed. If they're unsafe, shouldn't people be told about it?'

'Of course.'

'I rest my case. You did the right thing.'

They made good time; despite Rebecca's criticism of the trucks, she seemed to be driving recklessly fast. They were past the turnoff for Port Weller before Kate noticed a sign for the Canal. 'We have to go back. We've missed Lock 1.'

'Relax, there'll be another way. I'll ask someone.'

A gas jockey directed them to Government Road and from there Kate had her bearings. Rebecca counted three freighters beyond the scrim of trees.

'Two heading up and one down,' Kate said.

'How do you know?'

'God. Can't you tell the bow from the stern?'

Becks laughed. 'No.'

At Lock 1 a guy in a hard hat and safety vest told them the *Huron Queen* wasn't expected for an hour. He spoke to Kate but his eyes crawled all over Rebecca as she paced to the edge of the lock. She was wearing a short white linen sundress, creased now from driving, and lace-up roman sandals. She had her sunglasses pushed up like a hairband.

Towering above her in jeans and Docs, her hair in fuzzy braids, Kate felt like a farm girl. A hick.

There were no women like Becks on the boats. There were two dozen men and two old women and Kate. Sweeping and scrubbing from dawn to dusk. Like Snow White and her dwarves. But even in adversity, Snow White's hair looked good.

'Kate! Help! Oh my God. I can't move.'

'It's okay.' She grabbed Rebecca's hand and tugged backward. 'I've got you.'

Rebecca's eyes were huge and dark. 'I had no idea it would be so deep. It's like a canyon.'

'Yeah.'

'Let's go get breakfast. I need to sit down.'

At a McDonald's on the highway Kate had no appetite. She pushed her Egg McMuffin across the table to Rebecca.

'What's up?'

'I feel sick. I don't want to go back. But I have nowhere else to go.'

'Cheer up, sweetie. It's only a couple of weeks.'

'And then what? I'll have a week to get a place before school starts. And then I'll have another year of drinking too much on Friday nights and spending weekends in pyjamas. Why can't I be like you? Why can't I hang out with normal people and go out with men who went past grade twelve?'

Rebecca laughed bitterly. 'Oh, like the jerk I just broke up with? Smart guy, works for a newspaper.'

'I didn't know you were going out with anyone.'

'Just a guy I liked a lot. One of those brilliant screw-ups. Drinking too much, showing up late and climbing all over me. The first time, I made him sleep on the couch. Then I gave him an ultimatum. He blew it.'

'So you wrote him off.'

'Yeah. You have to do that sometimes. You know that, don't you?'

'Why don't you write me off?' There it was. She had said it. She swallowed against the dryness in her throat. 'Join the club. You and my parents.'

'Come on, Kate –'

'You're slumming with me, Becks. Like I was slumming with Boyd.'

'God, sweetie, maybe your parents are right. Did you ever think of that? Because, really, what the fuck are you doing? Now you're screwing another guy off the boats, a kid, and – news flash – he doesn't read books! Where's your self-respect? You have a gift. Your pictures are good, and you don't want to show them. What's the point of doing it if you don't believe in it?'

'That's the point. The point is doing it. Even when I don't believe.'

Rebecca slapped her palms against the tabletop. 'And I am furious that you haven't called the cops. You didn't tell the cops when Boyd assaulted you and now you're letting him get away with a break-in.'

'No,' Kate said wearily. 'I don't think it was Boyd. I don't think he cares that much.'

Calvin was waiting when she climbed aboard. He followed her to her cabin. 'I could've told you it wasn't Boyd. Kenny and Boyd are in Thunder Bay.'

'Doing what?'

'Nothing. They got fired.'

'From the self-unloader?'

'Mate caught them toking up.'

'So Boyd could be back in Toronto.'

'Nah. He's shacked up with someone.'

Kate stared at Calvin in amazement. He was leaning against her bunk, drinking a coffee. He said he had half an hour before the ship would be cleared for Lock 7. 'Then why the fuck didn't you –'

'Why didn't I what?'

She glared at him. 'Tell me.'

'I didn't get a chance to call till you were gone. Called the Thunder Bay hall. Talked to a buddy of mine.'

'So now everyone here knows I got off because I thought Boyd broke in but it wasn't him because he's shacked up in Thunder Bay?' She was thinking about Brian. He would love to have something like that to repeat.

Calvin sucked back the last of his coffee. 'How do I know? They never heard anything from me. Hey, got anything to drink?' He was eyeing her bag.

'Fuck off.'

It was his turn to look amazed. 'The fuck did I do?'

'What do you think? Do you think I like having my private life discussed by a bunch of old men?' They gossiped more than old women, the fucking dwarves.

Kate felt his arms slide around her as she stood at the porthole, his breath wafting coffee. He pushed his groin into her backside. She shoved him away with her hip.

'Give us a drink, then.'

'I think you should go.'

He watched her take a pile of books from her duffel bag and add them to her little library on the desk. She had brought a couple of Brontës and a Jane Austen. And a small volume of *The Odyssey*, chiefly because she liked the idea of a man spending years trying to find his way across 'a wine-dark sea', though she had never been able to get through more than three or four pages at a time.

Calvin picked up the book from her father. '*Two Years before the Mast*? What's this shit?'

She snatched it from him and tossed it onto her bunk. 'It's a book. You should try reading one sometime.'

'I read. I read plenty.'

'What do you read? *Great Shipwrecks of All Time?* Ever hear of literature?'

She turned back to the porthole. There was a city out there somewhere, but from the port side she could see nothing but trees. She yawned. She would have a hot shower and take a book to bed. A good book was all she wanted.

She turned and looked at him, a boy in ripped clothes, the Hulk reduced to human form. 'You'd better go. Ronnie'll be looking for you.'

He stopped at the door and turned back, searching for her eyes. She thought he would say something nasty now, but he only looked at her. And the look that he gave her was pure disillusionment.

In her bunk she lay in darkness, listening to the moans of the winch as the ship was secured, the rush of water as the lock filled. She was drifting into a dark dream place, standing at the railing on a river at night. Below her a skiff had come alongside. Someone threw down a rope ladder. Above her the sky was raining green fire; she could hear it crackle.

A pale figure appeared beside her at the railing. Slender, bandaged like a mummy from head to toe. She looked into the eyes, black hollows in the white bandages. They were all pupil, wet as a seal's, reflecting tiny flames. 'You forgot your luggage,' Kate pointed out.

'A navigator doesn't need luggage.' The voice was a woman's, low and amused.

The sky hissed above them. Kate looked up at a glowing funnel of orange. 'Why is the sky so loud?'

'It's the aurora.'

The river widened and they were passing a city, the oily black water a freeway of shattered light. Orange cartoon flames licked the skyline. Kate turned again. 'Why are they burning the city?'

And the woman's voice, laughing now. 'They're not burning the city. They're burning the bridges.'

She jerked awake. There was grey light coming through the porthole.

A squat silhouette filled the cabin doorway, barking at her.

'Hazel. What's wrong?'

'May missed the boat.' The cook's voice was shrill with indignation. 'You better get up. I'm gonna need you to do breakfast.'

Kate rolled out of bed and locked the cabin door. She lit a cigarette and turned the shower on full, grateful for the instant head of steam and the privacy to wallow in it. She left the washroom door open to warm the room.

Funny how you never knew how cold you were till you stepped into a hot shower. She was chilled to the core. Her whole body went slack, the blood blooming under her skin as she soaped herself, thinking about nothing beyond water, moving water, rain and waves and showers, washing away distracting details, washing things clean. Listening to the hiss of the shower, the patter of falling drops, she felt her brain slow down, felt things settling, becoming sediment, showing their patterns, like the ribbed sand under the waves.

Kate didn't make a practice of interpreting her dreams; dreams were just the brain doing its laundry, washing out the day's ideas. But this one had spooked her, the pilot swaddled like a mummy or a burn victim. She adjusted the hot tap, thinking of the porter she was replacing, the one who had scalded her hands.

She soaped herself with both hands, feeling their roughness against the soft skin of her belly. On the boats the women's hands took more abuse than the men's, always in heat or cold, soap powder, freezer ice, beef blood. The tips of her fingers had begun to peel; she found herself rubbing them together like some bag lady jazzed on speed, excising her own fingerprints, cell by cell.

There were fresh towels from the linen change so she used two, twisting one into a turban and laying the other on the edge of May's bunk, where she sat to pull on her jeans and socks. The thing was, you could forgive others for your injuries but that didn't mean you would be forgiven yourself. People are afraid of the damaged. They fear the contagion of recklessness. Or even bad luck.

Kate had been taking chances since she started climbing trees with Bobby when she was nine years old. Eating the stunted unripe apples that her mother warned against, though she spat out as much as she swallowed. It was the juice she liked: acrid, astringent, the taste of green.

To get the apples they had to shimmy out along scabbed old branches that creaked with their weight. Once she had refused to come back, clinging to a swaying branch in the dappled light. She said she would jump if he didn't love her. Where had she learned those words? And he said, of course he loved her. That was the day she had first let him push up her blouse.

Kate stood in front of the mirror and raised her hands to pull her T-shirt over her breasts. She wondered what had made her see what she had not wanted to see until now.

Calvin. Calvin was Bobby grown up, the coltish eager boy with apple breath and skinned knees, the boy they had taken away from her. And now she thought, They were right.

❡ 36. 'Pointe Noire to Indiana Harbour,' May said. 'One goddamn hole to another.' Kate and May were drinking Amaretto, a bottle she'd brought from the apartment. The porthole open to a circle of Erie sky, ridged with rags of white cloud, like ripples across a pond.

May was chain-smoking, perched on the edge of her bunk, tapping her toe against the linoleum. It made Kate think of the little yellow birds that sometimes flew aboard, pecking at the steel deck for a forgotten grain. Hazel called them wild canaries. Two weeks ago Kate had found one dead in the pantry linen drawer and carried it into the cabin on a tea towel. She wanted to photograph it, the exquisite little feathers, the tiny closed beak. A still life.

But May, thinking it had got in by itself and died in Kate's bunk, pitched it out the porthole. Just as well, she thought now. It was morbid.

All afternoon Hazel had been sniping about May missing the boat in Lock 7, as if Swede didn't routinely come back late, not to mention the second engineer. May seemed barely to hear her, going about her business like a clockwork doll, answering in monosyllables. She had a big ugly bruise on her right arm.

Hazel complained to Kate. 'Who's she think she is, anyway? It ain't my fault she went and got drunk.' It was the first time since Quebec that Hazel had really talked to her and she was careful in her answer.

'She seems upset. I think something happened.'

'Well, why don't she say?'

'I don't know. I could talk to her.'

Sitting at the cabin desk, Kate poured May a brimming shot to replace the one she'd just downed. 'Lord,' May said. 'I sure needed that.' She fished a fresh pack of cigarettes out of her drawer and lit up. 'Well, I'm done with him.'

'With who?'

'With Frank. I'm leaving him.'

'May, what happened? Did he hit you?'

'Oh no. Him?' May tittered. 'He's a mean, cheap bastard, excuse my French, but he's a coward, is what he is. Waits till I'm away, then pulls his tricks. Well, you know I bought new drapes. It was my money – Hazel give me a loan but I was paying her back. I got home yesterday and they were gone. The new ones gone and them ratty old things hanging there. Them old drapes belonged to his first wife. I hate those goddamn drapes.'

'What happened to the new ones?'

'Gone. But my dear, they were *custom*. If he thinks he can take them back he's got another think coming. Oh, I rue the day I met that man.'

'What happened to your arm?'

'Fell. Taking down her drapes. Now there's no goddamn drapes at all and we'll probably get robbed.'

May swallowed the last of her drink and squinted at the porthole. 'That's a real tasty drink. What d'you call that?'

'Amaretto. It's Italian. Made of almonds.'

'Frank would never let me buy nothing like that. I'll have to get me some. Maybe for Christmas.' Her face took on a distant look. 'When I move in with Maureen.'

From outside came a hooting like laughter, a tooting of toy horns.

'The geese!' Kate said.

She went to the porthole and craned to see a ragged V of Canada geese, noisy as a busload of sports fans heading home after a win. She wondered why they had to announce their progress so loudly, why stealth wasn't the better way. Maybe they had to encourage each other, because what they were doing was so hard.

They must be wild geese, not like the harbour geese in Toronto that haunted the quays all winter eating tourist scraps. Journeys they had made for millennia, abandoned for a regular supply of french fries.

It was the second southbound flock she had seen in as many days. Watching it dwindle she felt a wave of loneliness blow through the porthole.

'I always wondered where they go,' May said. 'Do you know?'

Kate shook her head, thinking about her mother. Geese meant fall, and ever since kindergarten, fall meant school. Crisp new exercise books, the fragrance of fallen leaves and pencil shavings, the smell of a fresh chance. A tartan skirt or a corduroy jumper sewn by her mother. And shoes.

The annual pilgrimage to the Hudson's Bay store, the ritual questioning of her choice, the pointy granny boots or the platforms or the flimsy ballet slippers. And then relief as her mother handed her a couple of new bills so she could pay for the shoes herself, inhaling the new smell of the leather, running her hands over the box.

Now fall was just fall, season of decay. The lake stank of fish and the field tomatoes that had come with the grocery order were flecked with black. Hazel was going to have to boil them into sauce. The geese were barely visible now, their flight chant no longer audible. She missed the brave hopefulness of it. They were going south, somewhere warm, but maybe less safe. She squinted against the slanting rays of the sun to see the last wavering specks.

'May, where did you take your girls to buy school shoes?'

May was snoring lightly, collapsed against the pillows, her head rocking with the motion of the boat. Her blind eye half open. Kate snapped off the bunk light and untied May's laces, gently removing her heavy nurse's oxfords, thick with many coatings of white.

She climbed up into her own bed and pulled the curtains shut. She tossed her jeans to the end of the mattress and tunnelled into the blankets. There was a chill creeping into the cabin, though as long as the engines were running it would never really get cold.

It was different at winter tie-up, May said. The engines were shut down, emptied and cleaned by the engineers after the deck crew had been paid off. They needed heaters then. They'd been lucky with tie-up on the *Huron Queen*; it had never been later than mid-December, which meant May could get home in time to shop for her daughters and grandchildren, she could fly back to Cape Breton and be there Christmas morning to cook a turkey with all the trimmings.

But now they were all going to be unemployed before December.

The union had got their strike mandate; May had heard about it in the bar last night. She said they were going to take the companies to task over safety, and that meant they couldn't let boats like the *Huron Queen* keep running. She had hesitated, then, and Kate knew there had been things said about her. 'It's not right what they done to you, using your picture like that,' May said. 'You didn't mean no harm. I know that.'

Kate was still awake when the tapping came. She reached for her clock: just past midnight. It came again, just audible above the engines, from the wind scoop vent above her head. Calvin, up on the boat deck. Kate tapped back with her lighter, as much to make him stop as to signal she was coming. She climbed down the foot of the bunk. She would get a tea. She wasn't going to sleep anyway.

He was sprawled on the bench, smoking a joint. She pushed his legs aside and sat, wrapping her hands around her mug.

'What's wrong? You still mad?'

She shrugged. 'I'm tired. God, it's cold up here.'

'Almost fall. It'll be getting rough soon.' He said it with relish.

In the darkness she could see what looked like flames through the trees. She yawned and smelled wood smoke. 'Where are we?'

'St. Mary's River. We're making good time.'

She could see a cabin now, its yard lit up by a blaze. Warmth or destruction? There were dark shapes of people moving around it. Laughter, a shout, a tattered bit of song. She took out her cigarettes, watching another camp of merrymakers, their tiny faces lit by the fire, squeezing the last drops out of summer. Calvin flicked open his lighter and she cupped the flame, inhaling deeply, feeling a hollowness fill her chest.

You could go past houses, past glowing windows and manicured lawns, past overgrown backyards full of rusty swing sets and cars on blocks, and you would imagine contentment in the lit windows and misery in the rust and you would be wrong. Quite often you would be wrong. She had to keep telling herself that. She had to remind herself. Watching the merrymakers through the trees, she imagined stepping overboard, swimming ashore with her clothes in a garbage bag clamped between her teeth. They would wrap her in a blanket and put her by the fire with a drink in her hand.

'Calvin. Give me your jacket. I've got goose bumps.'

She felt it spreading up from her belly, a sad sour rash of cold that made her shoulders rise and tighten.

'Hey man, you're shaking.'

The tea had already cooled to tepid. She finished it in one swallow and turned away from him, away from the wind. 'I miss ...' She stopped. What would she say? I miss my mommy. And then she remembered a time in Algonquin Park, her father by the fire with a drink in his hand, scolding her because she had eaten her marshmallow too soon, burned her tongue on the molten core of it, and Jenna was whining and her mother had gone off somewhere, to look at the stars maybe, to get away from the chaos of her family.

Kate was ten years old, weeping with pain and he was yelling, because that's what he did when things went wrong. And she thought, it's someone else's life I'm missing.

The river was widening now; there were no more bonfires. 'Cheer up, eh,' Calvin said, squeezing her shoulder roughly. 'Just think of the money.'

She stared at him. 'What?'

'You're worried about all this shit, man; the union, you got no apartment, no place to go back to. So what? You're free. You'll get a better place. Get enough weeks to go on pogey, you'll have it made. That's what keeps me going.'

Now she laughed, but there was no humour in it. 'Fuck off, Calvin; don't talk to me about money. You don't have a place, you don't even have a car.'

'Don't need one in Jamaica, mon.'

'What do you mean?'

'Buddy and I rented a place on the beach last winter. It was a fucking trip. Ganja. Rum. They sell these big sandwich things on the beach, rotis, fucking great. And the ladies. Oh yeah, I know some real nice ladies.'

'I bet you do.'

He squeezed her shoulder again. 'C'mon man. I'm just yankin' your chain.'

Kate wondered what her parents would say if she just showed up, knocked on the door with her duffel bag in her hand.

Calvin was talking. 'You'd love it, man.' His voice in her ear, almost a croon. 'At night the wind comes in and it's warm. You can lie in a hammock and watch the waves in the dark.'

'How can you see them in the dark?'

'You've never been south, have ya, babe?'

'Don't call me babe.'

His hand moved from her shoulder and clamped the back of her neck, hard. 'You're in a right cranky mood tonight, aren't ya?'

She elbowed him and he laughed

'The sea *glows* at night,' he said. 'It's got a green edge to it, phosphorescence or some fucking thing. I lie out on the beach and smoke my ganja and drink my rum and I think – you know what I think? Like I'm some fucking buccaneer, man, just landed on the island. Like Francis Drake and them, the dude with the earring. You'd love it. You could stay a couple weeks.'

She wiped her face with the back of her hand. 'You just told me I should think of my money. I don't have money to go down south.'

'You aren't listening, man. It's my place; I'm renting it again this winter.' He laughed slyly and put his face in her hair. 'Ever make love in the sand?'

Kate jerked her head away. 'You mean like your *ladies?*' She stood up. 'You don't get it, do you, Calvin?'

'What?'

'This isn't going anywhere, you and me. We're on a boat, a crappy fucking freighter, and it doesn't go anywhere. Just around and around. And that's us, okay? We're having a little ride. Around and around and then we get off. And that's it.'

Calvin drew hard on his cigarette, his eyes on the water. 'Whatever, man.'

¶ 37. Indiana Harbor squatted under a sulphurous fog, still rich with the stench of high summer, the soup of slag and garbage and diesel simmering in the heat of the steel plant.

But Hazel said it had never been this hot this late before, and she had been coming for thirty-five years. She sat red-faced in the pantry, holding a can of ginger ale to her forehead. 'Maybe I should just cancel dinner, whaddya think?'

'Oh lord, Hazel,' said May. 'That wouldn't go over too well.'

Kate rolled her eyes. She was sweaty and her thighs were sticking together under her skirt. Sometimes May was so literal she wanted to smack her.

It was just after coffee break and May was making pies; she would make pies for dessert whether the temperature was a hundred and twenty or twenty below. She put down her rolling pin and wiped her glasses on a tea towel. 'I got a better idea. Us girls should take a taxi up to the bar and have a few drinks. Come back tomorrow.'

'You mean catch it in the Soo tomorrow,' Hazel said.

'Well, why not,' May said.

Kate laughed. 'That sounds like mutiny.'

Hazel laughed too. 'You better believe it.' Then she took her pop can and put it against Kate's arm, making her shriek. Maybe it was too hot to hold grudges. Maybe Hazel had had good news from her bank. Whatever it was, Kate knew Hazel had forgiven her.

Calvin had not. He made himself scarce all morning, only to appear in the galley asking for a wrapped sandwich just before his watch ended. He was going ashore without even changing his clothes, heading for a cold beer and air-conditioning. It meant she would have to go ashore alone to buy cigarettes, and she dreaded walking alone in American ports, the men at the gate with their lazy accents and their guns, the way Americans could make you feel like you didn't speak the same language.

But the men at the gate were middle-aged and avuncular; they joked with her about tagging along for a cold one, and wasn't this a killer of a day? She had dressed more carefully than usual, a blouse instead of a tank top, and she thought, maybe I can do this. Walk through a steel town alone. Be a big girl.

She walked quickly past boarded-up storefronts to a shabby grocer's with large gaps on the wooden shelves. It wasn't the kind of store you saw in Toronto, at least not in the parts where she shopped. There was a hot thick smell of rotten meat and half the fluorescents were burned out or buzzing like the fat flies in the windows, one of which had been patched with cardboard and tape. In the wheezing cooler there was a breeze of sour milk but the cans of pop looked clean. Taped to the cash register a crudely lettered sign read, 'We don't take foodstamps without ID.'

There were three Hispanic-looking kids, maybe eight or nine

years old, ahead of her in line, counting out change to buy two cans of Coke and a pint of milk. The girl counted last and she was ten cents shy. Kate dug into her pocket, but the clerk was already handing the girl the carton. 'You pay me next time.'

The girl turned big dark eyes up to him. 'Mister, you got a bowl?'

'No, what you want a bowl for?'

'For the cat.'

'No, I have no bowls here. Go on.'

He was a brown-skinned man with acne scars and an eagle's beak of a nose and she smiled at him when she set a bottle of Seven-Up on the counter and asked for two packs of Camels. But he only glowered harder. He punched the numbers into the geriatric cash register and told her the total without looking at her and laid the change on the counter instead of her outstretched hand. She had stopped smiling.

Only why should an obvious fucking woman-hater make her feel embarrassed? She was angry now, she would go for a beer. But not at the sports bar where the sailors went; she hated the way they picked the same kind of place in every port, a dark bunker with a carpet smelling of beer, TVs and pinball machines flickering, a stripper on weekends. Like tourists who always stayed in a Holiday Inn, it didn't matter what it cost, as long as it looked the same.

Halfway up the block she found a sparse canteen of a bar with shabby pale walls and a high ceiling. She liked the fact that she could stand on the sidewalk and see the whole place through the dusty bay windows, could see right away where she would sit, at the end of the empty bar, just a step in from the open door.

There were only two other people in the place, both elderly black men wearing suits despite the heat, sitting at a table against the wall. They stopped talking when she walked in and flashed gold-flecked smiles. Kate took a seat and looked up at the tin ceiling, at flakes of white plaster floating down. A ceiling fan turned lazily, like an airplane propeller warming up. If she ever had a bar she would like it to be exactly like this.

She had finished her first cigarette before the barkeep came out of the back, a tall light-skinned black guy in a white T-shirt who might've been twenty or forty and had his hair in a couple of dozen cornrows. He ignored her studiously until thirst drove her to clear her throat and ask for a Pabst.

'You aren't from around here, are you?' he said.

'Oh,' said Kate, smiling, thinking he was joking, 'you don't have Pabst?' It was in Toledo that she'd had it – Ohio – but it was the first American brand that popped into her head.

He looked away and shook his head.

'No,' she tried again, feeling the sweat running down her neck, 'I'm off a boat. From Canada.'

'I've got Michelob. No Pabst.'

She nodded, hoping he would ask her another question, but he said nothing, just 'That's a dollar forty' when he put down her beer. She had almost finished when three other men came in laughing and looking at her as they took the table next to the old guys. Realization dawned then: she was in a black bar. She thought of the Portuguese sports bars along Dundas in her part of Toronto, bars she had never set foot in since the time she had gone into one to buy cigarettes and someone had spun a beer coaster at her ass. Maybe you had to be from somewhere else to go into places like this.

Well, fuck it, she was still thirsty. She caught his eye and asked for another beer, wondering if he'd crack a smile this time, but he didn't look at her as he set it down and took her money. Then he was gone, back to the back room. She drank the second one quickly, licking the foam from her lips, suddenly wanting to be on the ship. She could use a washroom about now, but she wasn't going to ask here.

One of the old guys caught her eye when she was sliding off her stool to go. 'Come over here, gal, we got to ask you something.' She hesitated in front of the closed faces of the other table, but he smiled her closer with his gold teeth. 'You got to settle us an argument here. It true you people don't pay nothing for an operation up there in Canada? All your hospitals is free? For everybody?'

The other man was shaking his head.

Kate smiled. 'Yup,' she said. 'It's true.' She raised her voice so grumpy guy would hear from the back. 'Universal health care. Everybody's treated the same. You couldn't even pay if you wanted to.'

'Man,' the old guy said, laughing. 'I got to take me a trip up there.'

Outside Kate concentrated on walking straight. In the heat the beer had gone right to her head. Inner ear, she thought. Inner harbour. Ha. I'm drunk. On two fucking beers.

She was straining to see the plant gates through the haze of the street when she heard a little voice on her starboard side. 'Miss, miss. You could help me? My cat, you could help it?'

It was the little girl from the grocer's, sitting on a wooden crate inside the mouth of an alley. The boys were farther in, kicking a Coke can. Then Kate saw that a marmalade-coloured kitten was lying in the dust by the girl's feet, a thin tabby maybe ten weeks old. She knelt and stroked its head and it mewed and struggled to rise on its front legs. The back legs weren't quite working. It wobbled and fell on its side, panting in the heat.

'She's thirsty,' said Kate. 'Did you give her some milk?'

'She's a girl?'

Kate laughed. 'I don't know, honey. I just think all cats are girls. Where'd you find her?'

The girl pointed back down the alley. 'Back there. In the trash. Somebody frow her out.'

'Did she drink some milk?'

'Yes, miss. She drink it. Then she frow up. Maybe she sick.'

Kate stood and wiped the sweat from her forehead. She patted the girl on the head. 'Can you wait here for a minute? Promise?' She sprinted up the street, past the gatehouse and across to the sports bar, into the cool air-conditioned dark and up to the counter where the lights were until her eyes adjusted. He was in the back playing pool.

'Calvin,' she panted. 'Thank God you're here. I need your help.'

'Fuck, man,' Calvin said. 'I don't know how you talked me into this. I had to give that guy my last five joints.'

He was drinking a beer on his bunk, watching her try to tempt the kitten with some mashed up sardines. It had come through the plant gates inside a metal lunch box belonging to one of the guys Calvin had been playing pool with, then on board in Kate's shoulder bag. The little girl had been clearly relieved to give it up, but Kate gave her five dollars and said to get herself and her friends a treat.

Stroking the kitten she could feel its whole body tremble, hunger she hoped, not distemper or something worse. Puking up the milk didn't mean anything; she'd heard cow's milk was no good for them. Little beady eyes popped open as she wafted her finger past its nose. Yes. It had noticed that. And then it was clambering to the edge of the cardboard box, licking and purring and biting the hand that held out little squashed bits of fish like hors d'oeuvres on a tray.

'Don't be giving it too much, now,' said Calvin. 'I hate cat puke.'

'Oh, calm down. Whatever she does, she'll do in this box.'

Kate had filled one side with the gravel they used on icy decks – Calvin said it was just kitty litter anyway – and the other with a piece of wool blanket. There was another box to go overtop, and she had fit it all in the space at the foot of the bunks Calvin shared with the wheelsman.

'You're sure Swede is okay with this?'

'Fucking right. I told him you'd buy him a forty-pounder of rum. It's only until the Lakehead.'

Kate plumped the blanket to make a nest and lifted the kitten to the centre, where it immediately curled up like a fuzzy yellow caterpillar. Its purr was as loud as a motor.

'Oh, you're happy now, aren't you?' Kate crooned.

Calvin held up a warning hand, turning his eyes toward the cabin door. Light footsteps went by in the corridor, along with a throat-clearing bark she knew was Brian's.

The cat looked up to the top of the box, then began scratching at the blanket, catching its claws in the threads. Kate lifted it over to the gravel, where it scratched and crouched to pee. It fell over mid-stream.

'God, something's really wrong with her legs. Somebody must have done something to her.'

Calvin shrugged. 'A cat like that when I was growing up, fuck, the boys'ld just set it on fire.'

She shot him a look of pure hate. 'Fuck off. Don't even joke about it.'

'I'm not shittin' ya. It's what they did.'

'What about you?'

'Me? Never. Made me sick.'

'But you didn't stop them?'

There. Now she had yelled. And if Brian was still up forward he would know she was in Calvin's room. He would spill it after dinner; let it slide out of his scummy mouth like a toad, plop it in front of Hazel and May and Ronnie so they couldn't ignore it. So Hazel would have to get on her high horse again.

Well, fuck them, she thought, walking down the deck with a towel over her head, because a hot wind was turning the ore dust into little tornadoes. Hazel wouldn't let her quit now. They were all stuck with her.

She would take the cat to the Thunder Bay animal shelter. And maybe she could see a doctor. Get some Valium or something. Something to keep her from wanting to cry all the time.

℃ 38. The sun rose at six-fifteen over a lake as smooth as brushed silver. Kate took her tea and watched from the pantry door, her face instantly warm with the glow, thinking people on land could not know such beauty, but that this morning it was wasted on her.

She raced through her breakfast chores and was down the ladder ten minutes after they tied up at the Thunder Bay terminal, jogging down the long narrow walkway beside the elevators to the phone booth at the end. The guy at the Humane Society sounded bored. They'd give the cat its shots for ten dollars but the vet would do nothing beyond that.

'He's not allowed,' the guy said. 'If it's sick you need to go to a regular vet.'

'It's not sick. It was probably abused. What's your policy on keeping them?'

'What do you mean?'

'I mean the cat might be a little crippled. What happens if no one adopts it?'

'We keep them a week. Then we put them down. We, uh, put down a lot of kittens.'

She didn't so much hang up as throw the receiver at the phone.

There was no answer at Carol's place and no machine. She hated Thunder Bay. She tried a vet's office and was told the consultation would be fifteen dollars; any treatment would be extra. She jogged back up to the ladder and found Calvin lounging on gangway watch.

'How much cash do you have?'

He squinted at her through his cigarette smoke. 'Some. Why?'

'I need to take the cat to a vet. I don't know how much it's going to be.'

'What's in it for me?' He nudged her knee with his.

'Fuck off, Calvin. I need thirty bucks.'

'Dunno, man. I need to score some weed.'

246

She huffed in frustration. 'Okay. Fine.' She started up the ladder.

'For Jesus sake hang on, will ya.' He handed some bills up through the steps. 'Come up to the bar tonight?'

'Maybe.'

After lunch she went up to do the second mate's room, which gave her an excuse to collect the cat. The box stank of pee. 'Come on, little thing, wake up.' It putt-putted a brief purr, eyes still closed. She had worn her bomber jacket over her apron; now she wrapped the apron around the cat and zipped it into the front of the jacket, belting it tight underneath.

Brian was on watch at the foot of the ladder, drinking from a Styrofoam cup. She went down fast, not looking at him, knowing he was watching her ass, getting ready to say something.

'Hey Brian,' she called brightly. 'Know where there's a drugstore?'

'Out of condoms, then?'

'Yeah, can't keep up.' Laughing to herself. God, he was an asshole.

It was the vet's office she had called that morning, a storefront on Simpson. The vet was paunchy and tired, a middle-aged man with wire-rimmed glasses and an Eastern European accent. He was also suspicious. 'This cat has been injured,' he said, probing. 'Kicked, probably.'

'I got it from a little girl,' Kate said impatiently. 'She said she found it in the garbage.'

'Where?'

'Somewhere in the east end. I don't know the street. I'm off a boat.'

He gave her a sharp look and set the cat down. 'I can try a cortisone shot. I'm not guaranteeing anything.'

She was amazed at how powerfully a thing that size could struggle. But it barely made a peep. 'It's still wobbly,' she said.

'The shot can cause a little irritation. You will see an improvement by tomorrow probably.'

She felt hope drain out of her. 'What?'

'Tomorrow, it will be better tomorrow.'

'Why didn't you tell me that? How am I going to find a home if it looks crippled?' Kate picked up the cat and put it back in her jacket. 'If I don't find it a home it'll be put down. It'll be killed. I could've just left it at the Humane Society.'

He was shrugging nervously and it occurred to her she was shouting. Her anger was filling the little room. He followed her out into the reception past two people waiting with dogs. They seemed grey to her, their dogs grey, the whole place grey and blurred and too small. She tried to control her voice as she marched over to the girl at the desk. 'I need my bill.'

'No, no,' the vet said from behind her, talking over her. 'No bill. No charge. Just go.'

Kate found a phone booth on Simpson Street. There was still no answer at Carol's. She slammed down the receiver. The kitten stirred, trying to launch itself up between her jacket and her sweater. She leaned against the glass wall of the booth, stroking the jacket and murmuring softly. But it was twisting around inside, emitting deep meows like the cries of a much larger animal. Through the glass she saw a pregnant woman stop on the sidewalk and look back at her. She pushed the door open and started walking.

She would try Nicole. Nicole and Stan lived just past the rip-off grocery at the far end of Simpson, on the second floor of a three-story building with peeling green paint over brick. The remains of a building-sized sign read: HIPS HANDLERS. Kate smiled despite herself: Ships Chandlers.

The kitten had gone to sleep. Kate went around to the back of the building and up a steep flight of wooden stairs that would be tricky for anyone toting one child, and now Nicole had two. Kate thought she might have found a better place by now, but here was the door with the same name on the mailbox. There were mice, she remembered. The cat would keep the mice out of the food, at least when Nicole's cupboards weren't bare. Kate would say that the little girl might like a kitten now that her mother had less time. She would give her Calvin's thirty dollars for cat food.

'Oh. It's you,' Nicole said flatly. She looked different, shinier somehow. She had painted her nails and streaked her hair. Kate thought of the super's daughter in Toronto, Brittney. Like someone playing dressup. 'You might as well come in. I just put the kettle on.'

Kate took in the room all at once, the same yellow paint, Formica-topped table laid with tea things and cards. But there were new flowered curtains over the solitary window and an upholstered rocking chair in the corner with a blue plaid diaper bag slung over the back. A shiny new stroller draped with a flannelette blanket stood next to the chair. It rocked once as the kettle started shrieking. Kate felt her heart skip.

Nicole added a bag to the Pyrex teapot sitting on the stove, still half full of black liquid from an earlier brewing. She poured in boiling water and swirled the pot once, carrying it casually over to the table as if Kate dropped in all the time, as if the cards spread there were from a game of rummy they were about to resume. Even the mugs that she took from the sink and rinsed were the ones Kate remembered. They dripped water where Nicole set them beside the pot. 'You gonna sit down?'

Kate sat gingerly, wondering how long the cat would be still. She would say it was just till she paid off.

Nicole lit a homemade cigarette from a pile on the table. There was a tin of tobacco and a box of paper tubes next to a little contraption that put them together. 'So you heard, eh.'

'Um, yeah. Congratulations. Boy or girl?' Kate swallowed a mouthful of tea: bitter and tannic as ever.

'Another girl.' Nicole smiled to herself. She was bulldozing ash into little piles in the ashtray with the glowing tip of her cigarette.

Then she looked up at Kate. 'I mean about Boyd and me.'

'About Boyd?' Kate repeated stupidly. 'And you?'

Her face went hot. Calvin had told her Boyd was shacked up and she hadn't believed it. 'What happened to Stan?'

'Back in jail. Did another B and E. He was still on parole.' Anger was flying off her in sparks; she was all in motion, tapping her cigarette, jiggling her leg.

Kate stood, feeling Nicole's eyes on the bulge in her jacket. Maybe Nicole would think she was pregnant. The kitten was too inert for her liking. 'Look, I have to get back. Good luck.'

Nicole tapped her cigarette and glared up. 'Good luck? I don't fucking need luck, okay?'

The baby started up as Kate shut the door, Nicole yelling now. 'Luck? Fuck you!'

Kate gripped the railing hard as she went down the stairs, feeling dizzy as she reached the bottom. She sat down on the last step until her pulse slowed, carefully unzipped the jacket. The kitten purred as she stroked its little triangular head, its eyes closed. Still asleep.

Then she thought Nicole might come out and yell some more and she got up and walked quickly toward the alley, toward the street where people and cars flickered by in the sunlight. She was breathing with her mouth open, the taste of diesel and dust coating her tongue. The animal smell of dead leaves.

Her body knew him before she did. The knowledge had not yet arrived in her consciousness when her heart began to hammer and her legs seized up. She put a hand against the wall. A silhouette, a cutout, a stickman rattling stick limbs through the shadows towards her. Smiling his half-buttoned smile. Bastard Boyd.

ℭ 39. He was a magnet with a negative charge, impelling her slowly back into the yard where the stairs were, where Nicole might still be watching, then into the narrow alley on the other side. There were thick shadows here, litter and debris. Daylight at the far end, she saw that as she turned to run. But he was faster.

Kate felt him grab her leather jacket and stopped, thinking of the kitten. She turned slowly and faced him, both of them breathing hard. She wondered if his heart was pounding the way hers was. She leaned against the wall to control the shaking in her legs. He slouched across from her, still panting. He hadn't shaved, and she could smell the booze and hash oil coming off him in waves. But his eyes were clear, flicking over her body and back to her face, bright fish darting in the shallows.

And then he lunged.

Laughing this time, at the last moment dropping his arms to his sides as she shrieked 'Don't!' Like a baby.

Boyd was enjoying himself, she could see that. She was on his turf, his woman up the stairs, his friends across the street at the bar. On his way home for a nap and maybe a screw, then back to the union hall. Looking for work but in no hurry. It was what he did, what he had done since he was teenager. And Nicole, Nicole would be at that table drinking tea when she was fifty. Fucking Nicole, she'd probably called the bar to scream at him, tell him Kate was here.

He was grinning at her, showing all his teeth, even the broken ones at the front that would now never be fixed, and she felt herself relax. He was going to make it all a joke. It was better this way. She'd tried to make him get serious and what had she got for her pains? She straightened herself against the wall.

'What's wrong, Kate?' The words croaked out, soft around the edges. An animal growl. 'Cat got your tongue?'

Laughing despite herself, she showed him the kitten.

'Poor pussy,' he said, stroking its little triangle head, but he was looking at her. Under his camel lashes, looking at her with pity. And then he let his fingers trail up for one brief instant against her neck.

'Don't.'

It was as if he had raised his cigarette and touched her with its burning tip. He had done this to her before. If she could just lie down in his arms in the dark somewhere, batten down the door. There were alarms going off between her legs. She was getting high on the smell of him. 'Don't,' she repeated.

'Why not, Kate? Afraid of what you might do?'

'No. I didn't come here for you. You are the last person I wanted to see. I came about the cat.' Boyd loved cats; she thought it was because they were like him, the velvet paw hiding the claws. But he said he couldn't give it a home. Nicole would kill him. Her three-year-old had asthma. They were looking for a new apartment.

'So you're staying in Thunder Bay?'

'Yeah. She's good to me.'

Kate, absurdly, felt a pang of jealousy. 'And I wasn't?'

They were talking normally now, as if they were old friends catching up over beers. War buddies, maybe, in an English-style pub, where even the furniture felt friendly. But she and Boyd had never been to a place like that.

'You're fucking kidding me.' Boyd laughed a throat-clearing laugh and then stopped. He licked his lips. 'I've never known anyone as spinny as you.'

Memory is like a drunk. It can go either way. It will lie barefaced, it will try to see the good in things. Or it will stoke the hurt till the truth has burned down to ashes, all in the name of clearing the air.

She heard a roaring in her ears. 'Me? You punched me in the face. You fucking tried to *strangle* me. Did you forget that?'

The cat reared up, startled by her raised voice, and tried to climb out of the jacket. She held it against her chest.

'You started it,' he said. 'You pour ice cold water on someone who's passed out, what do you think's going to happen? You had to have everything your way, didn't you? And nothing I did was good enough.'

'So why don't you leave me the fuck alone? Why are you leaving messages on my phone? Why did I get a call from one of your psycho friends? Why did someone break into my place?'

'Yeah, buddy told me he called you up. It's taken care of. But he never broke into your place. There's nothing in your place worth taking.'

'Oh, listen to you. *Someone* broke in. I had to fucking move out.'

Boyd shrugged impatiently, leaning against the peeling brick. Flakes of paint fell onto his shoulders, tiny specks of colour.

'And what about those fucking postcards? How could you send that shit through the mail?'

Boyd stood straighter, slapping his pockets for cigarettes. She could see paint chips in his hair. It made her feel better; if he hit her here, now, if he finished the job, if he choked the life out of her, the paint chips would convict him. She'd seen a show about it. But Boyd wouldn't want to hurt the cat.

'What did you expect? Eh? What did you expect?' His voice suddenly high with fury, a menacing singsong. 'The way you let me fuck you that time afterwards, like everything was okay.' He was pacing now, first to one side and then the other, making her turn her head to watch him.

'And then, *gone*. You're fucking gone. Fucking slut is what you are, you know that? You're lucky it was just postcards.'

And she thought, if they'd been two old friends having a pint in a pub she'd take her beer mug at that moment and crash it into his skull.

'Fuck you, Boyd. *Fuck* you.'

He grinned slowly through his cigarette smoke. 'No thanks, I got a better offer.'

Kate zipped up her jacket and headed down the alley. His voice came after her, full of scorn. 'Say hello to Calvin for me.'

She found a corner store a couple of blocks from the elevators and bought a catnip mouse and a plastic litter box and a box of cat chow. She smiled at the teenage girl behind the cash and unzipped her jacket to show her the kitten.

'Is it okay?' the girl asked doubtfully.

'Yes. It's just sleeping.'

All the way back down to the harbour, she had felt an arctic wind behind her, grabbing at her hair with cold fingers. She ran without looking back, sure that if she did she would see him coming after all. But she could not contain the relief, the sheer giddiness of being done with him. She felt buoyed. Un-Boyd. A weight had been pried off her and floated away, like the soot black clouds that were being pushed by a sharp wind over the lake, turning the world light-dark, light-dark as they passed in front of the sun.

And then she stopped abruptly. She knew who had broken into her apartment and the knowledge made her laugh so loud the kitten startled again.

It was obvious, when she thought about it. Process of elimination.

Brittney, the super's daughter. It had to be. The little girl who wandered the hallways unsupervised while her father dealt with leaking taps and blown fuses. The keys were all there in Jerry's kitchen; Kate had seen them, hanging in numbered rows inside the cupboard door.

The little girl who had lusted after her mother's old costume jewellery the time she had come to Kate's apartment for a tea party. What had Jerry said? Brittney, age eleven going on thirty.

❈ 40. The *Huron Queen* was low in the water, heavy with the wheat that still poured from the loading chutes. Chaff flurries glinted in the strobing sunlight. Kate zipped her jacket higher as she jogged through shadows to the foot of the gangway. It was deserted; it must be coffee break. No one in her cabin. She quickly emptied the bottom of her locker; room for the litter box and a folded sweater inside, a safe hidey-hole.

The kitten came out of the jacket like a biscuit from an oven, round and hot. It purred briefly, then recurled itself into a ball. 'You're going to be awake all night,' Kate told it in a low voice. 'Getting me in trouble.' It let out a long purr, like the last bit of fuel puttering in an engine.

She went into the galley to forage and found May being held captive by Swede, who was bending her ear about something. He was a quiet man except when he was drinking; then he liked to hang around the galley after his watch, looking for an audience.

He winked at Kate over May's shoulder. 'Yup,' he said. 'I go fishing for whitefish every year with two or three friends, and I'm telling you, everything we get is covered in those goddamn lamprey scars.'

'Well, you don't say,' May said politely. 'They're still good to eat? Well now, here's our porter. How'd you get on in town?'

'Fine. Where's Hazel?'

'You just missed her. She's gone up to use the phone.'

Kate went through the pantry into the storage locker and took two cans of sardines, one for each apron pocket. No one ate them any more; all the men wanted was tuna. In the galley she could hear Swede.

'Not too many sturgeon left. You know the lampreys got in through the Canal all the way back in the thirties?'

'You don't say.'

'You ever seen one up close? Looks like a fire hose with teeth. The teeth go around in a circle. Like a sieve made out of blades. Ugliest thing I've ever seen.'

Kate took down a box of Red Rose tea. There were two little tins of sockeye behind it, forgotten or misfiled. She added them to the sardines.

'People think it was the new seaway in '56. It was the third Welland Canal let them in. In the thirties. Took them twenty years to get up here. Killed the fishery, killed every goddamn fishery in the Great Lakes.'

'I thought it was pollution that killed the fishery,' Kate said, bringing in the tea. She put a teabag into a mug and dumped the rest into the basket next to the kettles.

'Ha. Maybe in Lake Ontario.' Swede's lip curled at the name. 'Erie too. But not the big lakes. No, that was a goddamn butt-ugly eel. I might have been a fisherman instead of a sailor, May, imagine that!'

'My,' May said. 'Imagine that.'

The galley stank of cabbage, simmering on the stove in a sulphurous stew Hazel called boiled dinner: hunks of corned beef and turnips and whatever else she could find. She said it was what everyone ate in Newfoundland, but there was only the captain and Charlie now from the Rock and Charlie told Kate he didn't care for it; he'd had altogether too much of it as a boy.

Calvin called it welfare food. Organ meats and offal. Liver and tongue and heart, pork hocks that floated in a greasy bath and fell apart when they were poked with a spoon. Food that had ceased to have any relation to the men's preferences but was supposed to keep costs down.

In fact it didn't, because plenty came back on the plates. It irritated Kate the way Hazel pretended it was what the men liked, even when she had to shame them into ordering it – 'I made ya salt cod, just the way you like it' – when most of them would have preferred a burger.

Not that they would ever miss a meal – even in port they'd come back to eat before resuming their drinking up at the bar. Except for Calvin. He made good money, so why would he come back for stew when he could order a nice steak? The rest of them were cheap fucking bastards, is what they were.

After supper Hazel poked her in the waist and told her to come in and sit. Kate dried her hands and made a toasted cheese and tomato sandwich and took it into the messroom with a cup of tea. 'Where's May?'

'She's in yakking with the chief and the Old Man,' Hazel said, spreading French's mustard on a slice of bright pink corned beef, a bubblegum island in a brown sea. She said it was the preservatives that made it go that colour. 'Them three should get married,' Hazel added, looking pointedly at Kate's plate. 'Nothing on the menu you liked? Thought you liked corn on the cob.'

Kate thought of her mother's corn, freshly picked and shucked and boiled for no more than five minutes, meltingly sweet and tender. Hazel put hers on at four-thirty and it simmered till six, turning the cobs into wrinkled spindles of starch. It was a crime against food, what Hazel did to corn. 'I'm not very hungry.'

'Jeez, I guess nobody was.' Hazel slurped at her tea. 'I seen all that corned beef in the garbage.'

'Maybe they're tired of it.' Remembering too late the clattering of pots after Hazel had come back from the phone booth, having had more bad news, her mortgage or her nephew or both.

Hazel stopped chewing. 'How would you know? I've been serving these men for fifteen years.'

'I'm sorry, Hazel,' she said miserably. 'I didn't mean –'

They both turned as May came in with her supper, looking pleased with herself.

'Did ya hear this?' said Hazel. 'I been a cook thirty-five years and this one's tryin' to tell me what the men like.'

'Funny you should mention it, Hazel,' said May, stirring her tea happily, blind to Kate's warning frown. 'The captain was just saying how he likes them stir fries. Chinese-style, like. It could be worth a go.'

'Is that right?' said Hazel, standing abruptly. 'All those fresh greens. Think the captain knows what broccoli costs out of season? Think I can get snow peas up here? Did you remind him about that letter I got from the company? I'm goddamn well over my budget as it is.' She stamped into the pantry, where they heard a crash.

May shot out her hand. 'Don't get up. It's best to leave her. She'll be going through the freezer now. Adding up costs and such. She'll be at it all night.' May thumped herself on the forehead. 'Oh, why'd I go and open me big mouth? I never learn, do I? It's no wonder he wants to get rid of me.'

'May, what are you talking about?'

May was rocking in her chair, staring into her cup. Kate wondered why she hadn't seen it before, the giddiness, the flush. That afternoon, with Swede in the galley, they must have both been spiking their tea. And then before supper she'd come out of their cabin smelling of mouthwash.

'May. Are you talking about Frank? I thought you wanted to leave him.'

But May's look was unreadable behind the thick glasses. 'You be careful, my girl,' she said a low voice. 'Someone's liable to take that little scrap of a thing you've got hid in the locker and pitch it overboard.'

So May had seen the cat.

'They did that to a dog on the *Mackie*, they did! Threw his little Scottie overboard to get the cook off there. They never caught who done it, neither.'

'Oh, for God's sake,' Kate said, standing to collect her dishes and smokes. She needed to talk to a normal person. She needed to get off this fucking boat.

❰ 41. Well, now she could. It was official: there would be two more cargoes, but this was the last time the *Huron Queen* would navigate the waters of Superior. The boat would end its sixty-year run at a Lake

Erie steel plant. Things were murkier after that. It might be left chained to a dock somewhere with a storage load; it might be towed overseas to a shipbreaking outfit in India.

The captain had got the orders just as they were readying to let go the lines. He came straight back to tell Hazel in person; he didn't want her to hear it from the watchman. Kate saw them with their heads together in the pantry, his arm around Hazel's broad back.

Kate had retreated to her bunk, where she lay in the dark with the curtains closed, ignoring May's entreaties to have a drink. It was her fault, whatever Haroun said; without the photographic evidence the company might have ridden it out. They were being made an example of.

She lay watching the green dial of her clock long after she heard May's snores, echoing the purr of the kitten in its box, the put-put of the tugboats pushing the boat out of the harbour. She could visualize it now without unfolding the chart; the chart had become fixed in her mind. She could see, as if from above, the *Huron Queen*'s progress across the pale paper water: from the harbour into Thunder Bay proper, past the Sleeping Giant and Thunder Cape, into the cold waters of Superior, what Swede called the sweetwater sea.

She felt the currents of her life converging, like depth lines on a chart, concentric circles closing in where the water was deepest. Water holes, the Old Man called them. It was where he took on drinking water for the ship, the cleanest water from the deepest holes, and she wondered if there was anything like that in herself, some well of purpose and goodness below the murk.

Kate reached down beside her mattress and felt for her father's book, laying it on her chest, running her fingers over the nubbly leather surface. There were tears running down past her ears and into her hair. She had never thought of how it must have made him feel, her scorn for his principles, her recklessness. And if deep down she had never doubted that he was a good and serious man, that he believed in certain things, she had never let that matter much to her.

She had needed someone to fight.

She wiped her eyes and snapped on her bunk light. The book was stained, worn on the edges, the colour of red wine. *Two Years before the Mast*, by Richard Henry Dana. A college boy, according to the preface. She leafed through the dry pages, bringing them close to inhale the warm musty scent. The smell of her father's books. The smell of home.

Her eyes fell on a line spoken by the cook. *Now, my men, we have begun a long voyage. If we get along well together we shall have a comfortable time; if we don't, we shall have hell afloat...*

The boat slowed, wallowed briefly, the wind buffeting, rain spattering the glass of the porthole. Her bunk rocked in the swell. She felt hungry now, and went into the galley and made a mug of tea and a cheese sandwich. There was no one about. The boat was pitching as she came back through the dining room and she had to steady her mug as she felt hot droplets hit her knees. Then she heard something heavy hit the wall of Hazel's cabin. A low animal howl.

She found the chief cook sitting on the floor of her washroom, in a chaos of spilled boxes. Cans of ginger ale rolled back and forth. Her face was grey.

'Hazel! What happened?'

'What does it look like? I fell. Get me up.' Barking, then whining. 'I can't feel my damn arm! What if it's broke?'

Kate tried to keep the fear out of her voice. 'It's okay, Hazel, it'll be okay. I'm going to get May.'

But the first person she saw was Brian, standing in the dining room doorway. 'Help me,' Kate said. 'Please.'

The Irishman took in the situation at a glance. He pulled the bedding from Hazel's bunk, piling blankets on her where she lay. 'Well now,' he said, kneeling to wedge a pillow behind her head. 'Got yourself in a jam, did you? You're going to be fine, dear. I'll soon have you out.'

Hazel's broad face collapsed. She was crying like a teenager. 'It hurts real bad. I think it's broke.'

'We're going to get you into your bed, dear. But first I think you need a shot. You still have that bottle of whisky?'

Hazel nodded, eyes squeezed shut. 'In the drawer.'

'Get it, Kate, there's a good girl.'

Kate danced across the dipping room to the dresser. She found the bottle and a glass tucked in among white cotton underwear. Brian put a hand behind Hazel's head and held the glass to her lips.

'Little sips, now. There's a good girl.'

Hazel slurped noisily, panting in between. Some of the colour had come back into her face but her breathing was laboured. She leaned back on the pillow, wincing with pain. 'I ain't a goddamn girl. I'm old enough to be your mother.'

'Go on, Hazel, you're in the prime.'

The ship was rolling heavily now, and Kate knew they were turning into the lee of the north shore. 'You're not going to move her, are you? I think she's better there until we get straightened out.'

Brian stood up and followed her out of the washroom. His voice was low and nasty. 'Yeah, you know so much about it. You ought to take a first aid course. It's shock that kills people. Fat old woman like that, she'll be having a heart attack next. She needs to feel safe. Now be a good girl and call the wheelhouse.'

'Asshole,' Hazel said an hour later. She was swaddled tight in her bed, the injured arm taped to a splint. Another shot of whisky and one of May's codeine pills and she was slurring. *Ashhole*. 'They're all fuckin' assholes. Men. Think we don't know anything. Think we don't know what they think.'

Hazel squinted at Kate, sitting beside the bed. 'Pour me another shot. You oughtta have one too. You don't look so good, honey.'

Kate went to the dresser. Outside the wind was still moaning, but the rolling had stopped. The captain would play it safe this trip, hugging the shore. Kate had brought Hazel a mug of tea, but she waved it away. There were pill bottles in the drawer. Heart pills, maybe. Painkillers for the arthritis.

'Are you sure you should have more rye? I don't think you're supposed to mix alcohol with pills.'

'Oh, for pity's sake,' Hazel barked. 'It would take a lot more than a shot of Seagram's to kill me.'

'Okay.' Kate poured three or four fingers into the tea mug and drank half where she stood. Then she poured a small shot into Hazel's water glass and put on her bunk shelf. The cook had closed her eyes, but she was still talking.

'I used to be a drinker. It was hard not to be, on these things. People say the truth comes out when you drink but that ain't necessarily so. It's meanness that comes out of some. You got no idea the things the men used to say to me when I was starting out. No idea. Now this. How'm I gonna get around with this arm? I won't be able to drive.'

'Hazel,' Kate said urgently. 'I am so sorry. For everything.'

The cook waved a hand. 'Water under the bridge now. I'll manage. I'll ask my doctor for some home help, somebody to come in.'

'What about your nephew?'

'Don't ask, honey. Well, hell, I'll tell you. He's got problems, Jamie does. Drugs. Can't seem to …' Hazel opened her eyes. 'All he does is ask for money. I feel like a goddamn bank. I know he's living there, in my house. He's not supposed to, but what can I do? I feel bad for him. Do you understand? I feel bad.'

She closed her eyes again. 'So no, honey, he ain't gonna be any help. And now I'm going to miss this old boat tying up. Fifteen years, honey, this has been my home, eight months a year.'

'That's a long time.'

'Get me another drink, honey. Get me some snacks while you're at it. In those boxes that fell. Cashews.'

Kate found the cashews in the third box, after the tins of king crab and jars of cocktail olives. 'It's the Old Man's fault,' Hazel said. 'All his fancy treats I had to hide in my budget. He likes to have it for the company men, the dock guys. Always wants to impress people, Felix.'

'Felix?'

'I was with him on his first boat. I've known him thirty years. He don't look it but that man is fifty-three. Prop me up, honey.'

'Was he the first mate?'

'Third mate.' Hazel heaved herself forward and drank, panting. 'There was a snow squall. We were in the river, just below Quebec. We got iced in at night. The noise was awful. You ever hear it? Like the ship's gonna crack in half. I was night cook and I was scared. Real scared. And Felix, he was only twenty-three, he gets a bottle and a deck of cards and we played all night in the dining room. Till the icebreaker come in the morning.'

Hazel chuckled fondly. 'Yup. Felix the cat. Oh, I know what you got hid in your room. In the old days lots of cooks had cats. Kept the rats out of the pantry. People say they're good company.'

She was drifting now, eyes closed, voice slowing down. 'It's just as well they're scrapping this old thing, honey. I've had enough of this life. Time to go home. Maybe you too, honey. Go home.'

¶ 42. There is that moment of waking. That long beat when sadness pours in, like seawater into a footprint on a beach, before you can remember why.

Kate flung back the bed curtains and craned over the edge of the bunk. It was dark and oddly quiet, quiet enough to hear May snoring into her pillow, and below her the engines muttering their old song. The porthole still shrouded in night. She fished under her blankets for the clock: just 4 a.m.

It was coming back now. She was looking up again toward the white-winged helicopter and its obliterating noise. So loud she could not really have heard Hazel wailing as it hoisted her up from the deck in a sling. Like a little metal coffin rising up through the scraps of fog that drifted across the black surface of Superior. Storm litter. The trash of clouds.

Most of the crew had gone out to watch it approach and hover, their grizzled faces closed against the cold wind. Calvin shivering next to her, because he had no insulation. Hazel had insulation at least. Kate wished she could believe they would be kind at the hospital. But a cranky old woman off a freighter, smelling of booze. They would think that was how she injured herself.

The crew turned as one as the helicopter swallowed up Hazel and flew off over the grey chop toward the Soo. Kate thought of Gram's funeral. There was a lump in her throat and it was made of all the things she'd left unsaid.

Things that cost too much to say. You had to be rich to say them. But Kate knew she was like Hazel: an emotional miser. A beggar.

The captain came into the messroom after breakfast. 'I just talked to the hospital. The doctor says it's broken all right. She won't be back on this boat. She's going to have to get herself home somehow.' He rocked on his soles and looked at Kate. 'Two trips left,' he repeated. 'Two weeks. We won't get anyone on here for two weeks. Not after what the union said about this boat. No sir.'

'What'll we do?' May asked.

'We'll go shorthanded. Young Calvin can give you a hand shifting things.'

Kate looked doubtfully at May. The second cook was nodding so hard she looked like a dashboard doll. She'd been drinking again, Kate realized. Or still under the influence from yesterday.

She shrugged. 'We'll do our best.'

'Fine.' He turned on his heel.

By suppertime she knew that she alone would be planning the meals. May seemed petrified at the notion of making a decision, even if it was only what vegetables to serve with the meatloaf. Kate spent too long on the salad, making enough for twenty, which turned out to be three times too much. After supper she found cigarette butts in the bowl on the messroom table. True, some of them had probably never eaten anything raw. Perhaps they really did think it was some kind of large ashtray.

She sat in the washroom and smoked after May had nodded off. The kitten climbed up her jeans, purring.

'You stupid little fucker,' she said. 'You have no idea.'

She wanted a drink. She had meant to buy vodka in Thunder Bay but she had spent everything outfitting the cat. She put on her shoes and went out to Hazel's room. The bottle of rye was still in her drawer.

Kate was in the galley getting ice when Calvin came in for his 10 p.m. coffee break. He prowled over to the door of the pantry and grinned at her suggestively. 'Hey, babe. If you're chief cook you should get the chief cook's room.'

She shook her head in annoyance. He was such a boy.

But then he came over to where she stood, setting down his coffee and laying his hand on her cheek. 'Hey, babe. I miss you.'

She closed her eyes, taking in the scent of him. The cold lake air that clung to his clothes, the yeasty smell of grain dust, the sweat. The warm cloud of sweet coffee-flavoured breath. 'Okay,' she said in a low voice. 'Okay. Come to Hazel's room after your watch. But don't let anyone see you.'

They did not use the bed. It felt too much like her parents' room. They locked themselves in the washroom and she stood still while he pulled her clothes off, laying wet kisses along her collar bone, her breasts, her belly, working his way down between her legs, until she couldn't stand it any more and demanded it right now.

Afterward they sat in the room in Hazel's two armchairs, wrapped in bedsheets, drinking and smoking. Kate's feet were in Calvin's lap and he stroked them absently. She felt light and happy in a way that was unfamiliar. It was astonishing, how sex could improve your outlook. People should have more of it.

Good sex, she mentally revised.

She had had a lot of sex with Boyd, and it had been thrilling sex, sometimes annihilating sex, but it had never been happy sex and she wondered now if it had been good sex.

'I saw Boyd,' she said. 'In Thunder Bay. I found out it's Nicole he's living with now.'

'You did, eh?'

'I should be mad at you for not telling me.' Her cheeks twitched into a grin. 'But I can't right now.'

'Was it all right? Seeing him?'

'Yeah.'

The next morning dawned bright and mild on Lake Huron and she transferred the kitten and its gear to Hazel's washroom. While she was there she rooted through the boxes of contraband and found ginger ale and a case of Export Ale. It was the best news she'd had in days.

For lunch she did sandwiches and tomato soup, for supper pork chops and pasta. They ate it.

After supper she pored over Hazel's recipe books, drinking a beer. If she could talk to anyone right now, it would be her mother. Her mother had routinely whipped up dinners for twelve; it was what a professional wife did. You just found a recipe and tripled it.

Calvin found her in the dining room. 'You got ice cream? I got the munchies some bad, man.'

She glared at him. 'Where were you at lunch? You're supposed to be helping.'

'Okay, I heard ya.'

'So why didn't you help?'

'They were bugging me, man. Saying I'm set for the winter now, going out with the chief cook.'

'What are you talking about?'

'Chief cooks, man, their freezers are full. Roasts, steaks, everything. They all take stuff home.'

'Calvin,' she said impatiently. 'I mean why were they saying we're going out? Did someone see you last night?'

'Ah, for Christ's sake. They know. Everyone knows.'

'Well, they don't really know, do they? Anyway, Hazel doesn't take stuff. I've been to her house. She doesn't even have a freezer.' Kate thought of Hazel's basement, the chair in the corner, the stereo boxes, the baseball bat. The nephew's lair. What kind of help would he be to an old woman with a broken arm?

After supper the next day – hamburgers, unfortunately overdone – the captain brought his dishes into the galley.

'You're managing, then,' he said, chewing on a toothpick.

'I'm trying.'

'I appreciate the effort.'

'Thanks.'

'We'll be in the Canal about eight o'clock.'

'Good. I can call Hazel.'

She could see why Hazel and May wanted to please him. He was vain and fussy but he had an old-fashioned gallantry about him. She felt unreasonably happy that he had come in to speak to her. But then she heard laughter from the crew's mess. Brian's voice. It was against her better judgment, to go and check the fridge so that she could listen outside the door. And then she heard a term that was new to her, but clear. 'That split tail thinks she can cook now,' Brian said. 'Look at these things. They're fucking hockey pucks.'

Fucking Irish. It was obvious to Kate why he hated her, she had known from day one he wanted into her pants.

But no one said anything in her defence. They just let him say it.

Split tail. Slut. Bitch. Cunt. Anger was good, anger made her strong. She wasn't going to cry on account of that prick, not when she still had the floor to do. Swab that deck, polish that steel, all around the circle. She filled the metal bucket and slammed it to the floor, sending steaming water, fragrant with Pine-Sol, slopping over her shoes. Ignoring the pain flashing in her forearms as she pulled the heavy mop across the tiles, back and forth, flooding the corners of the galley. Ignoring them as they stopped to watch her on the way out to the deck. Fuck them.

She was listening to her own breathing. Like waves at the seashore, loud and ragged, in and out, a storm rising. Sweat prickled along her spine as she launched the mop into every conceivable crack, the avenging mop, the killer mop, the mop that would vanquish entire colonies, entire *strains* of bacteria.

Her arms gave out as she frogmarched the bucket into the dining room. A breeze was pouring through the stern doorway and she stalled there, letting it cool the sweat on her skin.

'You're some good with that mop.' Calvin, a silhouette against the screen.

'Yeah,' she said wearily. 'I'm a fucking genius with a mop.' She backed the bucket up to the door and kicked it open with her heel.

'Gimme that.' He reached in past her, his arm sinewy and golden below the ragged edge of his sleeve. She stepped outside to let him pass and watched him empty the bucket neatly over the stern.

'I found some beer in Hazel's room,' she said. 'You want one?'

Calvin laughed. 'What do you fucking think?'

They sat drinking on the bench by the dining room door, not caring now if anyone saw them. May came out and sat too, wrapped in a pilly cardigan. She looked unwell, her little walnut face shadowed with fatigue. Together they watched the gulls crisscross the ship's frothy wake, diving for fish churned up by the propeller. Like tiny handmaids fussing over a queen's lace train.

'Red sky at night,' May murmured, lighting a cigarette.

Kate rested her eyes on the soft surface of Erie, blue licked by tongues of pink under a fuchsia sky. She hadn't taken out her camera since Thunder Bay. She pulled her eyes back from the busy water and watched the steel deck crawl with wavelets. Remembering the first time she had seen it, thinking she was hallucinating. Just a ghost image, like the last scenes inscribed on the eyes of the dead.

'I'm going ashore tonight,' she said. 'I'll get off in Lock 8. I'm worried about Hazel.'

€ 43. Ronnie stood glowering in his white mate's overalls, nursing a cup of tea. Above him the lights of Lock 8 glowed yellow, turning his pale lips blue. The *Huron Queen* had at least an hour to wait before going into the lock.

'It's a bloody shame about the timing,' he said. 'It'll cost you fifteen dollars to get to Hazel's from here. She's much closer to Lock 7.'

'It's all right. It'll be too late by the time we're in Lock 7.'

Charlie was waiting at the top of the ladder. He held out an arm to steady her. 'Watch yourself now. Give Hazel our regards.'

'Hang on a moment, porter.' The third mate came toward her, digging in his pocket. 'I don't suppose there'd be a shop open at this hour?'

Kate laughed. 'Yes, Ronnie. They're called convenience stores.'

He produced a worn, very flat leather wallet, and extracted a ten-dollar bill. 'A little something for Hazel. A box of chocolates, perhaps? From all of us.'

Calvin was waiting on the holding wall, pacing. He had taken down two of Hazel's bags, things she had left behind. They headed silently toward the phone booth, which stood on the far edge of the empty parking lot like a tiny lighthouse.

It was cold out here in the wind, out of the shelter of the ship. A smell of fish came off the water and she wondered why it was always stronger from shore than out on the lakes. But maybe that wasn't fish, just the rotted scum that collected on the edges, the water's refuse.

Or maybe it was just that her senses had sharpened in the dark. She could taste the clay in the dust being raised by her quickening footsteps, the vegetable smell of spent leaves. And Calvin's joint, a tiny ember in the darkness.

'Don't forget to check the kitten. And change her water.'

'Yeah, whatever.'

'And look, if anything happens, if I'm not back till morning, make sure she gets breakfast. Give her some sardines. You have to squish them up a bit, because she eats too fast.'

'It's all you care about, isn't it? Your pussy.' He laughed unpleasantly.

'God, what's the matter with you?'

They glared at each other in the light of the booth, him slouching against the glass, her standing stiffly, arms crossed against her stomach. The mother pose. Calvin licked his lips slowly, and grinned. 'You're really stoned, aren't you?' she said. 'That's idiotic, you know, getting wrecked when you have to work all night.'

Calvin flicked away his roach and laughed.

'Yeah well, I'm an eejit, aren't I?' She wondered if he did it consciously, heightened his accent when he was angry. 'Not good enough for a college girl like you.'

She stood with her mouth open, watching him walk away,

watching the long loping stride she had come to love, the aureole of gold ringlets gleaming as he passed a lamp pole. Then he stopped in the middle of the parking lot and turned back.

The words floated for a second on the wind before her ears reeled them in.

'You're just a fucking dishwasher!'

It was a sailors' phone booth, smelling of tobacco and desperation. She held the receiver away from her face as she dialled Hazel's number. Imagining the ring pealing through Hazel's little house from the heavy black phone in the hall. Thinking she should have just called a cab, because now she would be making Hazel come all the way downstairs, worrying.

But she let it ring on; she didn't want to be hanging up just as Hazel got there. When the voice came it was a shock, not least because she had ceased to expect it, had begun listening to the ring as an end in itself, its rhythm, its relentlessness.

Just one word, barked out breathless and harsh. 'Yeah?'

'Hazel?'

'Who's that?'

'It's Kate.'

'Who?'

She clutched the greasy receiver tighter, smelling the aftershave from the last caller. 'Kate, the porter. I'm in the Canal. Can I come and see you?'

'Wha' for?'

Realization dawned as she heard the slurring. 'Hazel, are you okay?'

There was blast of static, then a series of thumps, before the receiver was clattered into the cradle. The dial tone blared.

It was no surprise Hazel was drinking, but alarming all the same. Kate dragged up the tattered directory from where it hung chained to the phone. It opened itself onto the taxi listings; the pages creased and tattered, covered with scrawls and jottings, fragments of addresses, dollar figures, women's names. She called Seaway Cabs.

'Where will you be?' the dispatcher asked.

'Right here,' said Kate. 'At the phone booth.'

The dispatcher said they were busy; someone would be there in fifteen minutes. Kate lit a cigarette, watching the massed shape of the *Huron Queen* looming above the holding wall. The deck lights came on, making little cones of yellow in the fog that was now rolling in from the lake. The lake effect, the softening of the air when warm meets cold. All the cities crowding around the lakes, poisoning the water, ignorant of their debt. She longed for the wind on Superior, scouring everything away.

Calvin would be up there, smoking at the top of the ladder. It was too dark to see him now, but he would be able to see her. She thought of what he would see: Kate lighting a cigarette, Kate on the phone, like a doll in a glass case by the supermarket exit, waiting for someone to come along and win her.

He would see someone waiting for something better to come along. He wouldn't see the homesickness in her, the darkness curling up like fog through the gaps at the bottom of the booth. She felt it climb into her belly like the opportunist it was. People could get homesick for anything. For a school where no one really knew you, for a bad boyfriend, for parents who found you wanting. For a bunk as wide as a yardstick in a cabin smelling of soup.

She lit another cigarette. They had said fifteen minutes; that meant twenty at least. She thought of all the cabs she'd waited for, on docks, at the gates of plants. Cabs with Calvin, and he would always pay, and she would let him. Why had she let him? She could walk over now and have it out with him. She'd been honest; what did he expect? This wasn't her real life. Hazel knew that.

There was the mutter of an engine, headlights sweeping the gravel outside the phone booth. She stepped outside, but it was a pickup truck, hard hats silhouetted in the windows, a blast of country music dopplering as it disappeared toward the docks.

The silence had sharpened her hearing. There were crickets calling in the long grass outside the phone booth, three of them she could pick out, proclaiming their loneliness. Inside, a fat brown moth bunted against the light, its furred back like a tiny bearskin.

And then she remembered a camping trip to Sandbanks, when she and Jenna were seven and six and her father still fished. A great mating dance of beetles had appeared over Lake Ontario, thousands landing and dying in the sand surrounding the tents, fat hard-backed creatures with clawed legs. They called them June bugs, though it was probably July. And all the campground children ran through the firelight shrieking in predatory delight, collecting the insects in empty beer bottles for their fathers to use as bait.

Her father had found her cowering in the tent. 'Don't worry, love,' he said gently. 'The bugs are happy. They've come out for their last night of fun. They've had a big party and they're just worn out.'

She remembered what she had said. 'That's stupid, Dad. You can't die of fun.'

She still had change in her wallet. She dialled the area code for Ottawa. The operator told her to deposit a dollar fifty, and the number rang through. She could tell him she'd been thinking. Maybe he was right about some things. And then she wished it was her parents' station wagon turning into the parking lot instead of the cab, and she could just crawl into the back seat and sleep all the way home.

It rang five or six times before the answering machine clicked on. Her mother's voice self-consciously requesting a message. But she hadn't prepared a message. And now the cab had pulled up outside the phone booth. She hung up.

❴ 44. At nine o'clock the street was dark, the tidy bungalows tucked up and sleeping. Town life is too quiet, Kate thought, rapping on Hazel's door. The sound of her knuckles breaking the hiss that filled her ears, a million night insects calling across the damp lawns.

Somewhere to her left she heard what sounded like a mourning dove. The hair on her nape bristled. Doves don't sing at night. Not a dove, then. Something human.

A sharp smell assailed her as she pushed open the door. Alcohol. The ammonia smell of pee. And something else.

Hazel was lying on her back on the living room carpet. In her green plaid dressing gown. One slipper missing. Her white cast like a loaf across her middle. A low moaning came from her throat. The sound of mourning.

'Don't cry,' Kate said urgently, kneeling over her. Hands shaking, patting Hazel's hair. 'You need to breathe. Look at me, Hazel. It's okay. It's okay.'

Hazel had been drinking. She'd fallen. Hit her head. Tears ran down both sides of her face, making little runnels in the blood. Blood. Head wounds bleed the most.

But no. There were blood bubbles coming out of the flattened nose. Like tiny pink lungs. A laboured whistling. Hazel's pale blue eyes, huge behind the glasses. The lenses peppered with red.

Someone had done this to her.

Kate gently removed the glasses. She never realized Hazel's eyes were so blue. Cornflower blue. Against the red.

I must be in shock.

Brian: *Don't you know anything? It's the shock that kills.*

'Hazel,' Kate said, pulling a pile of May's afghans from the couch, piling them onto Hazel's legs. 'You're going to be okay. Help is coming. What's the address here? The number, Hazel. I have to call the police. The ambulance.'

Hazel stared at her. She was moving her lips. 'No. Police. He's. My. Boy. My *boy.*'

'Who, Hazel? Who?'

Hazel looked at her for a long beat and then abruptly shut her eyes.

Kate scrambled back to the hall. Mail piled by the phone. Dialled zero, gripping the receiver as it rang rang rang, scrabbling through the envelopes to find a number she could read. The printing on the paper seemed to tremble. Focus. Focus.

'Operator? We need an ambulance, we need it fast, it's an old woman ...'

'Your address. What's the address?'

And then she saw him at the end of the hall, arm raised up, brandishing some kind of stick. He must have been there the whole time, doing whatever he was doing in the basement, she'd known and not known all along.

She screamed something as he launched himself at her, a skinny mad-faced missile of a man, hair flying. No or don't or stop. Her hands raised uselessly against the blurred baseball bat just before it connected with her head.

Blood has a complex smell, she thought. Mineral, vegetable, animal. Blackened meat in blackened skillet on blackened stove. Hazel's swollen fingers, red sausages. In the pot the pale slaughtered organs, kidneys, I'm soaking the piss out of them. Hazel cackling like a witch, Witch Hazel.

The smell of iron and offal. Blood food. Through her eyelids a red glow. Sunset. No, fire. She is on the floor of a room watching flames, yellow feathers licking a red lampshade. A soft pop as something bursts. Above her a blanket of smoke. Beyond it a body in a green plaid housecoat, Hazel.

She lay listening. Subterranean thumps, an engine outside running.

How long had she lain there? What was that other, terrible smell?

Burning wool. Kate crawled over to the sofa and dragged a blanket down and tossed it over the cheerful little blaze surrounding the fallen lamp. Always put out your campfire.

It was dark now except for a swath of light from the dining room and a glow from the front hall where she had come in, where she had come in without thinking because she had heard an old woman moaning. The phone was where she remembered it, an inky beacon on the windowsill. Just beside the door. The smell of night air, fish and mist. The door was wide open.

Kate glanced back and saw Hazel's eyes swing wildly toward the kitchen and she heard footsteps up the basement stairs and then she was out the front door, scrambling across the damp lawn to the bungalow next door.

Water, water, water. She was floating above the lake. Trying to swim down to the surface, but she had never been a brilliant swimmer. Only she would have gladly drowned now, just to get a sip. I am so thirsty, oh please. Trying to force a whimper past the hot dry pain in her throat, a firebreak of seared flesh. But the noise she heard wasn't coming from her. Kate opened her eyes and stared at her mother in amazement. Her mother was crying. Her nose was red. It looked like a strawberry.

Mom. I need water.

Her mother leapt up from her hospital chair. 'Oh my God, Kate, we were so worried.'

Mom. Water.

'Hang on, Katie, I'll get the doctor.'

Suddenly there was a crowd in the room, nurses, a doctor in a white coat with untidy grey eyebrows. He smelled like her father, the way her father smelled when she was small. Old Spice. And then, as if she had conjured him up, her father was there too, standing at the foot of the bed, watching the doctor run his hands over Kate's skull. He caught her eye as she yelped with pain and he winked. *Winked.*

Water, she told him.

But her father was looking at the doctor, who had crossed his white-clad arms and was saying something about tests, smoke inhalation. Disoriented. Concussed. Cussed.

The doctor was back at her shoulder. 'How are you feeling now? All right?' He was shouting, as if she couldn't hear just fine.

Water, she said.

He turned back to her father. Maybe she'd only been thinking the word.

She took a painful, ragged breath and screamed. 'Water!'

There was silence as her mother filled a glass from a pitcher on the bedside table and looked defiantly at the doctor. 'It's all right, isn't it? She can have a drink?'

Idiots, Kate thought. But no, this time she hadn't thought it, she'd said it. She knew that because they were looking at her differently now. The doctor put a hand under her father's elbow and conveyed him out of the room.

Concussion can change your personality, her mother was telling the man in the suit. She was at the door, barring the way, explaining that her daughter was not herself, and who could blame her, just look at her. He took something out of his breast pocket and held it out to her mother. She nodded and told Kate he was a police officer. He looked like a bartender. Slicked-back hair, a scar on his forehead. He wanted to talk to her alone.

'It's all right, Kate,' her mother said. 'I'll be just outside the door.'

Up close she could smell the cigarettes and coffee on his breath and she thought suddenly of Calvin. Burned coffee, bad coffee, the only kind of coffee people like him had ever tasted. She longed for her parents' coffee, the dark Swedish roast they bought at a deli on Bank Street.

How long had she been in Hazel's house? She could only guess. It was eight-thirty when she got into the cab, nine-thirty when the police got the neighbour's call.

'You're a hero, dear, getting help the way you did. James Murray was going to burn his aunt's house down with both of you in it. Thought he could get the insurance money. They always think that.'

James Murray. The nephew. She still thought of him that way, easier to think of a nephew with blood all over his hands than a son. He had been caught that way, red-handed. Loading his van with boxes, bloody handprints all over the cardboard. The detective was volunteering too much, she thought. Enjoying his story.

'He was stoned on PCP, dear, but you never heard that from me. They'll probably try to use it as a defence.'

Kate began to cough. The inside of her throat felt coated in scabs. She covered her face with the sheet and coughed till she felt her ears pop. The cop's voice filtered through, worried now. 'Are you all right? Maybe I'd better let you get some rest, dear. Come back later.'

'Wait,' Kate croaked. 'Hazel. Where's Hazel? Is she okay?'

The cop hesitated, his body already turned to the door. 'You did your best, dear. You went beyond the call. You could have got out before you did.'

'What do you mean? Where is she?'

He ran a hand over a weary face. 'She's in the ICU. They think she's had a heart attack. You want my advice? Wait a few days. Don't make it harder for yourself.'

'I want to see Hazel!' There she was, screaming again.

Her mother barged back into the room. Kate glared at them both. 'This isn't a personality change, you know. This is the real me.'

She got the nurse to phone Rebecca the next morning, before her parents arrived from the Holiday Inn in St. Catharines. They'd been in her room most of the night, until she finally yelled at them to go and get some sleep.

Becks had already heard from Jenna. 'You're in a Catholic hospital?'

'Hotel Dieu. The hotel of God.'

'You're lucky you're not pregnant. They'd save the fetus first.'

'Yeah, I'm so lucky. I have such great fucking luck.'

Save the baby first. Well, it made sense. Except how could you be sure you weren't saving it for something worse? The son passed off as a nephew, inexplicably indulged by his aunt. The nephew passed off as a son.

Hazel's sister was sitting alone in the ICU lounge when Kate was taken up after breakfast. Her mother hadn't wanted her to see Hazel. But the nurse said it might be worse not to. They took her in a wheelchair, whisked her on rubber wheels past a little dumpy woman with grey hair and Hazel's nose, bent over a Bible, her black oxfords not touching the floor. Was this the woman who raised a child into a psychotic drug addict? Would she tell Jamie the truth? Had she already told him?

Who could Kate tell?

Hazel's head on the white hospital pillow was a cartoon, puffed up like a pumpkin. Kate put her hand over the cook's, gently squeezing the swollen arthritic fingers, willing Hazel to feel her presence.

And then the blue eyes opened, looking blindly beyond Kate toward another face, a little face she had cherished beyond any other.

'Jamie,' she moaned, gripping Kate's hand hard. 'Did he get away? My little boy.'

❰ 45. Hazel died at midnight. May said she died of a broken heart.

She was already dying when Kate came to and escaped out the front door onto the dark grass, staggered toward the lighted windows of the house next door. The night air sharp as a slap, filling her lungs with oxygen, pushing out a howl of animal terror. At the edge of Hazel's lawn she remembered words and the word she screamed was what Becks said was best to scream even if it wasn't true, but she knew it would be true.

Fire.

Twice now in her dreams she had seen him light it, the fire trail that would roar around the room and then snake up her pantlegs. In the second dream she saw the kitten running along the top of the sofa, a live torch with a birthday candle for a tail, while she screamed at it to stay away from May's new drapes.

She was still screaming when she woke. She'd forgotten the cat. Calvin would have forgotten to feed it. Her mother would have to go rescue it. She would have to go *now*.

But her mother knew all about the cat. If Kate would please stop screaming.

274

The kitten was still on the boat. The little woman with the funny eye and the big glasses, May, told them that.

'She's mine, Mom! You have to go get her!'

'Katie,' her mother said. 'You really have to stop screaming.'

Her mother would go back with May and fetch the cat. Her parents were going to bring Kate home with them to Ottawa once she was released from the God Hotel. Her mother lightly stroked her forehead, but she didn't want stroking. She was hollow. Why couldn't her mother see she needed to be held now, held hard? Why couldn't she see that? Kate pulled her head away from the stroking.

'May,' she said. 'Where's May?'

'She's right outside.'

May had chocolates and mail. There were letters from the art school. Kate left them on the tray, unopened.

'The police tied up the ship,' May said. 'They questioned us.'

'Is Calvin still on board?'

'Just till the end of the week. They're going to transfer the load. They're going to scrap her now.'

Kate put her hands over her face. 'Oh.'

'It's better this way, my dear. We all got to get on with things. You too. Go back to your school.'

'What did the police want to know?'

'Oh, just how did Hazel get along with her nephew, did she say anything about what he was up to. Did you know he wanted her to sign over her house? I told them that. And they wanted to know if I'd ever met him.' May was silent for a moment. 'Well, I did meet him. Couple of times. Never liked him much. But ...' May looked away, her little gnarled hands twisting in her lap.

'I know,' Kate said. 'I know who he is.'

May just nodded.

'She didn't want me to call the police. She would rather die than get him in trouble.' Kate's mouth twisted in a sob. 'Only I would have died too.'

'Oh no,' May said. 'Oh no, my dear. Don't you think that. No, she wouldn't have been thinking is all. Sometimes love makes you do awful bad things. And she blamed herself something fierce. For how he turned out.'

May said Hazel had told her the truth about Jamie the first time he went to jail. 'That was about five years ago. That was for drugs. The second time was drugs, too, and Hazel got him into a – whadyacallit – a twelve-step program in Buffalo. Otherwise she said she would disinherit him. But all that time, when she was paying for things, he never guessed.'

'Why didn't she tell him?'

'She was afraid to. She was afraid he would hate her for it.' Kate thought of the fury in the face of James Murray, coming at her in Hazel's hallway. The man was full of hate. Hazel had given him to people who could never love him the way she wanted to. So she softened his life the only way she knew how, by letting him walk all over her.

'Hazel never stopped blaming herself,' May said. 'He was six months old when she went back to the boats. She had him for six months, and she loved him. She was staying with her sister and brother-in-law out by Beamsville. They were trying out fruit farming. They thought they couldn't have children of their own. But then they did, they had two. Two of their own to raise. And Jamie was never easy.'

'She could have kept him. Raised him by herself.'

May shook her head. 'No, my dear, things were different back then. Hazel did her best for the boy. Small towns don't let you forget nothing. Anyway, she was on the boats and they were worse. Some of the stories she told me would make your hair stand on end. The cooks used to lock themselves in their rooms when the crew got drinking and even then they weren't safe. If they knew she had a kid and no husband they'd've been after her all the time.'

'Why didn't she marry him? The father.'

May shot her a pitying look. 'Because Jamie's father was already married. He was a mate, is all I know. She never told me his name.'

Kate closed her eyes. A terrible blackness pressed down on her forehead. She focused on the watch ticking on the bedside table. Her father's watch. The police had all her things. Her father spent most of the time in the smoking lounge. Afraid to look at her. She had two big shiners and stitches along her eyebrow and across the back of her scalp. Her nose was broken but they said it would heal all right. Just a little bump, the doctor said.

The sound of a chair scraping across the floor. May's smell as she came close: rosewater and Export A's. 'That's right, you rest, my dear.'

'Have a chocolate, May. I can't eat anything.'

May's voice brightened with pleasure. 'My goodness, I think I will.'
Kate listened to the cellophane being stripped from the box, the rustle
of the lid. May could take five minutes to choose a chocolate, reading
through every description. Whereas Hazel would have popped one
into her mouth in a heartbeat, closing her eyes and grunting with
pleasure.

It would peeve Hazel to know she had missed that last box of
chocolates, the one Ronnie meant her to have. His ten-dollar bill was
still in the pocket of Kate's jeans. They were evidence now, her jeans.
Stiff with gasoline and blood, sealed in a plastic bag at the police
station.

The cop said James Murray would plead guilty to all charges. It
would likely be knocked down to assault and aggravated assault, he
said with disgust, instead of what it should be, attempted murder,
conspiracy, arson, he could go on. James Murray would be out of jail in
a couple of years.

The doctors said it was the heart attack that killed Hazel, the one
she had lying on her living room floor. Watching the child she had
given life to set about extinguishing hers.

Kate sat up and covered her face with her hands. She was seeing
Hazel again, those blue blue eyes, like holes torn in a sunset. Her
animal defiance. Her last useless stubborn maternal act, to try to save
her killer.

'May. I need my mom. Can you get my mom?'

She began to bawl the moment she felt her mother's arms. It came
on her like a seizure, like a summer storm releasing the heat and filth of
days. 'I tried to save her, Mom. I tried to save her.'

Her mother folded her in, against her soft breasts, rocking her
steadily. 'I know, sweetheart. I know you did.'

Kate imagined that it was really Hazel who was holding her,
Hazel she had never told the truth to, because until this minute she
hadn't known it herself.

'I loved her, Mom.'

'Oh, Katie. You're all right now. Mom's here.'

The ship dropped into the dark.

Row by row the yellow portholes were doused, small eclipses in a constellation of rust. She could hear no voices now. There was a sound like an explosion that went on and on. It was the sound of water. Twenty million gallons emptying at once, on its way to the Atlantic, on its way to the salt.

Kate walked to the end of Lock 1 to watch the salty's glacial progress into Lake Ontario. It was a tramp sailing under a Liberian flag, heavy with Canadian grain. No one else watched it wheeze into the bay, a prehistoric creature on its long voyage back to sea level. There were no tourists this late in the year.

She shifted her attention to the big laker moored to the holding wall below, its deck lights glowing like Chinese lanterns in the mist. White delivery trucks roared up with their loads of meat and milk, clean laundry to trade for soiled. The blankets would be thicker on this boat, the food better. The MV *Superior* was the new queen of the Great Lakes fleet, a model of clean efficiency, everything streamlined into the five-story afterhouse, a gleaming terraced iceberg. There was even a beer machine on board.

Kate checked her watch; just past 8 p.m. Twelve hours since they left Ottawa, driving through valleys of red and yellow, the maples and oaks trooping the colours like the Mounties at Parliament Hill.

Her father liked to be early for things. He liked to have time to look around. They had stopped at the cemetery on the way and they had gone to the marine museum in town. She heard him come up behind her as the chandler's trucks peeled away from the boat. He put an arm around her shoulders, tightening his grip as the ship blasted its horn.

'One blast means let go the lines,' Kate said. 'It'll be coming into the lock now.'

Together they watched the *Superior* ease through the giant gates.

'It was mostly Irish who dug these canals,' her father said. 'Your ancestors, on my mother's side, anyway.'

'I didn't know we had any Irish in us.'

He laughed. 'Everyone's got some Irish in them.'

He'd been reading up over dinner at the Holiday Inn, studying a slim volume of local history he picked up at the museum. They reckoned thousands had died digging the early incarnations of the Canal, died of cholera and cold, of suicide and gang wars. The diggers were called navvies, after the great navigation channels that they dug, and they lived in a muddy slagheap of huts called Slabtown. No one remembered them now, just as no one would remember the East Coast migrants who worked the lake trade, once the lake trade was gone.

The lock yawned below them. Kate squeezed her father's hand and stepped back. It was a hole in the landscape, an absence. A miracle of engineering. A mass grave.

They had visited Hazel's grave. It lay behind an old Baptist church near Fruitvale, which first surprised Kate and then did not. It was undoubtedly the sister's church, the sister who had not been equal to the challenge of loving Hazel's love child.

Kate had gone home to Ottawa before the funeral, which by all accounts was mobbed with mourners. But she gave Bill Stone money for flowers when he came to visit her at the God Hotel. She had asked her father for ten dollars and given it to Bill, squaring the debt to Ronnie. Buy her a little something, he had said. From all of us.

Bill Stone sat beside Kate's hospital bed, turning an unlit cigarette in his big ruined hands. 'I'll tell you what I would have told her, dear. The union never meant to hang you out to dry with them pictures. We had to live up to our word. We ran our campaign on safety and we had to live up to it. We'd have taken care of Hazel. She was a good egg.'

'I know, Bill.'

'At least you've still got your teeth, dear,' he said. 'You just can't replace good teeth like yours.'

Kate and her father walked back up to the middle of the lock, where her bag sat waiting. The shorehands threw down their ropes and hauled them up again like fishing lines, dragging the captured loops of the boat's cables. They moved with the ease of long habit, pushing the loops over the bollards, stepping back neatly as the braided steel twanged tight, pulled fast by the rattling winches. She thought of Boyd, his grace tending the engines, a grace he found nowhere else in life.

There was a new clarity in the way she saw things, scoured down to their essentials the way the lakes had been scoured out of the landscape. The shrink said it was a response to trauma. It would go away. She would come back to the world.

But not just yet.

Her mother cried when Kate said she wanted to ship out again. It was her father who said they had to let her go. The companies had agreed to improve safety. The union wanted survival suits for crew members, you could live fourteen hours in the water of Superior in a survival suit, and the companies had agreed to that, too. And this was a new boat. She would have her own room.

'I'll be fine, Mom,' she said. 'It's only a couple of months till winter tie-up. And I miss the water.'

Bill Stone had fixed it. The *Superior* was state-of-the-art, he said, it was practically a hotel. And here it came, its white afterhouse sparkling in the floodlights of Lock 1.

Heart thudding so hard it hurt her bones, Kate pressed her palm against her father's, the way she had when she was little. Why was it harder now, with their blessing? She had lost her anger, the fuel of her rebellion, her exile. Dad, she wanted to say, I'm not ready. I want to go home.

As if he had heard her, her father put an arm across her shoulders. 'You'll be fine, love. You'll be aces. Bring us back some great pictures of storms. And we'll drive down and get you at Christmas. Get a tour of your fancy new boat.'

They watched the wheelhouse rise up, green instrument lights flickering in the darkness beyond the glass. Then the lifeboat deck and the officers' deck and finally the main deck, windows glowing. She heard the hum of the deck winches and then, through it all, the calls of the men.

'Dad,' she said urgently. 'It's time.'

A grey-bearded watchman in a baseball cap was standing at midships, directly below them. He nodded to her father and reached up for Kate's bag. Then he was level with her, and she gripped his gloved hand and leaped across, balancing for a wild second on the wire.

'Atta girl,' he said. 'You're fine.'

Kate wiped trembling hands on her jeans and stood looking at her father, a lone figure under the yellow lights, arm raised, his face turned up to the rising ship. Then she saw him wink. Letting go the lines.

'I think the cook's expectin' ya.'

She followed the watchman slowly between hatch covers to the port side, ignoring the mate and deckhands clustered at the winch. The ship was high in the water now, towering above the trees on the dark side of the Canal.

He stopped to wait for her in the bright port-side passageway, then turned left and left again along a shining linoleum deck into another hallway. Past doors labelled Night Cook, Second Cook, Porter, every one a private room. The Chief Cook's door, at the far end, opened before he could knock.

'You're Kate, I guess,' said the man in whites. He was in his forties, with a balding freckled head and a face creased by laugh lines. He did something she had never seen anyone do on a boat: he shook her hand. 'I'm Earl. We were all sorry to hear about Hazel. She was one of the good ones.'

Kate nodded, grateful. It was a good way to put it.

'Well, you come highly recommended.'

'Thanks. I'll do my best.'

'Freddy here can show you the room.'

Just before midnight there was a sharp rap on her door. She had been lying on the bed in her clothes, a drink still in her hand, drifting in and out of sleep, feeling the quiet thrum of the engines up through the mattress, feeling her heartbeat slow and her muscles unknot, feeling her head fill up with waves. Without a bunk above it the narrow bed seemed positively luxurious, though the curtains were the same institutional green as the *Huron Queen*'s.

He was at the door in clean white overalls, his green eyes full of shadows. Grinning his wicked boy's grin.

Calvin. Her whole body felt light. Calvin.

'Fuck, man, it *is* you. You're the new second cook? What happened to your hair?'

'It got cut. What are you doing here?'

'I work here, wheelsman now. Bill didn't tell you?'

She was laughing, backing into the room, everything suddenly clear. 'No he didn't. No he did not.'

'That sneaky bastard. Got anything to drink?'

'Help yourself.'

He went over to the desk. 'You gotta love this company, man. Real orange juice and everything.' He poured a generous shot of Smirnoff, added juice and fished for ice cubes in a bowl that was now mostly meltwater. He threw himself into the chair facing the bunk. They were grinning at each other, she was grinning so hard her cheeks hurt.

'You still reading that fucking book?' He reached over and picked up the copy of *Two Years before the Mast* from where it lay face down on the bedspread, open to page seven.

'Oh, that.' She shrugged. 'I'll never get through that.'

'Then why'd you bring it?'

'I guess I brought it for you.'

There were many helpers on the long journey to this novel, among them Don Coles and Clark Blaise, early guides and encouragers. There was also the kind young techie who got me a deal on a laptop, and my mother, Helen Olson, who paid for it. Friends who read early versions of the manuscript and gave wise counsel: Moira Farr, Iris Wilde, Kate Taylor, Charlotte Stein and Marjorie Harris. My father, George Olson, and his co-grandpa, Jack Batten, were supportive throughout, as were my sibs and the rest of the Olson, Swift, Harris and Batten clans. Anne McDermid and Anna Porter both raised my spirits at critical moments. I am also lucky to have good friends at *The Globe and Mail*, including Jill Borra, who provided an extra pair of eyes. And thanks to Tim and Elke Inkster, and my wonderful editor Doris Cowan, who made the book seaworthy.

Finally, to my boys and their dad, Chris Harris, deep and abiding gratitude for keeping me afloat.

Although based on my experiences on the Great Lakes in the early 1980s, this book is a work of fiction. As such it required research, which included haunting mariners' websites such as www.boat nerd.com. There were also a number of texts that provided insight along the way: *Ultramarine*, an early novel by Malcolm Lowry, and *Lakeboat*, an early play (also a film) by David Mamet. *The Women's Great Lakes Reader*, edited by Victoria Brehm, was an invaluable source, as was *A Sailor's Logbook*, by American sailor Mark L. Thompson. *A Wilderness Called Home*, by Charles Wilkins, explores Canadian lake history and geography, as do *The Wolf's Head: Writing Lake Superior*, by Peter Unwin, and *Into the Blue: Family Secrets and the Search for a Great Lakes Shipwreck*, by Andrea Curtis. Recent novels that inspired include *Voyageurs*, by Margaret Elphinstone and *The Shadow Boxer*, by Steven Heighton.

Lastly, I am grateful for financial support from both the Toronto Arts Council and the Ontario Arts Council. I am especially thankful for an OAC Works in Progress Grant that gave me time to sit by a shore, listening to the crash of the waves.

Sheree-Lee Olson was born in Picton, Ontario, a town on the shores of Lake Ontario. Six months later she crossed the Atlantic by steamer, en route to a Canadian military base in West Germany. As the eldest child of a career officer, she lived a nomadic life, attending thirteen different schools in four provinces. She has three university degrees, in fine arts, philosophy and journalism, financed largely by working on Great Lakes freighters. In 1985, she joined *The Globe and Mail* as an editor, and in 2007–8 she was a Canadian Journalism Fellow at Massey College, University of Toronto. She has published fiction and poetry in numerous literary magazines, as well as contributing personal essays to *The Globe*. She lives in Toronto with her family.